The
Heat
of
Lies

Also by Jonathan Stone

The Cold Truth

The
Heat
of
Lies

Jonathan
Stone

St. Martin's Minotaur
New York

www.minotaurbooks.com

ISBN 0-312-20604-6

10   9   8   7   6   5   4   3   2

Again, for my fellow commuters on the 8:08 out of Talmadge Hill.

And to the memory of my father, who was one of us.

(And of course for Rocco, the data retrieval specialist.)

Acknowledgments

I am particularly indebted to the monograph "Penetrating Gunshot Wounds to the Head and Lack of Immediate Incapacitation," *Karger, B., Int. J. Legal* 1995; 108: 53–61.

1

"Ahhh!!" *Jesus! Sonuvafuckingbitch!!!*

Lieutenant Palmer had just turned back from the big picture window of the cramped office six floors above Police Plaza, to hang up the phone after making yet another patiently irate call to Office Services checking on furniture ordered eight months ago, and there—seated silently in the wooden folding chair across the Lieutenant's crowded desk—was the first murderer Palmer had ever sent to prison.

Instinctively, the Lieutenant crossed her arms over her blouse to cover her breasts.

Her pulse surged. Her entire physiology sounded a well-orchestrated general alarm. Heart jumped, endorphins released, mouth went dry, stomach muscles clenched, in a fight-or-flight symphony of physical response. Memory came flooding back on a river of nausea. Five years, three promotions, twenty-four more murders and twenty-two murder convictions, had not, it appeared, sufficiently intervened.

Sonuvafuckingbitch, she thought. But she wouldn't say it. Wouldn't give him the satisfaction.

In a reassuring instant, she saw that Mendoza and Ng were in a state of high alert at their desks just outside her office, looking warily and protectively and not least of all curiously in through her open door. It calmed her somewhat. She felt herself relax a degree.

She regarded the huge man cautiously, tensely, like eyeing a still-armed bomb. But now that she'd recovered from the shock of knowing him immediately, she saw that he was in fact almost unrecognizable. In the intervening five years, he'd aged unimaginably. His body, whose epic size had once projected immense power, now projected simply immensity—sloppy, uncooperative, defeated mass, rolling over the edges of the folding chair.

"How'd you get in here?"

"Flashed a badge," he said. Adding, "Old one."

His hair had gone fright white, thinned from a proud mane to a strandy wispiness. The furrowed facial lines that once evoked character and experience had finally overwhelmed his features, becoming simply wrinkles, like any old man's. His skin was ashen, chalky, like a patient's.

Beneath the wrinkles, though, his eyes still harbored some semblance of that nasty, restless alertness—now even more startling, in contrast to the thick, loose, epidermal folds surrounding them. Rhinoceros eyes— steady, unblinking, uncaring, brute.

Apart from the eyes, he looked close to death.

Close, she thought, but no cigar.

She appraised him silently for another long moment before asking— carefully measuring her tone to be flat, without judgment or affront, like a disinterested clerk gathering information for a form—"What are you doing here?"

The unblinking eyes wandered aimlessly over the unadorned green institutional walls of the tiny room. He shrugged noncommitally.

She asked again—evenly, identically—as if he hadn't heard her the first time, which, given his startling aged appearance, he genuinely might not have—"What are you doing here?"

Another shrug.

She noted the rumpled white shirt beneath the open trench coat. Its collar, its cuffs, no longer crisply starched. "Wife finally threw you out, didn't she?" observed Lieutenant Palmer.

The man's eyebrows went up briefly, momentarily impressed with her deduction, then down again, sullenly confirming that it was correct.

She noticed the dirt ingrained on his shirt cuffs. Noticed that his left shoe heel was turned somewhat, askew beneath the rest of his shoe.

"Defense like that'll cost you, won't it?" she speculated further.

His lack of response was acknowledgment enough.

Whatever nest egg he'd managed to hide from the forensic accountants, whatever on-the-take money he'd augmented it with, had apparently gone significantly toward the fees of the famously brilliant and famously expensive attorney, one Lawrence Cooperman, Esq.

And it had been an exceedingly long defense, after all, longer than anyone could have predicted. Maybe he'd even had something on Cooperman as well—she had a nagging sense there was more to know about Cooperman's advocacy. His defense might have expended all his capital—the conventional green sort, and his deep hoard of black currency as well. Regardless, it had done its job.

Ladies and gentlemen, it is the word of one woman, a police officer at the outset of her career, against the word of another police officer, in the twilight of his. That's the cold truth of it. So do you believe the word of police officers, or don't you? Do they tell the truth, or are they liars?

Cooperman's cynical, sneering disregard for the proceedings in general. Inviting the jury to share that cynicism, cozying up to them.

Now if you think police officers generally tell the truth, then based on this little sampling at least, you'd have to rethink that, wouldn't you? And if you think police officers are generally liars, then this little sampling would suggest you're onto something.

The adeptness of the lawyer's delivery, coupled with the impression, the force, of slow, seamless, confident logic. She still heard it. It still pained her. . . .

She held now to her careful monotone. Continued to speak, firm, clear, her trademark gentle interrogative, a mere notch above a whisper.

"What're you going to do?"

He shrugged.

What happened to that young waitress out there in the snow, let's face it, we're never going to know. We have two conflicting versions of events, and we'll simply never know which version matches the truth, if either. . . .

"Where you gonna go?"

He shrugged again.

The alleged murder weapon was never found. Lost in an evidential mix-up in the small upstate police department that, it's been implied, he somehow controlled. I can only tell you that unfortunately and statistically, crucial evidence is lost and misplaced all the time, in departments of all sizes. . . .

She'd put him in prison five years ago, on the lesser charges that he'd pled to—tax evasion, financial malfeasance—and naturally she had gotten used to picturing him there. But it had proved particularly onerous for the State to find an acceptable venue for his murder trial, given his local reputation, and the sparseness of options in that sparely populated upstate New York county. Months had stretched to years. Legal technicalities and issues and delays had presented themselves aboundingly. Until at last, the trial had begun.

She's a poised, beautiful young woman. He's a powerful, hated, difficult man. Right there, that makes me doubt, makes me suspect, the easy version of events, the version the prosecutors are trying to serve up; right there, that makes me listen again to the less palatable version. . . .

Even then, there were further technicalities; another change of venue; witness-tampering and jury-tampering accusations and counteraccusations; false starts and full stops.

And the trial itself. Cameras banned. Access limited. Conducted during a brutal February of a brutal winter at the Canadian border. The venue inaccessible. A judge who would not allow a circus. This is no Heisman Trophy winner, the bald hawk-nosed judge had asserted with a smirk. The public has a right to know, yes, but not a right to watch. The reporters, and thus the public, could barely follow it. Soon lost interest in the legal tangle. Precisely what Lawrence Cooperman would have hoped.

No weapon. No real witnesses. I'm frankly surprised that the State chose to proceed on such meager evidential grounds. Political pressure? Pressure exerted by vocal friends of the young officer? By well-placed enemies of the famously difficult defendant? Don't discount it. It would at least explain why we're all here. . . .

And under the law, it had had to be divided into distinct and separate proceedings. Further diluting, further dulling, the incidents' sum of impact. The trial itself had solely concerned the murder of the waitress. In a few hours one morning, Julian delivered her testimony; her testimony was challenged; and that was the extent of her role and her presence.

The State chose not to proceed at all in the matter of the suspected murder of psychic Wayne Hill. No evidence. No body. And a long and documented history of erratic behavior, sudden self-exiles, even periodic disappearances, on the part of the purported decedent. There was little more than Julian's accusation: that Hill had been killed to cover up the waitress's murder. But she soon saw how that accusation—with little evidence behind it—undercut her credibility, even in the eyes of the prosecutors.

As for the accused's attempt on the life of Julian Palmer? Evidence nonexistent. Details extremely vague. Night. A blizzard. White-out conditions. Zero visibility. And because it was a matter between police officers, servants of the State, the State interceded on its own behalf. The career of a promising young police officer, in the State's view, should not be jeopardized; nor should the reputation of an acclaimed senior officer be needlessly compromised. In the absence of physical evidence, the State concluded, the matter should be adjudicated privately. Counselors to both parties—each feeling an advantage to themselves—unhesitatingly agreed. And so it became a closed hearing. An internal affair, thick with procedure, rich with technicality. Documents. Closed-door presentations. Arbitration and mediation panels. A police matter. And a muddling, obfuscatory mess.

Both of their versions are in some sense convincing, because we are here, after all, considering them each carefully. Then again, neither is convincing enough. Because neither version, I'll wager right now, has flatly convinced any of you.

It was all long ago now. Another place. Another lifetime. A handful of senior officials here knew of the events, and that was it.

In the intervening years, she'd become used to the world's grays. To its imperfections, to its drift and sway, the certainty of its uncertainty. She still didn't accept it. But she did now at least expect it.

You can't convict. Even if you think he did it, even if you feel somehow certain of that, you can't convict. Much as you might want to. Much as you might hate him. Because you haven't got one piece of credible reliable evidence with which to do it.

"You're a murderer," she said to him now. Reminding him of the fact—as quietly, as flatly, as matter-of-factly—as she had said everything else.

And only now did he finally turn his attention, his famous gaze, directly at her. And only now did he speak, the first words in that crusty, deep-mean voice she had not heard in five years. "But not a convicted murderer," he said as quietly back.

And suddenly, the smile. Brazen and infuriating, unregenerate and unchanged . . .

She pushed the intercom button.

Mendoza and Ng were flanking the strange immense figure before she even had to say their names. But they wore looks of confusion as loud as orange raid jackets.

"Detective Mendoza, Detective Ng, meet Winston the Bear Edwards. Former chief of police of Canaanville, New York, who I interned with five years ago. . . ."

Ng smiled broadly, relieved, before the rest of her introduction robbed him of his congeniality.

"He stabbed a waitress forty-six times. Killed a man to try to cover it up. And when I went tumbling over a ledge, he thought he'd killed me too. . . ." She could see the shock register on their faces. Big Ng looking incredulously at the old broken form seated in the chair, while the wiry, muscled Mendoza looked as incredulously directly at her. They knew she didn't lie. She didn't fool around. That's why they were having such a hard time with it.

"And not knowing where to go, he's come to see us. Like all the other flotsam and jetsam that washes up here. He doesn't know what he's doing here. Or he's not saying."

Now she was standing by the ancient crooked coat tree, lifting her own black trench coat off and swirling it onto her shoulders, having first, as always, strapped on the service revolver—an accessory, a necessity, like a handbag or wallet or keys.

"I want him watched, day and night," she told them. "I want a man tailing him everywhere. I want a man stationed in the hall of his fleabag hotel. I want someone beside him when he goes through restaurant trash. When he drinks rotgut, I want someone to know the brand. When he sleeps in the gutter, I want someone to watch him snore. He says he doesn't know what he's doing here. But we're going to. Every moment. Every move."

The short tirade had loosed her feelings, she discovered. They'd snuck out, leaked beneath the cold steel door of her professionalism, and now were gathering into a torrent she felt less and less control over.

She was as surprised as anyone to suddenly find the black muzzle of her service revolver sunk deep into Winston Edwards's mouth; before she could even process who exactly had done such a thing, before Mendoza and Ng could even respond with wide-eyed wordless shock.

Only Edwards seemed not to react. Looking up at her with big sleepy eyes behind the rhinocerative, pale, unhealthy folds.

You don't care, do you? she thought. A valuable perception . . . *store it away . . .*

Of course, she was now indicating how deeply *she* cared.

She was showing him—once again—the depth of her feeling for him.

She pulled the muzzle from his mouth.

And was nearly as surprised as before to find the same muzzle running high along his gums, making each tooth appear individually, sorrowfully, in a broken, ulcerative, yellowed periodontal parade. Livestock, examined meanly.

"He's a free man now," Julian said with mock gospel exuberance. "He can do whatever he wants."

Now she pressed the revolver muzzle hard just below his right eye, gathering up and pulling down the loose skin beneath the eye with it, opening the eye brutally, comically wide.

She put her own eye just above his brutally opened one, made a show of peering in, as if to see for herself the precise shape of the evil inside. A gemologist, appraising a strange brown stone in its crusted, folded setting.

She pressed the gun muzzle beneath his left eye now, pulled down, the folds of skin following helplessly obedient, a wake of stretched flesh. She made the same optometric inspection.

Mendoza shifted his feet uncomfortably. She heard Ng's breath come short and loud and nervous. Edwards never moved.

Now she pushed the muzzle against his right nostril. Lifted the outer edge meanly. Distorting the entire nose harshly for a long, held moment.

Lifted the right nostril identically.

Mendoza and Ng stood, transfixed.

She pulled the gun muzzle away, holstered it mechanically.

Regarded Edwards once more in the rickety folding chair.

Then reared her foot back and with all her gathered fury kicked the left front leg of the wooden chair. The same left front leg she'd seen threatening to give way on previous occupants for months now—eager clerks, nervous sergeants, Ng and Mendoza themselves.

The chair leg snapped crisply and cooperatively, and the two hundred eighty pounds of Winston the Bear Edwards puddled onto the floor sideways, gracelessly on top of it, aided in speed and awkwardness by the immensity and unpreparedness of the weight.

Beyond the sound of the broken wooden chair hitting the wooden floor, though, there was no accompanying sound from Edwards. No involuntary *huhn,* no raging curse, no strangled syllable of surprise, nothing. Only a studied, respectful, obedient silence. Maybe stoic and challenging. Maybe mocking. Maybe just stunned surprise.

Slowly, the huge form splayed facedown on the floor managed to turn its immense ursine head slightly toward her, to crane its neck just enough to present a coldly expressionless black pupil to her, peering out from behind the curtainous folds of skin.

She stood over the black pupil purposefully, to fill its vision with the bottom of her trench coat, to momentarily overwhelm it with her presence.

"Welcome to the big city," she said.

She adjusted the holster, buttoned her trench coat over it, clutched her handbag. "*My* city," she added. A perhaps unnecessary amplification.

She looked up at Mendoza and Ng. "I'm due at a deposition across town," she told them.

She headed briskly out the open office door.

It was frankly all she could think to do.

And with any luck, it would at least speed that furniture along.

2

A black-and-white took her crosstown: she knew the officers. It was a small enough city to know the officers. Julian had gone down into dispatch and hitched a ride. They were happy to take her, she knew. It gave some destination and purpose to their rounds. A city big enough to have officers in dispatch, small enough to know them: it was one of the many things that were right about Troy, New York.

Not too big. Not too small. Not overwhelming. Not claustrophobic. Troy's mix of ethnicities, expressed in faces and flavors, in the businesses and celebrations and cuisines, of each new immigrant group that somehow found its way here. Its sudden physical beauty amid its grimness and gray. Its mix of joy and glumness. Of noisy exuberance and contemplative silence. Its wind howling off the Hudson, sobering and incessant.

The manufacturing past that Troy had been founded on—textile mills, iron works, breweries, bell makers, carriage builders—had long ago disappeared. What was still made, was made cheaper elsewhere. It had left Troy downtrodden, identityless, adrift. Julian felt a lot in common with a city struggling to find its way. A city with struggle as a century-old theme. A city known only—if at all—as the birthplace of Sam Wilson, the local merchant who was the model for Uncle Sam. *Troy wants you, Julian,* she'd thought with a smile.

Albany and Schenectady were its better-off neighbors. Which said a lot. A city best known for being unknown.

All of which had revealed itself quickly to her, vindicated her choice of this city, when she had looked for, had needed a place—through no fault of her own—to once again start anew. She chose a place that was itself trying to start anew.

It was a manageable city. The officers riding in front could know its streets intimately—its landmarks, its crevices, its shopkeepers, it winos, its rhythms, its meanings. So did the passenger in their backseat, but she barely saw it now, was barely aware of it.

At the moment, her head was filled with the past. The past tumbling before her, collapsing thick and unsorted in her brain like a forgotten closet shelf, packed too heavy and piled too high, finally, suddenly, giving way . . .

Seeing him seated there, filling the straining chair with his two hundred eighty pounds of silent aggression, filling the room with mute smug threat, had brought it back smartly, crackling, instantly. At the moment, despite the admirably clean, clear rear windows of the black-and-white, despite the admirably crisp, clear cerulean blue November day beyond them, she could barely see.

Some of that past was sealed, of course. A protection provided by the State in any police proceeding. His flashy-ringed counselor Cooperman, her own quietly dogged state-assigned representative, had succeeded together—from their opposing sides—in at least accomplishing that. Her career to come, Your Honor, the gaunt gangly overworked state's counselor meekly reasonable, eyes and palms open, importuning, honest. His career too, Your Honor—countermanding, assertive, blustery, strutting, his bulldog insistence on fairness and balance. So that only the smallest piece of it necessary was a matter of public record. For anyone who might care to look, who might get interested anew.

Not just a murderer: that was the thing. A murderer, and a cop. The second denotation tending to ensure the memorability of the first. But even the prospect of a murderer cop, amid the world's assault of information, its barrage of data, held no particular command of the public imagination. It took up only its small place, delivered only its single portion, in the planet's daily diet of genocide and catastrophe, destruction and despair. The public's interest tended to move quickly to the next scandal, the next gruesome fascination. Killer cop. Diametrically distinct from cop killer. Inhabiting the opposite end of some lurid spectrum. Cop killer and killer cop, opposite and identical. And after all, not *really* a killer cop, said the record. A mistake. Sorry. Which tended to move the public interest quickly on as well.

Since then, she'd forced herself: forced herself to focus on the present.

Forced herself as a life-saving measure to see the city, look out at it, study and learn it, concentrate on its now familiar streets and shops and ancient brick edifices and hopeful and cheerfully chaotic new residential blocks. Her focus, her learning, had paid their dividends. In the narrow confines in which she'd applied herself, she'd succeeded wildly—full detective to detective-sergeant to lieutenant. Meteoric, yes, but within a vacuum, speed is inevitable, she'd thought cynically. Her quick lieutenancy probably said more about the size and needs of the force than about any innate ability. And her Homicide record furnished proof of her abilities, safely beyond any consideration of gender. It was a numbers game—and she had the numbers.

Through the rear windows of the black-and-white, she looked out on her city now—like the steadying orienting shoreline seen from a tiny, wind-rocked, wave-tossed boat.

This city had become a home to her. She was alone in it, but as alone in it as she had been everywhere in her life—no less so but no more so—and at least here it was a place she'd chosen.

Troy was her home.

And like its ancient namesake, it had been invaded.

What trick, what deceit, was Winston Edwards bringing to it? What wooden horse was he entering on?

Only she knew who he really was. What he was capable of. The judge and jury clearly didn't know. The police panels didn't. The world didn't. She hoped they wouldn't have to learn. She hoped she could prevent that. But for now, only she knew, so she was responsible. She knew what he was. She knew he was here. That was a lot to know.

She'd done what she could, having him watched. It didn't amount to much, but what more could she do? Under the law, he'd committed no violation. She could probably pull strings to get a restraining order, but that wouldn't accomplish anything, and his behavior so far could hardly qualify as harassment, if the issue ever came under scrutiny. In fact, if it came under scrutiny, she'd be the guilty party, leaving him—unprovoked—in a puddle on the station-house floor.

Running the gun along his teeth. Under his eyes. Once she'd found it there, she'd played the scene through. Played through the animosity and menace. But what was the gun doing out in the first place? To Ng and

Mendoza, discussing it now undoubtedly, it must look like a long-simmering vengeance. Like fury finally unleashed. But she knew—she knew it was only her fear.

What could she do? She could only go on. Press on, knowing that somehow Winston Edwards was back in her life, and somehow—as sure as night, as certain as darkness—he was about to figure prominently in it again.

Arching her back to get more comfortable in the rear seat, she saw the male officers' eyes drink her in quickly in the rearview mirror. Inspecting, as always, the God-given shape and underwear-catalogue curves that had brought her, she'd long ago concluded, a little more pleasure and a lot more trouble than the next female officer.

She rolled down the window, to let in her city, to draw sustenance and support into the police car with her. She let her thick black hair blow. Narrowed her eyes against the slice of wind, condensing further her already slightly pointed features. Features that sometimes exploded with animation and expressiveness, then retreated into their serene Cleopatra mask, leaving everyone longing for that expressiveness again.

Somewhere in her—shrouded, vague, murky and undefined—the thought unformed, the feeling only slightly more pronounced than the thought—she sensed it was one more opportunity to get him.

And equally shrouded and vague, murky and undefined, she sensed it was one more opportunity for him to get her.

Last time, he'd had the power. She'd been the outsider.

This time, it was the reverse.

Last time had been a draw.

But in matters of life and death, a draw was the exception.

In matters of life and death, a draw tended not to repeat.

3

Perfect day for a funeral.

Clouds bloated with gray, hanging, rolling slowly, like immense balloons in a parade of grief . . .

Julian, Ng, and Mendoza stood in the cold mist, heads bowed, cameras tucked into their palms.

It had been a long time since they'd been to a victim's funeral.

They were all quite proud of not attending victims' funerals.

Because the funerals always came about a week or so after the crime, and usually by then, they were well on their way to figuring it out; clues had compiled and compounded, were leading richly and relentlessly to other clues, and there was no reason for their strange faces to disrupt or unnerve a family in its grieving. No reason to impose, however slimly and diplomatically, a police presence.

But on this one, the Ryan case, it had been a week without a single break. Nothing. Which is why they were here in the drizzle, paying their respects to Francis Xerxes Ryan.

Of course, Julian generally got invited to the funeral anyway—the family's latest friend, their newest sympathizer and chronicler, and the surviving family was always eager to demonstrate the normalcy of what was left of it, to demonstrate its appropriate grief, to show this expert that the disaster at hand was only an aberration, a terrible mistake. What it really demonstrated, it had occurred to Julian, was the elaborateness of denial. And at first—mutely sympathetic, dutiful and appropriate herself, she had gone to the funerals, but soon—whether battle hardened and wearied, or out of some deeper and more genuine sympathy and understanding of the family, she had found ways to not go. Other work, other cases, she would say. Trying to protect and head off other families from this grief. Thanks for the invite, though.

So here they stood, identically, Ng, Mendoza, and Julian. All attired in black, heads bowed identically, hands clasped identically in front of them, the better for each of them to hide the identical tiny cameras clasped beneath their palms, the better to protect them from the drizzle.

Which was the real purpose of their attendance. The snapshot that was a long shot that had paid off before. A place to start, in finding Frank Ryan's murderer.

Julian stood a step in front, Mendoza and Ng flanking her a step behind. The unconscious ingrained police choreography of rank.

Of course, it put Julian that much closer to the hearse pulling up, backing carefully to the curb, its rear gate lifted; that much closer to the casket laboriously offloaded, delivered into position at the head of the deep perfectly dug rectangular hole by burly attendants swallowing their grunting effort in deference to the ceremony. That much closer to the eyes, to the tears, to the heavy silence, to the family.

They had taken most of their pictures already, employing a system the three of them had devised for getting at least a shot or two of every attendee. Ng was responsible for photographing the men, Mendoza for the women, and Julian for the children.

Which left Julian the most time and freedom to explore anything else, children being generally scarcest at a funeral, and the least likely to lead them anywhere.

And photography done—except for watching especially alertly to snap any straggler or observer lurking at the edges—they were now, as much as they could be at least, fellow mourners.

It was the two daughters, standing almost dangerously close to the edge of the pit—periodically, systematically, pulled back by an uncle's hand, then inching forward again—who held the interest of the mourners. Beautiful young girls, eleven and twelve maybe, a year apart, maybe two. It was their sullen curiosity, their instants of sudden vivacity, their awkward beauty, that, Julian could see, wrenched fresh misery from every mourner there. They were the locus, the centerpiece, of mourning.

Julian had witnessed far greater tragedy, far more closely, than anyone else at graveside, she figured. That was the case at every grave. An occupational hazard.

But this was something else. Something more. Julian stood immobile. The circumstance swept over her, enshrouded her like the misty morning, the long-ago events reawakened in her. Because these two girls—these sisters—were watching their murdered father being lowered into the ground. At the same age that Julian and her younger sister had watched their own murdered father lowered into it.

She was standing farther from this grave, of course. It was twenty-five years later and a thousand miles away. Yet it was, in every important sense, in everything that Julian could see and feel, the same funeral. And it was their stepping up to the hole and back, their curiosity, their irrepressible girlhood, even amid this sorrow, even trying as they were, to respect this solemnity, that was so heartripping. What was denial in adults, was, in eleven- and twelve-year-old children simply a dose of unreality—a complete inability to process the events, or feel the occasion. Long-unseen uncles and aunts and strangers standing silently around a hole, your dad inside a box, about to be lowered into the dirt. The girls' blank expressions masked no tears but reflected instead an altered universe in which tears would be too simple, too small a response.

Julian looked especially, of course, at the older girl. Her short black hair, pageboy cut, her exploratory, searching, swimming black eyes. It looked to be constant battle between curiosity and shyness, the way those eyes flitted around the mourners, fixed on the priests' raiments, appraised the undertaking staff's appearance and demeanor. Not to pass judgment on its appropriateness but to watch what they were doing, to overhear what they were saying. It was undoubtedly her first funeral, and, Julian hoped, her last for a very long time.

It could only be worse, thought Julian in passing, if this had been a funeral for one of the girls. But only a cop could even think that, she reflected. Only a cop could manage to make an event like this any bleaker.

And even if borne powerfully into the past, Julian was still on duty. She therefore duly noted the girls' matching blue raincoats, purchased especially, and obviously, for this occasion. She had of course looked at the cars—some sleek sedate German, some sensible Japanese. All to make some assessment, to get a sense, of the Ryans' socioeconomic status, their place in the world. Which wasn't necessarily valuable data, but wasn't necessarily meaningless, either.

In nomine Patris, et Filii, et Spiritus Sanctus . . . The priest alternately intoning and mumbling, swinging unpredictably between the two. All were conscious now of the increasingly insistent wind. Making scarves dance, sending the drizzle sideways. The wind like a mourner itself, strafing the small assembly with its moans and wails, like a message from the afterlife.

Pater Noster, qui est in coeli . . . Our Father, who art in heaven. As a detective in a long-settled American city, Julian had a grim knowledge of the ceremonies of all the major denominations and a number of minor ones, a knowledge not shared by most clergymen, who tended after all to specialize. Funerals in Arabic, in Hebrew, with Native American chants, in Hindi and Swahili. She had observed them all.

Finally, the priest invited each mourner to pass by the coffin, before it was lowered into the ground. It was a convenient moment for Julian, Ng, and Mendoza, permitting them a systematic, final review, a last confirmation of their newly gathered photographic evidence. *Got him, got her, got him* . . .

The mourners formed a line to pass by the casket. The two girls just after their uncle, each placing a rose as they saw their uncle do, following his example so closely that the younger girl cringed when her rose did not stay on top of the casket, but slid down its curved lid. Her mother's automatic, forgiving, blessing smile. All Julian needed to see from the grieving widow, to speak of the widow's brand of motherhood, and to know the girls would somehow be all right . . .

The mourners passed the casket shoulder to shoulder now, each dutifully, in strict Catholic fashion, taking the appropriate private moment for grief, seizing their allottment of time with tragedy.

As the last of them filed past, leaving the view to the casket clear again, Julian noticed the top flower in the growing, forlorn pile. It was a flower Julian had never seen before—purple and olive, with shocks and spots of scarlet, the edges of its petals black. Its colors almost unnaturally crisp, otherworldly; brittle and neon . . . it was, at the least, extremely unusual. A rose, but not a rose.

On the clergyman's signal, three gravediggers with shovels stepped silently forward. The heavy attendant at the coffin ropes struggled up from his seat, stood at the ready. The gravediggers buried their shovels in the dirt, each shovel shortly emerging piled high with a rich muddy loam, and they stood ready alongside.

And as the huge black box began its descent—creakingly but smoothly into the ground—Julian impulsively took out the camera, took a step forward, and quickly, quietly, unobtrusively, so a mourner watching might wonder if she really did it at all—used the last exposure on the roll to take a shot of the unusual flower on top.

One toss of dirt, then another, landed expertly, with a splattered drumming, on the wood of the casket.

The coffin's sling strained and squeaked as the box was lowered. Life's machinery turning again . . .

More dirt tossed: first ceremonial, now in earnest . . .

The widow's wail went up. Now in earnest, too.

In nomine Patris, et Filii, et Spiritus Sanctus . . . Julian watched the dirt pile on. But she was thinking about the last exposure on her roll.

4

His right ankle screamed with every step. His left knee would buckle without warning. When he moved, sat, stood, twisted a certain way, pain shot searing up his left side. Opening and closing the fingers of his right hand was a painful, intricate process. His cough sounded tubercular, a chronic soup-kitchen, sleep-in-the-street, get-to-the-clinic cough, a death rattle through his huge frame that set it shuddering. A cough like a rumble of impending terminality; a cracked bullhorn calling out the onset of the end.

It was a body whose upkeep he had abandoned long ago, and it had now in turn abandoned him. He'd always been strong, never sick a day, had always had vast reserves of strength and stamina that he'd taken for granted, and now it was all gone. Gone with a vengeance.

There was a continual throbbing against his brain that set a rhythm to his days. The chorus, the opera of pains, this one singing its aria, then this one, then this—an excrutiating accompaniment to his existence. He literally squinted against the pain, squinted to see through it, to not let it blind him because it would blind him completely, to keep moving against the thick wall and howling wind of it. Alcohol only dulled it, brought a forgetfulness of it, but not a relief. It had ceased to be a mantle of pain that he wore. Now it was in him, seeped into his bones and his being, part of him like his organs or his skin.

He sat drinking his fourth whiskey at the bright-lit bar. He'd found his way here by instinct. You felt your way to these bars, he'd discovered. A certain kind of bar. Brightly lit as if with no pretense—no thematic aspiration, no marketing plan. A certain kind of bar with no larger idea than drink. Once you were in the drinking subculture, you knew where they were, you found your way, as if the path were marked. In his work, he'd always seen the subculture. Now he was part of it, and it was honest in its bleakness, not sinuous and explosive and unreadable like the cultures of narcotics or the mob. It was frankly gloomy, forthrightly grim. So bare and simple as to be dumb, this subculture. He liked that, too. He could use a little dumb. He tipped back his whiskey, looked over expressionlessly, noncommitally, to a small table behind him, to the plainclothesman spending his shift assigned to him. The man looked back as noncommitally, like the blank slate he was supposed to be. It was like watching your shadow as a kid, he thought. Where it goes as you move, how it gets shorter, longer, sharper, paler. The plainclothesman had a paperback book with him, its title covered in plain paper, so that no assessment or judgment could be made, even based on literary taste.

The man had come prepared to do his job, as had the previous plainclothesmen assigned to him. Edwards turned back to the bar. They seemed to be generally well trained. He figured Julian had something to do with that.

Prison had given him patience, of course. Five years of prison had given him a convict's sense of time, closer to a Buddhist monk's or a Hindu yogi's than one might imagine. Five years of fate held in abeyance, of one's own life swinging just out of reach, gave you a perspective on daily events and on the movement of the cosmos that was vastly different from the one you'd entered prison with. The ability to wait literally a lifetime, if necessary, to make a move between stopwatch ticks. In that sense the worst lowlife, the dumbest-shit sixth-grade dropout street scum, became a Zen master. . . .

Age; vengeful prison beatings; withheld, then begrudging, medical help; that was the pedigree of his pain. He knew, he recognized, that the pain made him dangerous. The constant pain took away the fear of it, pain as a companion took away pain as a deterrent. It gave him the potential, the outlook, of the criminal.

His whole career, he'd demonstrated an excellent—indeed, a profound—understanding of the criminal mind. He'd been genteelly complimented on it, as if it were an intellectual victory, an academic exercise. *Remarkable how you knew he'd be hiding in the garage. Impressive how you knew she'd aim for him first.* Accepting the praise as genteelly, he'd known there was more to it, more connection to it, than that. Now, of course, the connection was robust and complete—if not proved in a court of law, then proved resoundingly to those who truly knew him.

Still, he would sit bolt upright, whether from a doorstep, or a gutter, or a holding cell floor—startled, straightened, disoriented by the vision of the lustrous black hair, the proud nose and cheekbones, the serene expression. Still he would sit bolt upright, whether from a tormented dream, or a blessed dreamless hour of sleep. In this, the usual pain did not mask or distract. This was a different pain. A pain that intensified his opaque desires. Pain like a carved and deeply scarred black border, framing her image.

I'll show her. The three simple words rose up into his consciousness now as if from some primal dark beneath it. They rose up in him as if out of nowhere, unsummoned, complete. Bearing a sense of order, of perfection, that was otherwise absent from his current existence. Three words that focused his fury, yet calmed it. *I'll show her.* Pure solution. Amid his derangements, pure solution.

He'd come here with nothing particular in mind. No plan. Random movement only. A random proceeding in the random affair his life had become. Her response—the probing gun muzzle, the furious kick, the hard cold linoleum floor—had meant nothing. Had been at least more acknowledgment than he'd received in prison beatings.

I'll show her.

Decorated, legendary police chief. Jailbird and criminal. Repository of pain, of penance, of resignation, of regret, of fury, of despair. Reliquary of a thousand deceits, a thousand ploys.

Arch-hero and neocriminal; god and devil. He was a strange creature now. A creature with little regard for its own fate. With nothing to gain and nothing to lose.

This was a strange, brooding, drifting, dangerous creature, he'd be the first to acknowledge, sitting at this bright-lit bar. He downed the rest of the whiskey, and then another, and in an hour, his head was on the counter, his eyes were shut, his mouth open and breathing heavily, raspily, slow and deep.

The bartender came over, leaned down to him. "Listen, pal. It ain't a hotel."

Edwards's head remained on the bar.

"Come on, ma man," said the bartender, a notch more urgently.

Edwards didn't stir.

The bartender looked up to the man reading at the table beyond the bar.

The plainclothesman's wooden chair scraped on the linoleum floor, a long loud scrape of annoyance and irritation. The plainclothesman joined the bartender standing over Edwards. There was a long silent moment while the two men studied the immense figure slumped on the bar, listened momentarily to the labored, deep, gasping breathing, as if lulled by it. "He can't stay there," the bartender asserted finally, and turned away, with implicit challenge, making it clear it was the plainclothesman's responsibility.

The plainclothesman, freckled, red haired, a short thick policeman who looked forward to the end of every shift, regarded the figure's incredible heft. His replacement wasn't due for another hour. "Ahhh, Christ," he said. The figure on the bar breathed noisily. The breath was animal. "Christ," the plainclothesman reiterated.

He headed purposefully to the phone booth at the back of the bar, tucked around the corner in the tiny half vestibule in front of the men's room door. To even see the old black rotary phone's half-scraped numerals in the vestibule's darkness, he had to huddle down to it, get close to the dial.

He began to dial the station house, watching and listening to the rotary dial's noisy clicking ancient return from each number.

By the fourth or fifth digit, the red-haired plainclothesman knew. His stomach wrenched and knotted.

He slammed the phone onto the receiver in time to hear the bartender's "Hey!"—weak, startled, ineffectual—"Hey!"

The plainclothesman launched himself out of the phone booth and around the vestibule corner, scanning the window furiously, racing for the bar door, all too late.

With the force of suddenness, like a caged animal freed, Winston the Bear Edwards—highly attuned and alert, despite his vivid head-on-the-bar impersonation—was gone.

5

In her tiny one-bedroom apartment, Julian stared out the window into the lit city streets below. She would find herself at this window often, the hours and minutes condensing and expanding until they were indistinguishable—time drifting, disappearing, time wafting—fragrant and appealing—stolen and precious—lost and found.

She'd taken the first place she'd seen, and vowed to decorate it cheerfully. But the big window seemed to serve as reminder that life was outside, and that inside was only shadow. The meager result of that conclusion: two prim, unmatched, uncomfortable chairs, a desk, a double bed, all bought secondhand, thoughtlessly, automatically, in a sweep one weekend morning.

She would stand at the window, never making it comfortable there, never putting a chair by it, and yet despite her self-imposed strictures, her defense against it, she would end up there hours. But it wasn't hours tonight. Tonight was different.

She looked down from the window. Saw Ng himself, immense, alert, in the passenger seat of an unmarked car directly in front of the single building entrance. He waved up to her, proving his alertness.

He'd slipped them midafternoon, while she and Mendoza and Ng were at the funeral. Slipped them easily, crisply. And in their little city, the city they covered closely, thought they knew so well, he had not yet reappeared.

But he was an old man now. He would not appear here tonight, she knew. He was shrewder than that. Far more complex. She did not know where he was, or what he was doing. But she sensed, at least, that it wasn't going to be here. She was four floors up, armed and aware. Ng and a night partner were armed and aware. Winston Edwards wasn't, she knew, coming here.

She wasn't afraid of his showing up tonight.

She was afraid of much more than that.

She was afraid that while she knew him well enough to know he would not appear tonight, she had no good idea why he was here, or what he had in mind.

The past, she thought again, staring out the window. The past, launching a sneak attack, cutting off escape into the present or the future. In the reappearance of the wretched Winston Edwards. And in the misted vision of two beautiful girls. The past in a guise of abject ugliness. And of sad beauty.

She hunted around on her crowded corner desk avidly, finally found the slip of paper with the number she knew was there, and after only a moment's hesitation dialed it. As the phone rang at the other end, she heard her own deep anxious breathing, pronounced in the silent apartment.

"Hello?" came the voice at the other end, as familiar as socks and bikes and ice cream, as distant as a lifetime.

"Steph?" she ventured, the syllable shy, as if looking on tiptoes over the top of a trim white picket fence.

"Julian? My God, what a surprise!"

Julian was always amazed to hear the strong vestige of the drawl still there. Julian had eradicated the Southern accent entirely. But there it was still, in her little sister Stephanie.

"Long time," Julian observed, hoping for it to land without judgment or criticism.

"Long time is right, Jules."

"How are your kids?"

"Growing, growing, growing . . . Robert is nine, you know. Sarah's seven."

"Paul?"

"Fine. Good. How are *you*? It's been . . . my God . . . since spring!" Her innocence. Her straightforwardness and levelheadedness. Julian cherished it and couldn't understand it.

To Julian, it seemed that both their lives had been paths of forgetting. Routes of personal eradication. But such different routes. Julian's had been an all-consuming career. Her sister's had been motherhood, convention, suburbia, absorbing oneself seamlessly and anonymously into mainstream America. Into conventional wishes and dreams and utterly unsuspect, conventional life. Julian knew that's what it was with Stephanie, because Stephanie, despite how she lived her life, never quite believed in her life.

She might not call it by the same name, but it was nevertheless her own escape. "So what's up?" Stephanie asked brightly.

"Just calling," Julian lied.

"Come on now, Jules," cheerful, attuned, "you do not just call. We both know that."

They would be bound forever by it, thought Julian again for the thousandth time. This link beyond sisterhood. This horrible link.

"I was at a funeral today," Julian said. Then a pause, a silent pause in Julian that caused, she noticed, a pause at the other end too. Julian could feel her sister's sense of burden—suspicious, cautious, not wanting to know more, but as the sister, obliged to. "Yeah?" said Stephanie. As measured, as cautious, as a single syllable can be.

"Two young girls, about a year apart," said Julian. "Standing there." She paused once more before telling her. "Their father was killed. . . ."

"Jules," her sister said with sudden exasperation, angry and annoyed, "Please . . . Let this stuff go."

Another silence. In which Julian did not respond, did not defend, knowing her sister was absolutely right, and knowing just as well that she could never do what her sister was suggesting.

"Jesus," said Stephanie, resignation now mixing in with, melting and softening, her frustration—knowing Julian would never let it go, was incapable of it.

"Cute girls," Julian went on now, the circle of silent understanding, of immutable behavior, implicit between them. "New blue coats just for the occasion."

"Don't go to funerals," Stephanie said.

"I stood there, and there it all was again," Julian told her sister, unable not to. "Not even like yesterday. Like . . . like *now* . . ."

"Julian, Julian . . ."

Julian could hear Stephanie's kids in the background—the murmurs, the eruptions, of manic activity, of child fury, of unalloyed hooting glee. She smiled. Warmed. With the thumb and forefinger of her free hand, she dabbed quickly at her own pinched tears.

She looked around her own apartment. Small. Silent.

"There's nothing you can do about it, don't you see?" said Stephanie, as if stating it once more like it was fresh and new, would change her. "Let it go."

"I can't." Said as fact. Without sadness. Adamantine. Granite.

"You have to. You just have to. You can't keep living in . . . I don't know . . . no-man's-land."

No-man's-land. Dim, unreal, ill defined. A habitation of ghosts and echoes and the infinite unfinished. It was Edwards's land, somehow, Julian thought.

"Jules . . ."

"Yeah?"

"You gotta call Mom."

"Oh. Trying to sidetrack me from my own morbid thoughts with a new one, huh?"

"Julian."

"What's the point?" Julian sighed. She did not want the conversation to head in this direction, but did not feel the right to stop it.

"Because you just . . . have to, that's all." As if it were self-evident.

"She's just gotten worse," Julian said. "She doesn't even know who we are. Doesn't even give any sign of knowing anymore."

"Doesn't matter," said Stephanie.

"How do you know I *haven't* called?" asked Julian.

" 'Cause I know you." She could feel Steph's smile. "Call her," the younger sister prodded gently. The noises behind Stephanie were louder now. Kids yelling at each other. "I gotta go," Stephanie said, "as you can hear, no doubt. We'll talk later. All right?"

"Yeah, all right."

Julian hung up the phone.

She tried to shut out the conversation's closing subject. Tried because she knew she almost could. Because she'd almost succeeded.

But to shut out the image of the two little girls. She knew she couldn't. Knew she never could.

6

The high vaults of the public library's main reading room reached upward with grand spirit and thick strength as if to some heavenly promise of knowledge; forever defiant of the cold and rain and ice and snow pounding at them from the outside; forever ignorant of the wild-eyed postmodern architects and egocentric local developers eager to assault them from within.

Silence, immensity, solemnity, swirled in the molecules that hovered dustily in the visible atmosphere beneath the soaring vaults; followed the thump of each footstep on worn stone floors, whose every echo spoke scholarship; rose from among the tomes stacked like bricks, fortress walls of knowing. At the north end of the immense main room, there were rows of cubicles, each with a terminal to summon up microfiche documents, to connect to the digital universe of the Internet, to facilitate the stunning depth and breadth of research that could be done from a single seat.

A public library, of course, inevitably got its share of drunks and eccentrics and the schizophrenic homeless; it was safe, warm, public property they couldn't be thrown out of except for cause; they used it like a church, and the less damaged and deranged came in each morning to read the daily paper for free, or to sit with a good book, and the library staff accepted them as part—the most difficult but colorful part—of its clientele.

And any of these poor and downtrodden—even with liquor on his breath—if he was polite, and quiet, making an effort to improve his mind, could even take his place at one of the terminals, for he was only a soul like any other, more visibly distressed perhaps, but no different fundamentally from any other library visitor.

So it was that Winston Edwards sat in front of the white box, scrolling silently, attentive, efficient, his various pains momentarily and cooperatively at bay.

They would look in the bars. They would look in the fleabags. They would check the alleys and side streets where he'd left a previous trail. But his bet was that they wouldn't check the library.

Now it was just him, and the ceiling vaults, his manifold pains, and the computer terminal in front of him—blinkingly alert, a portal of undigested fact. Now to turn it into a portal of truth.

No one involved in Edwards's trial or its aftermath had much procedural experience with a criminal cop. They took his badge, took his keys, locked him out of his office, couldn't think what else to do. Which was why Winston Edwards still had not only an expired badge but also, he was betting, his law enforcement computer access. His personal codes. In the midst of the erratic confusing trial and his long incarceration, he hoped no one had thought to take those away.

"WELCOME TO THE NATIONAL POLICE CRIME FILE AND DATA SEARCH CENTER. NAME?"

Winston Edwards, he typed. Hands huge and careful on the keyboard. And trembling, he noticed. But trembling only with age and infirmity.

"PASSWORD?"

He typed it: "BEAR." Hardly a secret password. The handle of his entire career. A nickname with staying power, he'd theorized, because it rolled together affection and fear, and didn't force the two to be distinguished.

He waited in the library's thick dusty silence for the computer to respond.

"ACCESS DENIED."

The rage welled up instant, alive. He wanted to smash the arrogant white box with a single blow. Hear the loud echo of its shattering demise rise into the vaults. He felt his fist form before he knew he'd formed it. . . .

No.

Of course. How stupid. It had been five years now. In the universe of computers, technology and data, several lifetimes. It wasn't the justice system or thorough policework that would foil him. It was time. The whole system must have changed. New codes were undoubtedly issued—maybe several times already. The information, the organization, the accessibility, were bound to be far superior now. Easier. Richer. More navigable. If only he could get on. That would be the toughest part.

Julian's code. He knew what she'd used before, but she might know if he used it, he'd bet there was that kind of tracking now.

Think.

No. Don't think. Drift . . .

He let his mind wander, called back, allowed out, the river of whiskey still in him, shunted temporarily to one side and now summoned again. He let his thoughts unmoor, let a sea of faces and interactions and experience wash over him in a Zen-like convict trick, a prison technique, where memory was a primary form of entertainment, so you learned to stir its various ingredients into new flavors and combinations, and then lay back and watched. He played it again now, his past in a thick, rich, unsorted parade . . . wife, children, employees, the good and bad, a rush of imagery, allowing an answer to come washing past him, unsummoned, unbidden, from the condensation of his police past. Chuck, the old cop who had greeted him every day . . . Richie, his pal from the academy . . . Simms, the dim-witted state employee who worshiped him, mimicked every mannerism, and cowered in his presence . . . Julian, of course, younger, bright-eyed, unhardened . . .

Wandering, drifting, the routines, the routine exchanges, the startless stopless parade of years continuing, washing over him, circling naturally, spiraling down to Chuck again, his daily weather report, earnest and inaccurate; Richie, lean and hunched, stamping his feet against the cold; Simms, the office's unauthorized biographer and gossipmonger, who'd imagined himself, absurdly, Edwards's heir. Edwards remembered discovering a pencil, a pen, or some other small item, mysteriously gone from his own desk, soon on Simms's desk, in Simms's hand. Some small silent obsession, not quite enough to bother or take issue with, just under the radar.

Edwards's eyes widened. Flooded with light . . .

"NAME?" the computer prompted again.

"LOUIS P. SIMMS," Edwards typed.

"PASSWORD?"

"BEAR," he typed, and in the computer's momentary pause to search, he crossed his thick fingers for luck, just above the keyboard.

"ACCESS GRANTED."

Through his manifold pains, Edwards couldn't help but smile.

Five years later, his instincts were intact.

Mostly, he figured, because five years later, the foibles of others were intact too.

A few screens and keystrokes and labored squints and leanings-forward to the terminal, and "UNSOLVED" opened before him. It was now a single national computerized file, he saw. He'd figured it would be at some point, since it was quickly realized and statistically verified that solving these cases—on the rare occasions they were solved—most often involved linking events and circumstances, similarities and echoes that jumped jurisdictions, crossed the country and even the world. There were eight thousand unsolved murders a year in the U.S. As raw numbers went, a particularly raw one. But at least you couldn't see the manila stacks anymore. The criminal justice failure was no longer so physical. That would daunt you, to say nothing of breaking your heart—for anyone in criminal justice who still had one.

It was truer now than ever, he saw: there were no data banks like police data banks. The FBI had made much of its own vaunted data accessible to state and local law enforcement. Which made the financial, behavioral, medical, and historic information available on individuals, families, marriages, purchases, and relationships, alarmingly thorough. It remained several leaps ahead of what you could discover on the Internet. Police data banks. Marketers would kill for them.

He began to weave his way through "UNSOLVED."

A small town. Within a hundred miles of here. Julian had said it one night five years ago at a candlelit dinner in Raleigh-Durham. They'd been investigating a particularly difficult case, had flown to the South for a day to do so, and it was, he realized now, only their accidental proximity to her past that had brought it up at all, that had allowed it briefly into the conversation. Her father's murder. Unsolved. It was all she had let drop at a dinner one night on an investigation six years ago. It was all he had to go on. But it might be enough.

He hadn't pushed her for details. Her message had been clear: don't ask me more. It was so patently her private silence, a private compartment, he didn't—wouldn't—invade. But the passing fact said so intimately—it had of course stayed stored within him, powerful, potent, churning. A single dangling fact to work with now. Plus one more fragment that made it considerably more difficult. *Another lifetime. Another life. I've even changed my name.*

So: a rough radius of geography. An unremarkable man's distant death. A single offhand reference to each. And not even a name. It was all he had. But thanks to this mute white box, thanks to the organizational mania and wholly surprising cooperative spirit of U.S. law enforcement, it might be all he needed.

Another click in "UNSOLVED" opened a "SEARCH" window.

At the "GEOGRAPHY" prompt, he typed in "NORTH CAROLINA."

At the "VICTIM" prompt, he typed in "MALE."

At the "AGE" prompt, he checked "35–45."

Then tapped "ENTER."

A huge list of names opened. Eight hundred twenty-five names, according to the total displayed in a corner of the screen. Murders, mayhem, of a half century. Victims high and low, refined and reviled, disturbing and deserving. He realized that the grim sum distinguished North Carolina law enforcement as neither particularly vigilant nor particularly inept. Probably put them about average.

He kept the file open. Shrank the window into a corner of the screen.

With Simms's password, Edwards now opened "U.S. CENSUS: LAW ENFORCEMENT ACCESS."

"YEAR?" the prompt offered. What could she have been? Twelve, thirteen? Try 1975. Didn't have to be exact, for what he was about to do. Just had to be close.

"1975 CENSUS" appeared, "SEARCH PARAMETERS" blinking below it, with a menu of options.

He highlighted "STATE"; typed in "NORTH CAROLINA."

"FURTHER PARAMETERS?" the census program prompted.

He clicked on the option "TOWNS."

"FURTHER PARAMETERS?" it asked again.

He clicked the option "LESS THAN 1000 RESIDENTS."

A long column of town names materialized. Only the A's and B's fit on the screen. Too much.

"FURTHER PARAMETERS?" it still offered.

A small town. Within a hundred miles of here. Dinner that night in Raleigh-Durham.

He double clicked on the "NORTH CAROLINA" prompt; a map of North Carolina instantly opened. He leaned in, squinted his eyes at the longitude and latitude numerals at its edges. He typed in 35° N, 78° W at the prompt, bracketed the longitudinal and latitudinal minutes, and then clicked "TOWNS" again.

Much better. Still about fifty town names. But more manageable.

He clicked "TOTAL POPULATION." A dizzyingly huge list of North Carolinians appeared.

Now.

He took a deep breath.

The computer now had both databases open. The names of the hundred thousand resident families of all of small-town North Carolina in a hundred-mile radius in the year 1975. And the names on the files of 825 unsolved North Carolina murders.

He pressed the "HELP" menu, followed the instructions on how to do it.

He merged the lists. And called up the tiny subset of duplications.

Four names appeared on both.

Just four names.

All within the right geography.

All the right age.

But one name caught him.

He would have assumed it was a black name, but what she'd said . . .

I've even changed my name. . . .

As soon as he saw it, he knew.

Vernon Blood.

Winston Edwards could feel his own pulse pound. His being crackle and sizzle. A feeling from before . . .

Vernon Blood. Old Southern name. Rendered in a single night too descriptive, too vivid, unfit and intolerable for at least one daughter of the South.

He clicked on the name. Opened the electronic file.

"Vernon Blood. RR 22, Tom's Bridge, NC.

D.O.D., NOV. 27, 1973. T.O.D. 2:00 A.M.–6:00 A.M. C.O.D., MLTPL STB WNDS TO CHST AND ABDMN."

Nearly a quarter century later, nothing more in the file. The barest of facts, tucked into a computer database as if folded deep and flat into a bottom drawer. Hardly summoning up the brutality of the moment. Delivered as if to negate, to dissipate, and to deny the nature of the actual event.

What would he do now?

He smiled. He knew exactly.

Intuition might say that a crime's insolubility twenty-five years earlier would make an attempt to solve it now even more difficult. But it was actually the crime's insolubility—its opaqueness, its mystery—which would help him now, a quarter century later.

Normally, he despised them. Their distortions, their errors; their hounding; their leering; their inaccuracies . . .

But this afternoon, he would come to appreciate them. This afternoon, beneath the ceiling vaults in the dusty municipal building, they would be his truest friends. . . .

The newspapers.

As much as they'd always been in his way, as much as they had altered, jiggled and jiggered reality, had twisted up, bungled—mostly bungled—the truth, they would now in an afternoon make up for their years of abuse. They would now become an invaluable and exclusive archive. They would be the missing file.

Because if a crime wasn't getting solved by the local police, you could be sure some hungry cub had written about that.

The curled bear paw hands aggressively punched the computer keys.

"PERIODICALS—NATIONAL REGISTER."

He entered the geography and the year.

And suppressed a smile.

There, suddenly, was the local paper.

"THE TOM'S BRIDGE NEWS." Weekly.

He scrolled through the paper archive to late November.

Huh.

No late November issue appeared.

No early December issue either.

Where the hell were they?

He scrolled some more. No more issues for the rest of the year.

Newspaper archives were often incomplete. Fragmentary. Particularly those of a Southern weekly from twenty-five years ago.

Still, it seemed impossible that there could be such bad luck. He wondered for a moment if the microfilm or microfiche could have been removed or tampered with; but here, in this library system, that hardly seemed possible.

But as Edwards naturally, vividly, began to imagine the editorial offices of *The Tom's Bridge News* weekly a quarter century ago, he quickly realized why *The Tom's Bridge News* wasn't published in that critical week, or thereafter.

He scrolled back to a *Tom's Bridge News* edition in mid-October, checked the masthead, and with a sinking sense of inevitability, confirmed it.

Vernon Blood was a newspaperman.

The *Tom's Bridge News* was his one-man paper.

An editor; an owner; a tiny town's one-man show.

His heart sank. A newspaperman. A thousand enemies. Corrupt local politicians. Slighted criminals. Those who felt they should have less coverage. Those who felt they should have more. The paranoid. The simply deranged. A newspaperman. An editor. The locus, the lightning rod, the punch toy, of the world's literate—even its illiterate—malcontents.

He searched for the closest local paper. "PARAMETER: GEOGRAPHY. PARAMETER: PERIODICAL." Click: "THE FAIRVILLE GAZETTE." A daily.

Bear paw fingers curled as if to pounce. Scrolling furiously, he got to the date when the *Tom's Bridge News* had stopped publishing: November 27. Nothing.

November 28. Nothing. The leisurely South.

November 29.

Editor Found Dead.

Responding to a call from the decedent's wife, local police found Vernon Blood, editor and publisher of *The Tom's Bridge News*, dead in his home, a victim of multiple stab wounds. According to Sylvia Blood, assailants entered the house moments before, while Mr. Blood worked at his desk. Mrs. Blood heard a commotion, and descended the stairs in time to see two hooded assailants flee the scene. No further details are available from police. Mrs. Blood is currently at Carolina Southern Hospital under observation. . . .

November 30. Some leads. Some suspects.

December 1. No leads. No suspects.

He followed the story over the next few days. Over the next weeks. Followed it to where it withered to a mention, and then evaporated altogether.

Fairly quickly in the progression of the story, he noticed, the articles began to bear a single byline.

He read, reread every one.

There was no conclusion, there was nothing to report. The trail had run dry.

He reread every article once more, then leaned back, crossed his arms, having arrived at his own inescapable conclusion.

Edwards could sense it—by the style, by the tone, by some of the sentence construction, by the literary decorum.

Not who the murderer was. On that, he had no idea. Had little idea, in fact, about anything further in the case.

He knew only, and with a fair degree of certainty, that the reporter knew more than he was writing. Might in fact know a whole lot more than was on the printed page.

It was twenty-five years ago. Bylines were still the custom for local crime reporting, particularly on smaller papers.

The reporter's name was Arteris Shore.

Twenty-five years ago.

Arteris Shore could easily be dead.

But Arteris Shore could easily be alive.

Edwards spot-checked *The Fairville Gazette* masthead over subsequent years. Arteris Shore, Arteris Shore . . . Never became editor. Or columnist.

Edwards returned to "U.S. CENSUS: LAW ENFORCEMENT ACCESS," still open on the electronic desktop.

Arteris Shore.

Unusual name. Luckily.

Unusual enough?

He entered the name in the U.S. Census data bank of living Americans.

Ten Arteris Shores. A relationship among them? All named for some character in a book or movie he'd never seen?

He entered one of the age options: "OVER 70."

Five.

Three in South Dakota. Family of them. Had to be. One in Maine.

One in Florida. Retired.

In the law-enforcement access version of the U.S. Census, next to "RETIRED" you could search "PREVIOUS OCCUPATION." Which he did.

Newspaper business.

Inside the immense body, the blood pulsed.

He heard himself thank God. With some strange mix of irony and authentic ardor, thanking God for having spared so far—through some fortuitous oversight in righteousness and the natural order—the life of a single lowly doubtlessly underserving newspaper reporter.

He could feel the excitement in him.

Now, how do we get to Mr. Shore's Florida address? . . .

"Sir?"

The voice startled him. He looked up, and was startled again to see the old woman's face leering over him.

What had he done? Who had found him? *Please* . . . He was so close, so close. . . .

"Library's closing in ten minutes. Have to finish up here." And she smiled down on him graciously, smiled at the tattered man expanding his mind, staying connected to the world for free.

He nodded silent assent and deference to her authority, and was back to his virtual search before she reached the next carrel.

He couldn't suppress the thought: he might be a criminal. But he was still a cop.

He was a cop again.

7

Julian began to scroll through the developed photos rapid-fire, Mendoza and Ng perched behind each shoulder, struggling to keep pace with identifying the subjects. It might have been a schoolyard game of trading cards, positions and stats of each card called out, but the stakes were considerably higher.

"That's the sister."

"Sister's friend."

"That's the friend from high school who's got the funeral parlor."

"Neighbor."

"'Nother neighbor."

When Julian came to the pictures of the two girls, she paused, stopped to look, set the photos down on her desk, side by side.

Ng and Mendoza were made to pause too. "Pretty," said Mendoza eventually, thrown off his rhythm, nervously drinking up the sudden silence.

In another moment, without explanation or expansion, Lieutenant Palmer continued scrolling through the photographs, and Ng and Mendoza picked up the rhythm again.

"Cousin's car."

"Boston aunt and Boston aunt's boyfriend's car, Escort."

"Interior of Escort."

Soon every mourner and every vehicle was identified. And they were nowhere again. But even further nowhere now, because it was a more complete and thorough nowhere.

It was a middle-class murder. Which usually made motive easier, more straightforward. Upper-class murders, you often had to sift through all the decadences first. It could be disgusting. It could be fun. The ghetto murders were drugs, incest, adultery, 95 percent explained by a small handful of the simplest motives and most obvious situations of human desperation. Murder was a surprise in the middle class, and middle-class lives were generally so ordered, so transparent, so appropriate, you quickly saw the missing piece, the jagged line, the element that didn't fit, that forced its way in. Here in the middle class, only rarely was it tough to make any headway, not to have even a direction to tilt off in.

She looked for suspiciously immaculate car interiors that had perhaps been cleaned up. It had worked for them before. She'd also scored on unduly filthy ones, whose discarded tissues and half-drunk sodas and pebbles and dirt in tires left a rich forensic trail that let her even reconstruct the roads they'd been on and the stores they'd stopped at. But all that had gotten her nowhere here.

She finally came to the picture of the flower. It wasn't quite as vivid photographed. It wasn't as startling as in real life. But it was still plenty unusual.

"What's that?" asked Ng.

"A flower," said Mendoza cynically.

"Ever seen one like it?" asked Julian. They shook their heads in somber near-comic unison.

"Me neither," she said. "That's why I took it."

"Beautiful," acknowledged Ng. "Interesting." There was silence.

She'd already asked, just after she'd snapped the picture, if Ng or Mendoza had happened to see who had put it on the casket. They'd shaken their heads no. But there it had been, balanced on, contrasting with, the casket's smooth, shining blackness.

Mendoza leaned farther in to the photograph. Then straightened, and smiled. "Interesting all right," he said. And looked at Julian. "But not the flower."

She looked back at him questioningly.

Mendoza pointed to the extreme bottom of the frame of the photograph. To photograph the flower, Julian had naturally aimed the camera directly down at the casket. So there, at the bottom of the frame, were the girls' prim Sunday shoes, lined up and glistening. There was their mother's sensible black footwear. And one other shoe—an otherwise unremarkable man's black dress shoe—with a single colorful petal of the distinctive flower stuck to its black leather upper.

"Most likely way that petal gets on your shoe," Mendoza pointed out dryly, "is if you're the one carrying the flower."

The three of them huddled more tightly around the photo, as if around a suddenly dug-up treasure.

Julian quickly divided the stack of photographs into three piles, placing one pile in front of Mendoza and another in front of Ng. They began silently cycling through the photos, looking, they knew without discussion, for a matching shoe, enpetaled or not.

"Nothing," concluded Ng at the end of his pile.

"Me neither," said Mendoza.

"Nell Ryan will remember," said Julian calmly. Nell Ryan, the widowed wife—cataloguing, adding up, a hostess keeping tabs on the grief. Or maybe even one of the girls—curious, finding the whole event memorable.

"Yeah, but . . . well . . ." Ng looked at Julian a little sheepishly. He shrugged his huge torso, the effect unintentionally comic. His huge face gathered into a frown. "I mean . . . what makes us think that flower means anything?" ·

They would go anywhere, they would with blind panting-dog loyalty pursue anything, but she had to give them the scent. They needed the scent.

And then Mendoza added quietly, in some mild mix of befuddlement and honest inquiry, but without any challenge in his tone, "Why'd you take the picture anyway?"

They looked at her, and calmly waited.

She considered her answer slowly and deliberately. It had been solely instinct when she stepped forward to take the picture, purely a nervous subneural alertness, a subcognitive signal. She thought now, carefully, seriously, about what that instinct might have been saying, might have been so instantly communicating; she considered how to bring into verbal reality, what had only, after all, run wordless along her forearms and down her spine.

She breathed once, looked confidently and yet at the same time imploringly at them.

"It took someone extra effort to bring a flower like that to that funeral," she said finally. "And *if* it took extra effort, some extra thought, to bring a flower like that to the funeral, then the flower might have some extra meaning."

But there was something more than that, too, something less dryly logical, yet oddly, potentially more meaningful. She looked at the photograph. "Think about this flower for a sec," she continued. "And think about that funeral. A funeral that was completely mundane, completely predictable, right down to the miserable weather." She tapped the photograph. "Except for this flower. It's the only exotic thing, the single unpredictable thing about that funeral." Now she picked up the photograph, fluttered it. "And murder was the only exotic, unpredictable thing that ever happened to Frank Ryan," said Julian.

She looked at Ng and Mendoza. It was the best verbalization she could manage, for the moment.

Somewhere deep in her, she was sure the stupid flower was nothing.

Somewhere deeper in her, she was sure it was something.

Something, anyway, to go on.

CRACK-CRACK!

Like a twin pop of rifle fire.

But actually thick fingers drummed twice, hard and quick, against the office door.

All three of them jumped on seeing him standing there, filling the doorway. Suddenly gone; just as suddenly there again.

Again, her heart clenched and fluttered. It was like a nightmare that repeats—worse the second time, in knowing all the fears unleashed the first time. Like a confirmation that the previous visit was no apparition. The same tattered clothes. The same rumpled superabundance. The same strange mix of presence and absence.

Although once again, Ng and Mendoza were here. Actually in her office, flanking her, as it happened, this time. Protective, reassuring, and ready to leap.

They'd lost him the previous afternoon—cops she'd trained—yet here he was. Wrinkled, folded in, downcast, outcast.

"Could I talk to you?" Edwards said, flatly, quietly. By which he clearly meant alone.

Mendoza narrowed his eyes with watchful wile.

Ng—as huge as Edwards, but far younger, and so far more powerful—brought himself up with slow and increasing effect to full height.

Cautiously, she nodded assent. Mendoza and Ng left the photos, left the office, left the door open.

Edwards's eyes once again roamed the institutional green walls of her office aimlessly, as if looking for something he was not eager to find, while her own eyes were never taken from his face. Then . . .

"I'm leavin'."

She looked at him, listening for more.

"Goin' to Florida," he said, with finality, with declaration.

Surprise and confusion and skepticism and giddy relief were all unleashed and skittering in Julian. "What . . . as in retiring?" She was surprised by her own sudden urge to smile at the preposterous mundaneness of it.

He shrugged noncommittally.

She settled back in her desk chair to sort the announcement against a moment of logic. "Retiring to Florida are we?" She grinned broadly at him now. The declaration was so obviously absurd. So patently an insult to her intelligence that it was undoubtedly meant to be. "I don't believe that for a minute," she said. "As you knew I wouldn't."

But she knew, she could tell, she'd get no more out of him on the true nature of his trip, whether to Florida or not.

"If you're going to Florida," she asked pointedly, "why are you here?"

He said nothing. Looked away, back to a spot high on the wall. But she saw his jaw clench tensely in the ensuing silence.

And suddenly she knew why.

She shook her head regretfully. Reached deep into her pocketbook that she kept on the floor beside her desk, drew out her checkbook, opened it to a blank blue check.

She looked at him, contemplating, curious. Then looked down again, to write and say as she wrote it, "There. Three hundred dollars. There you go . . ."

The check ripped loudly off the checkbook, as if protesting such a cavalier fate.

It was more than enough, she figured, for a ticket, seniors discount, plus a little money for a motel room. He couldn't complain. She was doing her part to get him out of here, wherever he was actually going, whatever he was actually going to do.

She folded the check, set it on the far edge of the desk, and quickly withdrew her hand.

The immense familiar paw scooped it up, deposited in the front chest pocket of the wrinkled shirt beneath the open trench coat.

Florida. She didn't believe him for a second. But she hadn't slept, knowing he was out there, unwatched. Three hundred dollars was worth getting him out of here. Wherever he was going. As long as he was going.

8

An indistinguishable, unobtrusive, decade-old green Buick Skylark cruises gently through the throb and pulse of a poor Spanish neighborhood in early evening. It cruises not quite aimlessly, but as close to aimless as possible, to still justify collecting a paycheck.

It is actually cruising the neighborhood around the cemetery, and Lieutenant Julian Palmer is at the wheel, alone, and gladly.

She felt safer here, in a nameless neighborhood, than at her precinct desk. She had the sense that she could understand life here, could understand the transactions, the needs, the moment to moment motives. In her desk life, her white life, the texture of need and motive and transaction shifted, hid, and dodged. But the greater truth was, she'd always felt safer in a place like this, where she knew half the residents were carrying guns and knives, than she felt within the thick clean walls and behind the gleaming locks of her other world. She had always felt safer, where she was more lost than found.

And Edwards seemed to be gone. That awareness played no small part in her sense of safety.

"Ever seen one of these?" she asked.

The elderly South American florist examined the photograph on his counter, and nodded sagely.

"What is it?"

The old man turned to the high bookshelf behind him, brought down a thick volume and thumbed quickly through it, stopped and turned the book to display the trophy to Julian. It was a richer photographic rendering, but it was clearly the same exotic flower. She couldn't tell whether he turned the book to her because of his inadequate English, or to display irrefutable proof and be particularly precise with the police.

"*Lilius macrophylla lupidus*," she read. He nodded.

"Ever had one in the shop?"

He shook his head, smiled with resignation. He held his hand out, rubbed his thumb against his other fingers and shook his head.

"Too expensive," she interpreted. So it was his lack of English.

He nodded vigorously,

From what she could imagine about his clientele, she knew he was right. It was most often in the poorest neighborhoods where cemeteries were located. Historically true for cities: that's where the land was affordable. There weren't many flower shops in this part of town. And it was looking less and less likely that the exotic flower had been picked up at a shop around here.

"But even though you don't order it, you do know the flower."

He nodded.

Julian leaned in, looking harder suddenly at the little man. "Why?"

He shrugged. He smiled uncomfortably. "Because I am florist."

Not only was his accent almost incomprehensibly thick, but his voice was cracked, weak, and odd. It was no wonder he chose to limit his speaking. But Julian was not letting him off that easily.

She picked up the thick floral reference book. She turned to a random page. She covered the name of a plant, and pointed to its photograph. "What's that?"

The man shrugged, smiled apologetically. "I dunno."

She flipped to another random page. "What about this one?"

Again he shrugged. "I dunno."

"It's a thick book," she smiled sympathetically. "Of course you don't know." She turned suddenly forcefully back to *Lilius macrophylla lupidus*. "But you know about this one," she said with aggression, clearly on her way toward outright anger, "and that's why I'll ask you again, and ask you just one last time. Why?"

His friendly mask came off. He dropped his smile. He was suddenly— beyond any language barrier—cornered, and intelligent enough to know it.

He looked at her, uncomfortable, not far from frightened. "They say . . ." He shrugged, smiled, then, she thought, shuddered a little.

"What?" she demanded.

"They say it means"—he paused—"another death. Another death to come." She noticed that his English was suddenly much better.

"Who says?" she demanded. What culture? What tribe?

He shrugged his shoulders, and she sensed, this time, that he truly didn't know.

Both regarded the picture in the thick book once more.

She left the shop. Looked out into the misty beautiful light—golden, red, and blue—the ironically golden light hanging above the downtrodden and struggling neighborhood—before getting back into the green Skylark.

Colorful, spangled, vibrant sky. As colorful, spangled, and vibrant as *Lilius macrophylla lupidus*. As unexpected above the gray neighborhood as *Lilius macrophylla lupidus* at a funeral.

Though whoever was carrying that flower, whatever family member or friend, might have had no idea.

But this was at least a direction to go in.

And *another death*. If that was really what it meant, then it meant the clock was ticking.

9

Winston Edwards perched at the edge of a cement fountain, in the fifth-floor open-air lobby of Sunshine Villas, a community of twenty thousand or so retirees thickly sprinkled across thirty or so six-story brick buildings. If there was ever an argument for dying young or staying north, Sunshine Villas was it.

But it was big enough, populous enough, that Edwards's pasty-faced bulk did not draw undue notice. He was simply a recent arrival, and he had already noticed a lot of them stayed out of the sun anyway, and were as pasty faced as he was.

Though it was still early morning, he'd already perspired through his shirt. His coat was folded in a lump beside him. He kept an eye on apartment 5C. Shore. Arteris Shore.

He used to be impatient. Used to want to bust in the door, get to the issue, not waste a moment. But now he had the inmate's Zen. Edwards had the sense that if he knocked, and the man looked, the man might not open the door. Retirees, after all. Old and frail. Older and frailer than himself. A retiree *and* a crime reporter. The man was probably more careful than most. Edwards figured he had a better shot this way. And the fact was, the sun slanted into the open veranda, and he could look out over this sun-soaked purgatory, and experience a few hours of Florida retirement, and still be working. Not bad. Not terrible. And the warmth even seemed to suspend his pains somewhat.

Late morning, the door to 5C finally opened. And a short, thin, wiry creature, gnomish, birdlike, sunburned red and creased and brown, like a menu item as much as a man, emerged—the inverse, the yang, to Edwards's pasty white bulk.

The man shuffled to the elevator bank, pushed Down, waited.

Edwards rose with a locally suitable laboriousness, kept his head down, watching his own footsteps seniorlike, as he ambled over to the elevator bank, nodded silently and disinterestedly at his fellow senior, and when the elevator came, got on with him.

They rode in silence for a couple of floors. Until Edwards asked, "Arteris Shore?"

The instant look of strangling fear on the man's face indicated that he'd been expecting and dreading just such a tolling of his name, such an intoning and invoking and accounting, for years. He lowered his gaze and did not look back up, Edwards noticed, as if not to face his executioner.

"Are you Arteris Shore?" Edwards had to therefore ask again.

"Yes, I am," a squeaky Southern drawl, tremulous, terrified—that drawl, for Edwards, a relieving proof of identity.

Edwards smiled, couldn't help himself. "I'm only after a story—same as you'd be."

And something in the words themselves, and something in how he said it, must have rung with truth, because Arteris Shore immediately took it as that, and visibly, physically, relaxed. By the time the elevator door opened onto the lobby, he was again merely a sun-browned retiree, and Edwards coud tell, even before stepping out, that if only in pure relief, Arteris was going to talk.

They sat at poolside, the huge white bloated specimen, the small quick-boned shriveled and wizened one, the meat before it's cooked and once it's overdone.

"I'm impressed you found me," said Arteris. "Here among all the birds a-butterin'." He had the Southerner's stretch and drawl, his sly weave of self-importance. "To what do I owe your company?"

"A case you covered." said Edwards, in contrasting briskness.

"One case among many," Shore warned Edwards gently. "To be recalled through the prism of a whiskey-drenched, arteriosclerotic, sun-numbed mind," the little man said, setting up, Edwards knew, excuse in advance for not recalling anything that shouldn't be recalled. A reporter's trick as old as Linotype.

"Vernon Blood," said Edwards.

"Vernon Blood." He repeated the name, as if to help locate the file in his mind, as if preparing to search memory's recesses, but only, Edwards knew, stalling for time.

Edwards smiled, looked at Shore, and summoning up his habit of threat, leaned closer. "I know you remember."

Arteris looked back at him, dropped the slow drawl a notch. "Remember it well," he said.

Shore settled back into the chaise a little. "Thing is, it coulda been anyone. So many enemies."

"Why was the other reporter taken off it, and you put on it?" Edwards asked.

"Scared us all," confessed Shore. "A newspaperman. I was just a little less scared than him." He shrugged. Edwards found himself immediately starting to like him. A rare thing, with a reporter.

"I read your articles," Edwards said. "As interesting for what they didn't say as what they did."

"What's your angle?" Shore's old reporter's instincts.

"I know the older daughter."

Arteris's eyes went wider, then narrowed, instincts sharpening. "How?"

"Became a cop," Edwards said.

"Huh," Arteris Shore said. He stared out at the pool a moment, and asked, "She a looker?"

Edwards's pulse jumped—in surprise, annoyance, a sense of invasion—but the broad heavy timbers of his body gave no outward sign. Arteris turned toward him. Edwards gave a short nod of affirmation, recognizing his duty to assist and further a shriveled retiree's fantasy life. Small price to pay for the information.

"Pretty clear you weren't writing everything you knew," Edwards said, through with the preliminaries, preparing to press in harder now.

"Coulda been anyone," Arteris Shore repeated, an almost singsong incantatory refrain. But then he suddenly smiled wickedly, or was it merely a smile of resignation. "But Chief Edwards, I can tell you got instincts." One eye was squinted against the bright sun. "And if you got instincts, you'da knowed what that murder was about the minute you stepped into that house."

The sun forced him to close one eye completely. He cocked his head birdlike out at the horizon, inspecting something from a new angle. "I heard the daughter looked into the murder, time to time. A cop, huh? Didn't know that. But I just smile at that. That makes it even better." The burnt little man leaned back in the deck chair. "See, cop or no cop, it don't matter how much she look into her daddy's murder. Because this kind of thing, even the widest-eyed daughter just don't see. Even a trained officer. Because no matter what, she's still a daughter. And that's why she can't see it."

Edwards had been growing frustrated, but suddenly, he felt the edges of it, felt the sense of it. *She a looker?* Now he understood. So that Arteris Shore's explanation coincided with Edwards's realizing it, making the moment stereoscopic, the realization doubly potent.

"You see, Winston," Arteris Shore smiled—wisely bitterly, angrily, resigned, "one look at Vernon Blood's wife, at those girls' mother, just one quick reporter-through-the-half-open-door look at her—and you'd know exactly what that murder was about."

10

It was a little stone house on a small dead-end road with a half dozen others. It looked to be from the twenties or thirties, solid, cherished, and unchanged.

Time to play Tell the Widow. The grimmest station-house game, one that existed only in their shared imaginations, with a black spinning arrow that theoretically could point to any of of them, but in reality—in practice—only pointed to Julian. She was perpetual winner-loser and still champion of Tell the Widow, and always would be. Tell the Widow was a task nobody wanted, nobody would ever volunteer for. And in this, the second round with Nell Ryan, it was a task no easier than bringing news of the death in the first place. Maybe worse.

Nell Ryan opened the door for Julian and turned away without greeting or acknowledgment. Still too deep in grief and denial and shock to be aware of the world and those around her, or else, she'd guessed the subject of today's visit, and was reacting already.

She was average in height, blond, and on a border between fashionably thin and delicate looking. Not built for tragedy, thought Julian. Tragedy that had compounded her fragile look. Or else legitimized it at last.

The house was immaculate. Bespoke the order that Julian had found in the Ryans' lives, deepening both the tragedy and mystery of what had happened.

She heard the girls upstairs, arguing, then laughing, felt relief at sensing a return to life. She heard their footsteps chasing one another. For their mother, of course, it might be much longer.

"It was a beautiful service," Julian offered.

The widow nodded acknowledgment. Then, whisperingly, "Thanks," unable, even in the disconnections of grief, to suppress or alter her innate civility.

Nell Ryan then drew herself up taller, braver. "So I assume you're here to update me on the investigation?" she asked, formal, distant.

"Yes, I am," said Julian somberly, hoping her very somberness would foreshadow what she had to say.

"And?" Somewhat challenging, all of a sudden brighter, alive. *She knows,* thought Julian. *She knows, and is making it hard for me.*

"Mrs. Ryan," said Julian.

The widow looked at Julian.

"Let me assure you, first of all, we've been on this case with all our resources, all our manpower. . . ."

There, now she could tell, thought Julian. Now it would be no surprise when Julian said it in the next few sentences.

Mrs. Ryan stared at Julian blankly—uncomprehending, fully comprehending; fully deflecting the information; fully absorbing it.

"So far, we're not where we had hoped to be. . . ."

"Meaning you're nowhere," she said now, not disdainfully or judgmentally, Julian noticed, but as a statement of fact.

If she were going to be that direct, Julian owed it to her to be as direct. "That's . . . correct. We're nowhere. We . . . have nothing, really."

"Nothing?" Now she was pleading, pleading for something.

Should Julian risk embarrassing both of them by asking about a suspicious flower, its suspiciousness based solely on her own equally colorful instincts? It would be unfair, immoral, to mislead Nell Ryan on this, to play with, knead her grief. Julian shook her head.

Mrs. Ryan straightened suddenly. "That's unacceptable," she said. "Unacceptable."

She walked away from Julian suddenly, huffily, distraught, down the hallway toward her kitchen at the deep end of the house, and then turned and looked back, in disdain, with incomprehension, at this inelegant woman in her home, at what the November wind had blown in.

It was now time for Julian to deploy the Stat: the Stat was part and parcel of Tell the Widow. They had to use it sometimes. In cases like this, they had to be armed with it. "Mrs. Ryan, thirteen percent of homicides in New York are never solved. Depite forensic science, despite our best efforts." Substats of the Stat, about solution percentage plunging with every day that goes by, she kept to herself for the moment. One Stat at a time.

This was painful. Especially painful for Julian, who knew whereof she spoke, who felt the pain particularly, again and again. She figured that's what especially qualified her for these visits, why she never shirked them, but why she especially dreaded them. Because she especially, she alone, knew the dose of pain they inflicted. It was the second shot of pain. The first one, the death itself, you didn't know what hit you, didn't know how much it would hurt, you had no idea, you were surprised at the degree of pain and suffering you were being asked to bear. With a second dose, though, you'd already experienced the pain's alarming depth and scope, so now you knew what you were in for, and knowing what suffering could amount to, it could be even worse.

"Unacceptable," repeated Mrs. Ryan, shaking her head school-marmish, resolute.

Then she came back toward Julian a different person. Without pretense or defensive formality, herself, all her anguish and distress, all her personhood, all her suffering in one moment on display, in one moment written across her face. "You've got to solve it," she said, stating it hoping it wishing it willing it, "you've got to somehow. I . . . I don't think I . . ." She shook off the thought. "Please . . ." And then Nell Ryan's legs gave way, and she barely caught herself by grabbing the arm of a chair, and Julian leaped forward to help her, lifting her, settling her into the hallway chair, feeling the psychological weight as physical.

"We'll do everything . . ." said Julian, witlessly, mindlessly. "We'll do everything . . ."

And Mrs. Ryan couldn't know that Julian was already doing it. Even while apologizing, even while consoling the widow, even while bumbling to explain, was already looking around the neat little stone house. Already listening. Already starting over.

While Mrs. Ryan sipped a glass of water, Julian knelt down next to her. "Mrs. Ryan," she began, "I need to ask you . . . to ask you . . . about a flower. . . ."

A flower. Good Christ. How embarrassing, how ridiculous, thought Julian.

Nell Ryan looked at her with sudden attention, sudden focus, waiting for her to continue.

"It was there on the casket when the mourners finally finished passing."

Nell was listening intently now, Julian saw. Julian felt her own heartbeat pick up; her spirit shifting.

"Bright, almost neon," said Julian. "Very unusual. I've never seen one like it. Did you happen to see who put it there?"

Nell cocked her head and regarded the end table next to the chair, then looked up at Julian. "I know exactly who put it there," she said.

"You do?" Julian felt her pulse jump. *A break.*

"Oh, yes," Nell Ryan confirmed.

Julian felt the excitement rise through her. A kind of arousal, intellectual and emotional and physical at once. An awakening. A feeling familiar from specific moments in cases past. A feeling satisfying enough to wait for. To look forward to. To even yearn for. *A break. A break at last.*

Nell sighed deeply, and looked up at Julian. "It was me."

"But . . . that's imposs—you weren't carrying it . . ."

"My brother, Arthur, was holding it for me earlier."

The petal stuck on the man's black shoe in the photograph.

"*Lilius macrophylla lupidus,*" Nell Ryan informed her. "The vivid color for our memories," she said.

Another death. Hah. The nervous florist knowing, from the photograph of the flower on the casket, that there'd been one death already. Concocting just enough to get the edgy aggressive lieutenant out of the shop. And just enough to shrug and claim it was only something he'd heard, if ever pressed about it.

Nell Ryan looked at Julian. It was a look loud with pity, broad with disappointment. She shook her head slowly, as if with the weight of the incompetence she had to bear.

Shame and failure poured over Julian. She resisted the impulse to remove the gun and badge, set them carefully on Nell Ryan's end table next to her, walk out into the world and never turn back.

11

The sun beat down on Winston Edwards, but he wasn't aware of it. He was somewhere else, somewhere deep in the poor South, where gossip is currency, traded and valued, where talk is like coins in your pocket, shiny, desired, offered up.

She couldn't investigate it because she couldn't see it, because she couldn't see how it involved her mother. Edwards sensed the truth of what the old reporter said.

"Tell you this," said Arteris Shore, "I saw that woman, and very next day, I started lookin' into it, askin' around, pokin' in here and there, and my instincts were right. Sure as shit, there were a good godly truckload of local men had slept with Sylvia Blood."

Arteris looked at Edwards, to gauge his reaction. But Edwards gazed straight ahead, staring once again, for the thousandth time, amazed and unmoved, into the maw of human behavior.

Somewhat disappointed, Arteris continued. "Those days, in small-town North Carolina, that was not the kind of information that anyone looked on too kindly. Editor could always ask what was its pertinence to the story; second of all, our little towns in those days didn't want to see themselves that way, wanted to get away from that image of themselves. Plus a newsman, guy we all knew and respected, nobody too eager to bury him twice, you know? Particularly for no good reason beyond selling papers, which we didn't sell many of anyway, and I'm proud to say, for a few of us, that wasn't a good enough reason. Tell you what, though. Lucky bunch of good ol' boys might've acted outraged and saddened, but same time they was relieved about Vernon Blood's untimely passin'. Point is, that kind of extracurricular behavior, so much of it goin' on in those days in those climes, it just ain't germane to the story, unless one of 'em killed him, and you better be pretty sure about that, before you go printin' it, and of course we wasn't."

Arteris Shore got up from the chaise longue, adjusted its angle to the sun as expertly, as naturally and silently as any sunbird, and sat back down. "And since my instincts tell me you're a man who goes by instincts, I'm gonna share mine," said Arteris. "Mind you, it's an old reporter's instinct, but mind you, it's correct." He didn't smile saying it, as if to convey that any humor was beside the point, and that what he had to say, despite it casual presentation, should be listened to acutely and intently. He paused before beginning, and then tossed it off. "Funny thing is, even though you'd figure with a killing like that, odds are pretty good one or more of those boys was somehow involved, I wasn't too sure any of 'em had the least thing to do with it. Fact is," he paused again, cocked his head to the other side, as if weighing it, "strange to say, I feel pretty sure none of 'em was involved. 'Course I didn't talk to all of 'em. Only got a few to talk to me. These was family men, ones I knew of. I know how crazy it sounds. How lazy and parochial of me. All I'm tellin' you is I'm tellin' you . . . I don't think any of 'em had anything to do with it at all." He added. "Hey, it's Southern tradition. Honor and chivalry even in your backdoor dealings. So here's the thing—I don't think any of 'em woulda let any *other* of 'em git away with it." He paused once more. "So they all kinda canceled each other out." He smiled ruefully. "Which canceled me out." Arteris looked at Edwards. A look that said, *Well, that's everything*.

It was a lot, Edwards would readily concede. A lot. But it wasn't enough. Because Arteris Shore had the mathematics, the algebra of human behavior, but he hadn't factored in the one element that Edwards could. That Edwards was uniquely equipped to consider.

As Julian had a blindness about her mother that Arteris had seen, Arteris had a blindness that Edwards could see. Because Arteris Shore seemed not to understand fully what a certain kind of man would do for passion. Whereas Winston Edwards understood it fully. Winston Edwards could understand killing for a woman. What could make that happen. What was involved.

12

When she left the little stone house, before getting into her car, Julian walked down the lane a way. She told herself she was looking again for how someone might have come in, how much cover they would have had, where they might have entered and exited. But she knew the other reason she'd walked out this far. She needed the air. She needed the silence. To think. To think very carefully about what she was contemplating. She needed to see the world this way, in this condition—unencumbered—before the world altered. Before she altered it.

She thought about it for a long time.

The bare trees swayed in the wind, whispering sinisterly.

She could feel the choice like a weight, a leaden lump in her.

She had to admit it. The investigation was nowhere. Zero. Zip.

She could stop. She could simply stop, put it in the unsolved folder, admirably thin from her own office and under her auspices, though depressingly thick from the station as a whole. Just stop. Or at least, pause. It wouldn't be the first time. It wouldn't be the last. It was an option. Cut your losses, go on to the next one, maybe a break would come, unexpected, later, out of the blue. It happened more than people thought. But stopping? It wouldn't be her.

Particularly knowing what never knowing put you through.

She knew a lot. In five years, she'd learned a lot. But she didn't know everything. She hadn't learned everything.

Frank Ryan's murder seemed to be tilting into the insoluble.

And Winston Edwards had reappeared.

And those two young sisters, standing at the funeral . . .

All conspiring to cast her, almost bodily it seemed, into the past.

Leaping and stumbling through the snow . . .
Feeling the beast, relentless, huffing, stumbling behind her . . .
Think. Don't think. Stop. Don't stop. All logic, all power, self,
everything, collapsed . . .
Behind her, a gun firing . . .
Bullets bouncing off a tree fiercely . . .
The snow thick now, a wall of white as she runs, so thick she cannot
really see.
Faster. Faster.
Looking behind her, for a moment to see . . .
No . . . Her leg gives way . . .
She screams.

She is rolling . . .
She is stopped.
Covered in snow. Her hip. Her knees. Her hands. The pain . . .
A ledge, twenty feet above her, where she fell . . .
She commands her breath to slow, to still . . .
Waits . . .
Waits . . .

And now, to stand near him? Next to him? Talking to him? Working
with him?

She felt dizzy, woozy, sick again. A sickness that brought back all the
sickness of five years ago. A sickness she thought she would never feel
again, that was returning, seeping back . . .

A wreck, a husk of a man, at the end of his days . . .

And a genius of criminal investigation.

She felt for the badge on her blue blouse. Its metal was cold to the
touch in the November air. She'd catch herself doing it occasionally,
touching it like a piece of jewelry—jewelry given without a pretty gift box,
without a seductive smile, commemorating not a special moment or a
special night but a special purpose.

What did she owe this badge? Did she owe it her sanity? What did she owe those little girls? Her dignity? Her health? Her well-being?

As she headed back up the lane to her car, she heard the back door slam, and saw the two girls racing each other through the backyard, no shrill screams that she'd expect from sisters that age, but in deference to recent events, silent—racing, it turned out, for their bicycles in the garage.

As they mounted up, and as she approached, they saw her, but didn't need to go appropriately silent since they were already.

Life did go on. She smiled silently at them as she reached for the car door handle. They smiled silently back, a shared secret with no secret there.

Back in the office, she watched the dusk gather in motes outside the plate-glass window six floors above Police Plaza.

When she could no longer see across the street, when the window was merely a black sheet—opaque, unforgiving, a visionless and smooth reflective surface—she turned and buzzed Mendoza.

"Yes, Lieutenant."

"Get hold of Winston Edwards," she said, confidently, flatly, as if the request were in the natural order of business.

There was a pause. "Lieutenant?"

"See if you can have him here in the morning."

She flipped the intercom button off, and turned back to the plate-glass window. But couldn't see anything through its opaque blackness.

13

At the door to 5C, the little burnt man's diminutive hand shook the big white bear paw. The feel of the uneven, uncomfortable clench held brief fascination for each of them. "Listen, you want to come in?" said Arteris.

Edwards shook his head. "No," he said, "but thanks."

Edwards hobbled out of Sunshine Villas, as if his pains had been held in abeyance at poolside, and had now returned. He'd catch a bus at the boulevard on the corner, which would take him back to his motel.

He wasn't sure exactly what he'd do now. Although he wasn't thinking much about it. He was thinking about Julian's mother.

Her double life. Loving mother, good mother, judging by her daughter. Grieving widow, following her husband's death. And unregenerate vixen, local toss, the local throw. But Winston Edwards wasn't wondering how you could lead a double life like that. He was wondering how you couldn't. About the people who didn't. The people who managed not to. Because he understood the double life, knew exactly and in minute detail how you led it, and what brought you to lead it.

Part of the secret was to be fully each thing, fully each character when you were inhabiting each character. Not to let one personality or one life judge, see, or even be aware of the other. Because then you'd get tripped up. Then one life would seep into the other, and each life would cease to make sense on its own. Then you'd have guilt, be contorted and strangled by it. The point was, you obviously needed this double life, or you wouldn't be living it. Because if you ceased it, something fundamental would cease, and in a profound sense, you would cease too.

When he got back to the twenty-nine-dollar-a-night motel and opened his door, the room appeared exactly as sad and bleak as he'd left it, with one exception. In the middle of the sagging bed was an airline ticket, Ft. Myers to Pittsburgh to Albany, NY.

He went down to the front desk, because there were no phones. "What's this?"

"Messenger brought it, said to leave it for you," said the acned clerk. Edwards looked at him. "That's all I know."

Edwards's eyes narrowed. He looked at the red ticket jacket. Looked at his name. They'd found him. Easily. How? Why? His jailhouse paranoia, his caution, his edgy worry, all ignited. What was she trying? What could this be?

There was more for him to do. New players to find. But he couldn't do any more from here.

He looked at the ticket again, shrugged. "Guess I'm checking out."

14

Unceremonially, Julian pulled the plastic wrapping off the new chair in front of her desk. Cautiously, tentatively, Winston Edwards sat.

"So how is it?" she asked, as casually, as carelessly, as if they'd never been apart.

"What? Retirement?"

Julian laughed short and sharp, shook her head no, and gestured toward the new chair under him.

Carefully, guardedly—barely detectably—Winston Edwards nodded his approval.

"Good, good," she said, leaning back in her own beat-up armchair. "Still waiting for *my* new one to replace this ratty-assed thing." It was his old technique, this needless banter. She knew he would recognize it. She hoped it would drive him a little crazy.

She saw Edwards looking at her blankly.

Julian stood up from her chair, came around to sit on the front of the desk, settled her skirt carefully, demurely, around her, took a breath, smiled, and waited a long moment before beginning.

She looked into his eyes, those empty wells where there appeared to be nothing left. But she pretended for the moment there was. She pretended for the moment someone was there.

She leaned forward toward him, put her head in front of his, and looked deeply at him, flat and unforgiving.

"Francis Xerxes Ryan," she said. "Age thirty-six. Wife, two daughters, eleven and twelve. Local businessman, two stationery stores, starting up a third, successful, only normal business debt. No gambling. No personal debt besides a modest mortgage. No romantic entanglements that we know of, and by now, we'd know."

She looked out the big picture window behind her: in daylight, the old familiar city buildings and roofs were there again. It was a view not truly breathtaking or commanding, but not without presence and aura. A view somehow honest, workaday, a decent slice of city framed.

"Two shots. Back of the head. Twenty-five-caliber handgun. Powder patterns around the entrance wounds establish a discharge distance from the target of at least six feet. So while consecutive shots with a twenty-five don't necessarily rule out suicide, the distance does."

She got up, walked a little around the office.

"Two weeks. Zip. Zilch. Nowhere." She looked at him. "I covered the funeral," she told him. *Just like you taught me.* "I checked the cars," she continued. *Just like you taught me.*

She crossed her arms, like a nervous coach trying to absorb and accept a team's failure. "A cold trail is growing frozen. We're nowhere."

And as she saw him begin to understand what was happening, what she was asking without asking, she watched for his reaction.

There. The amusement in his eyes. But only a brief flicker—momentary, inconsequential, incidental, gone—overtaken in the next moment by interest, by intensity and concentration. She saw him attach to it. Abandon his amusement at her and the situation, and begin to think things through.

"I've got to try everything," she said. "It's my responsibility to try everything. How can I live with myself if I don't?" She looked at him. "It reverberates for me. Unsolved murders anyway. And this one—a father—two girls." She was amazed. She knew she would never say it to anyone else. She was surprised to feel her eyes moisten. Her impulse was to wipe them. To turn away.

Why was she doing it? Why exactly? The motives stewed, stirred, simmered in her.

The chance to work with him again? To learn again? To reassemble, reconstruct what had been so attractive, so invigorating . . .

Or the chance to conquer him? To defeat him finally with superior thinking.

Or simply the chance to to master her own fears and terror. Put him to work alongside her, and he wouldn't loom in her thoughts. Put him to work next to her, to stop the nightmares about him. Normalize him, demystify him, desensitize herself.

The chance to understand him, understand his mystery?

Or to somehow make the case, the case of a murdered waitress, once and for all.

She had wondered cynically if any superior would accept any combination of these explanations, when she was finally called to task for having a felon on payroll. As she knew she would be, when it was inevitably discovered. The records from the proceedings were sealed. She would now find out exactly how sealed. The question wasn't if. The question was when. And would she have accomplished enough with him by the time it happened? There was going to be hell to pay. But a hell that might be worth it.

Why jeopardize her career this way, when her career was all she had? Was it merely a self-destructiveness she never escaped, never outgrew? A need to replay peril in an endless loop? An urge to rewrite life's rules, simply to see if she could?

In the end, she thought, it was simpler than that. Her life had been ripped away from convention, from conventional thinking and conventional solutions long ago. Why should it cleave to—have anything to do with—convention now? No one with a family would ever try this. A stunt like this. No one with a conventional connection to life.

There'd be no hearty welcome-aboards. No grateful thank-yous either, she was sure. No sense of team. No camaraderie. She felt sick to her stomach, as sick as she expected to. She was going against biology, against nature, against the protective instinct, against her own ambitions and well-being, maybe even against the law, for all she knew. She was looking at a man who had tried to kill her, and bringing him—*hiring* him—back into her life.

"So?" she said finally, challenging, exhausted. "Anything to say about this?"

Edwards looked at her, evenly, gauging, unreadable.

What was he thinking? She began to feel, with a reverberating, cavernous certainty, that she'd read him wrong.

"I'd like to get out to the house," Edwards said.

Rake. Liar. Monster. Murderer.

But cop first.

Just like you, she thought bitterly. *Cop first, just like you.*

"So now you can earn back that three hundred bucks," she said, returning to behind her desk, indicating the end of the encounter, the next order of business.

Keep your friends close. And your enemies closer.

She'd know where he was. What he was up to.

Why do it? Why exactly?

Because in the end, it was the only way.

When Edwards left her office, big Ng leaned into her doorway from his desk outside.

Julian gave him a deep, searching, soul-bare look unlike any she had given him in their year of working closely together.

"Don't leave me alone with him," she said.

15

Julian Palmer. A police officer, ladies and gentlemen. By all reports, an excellent, highly promising, if inexperienced one—I gladly give credit where credit is due. The point being, this is no everyday bystander. No casual witness. This is a trained police officer—who still can't provide us with credible evidence. The defendant is a lot of things. But he is not a magician. Local opinion to the contrary, he is not supernatural. Flesh and blood. As is the purported victim, Wayne Hill. Who, it is our firm contention, will eventually wander into view again. . . .

(But she had seen him kill Wayne Hill. The man pleading, begging, lying in the snow; a sudden single shot to the forehead; one moment alive, an existence proved powerfully by its own pleading, the next moment gone, evaporated, a corpse and mist. . . . She had never seen someone die before. The psychic, Wayne Hill, lying in the snow.)

It was almost sure that Hill had committed a murder of his own. So it was a kind of frontier justice. Swift, blunt. But how did that alter it? Edwards had done it . . . because he could. Showing Julian, at least, that he had killed the waitress . . . because he could.

In the State of New York Closed Police Hearing 9-104A into Report of Homicide of civilian Wayne Hill, and 9-104B Report of Attempted Homicide of Officer-in-Training Julian Palmer, no pictures of the waitress Sarah Langley had been allowed. Different case. Different rules of evidence. The murdered waitress became abstract, theoretical to the commission members, and even, somewhat, to Julian.

(But the psychic, Wayne Hill—she had stood where Edwards had stood, seen the same desperate expression Edwards saw, heard the same pleas . . .)

And as Julian had lain hidden below the ledge, caught there, desperate, terrified, shattered and incoherent after his pursuit of her, he'd had time to do whatever he needed to with the body. Bury it under the snow. Come back and rebury it after spring thaw. An entire night. An upstate preserve of uninhabited square miles. He knew the body would never be found.

My client is accused of not one but two murders: the young waitress, Sarah Langley, and this Wayne Hill. But this is perhaps a situation where two accusations are better than one. Because each helps reinforce the absurdity of the other.

The lawyer, Cooperman, perfectly playing the voice of intelligence, the impartial outsider, the light of reason finally shining its rays into this dark corner of the state, shaking his head as if incredulous at the outlandishness of the accusations, as if suspicious of their origins and purpose.

Not a shred of evidence. Not in either case. Entirely different MO's. No forensic department in the world would maintain this was the same murderer.

Blinding the commission with facts, to keep them from the truth. Excellent, Cooperman, excellent.

Julian squinted into the sunlight pouring brightly into her office through the plate glass window—suffusing its surfaces, streaking its ceiling and walls, with optimism, newness and promise.

She breathed deeply of the new day just once, inhaled the office air still cool and clear before its befouling and accumulating daily dose of sweat, activity, and decision. She took an inaugural sip of her morning coffee, turned to the small, focused, now slightly enlarged team assembled on the other side of her desk, and crisply summarized.

"Dead in his office. Two to the head," she said.

She smiled, brief and thin, acknowledgment that with her first words she had already sullied the morning's bright promise. She sat heavily into the desk chair, sinking again into its stains and frayed fabric of duty, burden, and responsibility—for whatever reason not even wanting, this morning, the overdue new desk chair. Feeling undeserving, maybe, or just focused elsewhere for the moment. "So what have we got?" she continued in a summary vein. "Beyond the fact that we have nothing, I mean."

She looked directly at Ng, but raised her chin toward Edwards, indicating to Ng in what direction he should tailor his review.

Edwards gingerly held the coffee he'd been handed between his two huge bear paws. As if waiting for its warmth to carry from the cup through his limbs, to penetrate the vast numb cold of his body. He sat silent, immobile, curled into silence and attentiveness. Listening.

"November twenty-first. Four A.M.," Ng began. "Windy out. Real windy. Forty- , forty-five-mile-an-hour gusts. Dry for days, too. So any footprints got dusted over," he observed in his odd mellifluous mix of Asian musicality and tough clipped shorthand cop-speak. "Forensic enemy, wind like that," said Ng. "Dead branches down, trash cans blown over, trash across the yard."

"It was a dark and stormy night," said Mendoza, but humorless, offhand, the next moment sipping his own coffee.

"Four A.M. He was at his desk," Ng continued, and watched Edwards's huge brow furrow slightly, the question forming mildly on Edwards's face, but Ng answered before it shaped itself into words. "So who the hell's at his desk at four A.M.? Guy who runs three small businesses is who. Apparently, was there every morning at that time."

"Which only certain people would know," offered Mendoza, as he had suggested before, now cocking his head hopefully, trying to enlist Edwards to this narrowing-down point of view.

"Yeah—plus anyone who happened to look through the window," said Julian, morosely and inarguably.

"Intruder entered," Ng continued.

"Entered or was already there. Had been there all night . . . or all his married life." Edwards muttered it into the coffee cup.

Ah, there it was. The put-down. Not long in coming. The veiled challenge to her competence. Did he really think that Julian wouldn't have begun with the wife? That she was that inept?

Julian looked at Edwards, shook her head with a half smile. "Ah, the wife did it! Of course! Our work is done," she said exuberantly, and turned broadly to Ng and Mendoza to explain. "Mr. Edwards's own marital turmoil may be coloring his view of things."

But she saw Edwards smile slightly, wryly, the smile hidden in his cup.

So he wasn't serious. He'd been joking, testing—and she'd proved humorless and shrill. You couldn't win with Winston Edwards. A bad start. She should have predicted as much.

She turned back to him. "Of course we started there," she assured Edwards formally. "With the immediate family. Interviewed each several times. You can imagine what a pleasant afternoon that was." She looked at him, shook her head. "But plenty of corroboration. And with two preteens, let me remind you. Beyond which, there's just . . . no motive. No reason." She leaned back, cocked her head, looked at him with at once gentleness and authority and a depth of understanding. "These people were happy."

Edwards smiled meanly. "And what would you know about it?"

But she could tell—in the roteness of his barb, in its lack of enthusiasm and bite—that he accepted that she was right, that the family was not involved. She sensed that her instincts—learned under his tutelage, developed and nurtured by him, after all—were now respected by him as well. That though he was teasing her a little, he trusted that she was right about the family at least, and that he'd already moved on.

So his put-down hid a compliment. Typical Edwards. His jab about her unhappiness. Typical too. She knew him that much. Maybe now could read him better than she had. She nodded to Ng to continue. But she saw Ng's expression linger on Edwards and on her. She saw that Ng was starting to pick up that there was something more, something deeper between them.

"All right. Perpetrator likely entered between four and four-thirty A.M., judging by both time of death and time of discovery. Perpetrator likely entered assisted by the volume of the aforementioned wind. Two to the back of the head. Shot A, occipital lobe, right hemiphere, shot B, same, half inch below, just above the cerebellum."

Edwards squinted, cocked his head. "How far apart, the two shots?" he asked.

Ng repeated. "Like I say, half inch."

Edwards now looked at Julian, and with what looked like an embarrassed smile, asked again. "I'm sorry. How far apart?"

"A half inch," Julian said it now, louder, enunciating more.

Looking at him—the lumbering, fading form, the slackening total of him—it would make sense that Edwards was losing his hearing. She was suddenly worried that that was the least of it. Was taking him on so quickly a mistake?

"Body discovered by Mrs. Ryan two hours later," said Ng, concertedly louder now.

"At first, we couldn't believe the family hadn't heard the shots," Mendoza offered.

"So I had Ng fire a couple of twenty-five blanks in there," said Julian.

"Twenty-five?" Edwards asked. His eyes suddenly narrowed. Had he not heard before? Did he not remember? Julian continued. "I listened from the bedrooms. Nada. You really couldn't hear anything. Great old stone house."

"Plus the wind," said Ng. "Plus . . ." With a grim smile, he began to snap his fingers in rhythm.

Edwards eyebrows rose, telegraphing interest again.

"Plus what might explain most of all," Julian jumped in, "why he never heard the approach behind him." Edwards looked at her impatiently, expectantly. "Played music while he worked," said Julian. "Always. CDs on a little desktop player, according to his wife. Classic rock."

"Couple extra beats that morning," said Mendoza darkly, distantly. "Ba-boom, ba-boom."

Julian ignored it. "His business's books were all there. I looked at them. Had a forensic accountant look, incidentally. Boy Scout clean." The accountant had explained the traditional little ledger marks—a check for plus, or credit, or money collected; a dash for minus—a debit, something still owed.

"Twenty-five caliber," she repeated, taking over now from Ng, it was apparent. "Street shit. Our streets aren't that busy, and ask Ng or Mendoza, we get pretty good four one one. The two slugs were fairly clean. But so far, the piece hasn't turned up. No transaction. So it's possible the piece is from out of town, and may have ridden back out of town, Clint Eastwood–like already. A twenty-five-caliber stranger. Even if the murderer isn't. Which is what I tend to think, given that nothing was stolen, nothing's missing, and the caliber size tends to say amateur, nonprofessional, personal. Or maybe professional trying to look amateur. Either way, judging by point of entry, someone who apparently preferred the victim not see them."

Edwards listened carefully.

"Fell dead at his desk," said Julian, with finality, leaning back, the puzzle laid out, generally at least, before them.

"Fell at his desk, yes," said Edwards. "Dead we don't know."

Julian felt the pulse of irritation. "What on earth is that supposed to mean?"

"Meaning dead at what moment exactly, we can't say," said Edwards.

She looked at Edwards, waiting, preparing.

"That's why I asked how far apart the shots were," he said calmly. "Not in inches," He looked at her. "In seconds." He paused. Cocked his head, raised his right eyebrow. "Or minutes." He shrugged, half dismissive of the idea, but his shrug did not shake off the meaning he intended, the picture that was beginning to form. "Time," he said, and let the word hang in the air for all of them to examine. Then adding, sarcastically, "I can hear perfectly well. Which makes one of us."

Still an asshole, she thought. She'd managed to turn his boorishness into a backhanded compliment a moment ago. Obviously she'd given him too much credit. Here she was taking him out of the gutter, for chrissake, and this was her treatment in return. It was as if he were inviting her, daring her, to toss him out, to be done with it before it began. Testing, poking, as blatantly as an adolescent, to see where the line might be. It was as outrageous as it was typical. But she would not give him the satisfaction of her fury. Because getting under her skin, for him, was at least getting next to it.

"There's no way to know how 'far apart' the shots were," she said calmly, levelly and correctly back to him, betraying none of her outrage or fury, "and you know there's no way."

"Of course there's no way," he concurred, as if to surprise her with his instant agreement, opening his huge palms in supplication. "But a case like this—when you're where you are with it—meaning where you aren't—you've got to at least start to think about possibilities like that. Not that you'll prove them. Not that you'll believe them. But just entertain them. They may take you somewhere useful." Painfully, laboriously, he shifted his heft. "Maybe it wasn't pop, pop. Maybe it was pop. . . ." He paused, looked at her, closed his eyes, opened them, and only then uttered a second, more ethereal ". . . pop." The syllable floated gently and strangely in the quiet of the office.

Ng and Mendoza, she saw, were listening to him. Seemed taken, charmed . . .

Oh, Christ, thought Julian.

Edwards struggled to put his feet up on the edge of her desk, tried to adjust and comfort his weight and his pains. "Because, see, I'm wondering right off about that second shot, and here's why. If it was professional, using an amateur gun to throw us off, okay. Two shots to the head, to be quick and sure, SOP. But twenty-five caliber, as you say, good odds it's amateur. And an amateur who knows the house is filled with a sleeping family is an amateur who wants to minimize the noise. So a second shot might have been only because Frank Ryan was still moving after the first. Twenty-five caliber," said Edwards dismissively. "That's no cannon, after all. That's a purse gun. A stun gun. So maybe his last thinking moments— second and a half? five seconds? more?—could tell us something." He smiled grimly. "The smaller the caliber, the larger the possibilities," he said ominously. "What else?"

"Letter opener on the carpet," said Ng, with, she detected, a new enthusiasm, an eagerness for reinterpretation.

"Picture of his kids knocked over on the desk," added Mendoza. And then, more slowly, with modest puzzlement, meaning rising mildly, hope- fully, "Nothing else disturbed."

She saw Ng and Mendoza looking at Edwards. *Oh, Christ. Look at them, following him anywhere.* She was losing them already. Good Christ. Edwards was doing it just to get to her, she was sure.

"For chrissake, he *fell,*" she reiterated, trying to gain control, rein in their imaginations, trying to make them cops again.

"CD player had shut itself off, by the time Nell Ryan discovered the body," said Ng, taking his boss's cue, obedient to her again. And in a show of thoroughness, added, "Eagles Greatest Hits of the Seventies."

"A hit of the nineties," quipped Mendoza, quietly.

" 'Course it doesn't much matter if he was just moving before the sec- ond shot," Edwards pressed forward undeterred. "What matters is if his movement indicates he was still *sentient*—able to think—before it. Because if he was still sentient, maybe he was aware and clear enough to leave us a message of some sort." A shrug. A shrug calculated to say *of course, maybe not,* and therefore to also say, *but maybe.*

A gruesome thought. But a possibility. Tantalizing the room with angles and interpretations. Classic Edwards.

And now, goddamn him, she too was thinking about the letter opener on the floor, the picture of the two daughters knocked to the edge of the desk. Before, they had been merely the objects swept to the carpet, swept out of place when Frank Ryan fell. Then why hadn't other objects on the desk—the pencil holder and pencils for instance, or the calculator or the paper clips or the blue box of tissue—been knocked out of place too?

Reaching for the letter opener . . . Had it been in the final seconds, a desperate, half-processed, futile effort to defend himself? The out-of-place picture—was it a last lunge toward love, to what mattered, as he saw his life slip from him?

Or just objects knocked by the way he happened to slump at his desk—some items brushed, some not—no subtext, no message. Dead at his desk as she had said, as reason, and the odds, both dictated.

And eerily, alarmingly, Edwards's thoughts were going the same place as hers, apparently. But going in his own inimitable way. "Two objects out of place," he said. "If Frank Ryan was actually reaching, he was reaching for only one of them. The gold letter opener versus the picture of his daughters. One his rage, the other his love, you could say," Edwards mused. "Rage versus love. The aggressive instinct versus the protective instinct. What's their relationship? What's their interplay? Did he knock over the picture while reaching for the letter opener? Or knock off the letter opener while reaching for the picture? What are they trying to tell us? What's *their* music at four A.M.?"

She would have howled aloud in derision, except for the expressions on Ng and Mendoza's faces.

"What did he know and when did he know it?" said Mendoza, summarizing succinctly, darkly.

She could see it in their faces. See it newly dancing in their eyes and heads. Ng and Mendoza each suffering a new vision of Frank Ryan alive, "sentient," not knowing what happened with that first shot, or knowing and unable to do anything about it. Each imagining what he might have said then, to whomever it might have been, what he might have felt. The crime took on in their imaginations a new gruesomeness and grimness. The death took on a new aliveness.

Oh, Christ.

Was Edwards doing it to mess with them? To make his presence felt in their imaginations as strongly as in this little office? Or only to mess with *her*, to establish, to assert, his primacy? Or because he genuinely felt it might get them somewhere?

The morning had begun with nothing.

Ten minutes later, she realized, they actually had even less.

Typical Edwards.

Welcome aboard, Winston.

16

The widow Ryan opened the door. There was Lieutenant Palmer again, once more flanked by the handsome Hispanic on one side and the big Chinese fellow on the other. Only this time there was someone else, a large, unkempt elderly man, who the widow first took to be a vagrant of some sort, an arrest made on the way, some other criminal matter, perhaps—Nell Ryan hoped—related.

She was sure she'd be asked if she'd ever seen this man, but at that moment, he was introduced only as Winston Edwards.

No further explanation was forthcoming. Lieutenant Palmer asked to look around the house again (the widow was sure it was only to convince her of the team's dedication, diligence and good intentions, and not through any genuine enthusiasm for finding something new). She looked with more curiosity at the old man, who looked not only ill but preoccupied with his illness, yet who nevertheless peered carefully and silently and with concentration for a few moments here and there, and then seemed suddenly, completely uninterested. If the others were wearing a mask of investigative fervor, he wore the most intense one, and then, in the next instant, let his drop completely.

The widow pulled Julian aside. "Who is he?"

"Mr. Edwards?" Julian asked, stalling.

"A detective?"

Julian paused. Mused. "Well, he . . . he was. He's . . . been . . . retired."

"You called him in to help?"

"He's very good at this kind of thing. He's a . . ."

"He's an expert," said Nell Ryan, confident, hopeful.

With any luck, Mrs. Ryan wouldn't mention it to anyone. Ng and Mendoza she could count on, except for an inadvertent slip. But she couldn't very well explain who Edwards was to this woman. *Oh, well, this is a man who should have been convicted for murder, and, oh, incidentally, who tried to kill me, but now he's on my payroll,* then ask her to keep it under her hat. She'd have no idea what was going on, no idea what to think.

Julian watched for a moment through a kitchen window as Ng and Mendoza made one more sweep around the yard, their standard-issue trench coats absurdly out of place wandering around the jungle gym and tire swing and looking around the base of the tree house, pointedly out of their element amid the specimen plantings and the faded lawn. Then Julian led Edwards through the narrow hallways of the stone house, trying professionally to see it through Edwards's eyes, meaning fresh and new.

Edwards obsessively checked every door handle, every door, more locksmith than detective.

They passed down a dark corridor, the ancient, slightly sloping wood floor of the old stone house cracking and squeaking under them. Edwards stopped to lean into the small lavatory to the left, flipped the light on, flipped it off, as if shopping for real estate, debating an offer on the place.

Julian opened the door at the end of the hallway, and there, suddenly, in a single sun-flooded moment, all the black-and-white photographs in the pile on her desk went suddenly into color, into sunflooded life. Everything was in place, bright, glowing, hyperreal, in Frank Ryan's office.

The sun poured in across the surface of the desk. The gold letter opener gleamed, returned now to its proper place. The ledgers were closed now, stacked neatly. The Lucite double-sided picture frame with the photographs of the girls, back where it belonged. Returned, with Julian's stalling but eventual permission, by the widow Ryan, to initiate what would no doubt be The Shrine.

The path of blood was still in evidence, but only a path of stain now, like a particularly forceful shadow, unremoved as yet at the request of Crime Services.

Winston Edwards, hands deep in pockets, looked silently, glumly around the office. Julian couldn't help but notice, it was the first place in the house he seemed suddenly comfortable. He had tiptoed, bent his head deferentially, in the dark hallways. Here, he seemed suddenly at home. Seemed almost to smile.

Edwards suddenly closed the office door behind them.

Julian felt a quiver, a frisson of fear.

Ng and Mendoza were here, nothing would happen, nothing was about to. But still, there was no stopping the echo of instinct, the body's memories.

He stepped over to the large window above the desk, pulled down the blinds.

Her heart rate accelerated. Her throat was dry.

She pictured the gun strapped to her hip. The gun she only fired on the police range once a month as required. *You're armed. He's not. Relax. Relax.*

He stepped over to the high small octagonal window, and wrestled off his trench coat. He stuffed it into the window's perfect octagonal recess above them.

The room was suddenly dark.

He turned on the desk lamp, stepped back.

Julian watched its shadows fall across the desk surface.

Suddenly, it was night again in Frank Ryan's office.

Edwards leaned over the CD player on the desk, leafed through the CD selections with his huge hands, squinting, pulled the Eagles Hits of the Seventies from its jewel case and inserted it into the player, touched Play, and stood back.

The music pulsed—tinny and low, whispery and insistent—through the small desktop speakers.

It was undeniably eerie.

Doubly eerie, because she sensed it was an eeriness intended only for her. Or did he truly mean it as a useful reconstruction? As an opening into mood and psyche. A path toward his famed and often-proved intuition.

Edwards seemed even more comfortable now.

He peered into the closet behind him.

Turned back to the desk.

Finally, he opened the office door behind him. Daylight from the hall ended the nighttime effect. He took a step backward into the doorway, stood there rocking slightly on his heels, staring at the desk broodingly.

"What?" asked Julian finally.

"Nothing," said Edwards, still staring. "Nothing yet."

Julian led Edwards upstairs.

When they'd arrived, Mrs. Ryan had called up to the girls that Lieutenant Palmer would be coming through, but that was ten minutes before, a lifetime ago for girls of eleven and twelve. So as Julian quickly showed Edwards the layout of the bedrooms upstairs, they glimpsed each girl in her own room; the younger one, Annabelle, lying on her bed reading; the older one, Alyshia, at her desk, painting her nails, Julian saw, a wild racy green color, and then—overcoming her quavering little-girl suspicion with a grown-up-seeming civility—smiling at Julian shyly, briefly, but within that shyness and brevity, warmly and winningly, through the open door.

"Hi," Alyshia managed curtly.

"Hi," managed Julian in return.

Edwards merely nodded gruff acknowledgment from the dark hallway, lumbered down it elephantine, like a mammal moving on relentlessly, unthinking, looking for greener pastures.

Julian had interviewed the girls before. Their answers had been exactly what she'd expected. The leaden, careful cooperativeness. The respectful silence, the hyperattentiveness to events around them. Doe eyes in the headlights. The newness, the excitement of disaster, at once energizing and embarrassing to them, leaving them flushed and attentive. And, Julian knew, the heartache—private, faced away—first a leaky tap of it, soon a flood of earth-shifting disaster—a depth of hurt and sorrow they were shocked to discover in themselves, an awful secret stumbled onto unwanted and unasked for in their young lives. The waiting, the hanging, the dependency, on adult words in this time of crisis. Reluctantly but dutifully, Julian had offered Edwards the opportunity to interview the girls again. But Edwards had read Julian's notes and transcripts, and had been satisfied enough to wave off another interview as an unnecessary infliction of fresh pain. She was no longer a trainee, and Edwards, at unpredictable junctures, seemed to accept and recognize that. To Julian's relief.

Julian lingered for a moment outside Alyshia's door.

Alyshia looked out at her as long as Julian looked in.

"Green nail polish," Alyshia offered shyly, gesturing to her hands, smiling a little uncomfortably, caught. Proving her twelve-year-old-hood, thought Julian, who made her own matching shy smile in return. Apologizing for the intrusion, for the police failure so far, for the sudden failure of life to live up to Alyshia's modest expectations and reasonable wishes.

The small square adjoining rooms, the narrow dim hallway . . . it wasn't so far from the upstairs of her own childhood, it occurred to Julian—visually receded long ago, but still viscerally present and felt.

The rooms were filled with the predictable changes, the cycles and seasons in the lives of their inhabitants. The little-girl dolls and stuffed animals, giving way to fan posters of music personalities and pink-and-lavender tape players, and in Alyshia's room, a computer. Clothing strewn about, Sunday best and jeans and T-shirts in ample evidence, hung primly or stretched langorously on the bed or over a white-painted rocker, echoing their wearers—and a dim, long-ago, playfully vivacious Julian and Stephanie.

Exactly, eerily, what she and her own sister had experienced. Until Julian had to squint her eyes against the similarity, the strange confluence of it, closing in on her physically.

In the Ryans' upstairs, Julian experienced the uncomfortable fascination of not just eavesdropping on a family's life but of eavesdropping on her own. Hearing, seeing, smelling, sensing, wandering through, her own past. There were differences, of course, physical and literal differences everywhere, but these only seemed to highlight what was essentially and timelessly the same.

Feelings, sensations, understandings passing between sisters in a dark upstairs hallway, the guarded words and commandments emanating from a beleagured mother at the bottom of the stairs—all those transactions hanging in the air, remarkably similar, sometimes identical.

Edwards emerged from the far end of the hall, nodded—his satisfaction, his dissatisfaction, contained efficiently in one nod.

"Enough?" asked Julian.

In answer, Edwards headed hugely, wordlessly, and rudely, down the shadowy staircase.

With little choice, Julian followed.

17

There was a petty cash account the department paid snitches and informants from. That was the money she used to compensate Edwards. It was
subsistence pay only. In dollar terms, a bargain-bin price for his expertise
and experience. In human terms, though, there was a much higher cost.
His gruffness alternately charming and annoying Ng and Mendoza. His
presence, his style, alternately fascinating and repelling them. But already
unduly taking up their energy and attention. In human terms, an extremely
high-cost temporary employee.

There was a cheap motel within walking distance of the station house,
one slippery and crumbling step up from a flophouse; a crash for Third
World and unskilled local workers, a beacon for the dispossessed and
transitory, the kind of place the beat cops found themselves called to
repeatedly, predictably. She herself had never been in it. She put him up
there.

There was a grim little diner a block east of it, she knew. A place for
him to get a bowl of soup, eggs with toast, for a couple of bucks.

Edwards was off the payroll. But not off the books. If push ever came to
shove. Which it undoubtedly would.

18

It looked like he was sleeping on the job, catching a few z's while no one saw him.

Except, that is, for the rivulet of blood running—as if knowingly, in a planned path of escape—down one side of his neck, across the blotter, over some papers, undeterred by a small pile of paper clips, pooling at the edge of the desk, as if to organize, before the red descent. There was a single, neat, eerily perfect circle pooled on the floor beneath. Frank Ryan's death, notwithstanding its method, seemed as orderly as his life.

The crime scene photos—a stack of eight-by-tens elaborating upon a handful of sixteen-by-twenty masters—were spread across Julian's desk once more.

Which made it almost appear, particularly with the correct border-to-border arrangement of the large and gruesome master photos, as if Frank Ryan were slumped across Julian's desk.

In the smaller photos, those without Frank Ryan's body, there was an even stranger effect: a duplication, an echo, between the black-and-white crime photographs and the surrounding reality of Julian's office. In one photo, there was a small stack of coins on Frank Ryan's desk. To the left of the photograph's edge, there was an actual stack of coins on Julian's desk. In the crime photos, there was a blotter on Frank Ryan's desk. Beneath the photos, there was a blotter on Julian's desk as well. A circular container of pens and pencils; a box of tissues; open manila folders: items on Frank Ryan's desk in the photos, surrounded by similar objects repeated in actuality. His desk on hers: it was an odd effect for anyone who might notice. Yet in the several times the photographs had been spread out here in her office, Julian had never seen it before. With Edwards here, she finally had. His presence seemed to bring her an added alertness. A hyperconnectedness. Was that good? Or bad? The mind working overtime, exhausting itself, hopelessly involuted at just the moment it needed to make a clear, crisp, instantaneous judgment?

The sharp gold letter opener. The double-sided Lucite frame, his daughters posing together. The fake wood burl of the desktop CD player. The open ledgers. The blue box of tissues. It was, Julian realized, the last tableau Frank Ryan saw. So that through the crime photographs, they continually shared Frank Ryan's last moments. Unconsciously, with mute respect, they treated it as a sacred trust, a sacred synergy between the living and the dead. With that sharing, too, they tried to somehow usefully climb inside the moment, but so far without any deeper understanding.

The fallen gold letter opener. The double-sided picture frame. Mutely present in the crime scene photos. Now the objects of speculation. The objects of their continual meditation, their visual mantra. She expected the objects to arrange themselves into an answer, into a comprehension of that night. A mere few objects, after all. A small, manageable number of permutations and possibilities. She tried to will them into a geometry of solution.

Means, motive, opportunity. A three-piece puzzle, a geometry as focused, as elemental, as those few objects. As she looked again and again at the photographs, the triumvirate hummed. Means, motive, opportunity. The holy trinity of police procedure. It chanted at the back of her consciousness, powerful, incessant, with the propelling rhythm of a full-dress regimental march. Means, motive, opportunity. The three commandments of the academy, simply, utterly, scientifically replacing any previous useless ten concerning respect, honor, obeying, and other archaic and outmoded principles. Means, motive, opportunity. The crucible, the mold, by which to measure and assess the evidence. By which to gauge and ultimately contain the criminal world.

Means, motive, opportunity—the template to lay over these objects. And yet she could see where his left elbow might have knocked the letter opener to the floor. Where his falling head could have knocked the picture frame out of place. "Look, there were no prints on the gold letter opener," she reminded them again. "There was no apparent attempt to defend himself."

"Maybe he was going for it when it fell, and *that's* why it fell, and that's why there are no prints," Mendoza countered again.

"Maybe the prints were wiped off it," said Ng this time.

"And it was left on the floor?" Julian asked. "If you wiped it off, you'd put it back."

"Maybe it was left on the floor to make it *look* like it had fallen," said Ng carefully. "And that's why it was wiped clean. When maybe it *had* been held . . ."

She shifted uncomfortably. Felt it all going too elaborate. Dancing at the edges of the byzantine.

Edwards was silent. Having started Ng and Mendoza down this path, seemed to be only half listening to them.

"Why just those objects?" he said finally—vaguely, ruminatively—as if only thinking aloud. "Why weren't other objects swept off the desk too?" He paused. Once again, it was her own silent speculation verbalized. But he never offered the opposing argument, she'd started to notice. Never offered the other side. Seemed to leave that negative role for her, she noticed.

"Who says there have to *be* other objects," she felt compelled to point out. "Think how he'd slump. He wouldn't necessarily hit anything else. It's those objects that happened to be in the path when he fell. That's all. Simple as that," she said.

Truth was, it wasn't clear, Julian knew. It wasn't absolute. Both views were possible. The letter opener on the floor: had he knocked it off accidentally when he slumped? Or was he trying to defend himself? The question circled—simple, insistent, so far unanswerable.

But it was as if Edwards were only feeding the confusion, pouring a new chemical into the bubbling compound of possibilities at just the moment when previous elements might begin to bind. It was as if he were using the opportunity of examining the photographs only to create new questions, vivid new scenarios.

She'd started to wonder. Was it all bluff?

He had been legendary. Had solved murders single-handedly. But in police work and police technology, this was a new era. And she was no longer the callow, credulous, eager intern. So was it all bluff? On this case, at least? A way of staying employed, living off his previous reputation? There were no prints on the gold letter opener. First shot, second shot, didn't much matter. There were no "clues" that she could see. Darkening Ryan's office. Standing there silently. Looking mutely at the pictures in her office. Setting them all against each other with theory. It was dawning on her slowly but logically—the possibility that it was bullshit.

Was he merely stalling for time? Already forestalling a dismissal he must know was inevitable? She felt disappointed. Let down. She looked at him skeptically.

Or did he really believe there was something here, in these insoluble opaque speculations, these unprovable gambits? She'd been fooled before by his remarkable abilities, by his remarkable insights out of nowhere. Should she be prepared to be fooled like that again?

She'd go along. She'd go along for a little bit. Maybe only for the chance to understand him. To understand him even slightly. To understand him finally.

The gold letter opener. The family pictures in the frame. The CD player. The blue box of tissues. Edwards shuffled through the photographs silently, studying the objects. Objects ordinary and totemic. Objects mute and revelatory. Each a silent witness, each with a story to tell. Would they remain silent witnesses, or reveal themselves? Speak, dance, in a concordant version of events.

"So what exactly are you lookin' at?" she asked finally.

"What's that?" he said, pointing to a dark spot on the carpet beneath the desk, visible in one of the photographs.

She smiled. Something domestic, comprehensible. "Not blood," she said. "Coffee stain."

"Then I'm looking at the coffee stain," he said, and said nothing more.

Ng carefully collected the photographs.

"Forensic neurologist you suggested will be here Monday," Julian told Edwards. She'd had no choice. Edwards's speculation about Frank Ryan's awareness before a second shot; it was at least possible. Her command of brain physiology was current enough to recognize that. Given the small weapon's low velocity, and entering the skull where they did, either bullet might have fallen short of the critical parietal lobe. Both bullets had appeared to lodge above the cerebellum—maybe hadn't damaged it. Any residual functioning probably depended on which bullet entered where first, and where exactly. She'd quickly dismissed the whole issue of which bullet penetrated first and where, for the simple and practical reason that it didn't seem to matter. Frank Ryan was dead either way. But granting, for the moment, some possible meaning to the positioning of the letter opener and the photograph frame—and given Edwards's point that they were otherwise nowhere—she'd consented to the idea.

Explore everything, she could hear him saying. *Don't you owe it to the Ryans, to yourself, to explore everything? Isn't that the pledge you made?* But he'd never had to utter a word. It didn't need his voice. It was the voice inside her.

"So we'll return to it then, I guess." No choice, really. She'd had to do it, despite her doubts. They were nowhere. She looked at Edwards, burying her own suspicions. "So what you gonna do this weekend?"

Edwards looked at her. "Head back up and see Stelly. Try to patch things up a little."

Estelle. His wife of forty years who'd finally thrown him out.

"She expecting you?"

Edwards nodded. "We talked. She knows I'm with you on a case. Can't believe it, 'course."

"Neither can I," said Julian.

"Neither can I," said Edwards, surprise and gratitude in some brief indecipherable mix.

"You know, you're such a ninth-degree black-belt asshole so much of the time, it's always a shock when you're not."

He looked at her expressionlessly. "Got any money to help me get home?"

She snorted in amazement. "You do that on purpose, don't you?" She shook her head, reached into her pocket. "An advance on next week."

Patching things up? If she checked with Estelle Edwards this weekend, renewed their acquaintance, talked over old times, would she really find him there?

But if she didn't find him there, wouldn't that be worse? The not knowing where he was, the wondering, the sleepless speculation . . .

She could have him followed.

Maybe she would.

But maybe it was better not to know.

19

Edwards had already bought a round-trip ticket to Florida when the New York State Department of Police had unexpectedly sent him a one-way ticket back. Leaving him with his original return from Florida still unused.

At an Albany County airport counter at dawn the next morning, he exchanged the ticket for a flight to North Carolina.

He was in sunny Charlotte airport by late breakfasttime.

He flashed his old, unconfiscated police badge at a terrified cab driver at curbside, and suddenly had a bewildered but obedient chauffeur for the day.

Edwards had gathered that for whatever the reasons exactly, Julian spoke to her mother only rarely. He had naturally become curious about her relationship with her mother, when, working for Edwards, Julian had revealed the murder of her father. Edwards was never able to ask about it directly—Julian had made clear the subject was out of bounds. He'd nevertheless gotten an impression. One of distance. That the relationship had increasingly degenerated, contact between them was less and less. He didn't know exactly why. A way for them all to efficiently forget, by building new lives? Some unconscious blame of her mother seeping into her behavior? In any case, it was now, he sensed, only obligatory, brief conversations. And if they now spoke so infrequently, if there was this distance he sensed, it was a safe bet neither ever brought up the murder in conversation, probably hadn't in years. One's father's murder: not something you keep bringing up with your mother, his wife.

Bu even if and when she had asked her mother about it, Edwards conjectured, she hadn't done it exactly right.

Nobody knows how to get answers out of one's own mother.

But Edwards knew that Sylvia Blood had answers.

And Edwards would get them.

Arteris's information was wrong, however. The group home where Sylvia had reportedly lived was gone, there had been trouble, the town had shut it down. And though Arteris had been diligent about past and present, here he had failed. Here, time had deceived him. He must have been years out of date. In the town hall, a young clerk, too young to really know, informed Edwards after a check of the records and files, that there was no Sylvia Blood anywhere near this town. No one else in the offices, or anyone accosted on the front steps, was even aware of the existence of the group home that Edwards mentioned. At the lunch counter, an older couple vaguely remembered the case. Knew vaguely, glancingly, who Edwards was talking about. But had no idea where she might be.

Risky as it was, he could attempt to find out from Julian. A look inside her address book. Find a way to pull her phone records anonymously. He should have tried it that way to start with. He shouldn't have counted on Arteris. He shouldn't count on anyone but himself.

Saturday evening. Edwards sat on a wooden bench in the center of the town. The rendezvous with his cab driver was in half an hour.

He had turned up nothing. Had come all this way, and got exactly nowhere.

The region was gripped by a freakish heat. A late Indian summer, that pressed itself fiercely into the land's low hillocks and flat fields in a last powerful hot exhalation. Edwards sat in shirtsleeves, the perspiration beading on him, ringing his scalp like a glistening bandanna. A remarkable contrast to the crisp cruel intimations of winter now in upstate New York. The heat, the cold. Equally cruel, descending identically on the unready.

He warmed the bench in front of the ice cream store, eventually making the proprietor nervous, he could see.

He watched a few of the townsfolk go back and forth, as if aimlessly, as aimless as he momentarily felt.

It was a town not unlike the one he had left, the little town that had been his for thirty years.

The cold little upstate snow belt town he'd ruled, first benignly and then less so, his private fiefdom for all his adult life. It had been a land unknown to others, to outsiders. Like an elaborate toy train set in one's basement, your visitors, your dinner guests, unaware of your little pastime, your secret, inexplicable obsession. He smiled. Maybe silly for a mature man, the proverbial, perennial small pond. But the pond was after all teeming with life, and greeted each season with its predictable changes, and best of all, he could fish it at will, anytime. The town he'd ruled and lost, when his rule had gone beyond reasonable boundaries, and had had to be reined in. Someone here in this little Southern town, someone or some small group, ruled this town like that too. That's what people didn't understand. He sat on the bench looking out over this town, thinking of that other town, so far away from him now, and yet so permanently within him. It was a southern town, at heart, he reflected, a southern town that happened to sit at the Canadian border, in the paralyzing cold. Which was why this town, although dripping hot and nearly nameless to him, a dot on a map, a passing mention from an unaware source, felt so familiar.

And then he saw her.

A woman in her late thirties, crossing the street, heading into the drugstore.

Probably only he could have seen it, he would later reflect.

Probably only someone obsessed with Julian Palmer.

Someone who had brooded about her, pictured her, compulsively, incessantly, who had summoned her image from the brick walls of his prison cell, off the springs and striped mattress above him, for months on end.

Someone who had memorized the single newspaper photo of her from the case, and then crumpled it in fury at its black-and-white inadequacy. Someone who had contemplated her unceasingly, bleakly, far past reason. Maybe it could only have been such a creature, such a man, who could so quickly, so certainly, have seen it.

Julian herself couldn't have imagined it.

Julian, Edwards knew, hadn't the slightest idea.

But it was unmistakable. The same slant and curve of jaw and chin. The same slender hands. The same gracefully alert arch of eyebrow and Cleopatra slant of eye, the same liquid layering of umber browns within it. The same flawless skin.

With his long-developed, once famed, and still-intact instincts, Edwards simply knew. Knew it, saw it, felt it at the base of his cerebellum, in the short hairs risen, once more aroused, at the back of his neck. Knew it, felt it, in his bones.

Living so close.

And with what he'd discovered from Arteris . . .

He was looking at Julian Palmer's half-sister. Had to be.

Two, three years older, maybe.

Her older half-sister.

Half, at least.

This being, after all, the South.

While the woman picked up several necessities at the old-fashioned wooden-shelved pharmacy inside, a half dozen scenarios jumped and danced, jostled nimbly in the mind of the old man now standing, pacing, apparently purposelessly, out front. While the woman paid at the counter, reaching unhurried into her purse, standing by the self-consciously antique cash register, her fictive past and present clashed and butted furiously, electrically, in the mind of the figure outside the single broad pharmacy window.

The woman emerged from the store, a small brown bag of purchases in one hand, and floated close past the old man, standing, waiting, she thought briefly, for his equally elderly wife, or maybe a younger guardian.

"Excuse me," she heard the old man utter rustily.

She turned, raised her eyebrows, with a small-town receptivity. "Yes?"

But the old man only looked at her blankly. A look that lasted a short moment, until, only mildly disconcerted, but more than that, feeling sorry for the man growing old and forgetting, she turned to go.

"I'm sorry," the old man said, this time not so rusty, a measure more competently, with even the beginning of a certain mellifluousness, she noticed. "It's just—" The man smiled shyly, and she noticed at least a certain alertness in his eyes. "You look so much like someone I know."

"I've been told that before."

"By who?" he said suddenly, a little too strong, the inquisitional tone leaping brusquely out. The woman recoiled somewhat, and began to look for some graceful escape.

She would not, though, simply turn and walk away, like a Northerner, like a city dweller. She needed some excuse, some small polite version of exit.

"Forgive me," the old man said, civilly, honestly it seemed, "I . . . I feel far from comfortable accosting a young lady in the street." There, dangling enough courtliness and civility to keep her from turning away, Edwards thought. "Forgive me," he said once more, smiling, and waiting for her smile accepting his apology, which in short order came. Emboldening, allowing, a next step. Anything, he thought, anything conventional, unthreatening, anything to engage her, continue the interaction. "Maybe you could help me," he said, a lack of threat, a pleasantry and convention readily apparent in his tone. "I was about to go in and ask . . . but maybe you could help me. . . ." He looked imploringly, hopefully, at her, dangled the twinkling courtliness again. "I'm trying to find accommodations for the night."

She regarded him defensively again, then smiled, he saw, at her own misunderstanding of his legitimate intentions, smiling, he saw, to deflect, defuse, her own defensiveness, which she clearly felt was inhospitable.

"Do you happen to know," he asked, overpolitely, "is there anything around here?"

"There's no hotel or motel in town," she told him, her voice, he noticed now, distinctively soft and easy but with that simple strength in the even tone, in just the same way, exactly the same way, startling aural confirmation. "Closest ones are down on Route Fifty-two," said the woman, the Southern accent not disguising the kinship of voice, " 'bout twenty-five miles from here."

The old man looked understandably distressed by the information. "Anything closer? Anything at all?" he asked.

She hesitated. Then shook her head no.

"But you were just thinking of something," he said, the old man's head cocked slightly to the side.

She looked at him, only mildly surprised by his insightfulness. She said nothing.

"Weren't you?" he prodded genially.

She smiled gently back. "We actually take people in, out at my dad's place." She paused. "And . . . well . . . we've got room." Her expression turned momentarily sober. "We get thirty-five a night."

"Sounds fair," he said.

"Where's your car?" she asked.

"In Canaanville, New York," he smiled. "But it's a beauty. Sixty-four Impala. Mint."

Her smile returned. "I'll give you a ride," she offered.

20

Tammy Smithers, she said, not taking a hand off the wheel.

Nice to meet you. Not offering his own name just yet.

She hadn't asked what he was doing here. He found that pleasantly intriguing. He steadfastly kept his eyes off her, would look only when spoken to, would discover more.

Somebody, something, was smiling down on him. Something in the universe wanted this crime solved, he thought, and he felt a sudden expansiveness and assurance that reverberated, pulsed with his former power, his former life. This could only have happened, it struck him again—struck him bluntly like a pole to the chest, with a sense of ecstasy, and yet with a sense of gloom—because of the face, the features, the being, that were so fiercely etched and ingrained in him, that he had been hyperalert, hyperattuned to their sudden echo, their unsuspected unknown kinship, in front of a pharmacy in a small town in North Carolina.

It was luck, pure luck, but as everyone knows, we make our own.

She would ask him eventually what he was doing here, she thought. She sensed that whatever it was, it was in some way illicit, unsavory, and yet it wasn't her business to ask. It hung over the transaction vaguely, mysteriously. But she liked that. In her world of utter predictability and sameness, she liked that.

Amid all her wild-minded speculations, she would never have guessed that he was here to see her.

Her father was away on business, she told him. There were another couple of guys, seasonal farm workers, already staying at the place. So she figured she was safe, she said smiling, without looking over at him.

The red Ford pickup, sensible and freshly washed, bumped along through the countryside.

"'Course, I want to ask you what exactly you're doing here, without even a suitcase or nothin', but I'm too polite for that," she said.

I want to ask you about your mother, thought Edwards, *and I'm not too polite for that.*

"A guy can't be just travelin' through?" he suggested.

"Not a guy as old as you."

"Oh, age discrimination," he said jovially. "I'm gonna report you."

"Tryin' to pick up women half your age. I'm gonna report *you.*"

They rode in silence for a while. Edwards aware of all his pains, and freed, liberated from them, alert, alive.

"So who do I look like?" she asked.

"Oh, well . . ." he looked out the window. "I'll confess . . . someone special to me . . . as I'll bet you already guessed."

Your sister, he thought. *You look like your sister.*

"So really . . . what are you doin' here?"

"I'm a detective, and I'm workin' on a case."

She hooted with laughter. "Come on. You can do better than that."

He shrugged.

She looked at him teasingly. "You're a awful old detective."

He squinted his eyes. "It's an awful old case."

"So that's why you had no place to stay," she said, realizing, it seemed, that he might be leveling with her.

"Hey, you're a pretty good detective yourself," he said, complimenting her observation.

And that's why I've got no car: no budget, no clues, no more than instinct: because it's a case that's been officially forgotten for years.

She looked like her, sounded like her. Uncannily. Eerily. Like an uneducated, parochial, less sophisticated version of Julian.

He still didn't know for sure. But riding with Tammy Smithers, talking to her, made him more and more certain, and cast the story in more and more shades and shadows.

Had Julian's mother had this daughter before her marriage to the deceased Vernon Blood? Motherhood at sixteen or seventeen, a fresh start after; it was hardly unlikely in this part of the woods, or anywhere else for that matter. And Vernon Blood, small-town newsman. Did he even know? Or was it one story his newsman's instincts had completely missed?

Or was it more complicated? Given everything Arteris had said about Sylvia, was this daughter the result of an affair? Maybe she gave birth during a separation from Vernon over exactly this. In some angry arrangement between them. It seemed only too possible, in rural North Carolina. Edwards could taste his own curiosity powerfully on his lips and tongue.

He could imagine the affair, too. The disappearing into the middle of the day, when Vernon was at work and the girls were at school.

But he was ahead of himself.

Whatever the truth was, it had something to do with Vernon Blood's murder. Not necessarily. But the likelihood was rearing up smartly. The likelihood . . .

"Here we are. . . ." Tammy Smithers said, turning in.

An old clapboard farmhouse, large and white and somewhat beaten down and ramshackle. The house looked to be an inheritance, a legacy of what family exactly, he couldn't say, of course—and although it had seen better days, it could be seeing worse.

Though it had a telltale downbeatness to it—a car on blocks in the driveway, a couple of broken gutters—there was some diligent attention to it as well. Fresh paint. Tended stone walls. Effort was evident. The jury was still out.

She continued driving past the house, steered the truck around the house's far edge, revealing two smaller cabins set at the back of the lawn behind it. She pulled the pickup to a stop at the sudden end of the dirt driveway, and gestured with a slight raising of the chin to the guest accommodations.

"And I'll take the thirty-five dollars now," she said.

Edwards reached for his wallet, pulled out the agreed amount of cash, and passed it to her.

"And where does a guy get somethin' to eat around here?" he asked.

"A guy comes to my kitchen," she said.

It was as if there were some natural connection between them, based on his connection with Julian.

As if he were with Julian—suddenly, unpredictably—in an alternate world, in an alternate way. The curve of jaw. The slender hands. The alert arch of eyebrow and slant of eye.

But there was a strange effect that accompanied it. He had the sense of fate dealing him his final hand, his final chances, his last reckonings. It was dreamlike, this encounter, and had—uncomfortably, strangely, float-ing—the timeless feel of afterlife.

She made him a sandwich, gave him some cream pie, a flavorful ges-ture of the most local hospitality. He could tell, by the plates and glasses stacked on the counter and not on any shelves, by the calendar and frag-ments of notes and reminders tacked haphazardly to the kitchen walls, that hers was a loose, catch-as-catch-can existence.

"So tell me more about your case," she said, smiling coyly, still, it seemed, only half buying it.

"Murder case," he said, and looked at her to gauge her reaction.

"Of course," she said, her smile bright with sarcasm, to demonstrate she still only half believed him, and maybe trying to prove it to herself, too—but revealing instead, that deeper down she was actually believing it a little more.

"Murder of a father," he elaborated, watched her wipe the counters as if she were paying only vague attention.

"Took place around here?" she asked.

"Years ago. Like I said."

"So how do you find anything out years later?" she asked reasonably.

"Not easy," he admitted. "You're reduced to instincts, town records, casual conversations. . . ."

"Like this," she said wryly.

He smiled. "Like this."

He had looked around the house as they'd come in, of course. Checked on the mantle, the living room and hallways and kitchen walls, for a tell-tale family photograph, for a picture of Tammy's mother. Father and daughter, father and daughter, conventionally posed with her horse, her dog, his new car, in bathing suits at the beach. Her mother was conspicu-ously absent.

He decided to push carefully, gently, to the next emotional level.

"He was the father of girls who are just about your age now, actually. . . ." he said, as if it had just occurred to him. He paused, before saying, "They were just kids when he was killed, of course."

She nodded, accepting Edwards's words and tone gradually as the truth. "I know a little something about that," she said, suddenly more quietly, with no banter to it, no bantering cheerful challenge this time.

His eyebrows rose. He was listening, attentive, but did not say anything, stayed silent in Tammy Smithers's kitchen, left the conversational surface clean and clear for whatever might serve itself up, however long it had been stored away.

"Not murder," she said quickly, correctively, "but just . . . how it feels not to have a parent." She looked at him. "With all my talk about sharing this place with my dad, don't tell me you didn't notice or wonder about my mother."

"I am a detective," he said. "Sure, I've been wondering—and I did see the photographs of you and your dad on the walls."

"I don't remember her at all," she said, somewhere between shrugging and sadness. "She died when I was very young."

You don't remember her, because you weren't allowed to know her. Christ. The deceit of it, he thought, the deceit of depriving a little girl of her right to a mother, and a right to the truth. Simply erasing her mother from her life. He was surprised to feel how the powerful, blanket wrongness rose up in him, gathered and accelerated into a fury inside him he barely succeeded in hiding. No doubt because of her kinship to Julian, and his own morality eccentrically obtruding.

"She's buried just a short walk from here."

Wait . . . *what?!*

Edwards's grip tightened on the kitchen counter for support.

"I visit her grave every day—try to be with her," she admitted shyly.

Edwards's mind spun. Had he been entirely wrong about Tammy Smithers? Had he willed the shocking coincidence of her appearance, and the confirmation of a missing mother, into the text he needed, the solution he craved? Was Tammy Smithers's only relationship to Julian Palmer coincidental, as another tragic Southern girl? Had he imagined into being, out of some need in himself, the striking physical similarity?

Quick math only hardened the confusion: according to what she was saying about her mother's dying when she was very young, Tammy Smithers's mother *could* have been dead before Julian was born. In which case it wouldn't be the same woman.

Had he been wrong? Were his instincts, at last, failing like the rest of him? It must be the wishfulness on his part, the obsession, overwhelming him, making things unclear. He felt defeated. Diminished.

He tried now to see Tammy in a different light, as just another Southern girl.

He began to rethink whether he'd been wrong about Julian and her mother entirely. His strong impression of distance, of curt and strained conversations between them; but at this moment, he couldn't recall any specific conversation or reference. It had been instinct. He didn't know. He'd assumed. Had he been wrong? He felt unsteady, off-balance, panicky. The first panic of the elderly, he sensed, a rite of passage—not trusting oneself or one's own thinking, the world suddenly too taxing and overwhelming.

Was Sylvia Blood even alive? Arteris had said Sylvia Blood was institutionalized, but that information had turned out to be wrong, or at least out of date. Was she dead? Illness? Suicide? The double life he'd vividly intuited finally taking its toll? Had he too vividly imagined everything? He felt stricken.

It was all Edwards could do to hush the screeching possibilities, herd their swirling to a corner of his mind enough to hear what she was continuing to say.

"I don't remember the funeral. I was too young. But one time I insisted on knowing about it, and my dad told me, though I could tell it made him uncomfortable. The casket. The procession. I feel like I vaguely remember it. But I remember it as a parade." She smiled wistfully. "I was only a little kid. So of course I'm confusing it with a parade."

He felt dejected, demolished. He had tried madly, in a mental flurry, to put it together, to make his theory work, but then realized, accepted—he was just plain wrong.

Unless. Unless.

The night is cloudy, therefore moonless, therefore an inky, murky dark. The creatures of the woods and hills, far off and close by, intermittently howl and bray, squeal and squall, crying the fact of their existence against the blanket of blackness—periodic, repeating affirmations of themselves, somehow necessary against the oceanic night.

There are other sounds, too, a mumbling muttering chorus of them generated by the wind. The remnants of old wind chimes, hanging broken off the back porch, reduced now to a syncopated single pitch, a dirgelike monotone in the wind. The irregular knock of a shutter swinging slightly against wooden shingles. The full, hotblooded whisper of ten thousand rustling leaves, swelling up passionately with each uptake of breeze, then settling, as if sated and spent.

And now, a third set of sounds.

The side door to the barn-style garage swinging open—the wind again?—and now the single clang of a shovel against a rafter in the dark.

Maybe just a mouse in there, or wind making something fall, because now there's silence again.

But now a dull footfall, the ancient, primal rhythm of man's motion over ground, across earth.

The slowly rhythmic pound of shovel into dirt. A slight soprano-pitch scrape to the metal of each thud.

And soon, the breathing with it, labored, immense . . .

Stopping . . .

Silent . . .

Maybe imagined . . .

There . . . starting again . . .

Perspiring in the still-hot night, determined, surrounded by blackness, a terrifying vision in the dark, Winston Edwards shoveled straight down into black North Carolina dirt, keeping the circumference of the hole small. It was only dirt here fortunately, this time of year, no covering grasses, so he'd feather it in, and by morning the color of the new dirt would blend with the old.

When he'd reached a couple of feet, and the soft earth began to resist him more substantially, he switched to the stake. About six feet long.

Swifter, more efficient, but the hammering noisier, and therefore riskier. But the wind would blow the sound this way, away from the house, and that would help.

The focus of his labors distracted him completely from his pains. Distracted him, too, from his feeling of foolishness and obsession, at his ghoulish, gruesome investigation. *Trust your instincts.*

He blunted the sound of his hammering with a folded piece of rag he'd also found in the barn garage, draped over the top of the stake.

After each set of hammer blows on the stake, he waited. Rhythmic it would give itself away. Single blows took longer but might seem random—creating less chance that a young woman awakening might hear one.

Within fifteen minutes, the stake was submerged at least five feet in the soft dirt. With the two-foot hole, it was seven feet total.

Seven feet straight down. And two feet directly in front of the simple headstone.

Judy Smithers. B. 1942. D. 1966.

The stake had hit nothing. No box. No container. No obstruction. Nothing but rich, worthy North Carolina dirt.

As he had only half suspected, there had never been a coffin there. Never been a body there.

It was only a useful shrine. A useful fiction. Composed undoubtedly by the girl's father. And bringing Edwards one step closer to the facts.

The fake grave didn't make Tammy's father a killer.

But it sure took him a giant step toward it.

By proving the man was willing to go to some lengths to mount and maintain an elaborate deception. Why so elaborate? one had to ask. Merely for the sake of a little girl?

Once he had filled it in, he inspected the spot as best he could in the moonless night. Smoothed the dirt over. It would dry by morning.

He stood up, arched backward. The perspiration of the effort still poured from him.

He looked up at the stars. Looked to the dark house, the woman asleep.

Winston Edwards in the night. In the night once again. The night that had always held him. The night that had sheltered him. Hidden him. And finally, had accused him. Winston Edwards. Werewolf cop.

Tammy Smithers watched—with an unwarranted and close fascination—as he sipped the morning coffee she had brewed.

"You're off, aren't you?"

"Mm?" he asked.

"I can tell by the way you're sipping the coffee. The hurriedness. The quick gulps. There's some other place you're thinking of. Some other place you've got to be."

He smiled. "Ah, the detective again," he said. He sipped once more, and smiled. "Entirely right. I should put you on payroll."

The sunlight streamed in through the bay window into the antique kitchen, antique but functional. It was an idyll. Peaceful, time suspended . . .

"I'm due back," he confirmed. He took one last sip.

She looked at him a little sadly, concerned. "But you didn't find what you were looking for," she observed.

He put down the cup carefully, leaned forward, looked at her, gently, warmly. "I found something, didn't I?" he asked sweetly. "Wouldn't you agree, I found something?"

She smiled, and nodded agreement.

A few minutes later, she drove him in the bright red Ford pickup back into town.

21

The diminutive bespectacled elderly woman stepped off the train at the old downtown station in a red vinyl raincoat, holding a pendulous over-sized purse, energetically befuddled, quite obviously and amply a bundle of neuroses leaping and protruding like a sackful of cats.

Julian stepped up to meet her.

The forensic neurologist.

The brain brain.

Arguably the foremost brain brain in the country.

Ida Cornell.

She had a research arrangement with Johns Hopkins, and had taken the train up from Maryland. She refused to fly. As steadfastly and ungraciously and vociferously as she refused to eat cooked or packaged foods. As she refused to wear seat belts. As she refused to remove the latex gloves that she had apparently traveled wearing. Her own brain might provide rich research data for singular neurological findings and advances. But in any case, Julian had been warned.

The idea of a second shot fired seconds or more later because the first hadn't done an adequate job, a notion at first summarily dismissed, then allowed to enter, then genuinely entertained. And now, here was the brain brain.

Julian knew the story. Everyone did.

She was primarily an academic. Had done extensive primate work, and had then had the good fortune, and misfortune, to find herself among the Hutus and Tutsis, in a living albeit bloody and horrifying laboratory of ethnic genocide, wherein the crudest blows from the crudest weapons—hatchets, clubs, bicycle chains, donkey whips—were sustained by millions of victims. So she could bring her modern methods and modern examinations to this primitive national nightmare, and not only benefit from performing hundreds of autopsies, with no living relatives to intervene or claim rights or burial interests in the body, but even better, an added bonus, observe the still living—gruesomely injured, but still living—who were functioning mysteriously, remarkably, in defiance of conventional scientific wisdoms and tenets.

It was happening brutally, daily, and research science, unable to deter it and unresponsible for deterring it, was free and unencumbered to observe and learn from it.

Then, she'd returned to the academy. As if the genocide were one more field study. Returned to the ivy enclave with her films, her pictures, her studies. And had startled the neurological community with her filmed intimate discussions and native meals with men and woman with their heads half caved in, men and women graciously and cooperatively bowing their heads and pointing to their afflictions. And she startled them a second time with her findings.

She demonstrated ample new evidence for the human brain sustaining physical damage, and compartmentalizing it, adjusting to it. For traumatizing brain injury, and the heretofore unsuspected pathways that the brain employs to compensate. Evidence particularly riveting, of course, as presented by her war-tossed subjects.

Julian wondered if the challenges to Ida Cornell's research were fewer—or greater?—because she was black. Did her color aid her in carrying out her research, or hamper her? Either way, Julian imagined the resentment, the grumbling, the silent seething of Dr. Cornell's academic colleagues and competitors, and imagined that whatever they thought about Ida Cornell's color, they thought something.

Dr. Cornell soon found herself testifying in a case in which a man who had been shot in the head—a victim of attempted murder—had himself committed a retaliatory murder moments later. Was he in possession of his faculties, or wasn't he? She proved neurologically and rivetingly that he was.

She had testified in a case where a man shot in the head on one city block had been found in another part of the city, with no evidence of his having been moved. She showed convincingly that, unaware of his injury, or at least unimpeded by it, head covered by a hood, the man had taken mass transportation—a subway, and a second connecting subway—to a second location, established as intentional, before expiring.

To Julian, it was all gruesome stuff.

But Ida Cornell was a woman operating uncompromised and independent in a man's world, and earned points from Julian for that.

It was all particularly unlikely stuff in the life of a midwestern grandmother, as she revealed herself to be on the ride to the station-house forensics lab, but that is how she presented herself—her sole personal credential on the ride over. The rest of her conversation was about the advantage of trains, germs in America, the rudeness and inconsideration of the young—in fact, particularly grandmotherly stuff.

"Ida Cornell, my detectives, Walter Ng, Juan Mendoza. And this is Winston Edwards, who suggested we call you." Julian made the introductions.

The diminutive woman and the big man nodded sagely at one another.

"Here you go, then," said Julian, pushing the close-up crime photos expertly and deftly up into the hanging clips.

"Point of entry, occipital lobe, about, mm . . . let's say three hundred microns off the longitudinal sulcus," said Ida Cornell in her flat midwestern accent. "Second point of entry, about, oh . . . a hundred fifty microns further southwest." She smiled cheerfully. "Consciousness after the first shot? Or even after the second? Depends on angles. On depth. On tissue damage." She craned her neck at one photo, squinted. "Depends a lot, though, on which bullet was first, and which was second." She turned and looked at them, smiling at the academic neatness of the problem.

She looked back. "And that can be determined. By which bullet path crossed which bullet path. Particularly if they overlap. But even if they're only close, because some of the brain matter gets bunched on top of other brain matter—not to get too graphic. Think of a sandbox. Somebody drew intersecting lines with their fingers. Well, look closely where they cross, and you can tell which line got drawn first, and which got drawn second."

She stood patiently. As if awaiting the next display.

Then Dr. Cornell looked aghast at Julian's empty hands. "This is it?" she said crankily, incredulous.

"Yes."

"No closer shots?"

Julian shook her head. It wasn't procedure to have closer shots.

"But I can't tell from these photos which bullet entered first or second," Ida Cornell said, annoyed. "So *you* can't tell if he still had residual functioning after either." She looked at Julian. "Don't you want all the facts? Don't you *need* them, don't you *deserve* them, particularly since you're otherwise nowhere?"

To see whether there was meaning to the positioning of the objects. To gain some new insight, any insight, into Frank Ryan's final moments.

Ida Cornell pursed her lips. "How long since the murder?"

"Three weeks."

She weighed it. "Ten feet under. The ground is fairly cool right now, that far down." She looked hard at Julian. "I could still see what I need to. The tissue would still be intact enough."

Julian had a sinking feeling. "What . . . exhume the body?" she said, the dread rising in her. Could she really take such a drastic step, based only on Edwards's and the neurologist's speculations? But she'd brought in Edwards to begin with. Obviously, she'd do whatever it took.

"Exhume," commanded Dr. Cornell suddenly with an odd fluttery wave of her hand, as if surprised that it should warrant any further discussion. "Exhume."

22

Once again, Julian stood on the broad porch of the solid stone house, and rang the bell.

Ida Cornell had pushed to get it taken care of over the phone, so she could get started right away, but Julian had refused. Much as she herself would have preferred a quick phone call, for how much easier it would be. Instead of a grim visit to the widow once more.

Mrs. Ryan opened the door and raised her eyes with a momentary glimmer of expection, before taking the measure of Julian's expression, and knowing this was nothing—an update, an administrative errand of some sort. Julian felt a physical pain on dashing those expectations.

"Hello," Nell Ryan said, guardedly.

"Hello, Nell," said Julian. They were familiar by now. Familiar enough to be friends. But were still, would always be, strangers to one another.

"Nell, we've . . ." it was a sentence Julian had not expected to utter in the course of this investigation, nor of any investigation of her career, and she stumbled over its unfamiliarity. "Nell . . . I'm afraid we've got to exhume your husband's body."

Nell Ryan stood, looking uncomprehending. "But you did an autopsy!"

"Yes . . . but, well, we have a forensic neurology expert, and she—"

"She! Is it all women in your ghastly work?!"

Julian took a breath. "She needs to perform her own neurological exam."

There was silence. Then a pained, small, weakened, "My God." Then silence again.

Julian waited for her to say something. But no approval or disapproval was forthcoming.

She waited, listened into the silence.

"Nell?"

"All right," said the voice, defeated.

"There are several legal details to a procedure like—"

"Take care of them," Nell snapped.

"I'll have a power of attorney dropped off for your signature," Julian said quickly.

Julian felt ugly. Incompetent. Worse than all that, she feared this was a fishing expedition. All for nothing.

Nell Ryan raised herself up slightly, straightened her back against this latest indignity, this fresh onslaught of fate. "By the way," said Mrs. Ryan, tone shifting only slightly, "my daughter has something she wants to ask you."

Julian felt an unexpected lightness. Felt the weight of the preceding conversation lift somewhat, and was curious to know a little more, to connect a little further, with the girl who had smiled out at her so engagingly from the bedroom. On the heels of the topic of exhumation, Julian managed to suppress her smile. But she felt a warmth, a warmth of flattery. And then realized it might be the younger daughter . . .

"Alyshia," called Mrs. Ryan up the stairs.

The older one. Julian kept the smile inside.

Alyshia came to the top of the stairs.

"Officer Palmer is here."

"Oh." Alyshia stood suddenly nervously, swinging one toe anxiously against the carpeting of the top step.

"Aren't you going to ask?" prompted her mother, annoyance mixed with affection, a habit of their life together. "Come down here, please. Be polite."

Alyshia descended the steps halfway, met her mother halfway, literally. She nervously toed the next step. She tried to shrug off her mother's prompting, her mother's very involvement, her too-closeness—a twelve-year-old amid tragedy, but a twelve-year-old nonetheless.

"Hi, Alyshia," Julian said up the staircase to her, "And you can call me Julian, if you want."

"Oh," said the girl, the thought a new one, obviously constituting a slight shift in her understanding of the world, that understanding being an evolving, mutable thing, and then, obviously pleased, upbeat. "Okay. Well, the thing is, at school we have this project? Where we have to interview someone in an interesting job? And I just thought . . ." and here the sentence broke down, relied on adults to take up the slack.

"I'd love to," said Julian, jumping in to cut off the girl's embarrassment in asking—flattered, pleased, relieved to be able to salvage something, to offer something, anything, to the Ryans besides heartache.

23

As Julian had expected, the flaky, disorganized, distractable midwestern black grandmother became transformed with a scalpel and forensic forceps in her hands. She was suddenly a commanding presence, a titanic force of intellect and a supreme demonstration of competence, in the amphitheater where she seemed to be more comfortable, Julian was sure, than even in her own home with her own family. She spoke fluently and unhesitatingly into the ancient microphone suspended above the mercifully covered corporeal remains of Frank Ryan.

Her gleaming instruments were arrayed carefully in three sparkling trays beside her. Spectroscopes, precise calipers, optic probes, unique optometric devices, stood in stark contrast to the crude saws, blades, clamps and forceps typically employed by Myron Caterwalk, their own medical examiner. Her cuts into the brain were crisp and aggressive, even though minute and precise. Caterwalk assisted silently, appropriately meek and subdued.

With her own training, Julian could follow Ida's medical pronouncements and commentary initially, but once Ida was deep inside Frank Ryan's brain, all bets were off. The terminology became technical and arcane, and Julian, out of her depth, gladly retreated from the harsh glaring lights and choking disinfectant smell and hard cement floor through the swinging doors. To be thorough, to avoid ever having to do this sort of exercise again, Ida Cornell was performing a complete neurological exam. Julian sat silently in one of the uncomfortable seats outside the ancient amphitheater, and took a deep, welcome breath of air.

In less than an hour, Dr. Cornell emerged, pulled off mask and gloves, and, still assertive, still commanding, made Julian and Myron aware of her further plans.

"I'm going to head to the hotel, take a nice long hot bath, have a nice salad for lunch, write up the case this afternoon, and deliver it to you this evening, before I depart on the 7:19," she said, nodding to Julian, indicating the ride she would need.

Then her demeanor shifted. She became suddenly human again. A midwestern grandmother once more. She looked at them with concern. "But I do have this to tell you." She studied each of their faces, as if to look deep into each of them, to see if they could handle, would understand, what she was about to say.

"Fortunately for our purposes here, the trajectories of the bullets intersect. Not that the bullets themselves ever crossed paths, you understand. The bullets were lodged in the brain matter. But their invasion disrupts the brain matter in such a way that I can see which disruption is underneath—that would be the first shot—and which is on top of it—that would be the second. Remember my finger paths in the sand?" she reminded them, schoolteacherish. "So that's how I know the occipital lobe's anterior third sector took the first shot." She looked at them. "And given that the first shot, with that little twenty-five-caliber, was through the occipital lobe's anterior third sector"—she paused, looked at them— "it's quite possible Frank Ryan looked up to see what all the commotion was about." The picture that Edwards had proposed tore through them again. But now with Ida Cornell's authority.

"You mean, maybe he didn't even know he was shot?" It was one thing when Edwards proposed it offhand. It was another thing coming from her.

And yet, Julian thought, maybe that's exactly what Edwards intended.

After all, she wasn't saying it was what happened. She was only saying it was possible.

"He might have been entirely sentient." She reached for her red vinyl coat, began to button it almost abstractly, aimlessly, with no more motor skill or adeptness than the next grandmother, Julian noted. "Like a trauma injury. I've seen it a lot now. You're mysteriously, entirely functional."

"So he might not have felt it."

"Worse than not feeling it," said Ida Cornell, "he might have not *felt* it, but saw it, knew it, and could see who fired it."

"But the second shot is to the *back* of the head," Julian pointed out. "Sure doesn't look like he knew or realized anything."

She shrugged, closed the collar of her coat.

"I wish I could tell you that has to be true. But a lot could have happened between the first and second shot. He could have been forced to turn back to his desk. He could have turned back because he chose to. Or, as you say, because he wasn't aware of being shot at all." Ida Cornell sat heavily in the little folding chair in the waiting hall off the amphitheater. "But this is where it gets tricky. Because the second shot could have been fired a second later." She looked at Julian. "Or five minutes later."

"Five minutes!"

"I'm not saying that's what happened. I'm saying that's the outer parameter of what's medically possible. That's approximately when the blood loss from the first wound would have begun to have a deleterious and fatal effect. You saw the blood flow. Not terribly fast. Consistent with a head wound in that area. And because of how the blood was flowing, down the back of his neck, down his collar and shirt, it's still possible he simply didn't know he'd been shot."

He might have recognized his assailant, Julian realized. Might have turned calmly to the assailant, and asked confused, puzzled, "What was that? Did you hear that? Why, why did you do that?" And then for whatever reason—not knowing, or choosing to, or forced to, turned back. The baroque possibilities of the scene danced. Only one thing could be worse than being killed at your desk. Being killed, and being around to see it.

Julian felt physically sick with the vividness of the thought. From being unable to imagine a scenario in which the elements fit, to a scenario that was dizzyingly appalling. The imagination unleashed . . .

"Now, let's face it. The likelihood in these things is that the second shot is fired pretty damn close to the first," Ida Cornell said with midwestern practicality. "In reaction to the victim's moving after the first shot. Or maybe not even waiting for that." Ignoring, however, certain desktop objects out of place, thought Julian.

Ida Cornell doubled over with strenuous effort to reach her black boots. "I'm good on the whats and wheres," she said, struggling with their buckles. "You have to handle the whys." As if she could read the chaotic tossing of Julian's thoughts.

From too little to too much, in a way. All this possibility—it was directly opposed to intuition, Julian realized. It was in direct contradiction to, flew in the face of, what Edwards had always taught, the way he'd always worked. Was it planned on his part? Adding expertise to the confusion? Adding legitimacy to the wrenching vision?

Yet at the same time, making himself look good, building his credibility.

Because Edwards had posited it, offhand, in passing. And the little expert had confirmed it.

Confirmed it as only a possibility. Which gave them nothing. Except sleepless nights.

24

With a smile, the Captain motioned Julian to sit, and closed his office door behind her.

He continued sporting the smile as he seated himself in his large office chair. Academy green leather. Brand-new, she noticed. Its delivery probably not held up for eight months.

He even held the smile—remarkably consistent, remarkably durable, a muscular smile—as he said to her, foamy with fury, "What in fuck's name are you doing?"

He was of Irish stock, famously handsome, with a famously large brood, and famously straightlaced. And while his own boss, the commissioner and chief of police, was a transplant who'd been with the department only a year, he'd been on the force for thirty, and ran much of it day to day, and knew far more, and presumed to know all.

He was always impeccably dressed. Like a successful broker or real estate developer. Someone regularly in the gym. Unremarkable, perhaps, except compared to the incipient, creeping dissoluteness of other police captains she'd had the misfortune to know.

"Your court files are sealed from the public. But I assume you're aware, they're not sealed from me," he told her. "Did you think I wouldn't find out?" he asked, incredulous. "Did you think I wouldn't be utterly shocked?"

Julian said nothing.

The Captain shook his head.

"What are you doing? Do you have any idea how quickly you could be dismissed?"

She stayed silent, but looked unsurprised, indicating that she was very well aware.

He breathed in sharply.

He had never liked her. She had picked it up from day one. He'd taken an instant and irrational dislike to her that was as obvious as his pasted-on smile. And so they'd avoided each other. But with this—with this he'd felt compelled to deal with her.

Julian smiled.

The Captain seemed startled by the smile, shifted uncomfortably, but recovered.

He settled back into the green leather. "Presuming that you knew all the risks, you obviously believe in this guy's abilities."

Believe in his abilities? Beneath the theatrics, Edwards had so far run into the same brick walls, had accomplished no more than she had. Julian had expected to feel some pride, some vindication in this. But she found she only felt worse, more cornered, more trapped, even less competent. Because having opened the Edwards can of worms, having opened herself to criticism and derision for taking Edwards on, she so far had nothing to counteract it, to stave it off, nothing to show for it.

The Captain's next pronouncement was one that he obviously expected would greatly startle his subordinate. "Well . . . I'm going to let you continue." he said grandly. "It'll be our secret."

But his subordinate understood him better than he thought. "You're going to let me continue," said Julian, "because you'd like to see me fail. You're going to let me continue, because you can easily claim you knew nothing about Edwards being here, because I've set it up so there's no paper trail about Edwards's employment. You're going to let me continue, because you figure this'll be the perfect catastrophe, the perfect chance to finally get rid of me. Because you don't like me, you don't like what I represent, you don't like anything about me, and you don't like having to pretend you do."

The Captain leaned back, rubbed the palms of his manicured hands over the smooth leather surfaces of the big green leather chair. His new chair. Spanking new.

He paused to consider her in light of the sudden honesty that hung between them. "If you somehow do get yourself out of this mess," the Captain said, "I promise you, I'll be the first to recommend you for promotion. Because based on this exchange, you see, I think your insights are utterly brilliant."

He looked straight at her—authentic, challenging, and real for a moment—then pasted his plastic smile back on, and briskly slapped the top of his desk with two open palms. Indicating to Julian the meeting was over.

It occurred to her in the dim cement stairwell that brought her back down to her own floor:

Once you're operating outside convention, it seems that you have less and less to lose.

Maybe that was the crazy kinship she felt with Winston Edwards.

25

Edwards lay on his side on the single bed in the downtown motel they'd put him up in, rocking a short whiskey philosophically in his hand. His third.

He could also tell it was his last. Though he couldn't tell you why.

He lay brooding about, imagining, a father who would arrange that elaborate deception for his child.

For the sake of his child?

He knew about deception. It was an area of competence. Of expertise. He knew quite well the deception meant to protect—the deception that gave the deceiver the sense of conviction and fiber, a singing sense of morality—and he knew that that sort of deception had with it a strong accompaniment of self-deception. It was more often an effort to control, not protect. To control the situation, not protect anyone from it.

Was the deception for the sake of his child? If the father told himself it was for the sake of his child, Edwards was sure it was for the father's own sake too. He reached for the phone, and dialed.

"Arteris?"

"Yes?"

"Edwards here."

"Ah, the big chief." Drawly, alcoholic, dissolute—and utterly honest, if not utterly reliable. Winston Edwards found himself smiling at the little man's obvious pleasure in Edwards's contact. He liked the eccentric little guy. It might be the first time Edwards had cared about a source.

"Philip Smithers," said Edwards, and listened for the response, imagining the bright Florida prints, the humid heat, Arteris Shore padding around in his slippers.

"Philip Smithers," said Arteris. "Sure."

"He was one of 'em?" Edwards asked. "One of that pack of good ol' boys?"

"Hell, no," said Arteris confused. "He was a *real* good ol' boy. He was a gentleman."

"Arty, they had a daughter together. Philip Smithers and Julian's mother. I've seen her."

Arteris was silent.

"They had the daughter *before*, Arty. Before the marriage to Julian's father. Before the lovers." All the lovers that were a reaction, a young Southern girl's self-loathing and self-destructiveness and self-image of defilement, for bearing a secret child. For getting away with it. "That's why nobody ever found anything. You, the first reporter, everyone, concentrated on the affairs. That had to be it. But it wasn't. It was this guy, this guy from before, who couldn't stand it when she went on to another life, nearby enough to make him stare at his broken dreams every day. Probably he even learned about the lovers, and it only aggravated his anger." The whiskey lubricated Edwards. The words poured out. "The guy was cut out, cut off in every way. He would see her with her beautiful new daughters, reminders of the life he might have had, as this guy Smithers's life swung lower and lower from its high point with her. And he couldn't take it anymore, and he knew he had the cover of a dozen likely suspects, prominent guys who the local deputies would never sort through and would be reluctant to take down anyway. He had the cover that let his rage get the better of him, and one night it did." In the ensuing silence, and with the lubricating whiskey, he freely felt an enormous identity with that rage. Felt the dispossession, the omnidirectional fury, that Smithers felt. A brotherhood of fury that assured Edwards beneath his skin that he had the right man.

"Then who was the other guy that night? The other hooded figure?"

Trust a reporter to wreck the moment, to divert it, shut it down.

"Don't know," said Edwards. "Don't even begin to know."

Arteris was silent. Then, taking it on instinct as correct, asked what was, Edwards knew, the single remaining relevant question. "How the hell you gonna prove any of that?"

"Don't begin to know that either."

How would he? Why should he? Why should he bother?

His last case. So clearly.

Edwards lay back on the pillow. Idly he spun his glass with his fingers.

He had solved it. He knew who. He didn't know yet whether to try bringing him to justice, or whether or when to tell Julian, or even if—but he knew who.

In a way, it could only have been he who solved it. Julian could not see it. And he and Julian were the only ones left interested enough to solve it.

An unsolved murder with only one possible detective. That narrowed the chances it would get solved. But it was solved.

In fact, with a little luck, it had been easy.

So easy he had begun to wonder if Julian, after her initial efforts at it—if Julian, learning more about life, about what people do and who people really are and how those close to you can surprise you—if Julian had really wanted it solved.

Three whiskeys in, he reached for the phone, unfolded the slip of paper tucked into his wallet.

He'd jotted down the phone number.

Winston Edwards made a call to the farm.

A man answered.

Good.

"Hello?"

"Hi, Mr. Smithers?"

"Yes . . ."

Guarded. The habit of guardedness. Of meanness. Edwards could hear a lifetime in a single syllable, digitally disassembled, transmitted several hundred miles north, reassembled for Edwards's ear, with nothing lost in the translation. He could hear a lifetime. Or else, only wanted to.

"This is Detective Edwards." He waited silently. A beat. He would lay out each line. Let each build implication, let each have its own power, examine where each shot landed, before discharging the next.

Silence. "Yes?" Completely different from the first yes, Edwards immediately noticed. This one acting suddenly friendly, cheerfully cooperative and utterly false. It would not have given itself away were it not for the suspicious, guarded yes preceding it.

"I'm a friend of your daughter's," Edwards said, and listened carefully for a catch of breath, for an exhalation. He now knew he had the man's full attention, so he knew any reaction would relate directly to his words.

"Aha. Yes," Smithers said, unrevealing, uncommitted, implying slightly that she'd told her father about the overnight guest, but not implying it very much.

"Oh—she mentioned me?" Edwards asked pointedly, to show him he could read him, to rattle him a little.

"Well . . ." And here the man, in that beat, proved he hadn't decided exactly what to say. "Yes, I think she did, in fact. Yes, I think so." Trying to recover, to save the moment.

"Well, I just wanted to call and thank her. And thank you. Philip, is it?" *I know your name.*

Edwards could hear the mix of nervous silence and slight anger, an anger quick to materialize, quick enough, strong enough, to well up uncontrollably. "I'd a been stuck without her help. So I wanted to thank her. And you."

"Mm," he said, assent.

"Is she there?"

"Yes, but she's not avail—"

"Who is it, Daddy?" Edwards heard it called out suddenly from a distance.

"It's nob—" the man began to say, preparing, Edwards bet, to hang up.

"Who is it?" Brighter, closer, the woman's voice now next to the phone.

"It's the detective," said Tammy Smithers's father grudgingly.

She took the phone. "Hi." Brightly, cheerfully.

"Just wanted to thank you again," said Edwards.

"Well, that's awful nice of you." She paused. "Daddy," teasing, affectionate, Southern, "it's a private call."

Private call? What? Why is she implying to her father there's something between them?

To mislead . . . precautionary . . .

Then, in a moment, quietly, harshly, furiously, "You dug up the grave."

Edwards made no reply.

"Your case was here," she said, "wasn't it?" Harsh, angry.

There was a silence in which Edwards was accused. A moment in which he understood he would probably never see her again, or if he did, it would be adversarial, and their friendship, started so instinctively and promisingly, was ended before it began. He wasn't surprised to feel a blanket of sadness.

"I didn't tell him," Tammy Smithers said suddenly in a quick whisper, and hung up.

So she knew.

No, didn't know, necessarily. But sensed something. Had always sensed something, and had her sense of something confirmed on her discovery of Edwards's presence at her mother's grave.

Didn't know exactly what he was doing there. But knew it was something. Knew—knew herself—something wasn't right.

And she was letting him go ahead.

I'll show her. The three words rising up again. The dark thought loosened into consciousness by the whiskey. *I'll show her.*

26

Ng led the older Ryan girl into Lieutenant Palmer's office, the girl leaning around the edges of the doorway, around the huge back of Ng, like a frightened animal.

On seeing her, Julian issued a megawatt smile, realizing that a smile that broad, that pleased and uncalculated, was a rarity in this office. In fact, she couldn't think of another time she or anyone else had issued one.

"Come in, come in," said Julian expansively, imagining the girl's discomfort amid this grim brick, this oppressive flat fluorescence. "Take this seat. Thank you, Ng." Julian was up, pulled out and held the chair for Alyshia, who was clutching her kitten-theme notebook and her colored pens.

"Thanks for doin' this," the girl said uncomfortably, reluctantly, like all preteenagers, Julian instantly felt, at having to temporarily conduct herself as an adult, but obviously infinitely capable of it when pressed. Julian smiled inwardly, remembering so clearly. You could act insecure. You could act secure. You could act any way, really, because you didn't know who you were, didn't know which one was the real you.

Mrs. Ryan had called Julian a few days before. "It's really nice of you to do this."

"Don't be silly. My pleasure." *Are you kidding? It's something I can do, at least. Something. Anything.*

"I'm very glad she wanted to do this with you. I was going to call you about her anyway."

"You were?"

Nell Ryan had taken a breath, exhaled her exasperation evenly, measuring it out, suffering the matter maximally. "She hasn't been doing any homework. She's been disruptive at school. Staying out late." Her exasperation vented in another sigh. "I know you're not a guidance counselor, but guidance counselors don't deal with murder."

"Something like this happens, it's hard to imagine the effect on a kid. Give it time," Julian said, flattered by Nell's confiding in her, knowing that that was the right response.

"Was always an A student, top of her class. One of those dream kids you never even have to think about. Did everything right. Loved by everyone. And now, well, now I *do* have to think about it."

"How's her sister doing?"

Julian could hear the parental surprise in Nell's response, the somewhat amused parental observation: "Her sister seems to be going the other way. Never a student. And now she's hunkering down."

Julian recognized that. That had been her own way. Blinders on. Narrow down. Dig in. Alyshia might be doing it the better way—letting it all out, letting it all in, feeling it all.

"They're both reacting, though, aren't they? Dealing with it the best they can. It's probably going to take some time."

"She looks awful. She's gaining weight."

"She's a teenager, Mrs. Ryan. Go easy on her."

"You sound like you've seen this kind of thing before."

"Well . . ." the word stumbling, stalling, falling limply. *I was your daughter. I was her. I suffered the same catastrophe, the same inconceivable alteration of the universe.* "I do . . . I do have experience with this kind of thing."

"Well, I don't mean to burden you with all my kid's problems. I just called to say thanks that you're going to see her."

And now she sat in Julian's office.

Julian was surprised by the inconsistency: the girl's acting out at school, and yet her intensity, her focus, on this school project. But maybe Julian's world smacked of reality, of the real and brutal world that the girl had been delivered too heavy a dose of, and after what happened, school seemed so artificial, so isolated. The real world had obtruded. It had brought ruin, and yet, in that same moment, the girl had learned of its existence, and was intrigued, pulled in. And Julian, given her profession, represented in a sense something ideal—a safe escort into that brutal world, and a close observer and participant in it.

"So . . . I mean . . . how did you get into police work?" The pink kitty-cat notebook opened, a colored pen poised.

"How did I?" Julian looked at the girl for a long moment.

A twelve-year old, who'd been through so much so suddenly these past few weeks . . . What might it mean to her, to know how much she happened to share with the lead detective on the case?

What healing might there be, in the relief of a little girl's sense of aloneness?

Julian got up, went over to the door, shut it gently, as gently as she might the cover of a book she'd just finished. Finished forever . . . and yet perhaps she'd carefully open its cover one last time.

"How did I get into police work? I'm going to tell you. But I want you to know . . . it's something I haven't shared with anyone, because I haven't felt that it's directly relevant. Until now . . ."

The girl wrinkled her nose and brow, not understanding exactly. That was okay. She would in a moment.

"When I was your age, exactly your age"—Julian paused, took a short breath, looked hard at the little girl—"my own father was killed very much like yours." Her words flat, clear, staid, the arc of feeling having not yet begun its ascent behind them.

The girl looked stunned, stayed silent, regarded Julian in amazement.

Julian felt a pride, a release, a connection she hadn't expected.

It helped Julian to tell it.

A door. Footfalls. Blackness. The creak of the springs, the breathing of her sister asleep in the bunk above her. Something smashes near the front door. A thump. Silence. A scream. Sirens.

Frozen. Frozen in the bed. Immobilized. Amid the choking heat, the pooling sweat, the new rise of screams.

The door flung open. The sheriff filling the doorway. "Get up girls."

No, I can't.

Pulling them, prying them up. Her sister screaming. Herself, frozen.

Holding the knife. The sheriff. In plastic. The knife . . .

Red cherry light sweeping doom across the kitchen. The pounding of uniformed boots and her own heart, the sudden bright flood of light after the bedroom dark, the indecipherable crackle of the radios; and men—men, nameless, faceless, looking through her nightgown at the first bloom of her breasts . . .

The wail of her mother . . . howling, incalculable . . .

The warmth and wetness of her own urine down her leg . . .

And in the middle of the floor, the lump of body beneath the tarp, like a sack of sand.

A frantic, crescendoing crackle of radios. The rush of exit. Quickness to the trail. The evaporation of disaster. Instant. Dreamlike. Unreal.

But the trail had soon stopped. The trail had soon frozen.

Frozen like a little girl, on a suffocating night of Southern heat . . .

Frozen in her bed.

Could I have saved you, Daddy? Oh, Daddy, could I have saved you, if I hadn't stayed frozen in the bed?

The interview was clearly over, but they both remained seated, Alyshia and Julian, not moving, somehow held.

The girl was alive, engaged. Julian wished that Nell Ryan could see it. It was something, at last, that Julian was doing for the Ryans. It was startling, how immediately relieving it felt to her, to be able to do something for Alyshia. And given Nell Ryan's phone call about Alyshia's troubles in school, it occurred to Julian that she could easily do more.

"Listen," she said to Alyshia, and felt amused to find herself uncomfortable, embarrassed in asking, after setting aside this time and making this effort on the girl's behalf. "How 'bout . . . uh . . ." But it felt natural, right, a good idea, to ask. "How 'bout I take you out to see a movie this weekend?"

The girl looked in surprise at Julian. Seemed a little stunned by the question, and then to honestly consider for a moment. It was apparent from her expression of pleasant startlement, that she had never even thought of something like that. But as she thought about it, a smile crossed her face warmly.

"Yeah," she said, realizing it freshly and more deeply as she said the word. "Yeah, I'd like that."

"Saturday?" asked Julian. "Friday? What's good for you?"

"Either," she said, sprightly, getting more used to the idea.

"Saturday at seven. I'll pick you up." Adding sternly, "Clear it with your mom."

I can do some good here, thought Julian. *Do some good for both of us.*

27

All week, Julian fretted ridiculously about the movie. She had initially decided on some new Disney fare, but then had worried in the end that the choice would insult Alyshia's intelligence. She had scanned the listings, researched them with a couple of media-obsessed moviegoing secretaries in the station house, eliminated any sex or violence—a police lieutenant, after all, in charge of a minor, there were moral choices to make, moral standards to uphold. It had left her with nothing. Eventually, she had laughed at herself, a parent by proxy, obsessing about the content, the appropriateness of a movie, when the girl had just lived through an experience that would make the two-hour artificial experience seem like nothing. Don't worry about the morality. Let the girl enjoy for once the advantage of being with an adult who is not her parent. And if Julian was more relaxed, it was bound to go better anyway.

She was surprised at her own nervousness. Like a date. Well, it *was* a date. A date with her own competence—as an adult, with the charge of a child.

Although she knew it was more than that. She liked Alyshia—beyond the circumstances, beyond the tragedy, beyond seeing herself, her own past, reflected, repeated in her. Beyond this friendship's offering an oblique way of somehow addressing, of rectifying, the emotional chaos that had followed her own father's murder. Julian recognized all that, but that wasn't it.

Julian just liked her, period. Saw and sensed from her curiosity, individuality, simple and irrepressible girlhood, climbing out from the tragedy, her innocent arms and hands reaching heroically out to pull herself up over the fiery lip of it. Inside the brittle fractured shell of tragedy, she sensed a terrific kid.

Julian was getting older. She wasn't seeing anyone romantically. The clock was ticking, and the oddness of her life, the choices and the circumstances, were making it less and less likely that she'd have the experience of a family. An experience that, ironically, she was finding feeling for, and aware of, more and more acutely.

So this was more than someone's daughter. It was the daughter she would like to have. The daughter she might never have. But Jesus—not to burden the relationship, thought Julian.

And she realized why she had fretted so about the movie. Something further about it. She felt protective. Wanted to protect Alyshia's childhood from any further invasion, any further harm. She thought briefly about the crime. About someone who had apparently entered and exited leaving no clue, no trail. Almost as if to show, to prove, they could do it again. She pushed the thought away.

Seven o'clock sharp, she pulled into the Ryans' driveway. The sturdy stone house, grown so familiar during several close inspections and investigations, looked completely different and unexpected to Julian at night. With a mild jolt, she realized that this was how it had looked to the killer.

The realization made her walk up slowly. She regarded for a moment the stone house's outline, its hard black edge against the gray night sky. After a moment, she rang the doorbell. "Come on in!" yelled out carelessly, automatically, the teenager's voice. Julian was surprised Alyshia would be so trusting, although Alyshia, after all, must know it was her. She entered to see Alyshia slumped in the living room in front of the television, a junk game show, no head turn of acknowledgment, eating ice cream out of a container.

Maybe she was shy and uncomfortable.

Maybe it was the nearness of her mother.

Whatever the reason, Julian was suddenly in the presence of a slovenly, rude, willful teenager. This was not the sprightly kid who had come to interview her in her office.

Mrs. Ryan came out of the kitchen, looking in frustration at the back of Alyshia's head.

"You're not going to greet Miss Palmer?"

"Julian, please." Julian requested her first name gently—not to play a part in this moment of domestic drama.

"Alyshia . . ." said Nell Ryan, in some broad accustomed space between pleading and warning that Julian sensed, many of her communications to her daughter existed within.

No response.

"Alyshia, she's come all—"

"In a *minute*, Mom," exasperated. "Just after this part . . ." And her head pivoted slightly above the couch, and she caught Julian's eye, and smiled broad and kidlike, mischievous and alive, and Julian knew the evening would go just fine.

The next moment, there was a flush of the toilet, and a gangly young boy about Alyshia's age emerged from the guest bathroom, hands in his jeans pockets, stood in the bathroom doorway, and looked at Julian.

"Aren't you going to introduce Rick?" asked Mrs. Ryan, her irritation finding easy, ample reason to ramp up again.

"What's the point? We're breaking up," said Alyshia, with teenager's calculated outrageousness.

Her mother shook her head in exasperation, looking at the back of Alyshia's head, and not at Julian for support or commiseration.

Nell went over to Alyshia, pulled the ice cream container roughly out of her hands, and said, as if unfazed and unrattled, "Rick, this is Lieutenant Palmer."

"Julian," said Julian gently again.

"Julian, this is Rick Boyko, Alyshia's friend."

A friend Julian had never heard mentioned when she'd initially interviewed the girls.

Deep down, she felt a tingling, an inkling. A massing of the senses. She felt Rick attaching himself to the Ryans'. It was like a simmering soup stirred, new ingredients rising from beneath the surface.

She realized later that she was literally feeling the plot thicken.

28

They stood outside the multiplex after the movie in the fresh air, stars swirling above the concrete videodrome, milky in the cool dusk. The movie had been perfectly innocent. It had hardly enthralled Julian, but it had, she was pleased to see, held Alyshia rapt—and so Julian had found herself studying Alyshia sidelong in the movie screen's flickering light.

It was true about the weight gain, she saw. But pubescent girls even in the best situations fluctuated wildly. And as far as her suffering school-work—the girl obviously was not only plenty bright but had, when she chose to use it, a winning way. Armed with those two skills, Julian wasn't concerned.

"So . . . ice cream?" Julian asked now.

The girl looked suddenly sourly away. "You're making fun of my weight."

Julian felt stricken. "No, no . . . I . . . that's just what you do after a movie. Get an ice cream. That's the law, isn't it?"

"But you do notice the weight. You just proved it, when you got all nervous and jittery when I mentioned it." As the other moviegoers filed past, Alyshia crossed her arms hard, stood with her legs apart, planting herself in her moroseness.

"Boy, you read me perfectly on that. A junior detective," said Julian, trying to defuse it. "Is that the real reason you did the interview?" she teased. "You're interested in the job?"

Alyshia smiled, and then pushed it one further, continued the game a little. "And now you're trying to distract me by flattering me about my skills of observation. Well," the girl smiled now, couldn't help it, "it's working." She uncrossed her arms. "And ice cream does sound good." Mock accusingly now, playfully, looking at Julian. "Just like you knew it would."

She was smart. Observant. Bright and alive.

And there was a connection between them. An instant intimacy that Julian had only dared to vaguely imagine, had only hoped would be there. And suddenly, it was. Real. Here. Delightful.

The ice cream parlor glimmered, buffed and gemlike with bright confection. Julian and Alyshia sat in a booth across from each other, eyes on their ice cream, absorbed respectively in mint chocolate chip and butter pecan splash, spooning silently, satisfied.

They remembered at a certain point to look up at one another, and laughed spontaneously to see the perfect mirror, the reflection of each in the other engrossed for a moment in cold sweet melting goodness.

"So . . ." said Julian, pausing for a moment, wiping the mint chocolate chip off her lips.

"So . . ." now extending verbally the image of identicalness.

"So who's Rick?" idly, teasingly.

"Rick?" She shrugged. "He's nothing. He's a friend."

"Seemed pretty comfortable there. How come I never heard about him before?"

She shrugged again. "Why would you? He's . . . a boy. . . ." Shrugging again, as if it were of the utmost insignificance. As in, another boy, boys are boys, nothing more, they don't rate. . . .

"Now let me point out: You followed the word 'friend' with the word 'boy'," said Julian, and smiled. "Those two words came out of you awfully close together."

Alyshia smirked. ·

"He seemed to be part of the fabric there, from what I could see," Julian observed. "Old comfortable Rick."

Alyshia suddenly frowned, set down her spoon hard on the shiny table. "Why are you trying to get under my skin?"

It was as if Julian, not looking—walking blissfully, carefree, singing through the woods—had suddenly stumbled against something. A completely unidentified object. What it was couldn't yet be said. But something unexpected. That much was sure.

Julian managed to turn the conversation elsewhere. To the movie. To classes. Alyshia soon picked up the spoon again. As if she'd already forgotten. But Julian hadn't.

"Well," Julian said at the door, feeling at once datelike and at the same time ridiculous for feeling it, "hope you had a good time."

Alyshia smiled. A smile that clearly telegraphed, *You know I did,* and to confirm its meaning, she stepped with deliberation and surprising sudden confidence over to Julian on the porch landing, and gave her a spontaneous, unmodulated hug.

She let go, looked up at Julian. "Thanks." Suddenly politely, obviously authentic, gratitude extending beyond the movie and ice cream, it seemed. Alyshia turned and went inside.

Julian looked up once more at the stone house. Quarried from somewhere near, three-quarters of a century ago. The house that had become so familiar to her by now, going through its rooms, imagining its life, first purely professionally, then with something more, some other more complex motive.

She looked up again at the stars, still hovering over her. Watchful, bright and without judgment, the same stars in the sky above the movie theater. She began a chain of thought that came and went in her, drifting uninvited in and out of her consciousness—vague, then clear, hovering like those stars—on her drive back to her apartment, and as she sat familiarly, timelessly at her apartment window, staring out at the park across the street.

It was a meditation on loneliness. A drifting meditation on being alone. Begun by the realization that being with someone, connecting to someone, anyone—even in a small way to a shy, troubled junior high school girl—only highlighted her loneliness. Connection highlighted her aloneness. How ironic. How brutal.

The loneliness that the circumstances of her life now played into, reinforced. An officer in command, who must make command decisions alone. Who, by the written manuals and the unwritten code of her position, must maintain her distance to maintain her authority. A city chosen almost at random, chosen only professionally, where she must exist alone. A life that had conspired to force her early, and therefore to teach her quickly and of necessity, to live alone. And when she saw that she could do it, it might have been the turning moment, because from then on, she did. Like a certain stupid expression, like an unthinking habit, like a certain ritual before a kill, it was her MO.

There was in her meditation, she noticed, no sadness particularly, in the observation of her own aloneness. It was, emotionally speaking, for the moment at least, merely observable fact. A fact of her life, a fact of her personality, like Ng's inborn enthusiasm, like Mendoza's inborn suspicion, like an item on the checklist of personality, of personal definition. Her inborn aloneness. Not aloofness, or lack of connection, or inability to communicate. Simply, resoundingly, aloneness.

Like Edwards's obliqueness, Edwards's brooding, Edwards's deep separateness—she couldn't avoid the comparison—like his aloneness, too.

Her aloneness was private and quiet, moving lightly between visibility and invisibility. Diaphanous. A shawl. Whereas Edwards's was yawning and cavernous. Oceanic. If hers was a small cry, his was a howl. Or was hers a howl too? A silent howl, but a howl nonetheless.

She was so alone, the detective in her observed, there was hardly evidence of herself in her own life. There was the coffee picked up on the way in to work, but no enjoyment of the coffee. There were the CDs playing in the apartment, but no recognition, no sitting and listening or even noticing the music. There was the drive in the country, but fast, not looking too closely, knowing only that you were there, that the trees were beside you. There was the walk in the woods, but without awareness of your footsteps, of your path, of your own presence. She could find only the briefest glimpse of herself, which was worse, in a way—a glimpse of what could and should be.

Then, feeling crept in; at her apartment window, in the dark and quiet, her self appeared to her. It probably required the quiet. It probably required the dark. To bring forth the tears, isolated, silent themselves, single at first, almost pretty, then plentiful, and not pretty at all.

Alone. Not just a fact. A life sentence. Alone. Maybe that was what Edwards was doing on her team.

Alone. Not to unduly burden Alyshia—glimmer of light, light of reflection.

Alone.

29

She'd had Ng call the high school, get the transcript of one Rick Boyko just to satisfy her curiosity.

"And ask your kids about him," she'd added. Anything to do with the schools, Ng was a fantastic resource. His six kids were all straight-A math types, 100 percent confirmation of the achieving Asian stereotype. Ng the burly cop was a stranger in his own home. Julian had seen how they looked at him uncomprehending. But they were utterly trustworthy. If they were told once by their immense dad not to say anything, they didn't. Wouldn't ever. They were the cutest little informants.

The school transcript and Ng's kids' report confirmed one another. Rick Boyko was a shop-and-mechanic kind of kid, usually at the margins of high school life, who only got into the margins of high school–style trouble, rarely in the middle of it, and rarely very serious. A schoolyard fight. Talking back to a teacher. Drinking in the parking lot once. A handful of detentions. No suspensions. Not a particularly good or cooperative kid. Not a particularly bad one. A nice, surprising stick-to-itiveness, every so often, on something he was interested in, according to one teacher's notes. With a little harmless roguish charm, Julian gathered. And that, she figured, was what he was doing hanging out in Alyshia's living room, with his slow smile.

She scanned the transcript. Even looked at attendance. "Attendance pretty good," commented Julian. "Although look at this. Missed two solid weeks in November." She shook her head disapprovingly at Ng. "And look. Nobody ever called from home. Nobody said anything. What do you think? The flu? Or just skipping some tough tests?"

Ng, brow furrowed, turned the transcript to look at the attendance record, then looked up at Julian.

"Those two weeks in November." He looked at her. "That's hunting season."

Out getting educated, thought Julian grimly.

Predictably, the Boykos did not live as neatly and properly as the Ryans. A van on blocks in the yard. An inexplicable and significant bluestone quarry at the end of the dirt driveway. Julian was about to enter unwelcome as always into the lives of another American family, one that helped demonstrate the breadth of America.

There was no doorbell, of course. She knocked on the door's peeling frame. A gargantuan figure who could only be known as Old Man Boyko came to the door, but stayed shadowed inside the decrepit screens.

Julian had seen the gun rack mounted on the pickup truck. Now she could see past Boyko to the gun case in the living room—its most singular and beautiful piece of furniture—plainly visible from the front door, as if Old Man Boyko were daring anyone to make a disagreeable demand, or to attempt making off with any of its contents.

He stood at the screen door silently, full of harsh judgment, somehow, staring down, assessing this neatly dressed young woman standing rather fearlessly but nevertheless alertly here in the piney woods south of town.

"Yes?" he said curtly.

"Mr. Boyko?"

"What you want?" Acknowledging quite efficiently, if not very politely or happily, that he was indeed Boyko.

"I'm Lieutenant Palmer."

She could see him processing the word "Lieutenant." Almost visibly. Deciding what box to put that knowledge in.

"May I come in?"

"Why?" he said, his habitual belligerence not masking his genuine confusion.

"May I?" she asked politely again, looked at him, still, silent, daring him to defy her.

But he was smarter than that. He gestured her in.

She looked around briefly. Inside was precisely what outside would lead anyone to expect. A bric-a-brac chaos, a tornado of objects in attic-like plenitude and arrangement. With the exception of the beautiful mahogany gun case center stage. "Nice case," she commented with genuine admiration. "I see an old Winchester thirty-eight forty in there, don't I?" she added, offhand.

Now he was stuck; his grudgingness, his surly, careful silence wrestled with his enthusiasm, with the presence of someone who potentially shared his passion. She could see him almost physically tussle with the problem.

"Yeah, well . . ." He looked at it pridefully, couldn't help it. "Not as rare as the forty forty-four."

"Shoots better, though," she said, authoritative and correct. "You could take a summer buck quick with one round. Quicker with two. Eye and neck," she advised. She had made it her business, in the past couple of years, to learn the patterns, the hierarchy, of hunters—of the professional and the hobbyist, the expert shot and the rank amateur. This was hunting country, and inevitably crime and hunting had an unfortunate intersection in the matter of firearms.

He stood in silent respect. Her expertise had the effect of ratcheting up his silence, she noticed, not loosening it.

"Anything small-bore?"

He shook his head no.

She moved closer to the gun case, looked over its lip at hip level, and saw two pistols lying prone, as if hiding. She picked one up. "Thirty-two caliber? I'd call that small bore."

She had caught him in a lie. She hoped it was implied that she would not accept another.

She looked at the other pistol. Pristine. Shining.

"Your boy's a friend of the dead man's daughter," she said, hoping to create some mutual respect by cutting out fussy preliminaries.

"I never know where he is. He gets in a little trouble. He's not a bad kid," said Boyko senior.

"What's the bore on this?" she asked.

"Twenty-eight."

She looked at him evenly.

Looked down again at the gun.

She opened her purse, took out a handkerchief, picked up the pistol, weighed it and balanced it contemplatively on her palm, peered down the barrel intently.

"I'm taking this with me," she said evenly, without looking up at Boyko. Adding warningly, "Don't make me get a warrant."

Boyko shifted uncomfortably. His jaw clenched. She saw his left eyelid start to flutter. But then, one edge of his mouth turned up like a smart-ass school kid's. "Can't imagine what good that'll do ya."

She looked at him inquisitively.

The smile spread carefully. "I fire 'em every Sunday out back," he said. "Every one of 'em. My babies. Wipe 'em down after I fire 'em, get 'em nice and clean. The neighbors hear me shootin'. They'll tell you. They want to complain, but they don't dare," he said with a mean smile. "It's legal."

Julian suddenly picked the gun up off the handkerchief, gripped it hard, and turned the barrel at him. Boyko flinched. Stepped back instinctively. Then appeared quickly and broadly resentful of stepping back, momentarily caught off guard, fooled.

Now Julian smiled back at him. "I got a complaint, too. My complaint is, I'd love to nail you, but I won't be able to."

She put the gun down gently and respectfully where she'd found it. "Murder was with a twenty-five," she told him.

He looked confused.

"You figured the murder weapon was small bore," she said to Boyko. "So you figured you'd play it safe and just say you didn't have any hand-guns. When I could just look over the lip of this case and see you did," she said. "Right there, I knew you were stupid," she explained. "I knew I had to dumb down my strategy."

"So when you tell me that's a twenty-eight," she continued, "I imply the murder weapon was a twenty-eight. And all of a sudden you're defending this twenty-eight so hard, because you're thinking this might be it. That your kid might have used it and returned it without your knowing. You're thinking fast, to cover for him. But I know what I need to—that you don't have the real murder weapon. If you did, see, you'd have just gently given that twenty-eight to me, knowing ballistics would show it wasn't the weapon."

She closed the gun case politely, looked admiringly at it once more. "I needed to be sure you didn't have a twenty-five here. The way you defended this twenty-eight, I know you don't."

Boyko could only stare at her.

"You're not hiding anything," she told him. "Nothing important, anyway. I know guys like you." She smiled. "You wish you *did* have that twenty-five."

You're not hiding anything. The question is, is your kid? The little gun expert you created.

"He's not supposed to skip two weeks of school to hunt, you know."

Boyko didn't answer. Looked evenly at Julian, an interesting new specimen of law enforcement, a slippery new incarnation of the state's devilry. The right to bear arms, the right to raise his child as he saw fit, the right to defend himself, a man sovereign in his own home—all that backwoods conviction and justification silently in his expression—but saying nothing because she was a lackey of the police state, a robot, an automaton, if a damn clever one. Julian knew how they thought. "Careful, there, Boyko, I can read your mind," she said.

It worked. He looked momentarily startled, as if she could.

She smiled, shook her head. "No, I can't Boyko. You're just paranoid. And stupid. As you've proved again."

The sudden appearance of little Ricky Boyko. Father: a misanthropic gun enthusiast.

It was improbably neat. And though she was sure Boyko Senior didn't have the .25, she was somehow sure she wasn't done with Gun World.

She was thinking about the world's Boykos when she got into her Skylark, backed it out, and in a last cursory scan of the yard saw it growing wild and unkempt and beautiful at the end of the Boyko property.

She flung the car door open and leaped from the driver's seat as if after a perp.

She stood in front of it, filled with the admiration and wonder and adulation of a garden club matron.

Lilius macrophylla lupidus.

30

The exhumed body of Frank Ryan only revealed so much. Julian, Edwards, Ng, and Mendoza, aloud together briefly, and then individually, silently, and lengthily, brooded about the man still alive after the first bullet. The forensic neurologist had been reluctant to assign a percentage chance of sentience. "A significant chance," was all she would say. A significant chance of knowing the life was running out of you.

"It couldn't be," said Ng. "Then why didn't he reach for the phone? It was right there on his desk."

"Maybe it was the second shot he was afraid of. Afraid that reaching for the phone, moving at all, would only bring it faster." There was no way to know. But it did not stop the imagination. Five minutes max, said the forensic neurologist. What could have happened in those five minutes?

Might have been sentient. Aware. Assailant might not have known he was sentient and aware.

"I think that Cornell woman put a voodoo fear into us," Mendoza said.

They looked again at the photographs. The sharp gold letter opener. The Lucite double-sided picture frame. She couldn't help but see Frank Ryan still talking. Still alive. Frank Ryan, she thought: the man now gone who should still be in the world. Winston Edwards, she thought, looking up at him: the man still in the world who should be gone. The man still free who should be locked away.

She regarded Edwards. Used up. Crumbling.

It occurred to her: he, too, was a man alive after the first bullet, before the second.

Any way you look at it, it's a special time for a man.

31

Back at the computer.

Edwards anticipated no problem hunting down the mental health facility where Sylvia Blood was. Not to be seen exploring it at the station house, he returned to the library computer terminal, where no one seemed to make any comparison to his earlier, less sober state. The cleaner-shaven, neater, more stable, temporarily employed version of himself sat gingerly at the terminal, once again logged in his former code, held his breath for a moment to see if his last foray had been discovered and his access denied—it hadn't—and entered the extraordinary police database and search mechanisms, the pride of departments, the sine qua non of the Web. He went to work.

He searched first within patient databases, then controlled-medication and controlled-substance records that had to be filed with each state, then other state medical filings and records. In a rigorous, methodical hour, he stumbled across patient Sylvia Blood, aged fifty-five. Diagnosis: manic depressive psychosis.

From file to file, screen to screen, record to record, he followed a ten-year, multistate trail of medical facilities, two-day forced residencies, voluntary and involuntary incarcerations, patient clearance lists for controlled substances, psychiatric reports filed from and to various states. In fact, reflected Edwards, it would have been harder *not* to pick up the trail of Sylvia Blood.

He double-checked the last entry and cross-referenced it with medical records and state psychiatric reports just to be sure.

Sylvia Blood. St. Mary Southwest Virginia Rehabilitative Center.

Where everything converged.

Medical and patient records.

And, he hoped, some portion of the truth.

Armed with just enough of it, with just a glimmer and hint of it, he figured he'd have enough purchase to haul open a whole wide gaping door of
it, and that its contents would spill forth like an overstuffed back hall
closet.

"Mrs. Blood?" said the pleasant, elderly nun nurse, more to discharge her
responsibility and go home feeling clean and good and whole than with
any hope of clear, unencumbered communication, which she'd given up
on with this patient long ago. "There's a gentleman coming to see you."

"There's no water in the pot, and that concerns me," Mrs. Blood
responded grandly. "No water in the pot, no God on his throne, no devil in
shirtsleeves. I don't know. . . . Gentlemen are a race," she informed the
nun. "They're a breed of breeders. I knew a gentleman once. I knew several. They were a thousand thundering chariots, crossing the Plains of
Dardemagne by the Caspian Sea." Mrs. Blood expectorated ven-
emously—into the metal trash can, at least.

The nurse hardly flinched. She'd seen it before. "His name is Winston
Edwards."

"*My* name is Winston Edwards," said Mrs. Blood bitterly. "You should
have seen the peonies. Blue, gold, vibrant, violent. Violent colors. You'd
look around the corner, and catch the colors attacking one another. But
they'd never do it right in front of you."

"He'll be here at two," said the nun, and took a deep breath, as always,
to recover from the encounter. Adjusting the medications of these kinds
of patients, finding and maintaining the most beneficial mix, was always a
delicate balancing act—but it seemed particularly difficult with this
patient. The nun hoped the doctors would soon get it right.

The nun turned, and headed down the hallway. Sylvia Blood stared
vacantly at the empty doorway that she had just left. "At night the colors
would dance, to that crazy palette music, that crazy French horn jazz," she
muttered, and shook her head in amazement at the thought.

In a moment, she moved slowly to the door. Slowly, quietly closed it.
Slowly, quietly, propped a chair beneath its handle. "Like an old orderly,"
she said aloud. "Moving slow and deliberate like an old orderly."

She bent down in front of her bookshelves. Reached her hand behind a certain book there, retrieved a crumpled baggie, uncrumpled it carefully and dumped the handful of pills into her palm. White pills. "Too colorful," she said, irascibly. "All too damn colorful," and with a long sigh, she sat heavily on the bed. She shook her head. Her eyes filled with tears. The tears made the room around her blur.

In a single motion, she upended the fistful of pills into her mouth, swallowed in two expert gulps, from so many years of swallowing pills. In a blink, a heartbeat, had downed them all.

She sat on the single bed, leaned against the wall, looking out the familiar window.

Soon, the tear-blurred room began to spin.

She had no idea how long she sat there.

She never would.

Neither would the pleasant old nun who discovered her on returning.

"I had told her you were coming," Winston Edwards heard the nun say, as he stood stunned, shaken, in the administrative doctor's office two hours later, the same nun in front of them, distraught, filled with self-reproach, fighting back her own chaos of tearful emotion. "That's all I said. A Mr. Winston Edwards," and as the nun began to fall apart, the administrative doctor sat her down, and looked up at Edwards.

"She obviously had more of an understanding of things than her outward demeanor indicated," the doctor said. "I had a sense of that, but I couldn't prove it, and I couldn't do anything about it." He looked at Edwards, authentically dejected, dejected beyond his authority as hospital administrator, dejected as another human being. "This was a failure," he said. "A failure on this hospital's part. On all our parts. She had such a difficult life." He shook his head with regret. "Something in the prospect of your visit . . . You're certain she didn't know you?"

Edwards nodded, confirming it again.

"Well, we've already notified next of kin," said the doctor, leaning down to check the folder on his desk. "A daughter . . ."

Edwards felt his pulse surge.

"Stephanie," the doctor said, squinting at the file. "Stephanie Holmes."

Edwards looked at him. He felt his hands tighten. He loosened them consciously, with difficulty. "Did you, uh . . . did you mention that I was on my way to see her?" *Did you mention my name?*

The doctor shrugged. "Don't remember, to tell you the truth."

Edwards managed to nod.

He turned toward the door.

He had killed Julian's mother.

Inadvertently, yes—but she was as dead as if it were meant.

This would change everything, he knew.

The heavy form, the leaden figure of Winston Edwards, continuing to carve its swath through the landscape, wreaking destruction as it lumbered along.

Nicely done, Edwards thought blackly to himself. Nicely done.

32

Pop!

What was that noise? Frank Ryan blinks.

Was I asleep?

Everything knocked over. Why?

Stooping to pick it up.

How did it all get down here like this? Why is there such a mess here? Did I make this mess? Did someone else?

Reaching down.

God, look at this. What is this? It's blood.

Sitting up. Confused. *How did this blood get here?*

Pop!

Pop!

What's that popping? Something fall? Door opening?

Hey.

Head down on my desk.

Pencils in front of me.

What's going on?

Strange, strange angle to find myself at. Strange view.

Got to sit up.

Hard to sit up.

There.

Pop!

———

Pop!

Huh . . . warm at the back of my head.

Reaching for it.

What?! Blood!

Turning . . .

You! You shot me! Why!?

How could you?!

Put it down! For God's sake!

Turning back, hands on desk, trying to get up.

Can't.

Hard.

There. Up.

Pop!

Down. Into the chair.

Get up.

Can't.

Can't.

Scenarios played in their various imaginations, vivid, irrepressible. For a simple reason: one of the scenarios had to be right.

33

It was evening by the time Julian was back in her office. She'd spent all afternoon giving testimony in a drug-trafficking trial fifty miles away. She looked for only a moment out her plate-glass window above Police Plaza—blacked in by now in the gathered darkness—before spinning the beat-up chair back to her desk. She quickly sorted through and arranged the folders for the morning, and leaned in to her computer screen to check her e-mail once more before leaving for the night.

She smiled. Another from Chief Richards. The person she had gone to, stumbled through the snow to, that horrifying night five years ago. He'd attempted to catch Edwards in his deceits. And throughout the trial and the hearings, he had stayed in touch with Julian. Richards was Edwards's contemporary. Had gone to school with him. And like Edwards, was now growing old, appreciably, noticeably, but with his spry spirit undampened and unswayed.

This e-mail, she saw, however, came from a different address. Not his office. His home. "Not going in to the office anymore. Going to be staying at home now. I've loved our correspondences." And the message's next sentence. There, perhaps, so as not to be accused of deception, nor of self-pity, nor of moroseness. There to be as explicit as necessary. Not more so, not less. "It's happening fast."

It's happening fast. Richards's small-town taciturnity, summarized and writ large. Dying. Cancer, undoubtedly. No spring chicken, after all, into his seventies somewhere, but still so full of life. She realized, with an aching, that he had known for months, had e-mailed cheerfully nonetheless, never mentioned it, never burdened her with it, until he felt he had to. "Come up and see me sometime," the e-mail continued, archly, sweetly. She was flattered, moved by the invitation, and instantly subdued

on reading the rest of it: "And bring your pal Edwards." Boy, word got
around. She felt instantly ashamed. She had never mentioned it. What did
Richards think? How would he judge it?

And thinking about that, she had got up to leave her office for the
night, when the phone rang once more. Ng was still at his desk. Julian
debated letting him get it, but picked it up herself.

"Julian?"

"Steph?"

"I've been trying you all day, but they said you've been out at a trial."

Julian knew immediately. The news was already in the urgency of her
sister's voice.

She listened silently to the brief report. Facts without detail. A brief
discussion about cremation. Vague talk about organizing a memorial service. Then, their mutual silence. And hanging up. Nothing more to say.
Too much to understand . . .

She looked out the window. Thought—briefly, formally—about a
wasted, ruined life. And was silently ashamed by the insistent single
thought that kept intruding.

That it would never be solved.

Another death. That's what the old Spanish florist had said the neon
flower meant. And although she was sure he'd made up the meaning, it
turned out he'd been right. *Another death*. But she had thought about it
only in the context of her current case. Not of a death related to her. Not
of death so purely personal.

34

They rode large silently, Julian driving the Skylark, Edwards beside her. She had made their itinerary clear to Ng and Mendoza, and made clear to Edwards that Ng and Mendoza knew it. The two-way radio mounted under the dash stayed dutifully and protectively on. Though she'd begun to gather, to somehow sense, that bodily harm wasn't the agenda with Winston Edwards. And this morning, it didn't much matter to her that she was alone with him. She didn't much care. She'd just as soon he pop her and drop her at the side of the road. She'd just as soon be staring up lifeless from a ditch somewhere. Never to be found.

Push it away. Push it away for now. You can't . . . you can't deal with it now. If you haven't been able to deal with it for years, you certainly can't handle it now.

Keeping to her life in the short term. Focusing on the yellow line in front of her. Riding up to see Chief Richards as scheduled. Because there might not be another chance. Clearly that was the lesson: that there might not be. *Push it away. Push it away for now.*

Push it away. Push it away for now.

She looked over at Edwards in the passenger seat next to her. Tubercular looking and sounding. White, old, but in some small measure at least, newly alive, coming back, his boorish incomprehensibility resurrected, his health and vitality returning as naturally and steadily as they had diminished and disappeared before. While Chief Richards, civil and moral to the marrow, lay dying. And Sylvia Blood, shattered and unreachable, long untethered from reality, lay dead. *Push it away. Push it away for now.*

They drove silently, Julian anticipating the visit with Richards, the conversation, the dynamic, the math of the three of them in the deathbed room. Hearing Richards say certain things, hearing herself say certain things to Richards. And what was Edwards thinking to say? It occurred to her only then: Did Richards have something? Something on Edwards at last? Was that why the invitation, and for some reason, the request to bring Edwards along?

Edwards, hulking, aged, silent beside her, was picturing himself in a ditch too. Fully ready to occupy the hard earth, to stare up lifeless out of it. The next of kin had been informed, according to the St. Mary's hospital administrator, Julian had to know by now. Yet she said nothing. He must not have been part of the information. For whatever reason, his name must not have been involved.

Unless she was keeping it in. Planning it silently. Waiting for the perfect roadside ditch.

But he knew that wasn't it. He could read her better than that. He knew that for whatever strange reason, he'd been granted a reprieve.

She pulled the Skylark into the bluestone driveway. The house looked the same. The same as the night Julian found her way to it, bloodied, frozen, probably technically in shock and yet pushed on by some force in her that she had never suspected before and had doubted since, a force that could not be summoned except in the face of death, and thus a force one naturally sought to avoid summoning, to avoid even knowing of. It was daylight now, a cold but bright and pretty morning, yet she would know the house anywhere. It was a snapshot, a frame, a vivid visual element in what had been her salvation, and so it would always, day or night, give off an aura of safety and home to her.

But Mrs. Richards opened the door this time.

And this time, the man who had tried to kill her, the man she had narrowly escaped, stood right next to her, and stepped into the Richards home beside her.

As if recognizing the significance of the tableau, Mrs. Richards simply smiled, sweetly, resigned and wise, all words spoken and all understanding needed conveyed in that smile, and motioned them up the stairs.

He lay prone in a hospital bed by the window, one obviously brought in for the occasion. He'd been there for some time, because the objects, the room, had a settled-in look around the hospital bed. He was staring up at the ceiling. The big computer was by his side.

Without thinking, unaware of and unchecked by her own usually guarded actions, Julian went over and hugged and kissed the emaciated, barely recognizable form.

Edwards stood there, not awkwardly, not obediently, but simply a presence, a hulking presence in the room.

He would have been a presence in the room even had he not been there physically.

Richards turned, looked at Julian, at Edwards. Morning visitors—maybe the only visitors—to his dying.

He smiled wanly. "Well. I see you did bring him," he said to Julian. "But he sure don't look the same, do he?" The put-on upstate ungrammar. He brought his failing, yellowing eyes, the eyes of a dying man, into focus—and studied Edwards from a new perspective. The perspective of finality. The perspective of infinity. "How you doin', Winston?" he finally asked, with no warmth, no forgiveness, no quarter.

Edwards nodded. "How 'bout you?" Mockery? Was there really mockery in it, or did Julian imagine the tone? Subtle enough, guarded enough, that you could never accuse Edwards of it, but present enough for you to suspect it.

Richards snickered. "Not too good. Figure a few days." Richards looked down across the expanse of his own diminished body, as if across a mountain range that could not be traversed. "A few days at most."

He looked up, narrowed his yellow eyes into focus again. "I want a word with Julian."

Edwards stood mutely for a moment, moved closer to the bed, like a killer who would now strangle the patient, like an angel hovering above its charge, and then turned silently and left the room.

Julian moved closer again. Richards looked up and smiled. Smiled with a warmth that Julian would have doubted still existed in the dying body, though she had discovered how deeply it existed in the living, vibrant version.

"It is a pleasure to leave the world to the likes of you," he said, confidently, peacefully, and they both listened to the words a moment, like listening to a running brook, its water flowing ceaselessly from upstream where you could not see it, to right in front of you where its sparkle and glisten filled your vision, to downstream, farther down-stream, where you could not see it anymore. Its burble of busyness. The burble of a life.

"He don't seem so bad, now that you're with him again, right?" Richards smiled, eyes half-open, but fully friendly. "Seems okay, right? Makes you wonder if you was maybe wrong about him. He ain't so bad. Chastened, different now. You're in charge now. Right?" He knew her. She nodded affirmatively.

He shook his head. His expression hardened. "He is evil, Julian. Evil incarnate. You know that, don't you?" He looked at her, eyes fully open now, and seemed to be waiting for a nod, for a confirmation. Obediently, Julian nodded. Richard nodded too, in solidarity, satisfied. "Part of evil incarnate is you forget it. You accept it. You allow it. But don't forget. Don't relent. Don't let him seep around the edges. You hear?" Again he waited for her response. A father and a schoolgirl daughter. The father she had lost. The father Alyshia had lost. The father Edwards had once fooled her into thinking he would be. "You watch him. That's all. You promise me."

Julian nodded.

"Get him in here," Richards said with sudden strength, the strength of annoyance and irritation.

Julian motioned him in, stood back a respectful step.

Edwards looked down again at Richards, revealing nothing. Richards looked up at Edwards, revealing everything.

"I'm lyin' here about to die, and you're up and around, as if rehabili-tated and reconstituted." He smiled. "Don't that beat all." Adding, " 'Course. It's life, ain't it?"

Richards looked at the ceiling. "I don't know where I'm goin'. I doubt it's anywhere really. But I tell you this. Wherever and whatever it is, if it is, I give you my guarantee I will beset and bedevil you mercilessly from there, if that power is in any way granted me. If I can, I will haunt you to the end of your days.

"We both know you did it, Winston. It can't never be proved, but we both know you did it."

Edwards said nothing.

"You are the worst that life has to offer," Richards said, with the conviction and conclusiveness of having experienced everything to compare, of having seen and known all of life. "You think this cancer is bad, eating away at me like a wolf at fresh kill?" He shook his head. "It's nothin.' Nothin' compared to how you eat at my insides. How the knowledge of your evil devours me." All his rage, all his bile, seemed to gather into his yellowing eyes. "I will haunt you," he promised. "So help me, I will hound and haunt you, and swarm around and mock your sleep."

Edwards leaned down, brought his huge face alongside Richie's emaciated, withered head and neck and shoulders. "Looking forward to it," he said. Simply, unrevealing, except for a small smile at one edge of his mouth.

Julian couldn't believe it. Her heart pounded. The atmosphere of the little room was incendiary.

Richards looked at Edwards once more, as if fixing his image to do battle from the other side, then looked to the ceiling and peacefully closed his eyes. "Nice to see you, Julian," he said mildly, and fell in moments into a deep, untroubled sleep.

"Looking forward to it, Richie," said Edwards again, now only for Julian's benefit.

Julian looked at the sleeping Richards. She would not, could not, bring herself to look at Edwards.

She heard Edwards leave the room behind her.

She looked at Richie sleeping another moment, and followed soon after.

They drove back in silence. Not a single word exchanged. But in their silence, fully communicating—Julian her fury, Edwards his insolence.

Three days later Richards was dead.

Julian attended the funeral. Edwards did not. From respect or disrespect for his old friend, Julian would never know.

Richards's vehement promise of retribution from the other side—she tried to see it as his rage for justice intact and not as the sad ranting of a dying man.

His rage for justice from the other side.
Did it say there was no chance for justice on this one?
Chief Richards was dead.
She was on her own.

35

The Ryans' front door blasted open, and Alyshia bounded out of the house and down the porch steps to Julian's car.

Julian smiled, thoroughly infected.

Amid all the death, Alyshia was life. She was an antidote.

And her school problems, her weight, her mood swings. For Julian they were just part of who she was, and best, they were the chance for Julian to help her.

"So what are we gonna do tonight?" Alyshia asked Julian, hopping into the seat, even with the weight gain as agile as a junior high school girl can be.

They'd discussed possibilities on the phone, but hadn't settled on anything yet.

"I like getting together with you," Alyshia gushed spontaneously, as if surprised to discover it at that very moment herself. "If I go with a group of girls and boys, I'm so conscious of my weight," she said. "Plus they still don't know what to say to me, how to treat me, and I don't know what to do about that."

"Don't do anything," Julian shrugged. "Give it a little time. They'll figure out how to be with you soon enough," she said confidently. Then asked, upbeat, flowing into it as if undifferentiated, "What about Rick? How is he about your weight?"

She smiled. "Rick . . . he's real understanding. He doesn't bother about stuff like that." She looked glumly out the window. "But you're so obvious when you switch into detective mode," Alyshia said, running a finger idly along the side window. "It reminds me who you are. It makes me sad." Alyshia looked out the window. "You went to visit his gun-crazy dad, didn't you?"

She was a smart little girl. Respect that. Be direct. Be honest. "Well, there's two things, Alyshia. I want to be friends with you, I like being friends with you, and I know you can tell that. But I have to feel I know about you and Ricky, too. I have to feel that I understand."

It was a Friday night, and the bowling lanes were crowded, but a quick survey showed there were no fellow cops, and no fellow junior high schoolers, and so they each felt safely unnoticed enough to enjoy themselves.

Alyshia threw carelessly and smiled, seemed the better equipped of them to have more fun, seemed to be returning to a habit of fun with a noticeable aptitude for it. Julian brought the science to her bowling that she brought to everything, and had to remember to smile, had to remind herself to enjoy it, which Alyshia did naturally and infectiously, which Julian was glad for. Alyshia moved well. She had her shirttail out, to hide her weight, Julian could tell. But the truth was, it worked—you couldn't see the extra pounds—she was just another healthy, normal, beautiful glowing young girl.

Both were genuinely shocked and genuinely pleased to discover they had tied. "Another?"

"You betcha, girl."

Midway through the second game, Alyshia threw a strike, slipped, and was suddenly sitting on the bowling alley floor.

Julian jumped up, ran over. "You okay?"

Alyshia swallowed and nodded. "Yeah . . . I just . . . I just fell, I guess. . . ."

Julian took her by both arms, began to lift her up.

"No, no," said Alyshia, strongly, panicky. Julian let her go, and Alyshia sat back down. She smiled. "I . . . I'm still dizzy. . . . Just . . . just wait . . ."

Julian felt a stab of worry. "What's going on?"

"Nothing," she said. "Just . . . just wait a sec."

Julian waited. A few other bowlers looked over, could see there was no laughter, no typical uproariousness at someone slipping. Alyshia finally nodded, and Julian lifted her up off the floor, held her as she walked her back to the plastic bench.

"I'll . . . I'm okay," Alyshia said as she sat down and smiled.

"Maybe we'll call it a night," Julian suggested.

Alyshia shook it off. "I feel fine now. We can keep going."

"Maybe we'll call it a night," Julian said again, meaning this time that they would. "It's getting late anyway."

"It's okay. It's not a problem. I'm really okay," insisted Alyshia. Julian looked at her sternly, doubtful, undecided. "It's no big deal." Alyshia shrugged and smiled. "I got dizzy like this a couple of days ago at school, too. I wanted to throw up. But it went away . . ."

"You did?"

"It's nothing. I'm fine."

And suddenly Julian knew. Julian the detective. Julian the idiot, she thought to herself with disgust. Julian the deluded. Julian the blind.

Ice cream.

Weight gain.

Dizziness.

Nausea.

The changed attitude in school. The lack of concentration. Neglecting her homework. The swings of mood.

Alyshia Ryan was pregnant.

Twelve years old.

And somewhere deep in Julian, somewhere deeper than mere observation, where observation connected to emotion and mixed primally with rage, she watched Ricky, that insolent little bastard, lazily zipping his fly as he emerged from the bathroom. Indolently presenting the evidence to her the moment she first laid eyes on him. "Well, he's not really a boyfriend," she had said. "Not really."

No, not in the conventional twelve-year-old sense. Not in the ice-cream-soda, homework-together, junior-high-dance sense at all.

She wanted to knock him around the room, show him another side of womanhood, forcefully and forever demonstrate that womanhood was not simply a twelve-year-old receptable. That it involved a little more than that, Ricky, my boy.

Pregnant.

Twelve years old. Pregnant.

And not only that.

I'm okay. It's nothing.

She realized—Alyshia Ryan might have no idea.

Twenty-five caliber . . . A stun gun, after all.

Stunned, for sure.

The night of Frank Ryan's murder opened anew, jumped and mirrored and careened with possibility, loud, sheer, screeching.

Their relationship threatened by Frank Ryan? The pregnancy discovered by him? Or to keep it from being discovered, a preemptive strike against Daddy's suspicions. A teenage pact? Or Ricky acting alone? Or someone else entirely, on their behalf? Alyshia, twelve. Ricky, thirteen. The cusp of adulthood, under the law, the edge of responsibilities, a wide range of possible consequences, particularly with capital crimes, under current state law. The law, the consequences, tricky, mutable . . .

Julian tried to focus on the road ahead. Felt dizzy. Confused. It couldn't involve this twelve-year-old next to her. It simply couldn't. This twelve-year-old who, it appeared, had no idea she was even pregnant. It just didn't fit. Didn't make sense. Didn't seem right. She gripped the wheel firmly, kept her eyes on the double white line. Never letting them wander to the twelve-year-old next to her, legs curled under her, staring out the passenger window.

What to do . . . what to do . . .

She dropped Alyshia at home. Gave a smile, a hug, watched her disappear into the dark, shadowy house.

Pulled out to the end of the driveway, turned off her headlights and engine, took out her cell phone, and made the only call that felt right, that made sense somehow.

"Winston?"

"What."

"That diner down the street from your hotel. Now."

36

The matter did not wait for coffee. It did not wait for greetings. It did not wait even for a cursory look around to drink in the atmosphere. The table bare between them. Not even a glass of water.

"Winston."

"What."

"Ice cream. Weight gain. Mood swings. Dizziness. I'm an idiot. Alyshia Ryan is pregnant."

He looked at her. Half closed one eye strangely, involuntarily, to focus down, to narrow. He stayed silent.

"I want to punch that little bastard Ricky." Julian felt the rage rising in her, a tide that had to be shut down, clamped, held in check for the moment, and then couldn't be. "Arrogant little shit." She watched herself, felt herself, slapping him around the Ryan house, slapping him around her office, slapping him around anywhere and everywhere he intersected with her enraged imagination. "I feel like killing that little kid."

"Why?" said Edwards.

"Why!" It brought her up short. And she saw, saw and felt cutting her once again, the knife-sharp, mortally wounding Winston Edwards smile.

Julian looked at him confused. Looked and saw the sum of Winston Edwards—a sum of conflicts and pains and torments, a sealed vault of human darkness.

And strangely, clearly, by the mere fact of his presence so close to her there in the diner, by the mere fact of his hard eyes, she suddenly knew . . .

But the brooding, hulking figure across the diner table uttered it anyway, confirmed it between them nonetheless. "He's not the father," said Edwards, flatly, curtly.

As if to resist, to somehow protect her, her mind went momentarily blank.

Then flooded. Flooded with imagery, with a blinding brightness of realization, while her body flooded with an accompanying terror . . .

"The father is the father," Edwards said very quietly, the sentence sounding obvious and natural spoken, somehow necessary to say, its simplicity seeming heraldic and strong, rather than demented and inhuman.

The father is the father.

The simple sentence now strange—a misuse, a mistake, a syntactical deformity—signaling a deeper misuse, and mistake, and deformity . . .

The Ryans, the beautiful brave Ryans, disintegrated before her eyes.

And the word "father"—so rife in Julian's father-robbed past and fatherless adulthood, so freighted with meaning and steeped in significance, took on immediately and forever for her, another meaning.

Julian felt her hands go limp. Her breath was short. She sat there in the hard chair, felt her breath catching, felt her cheeks, her body, flush with blood—rage, embarrassment, realization, charging through her body.

Of course. No sign of entry or exit. Because the killer was already in the house. Because the killer lived there. Because the killer was Frank Ryan's older daughter.

Means, motive, opportunity. The sacred triumvirate, the three sirens, singing harmoniously at last. The three notes of the triad aligning, at once celebratory and sorrowful.

Means, motive, opportunity. What may seem complex turns out to be simple. It had always been Edwards's mantra.

The father is the father. She knew in an instant that Edwards was right. She'd missed the possibility completely, for every reason in the world— her emotional involvement with the family, her admiration of their strength amid tragedy, her separate and special admiration for Nell Ryan and Alyshia, her own weighted and idealized feelings about fathers.

But beyond all that, was it an inability to recognize or accept evil? To adequately sense it as part of the daily human equation? Her optimism, her Pollyannaism, had certainly served her, but also might work powerfully against her. Her inability to see and sense evil: Edwards's conversancy with it. His instinctive recognition of it. His familiarity with it and belief in it.

The events spun out in her mind quickly. The near and distant future presented itself in a matter of seconds. A state recommendation of leniency. Mitigating circumstances. Maybe juvenile time, maybe even a suspended sentence. She knew these cases went both ways, but that this case would in all likelihood go the lightest way.

Why didn't Alyshia go to her mother? Because when it's the father, the child almost never does. Because it *is* her father. Her mother's husband. A juvenile court judge would undoubtedly accept that.

"So what do I do?" she asked, knowing as well as anyone what had to be done.

"You get her in," Edwards said for her, as if saying it aloud was the way to make it happen.

"But Winston. Twelve years old." She shook her head. "A minor." She began to talk her way through it. "She's presumed not to understand her rights. So she's supposed to have a guardian present for any questioning, to understand them for her. We can't assign a guardian besides her mother, because her mother is competent and available. But we can be pretty sure she won't tell the whole story in front of her mother. Since she never has." She tapped her fingers nervously on the shiny table. "And if we're wrong in guessing what happened"—she was thinking again, vaguely, about Alyshia and little Ricky—"or if we're reading something, anything, wrong about all this—and it's all speculation right now—then any admission from her without a guardian here could end up legally useless to us."

"Figure the worst," said Edwards, agreeing darkly. "Figure it's going to have to hold up in a court someday, a juvenile or a criminal or even a civil court, for some unforeseen goddamn reason, who the hell knows what."

Their both having seen firsthand how the system could spin and pretzel a case into unrecognizability. Though for the moment, it went unsaid betwen them.

"So what do I do? Ask a court to assign a temporary guardian?"

"That might rattle a twelve-year-old even more," said Edwards. "Might not get anything from her at all." And Julian knew he was right.

"But you do have something here," said Edwards slowly. "Something you're goddamn lucky to have in a situation like this." He looked at her, cocked his huge ursine head. "Your friendship."

He regarded her more deeply. "Friends do ask friends questions," he said. "It's your prior friendship that gives you a way to get her testimony, that gives you a chance," said Edwards. "And the only chance you'll have—and the best chance *she'll* have—is if there *is* testimony, supported by evidence." He sat up straight, grimaced against some pain or other, and pressed on. "You have to talk to her alone. Obviously it has to be you. You'll have one shot. Don't blow it." He smiled sarcastically.

Julian noticed how her body had tensed.

"There's the chance," he warned, "that she can't verbalize anything at all about what happened. It's her father, for chrissake. Maybe she's blocked it, and it won't come. Maybe she understands what happened, but doesn't understand the consequences. . . ."

Julian considered. "Sometimes she seems sophisticated and sharp. But other times like a child. Maybe it's the strict Catholicism. Who the hell knows."

"You can probe a little within the friendship," Edwards advised, "but then it could serve as evidence of your crossing the line, of your not giving her her rights. Keep it in the form of questions, don't accuse her of hiding anything. Ask her nothing, I repeat nothing, about the shooting. Ask as if you know nothing about the crime. Ask, probe, only about her relationship with her father. If she offers up something about the gun or the shooting, then you can follow up. To understand. To clarify. But you can't lead."

It was the other Edwards. The Edwards without ego or bluster. In the midst of the moment, she couldn't help but notice.

He was clear. "It can't be an interrogation, or coercion, or it'll be thrown out. Of course, by the time you get to a hearing or a courtroom, you'd presumably have more hard evidence. But there may not be much. So you have to be cautious, assume the worst. She has to confess. You can't push. You have to gently coddle. If there is ever an argument in this case, if speculation here is wrong, this will be what her lawyer will seize on, this conversation you're about to have—and you have to be ready for that."

"It's so risky."

"It's a risk you have to take, Julian."

She looked at him. She knew he was right.

37

Who is it? Oh. Hi, sweetie. It's four in the morning. What are you doing up? Well, I'm glad you're here. Really glad. Daddy has something for you, sweetie. Let me just get it ready for you. It doesn't need much help getting ready, since you're such a sweet little girl. . . .

Pop!

What?

What happened?

What was that noise? Did you hear? . . .

Pop!

Pop!

What?

You? What are you doing here?

Turn back to my desk? What do you mean?

What is that?

My God.

I love you. I don't understand. I love you. You know I do.

Pop!

Julian invited Alyshia out to the regional high school championship basketball game.

She picked her up at seven.

She told her she had to stop at the station house to pick up the tickets.

There was an old storeroom at the end of the hall. They had wired it for sound haphazardly, and used it for interrogation. Brooms and buckets were still kept in it, moved out only when there was a violent criminal. It was the only space they could spare. It didn't look like an interrogation room, which Julian thought probably increased its effectiveness. Four hard chairs from the Department of Education. An old cassette player. A small window cut crudely into the top of the door, which, when the hall lighting was lowered, was actually a one-way mirror.

Julian seated Alyshia in the room.

She closed the door behind them.

Edwards, she knew, had stepped quietly out of the shadows, to stand on the mirror's other side.

"Alyshia? . . ." gently, as gently as possible.

"What—what am I doing here?" Alyshia asked, the fear beginning to simmer, starting to bloom.

"Let's talk about your dad."

"What . . . what do you mean?"

"You and your dad . . ." said Julian. Her insides were jelly.

"What about my dad? He was . . . he was my best friend."

She felt the doubt rise up instantly. She wanted to flash Edwards a questioning look out the little window, a questioning look and something stronger, but wouldn't risk Alyshia seeing it.

She felt a sense of shifting. That Edwards had been wrong. That it wasn't Frank Ryan who'd got her pregnant, but Ricky, after all. Little pricky Ricky. What starts out complex turns out quite simple. Why didn't she follow her original instinct? Then, a sinking feeling, her stomach falling: Maybe Alyshia wasn't pregnant at all. That had been Julian's own conclusion, really. Had she and Edwards done it to each other, fooled each other, too smart for their own good?

All speculation. Which they'd both said. Then both ignored. Plunged ahead. Excited. Tasting it. *Christ.*

Julian wanted to get up, open the door, take Alyshia to the basketball game, forget it all, but she felt Edwards's stare, his intensity, behind the little cutout window . . .

"Alyshia . . ." said Julian gently.

There were experts at this kind of thing. Child psychiatrists, adolescent specialists. But Julian was who Alyshia trusted, so Julian was their best shot.

"Alyshia, your weight. Your dizziness . . ."

Alyshia looked up at her. A twelve-year-old, waiting for an explanation, waiting for instruction, waiting to be told something.

Was it a mistake? Had they imagined it all? Julian and Edwards, a complicity of bleak, dank imagination.

"Alyshia, did your dad come in your room sometimes?" To which Julian assumed there'd be no response, because her father would have coached her against it, prepared her for this kind of question. Whereas, Julian knew, Frank Ryan would not have prepared her for the next.

"Alyshia, do you know you're pregnant?"

Alyshia Ryan looked at her. A snap of shock. And of recognition. Of offense. And of knowing it was true.

Her features scrunched together, gathered as if into a fist of rage, of last resistance against the leak of feeling. But it didn't work.

She began to weep. A high, strained, pained note emanating weakly.

Julian shifted. Did not know what to do.

She had seen grief. But not the grief of a twelve-year old friend.

She suddenly knew there was something here—but truly did not want to know what. For once in her life, she did not want to know the truth.

She was wrenched. Felt close to weeping herself. And yet she needed the story, needed the truth.

"Alyshia." She said her name, could think of nothing else to say or do. Wanted to leap across the table, hold her, but could not. Sat there.

Alyshia began to sob. A stuttering at first, guarded, then collapsing, deepening, finding a rhythm.

Then a spilling, a torrent, like a vessel overturned.

The pattern of rape.

The repeated visits.

The story pouring immense, unstoppable, out of her—as immense, as unstoppable, as the tears carrying it, slick down her cheeks, thick across her tongue.

Disorganized, jumping in time, but brutal, riveting.

And Julian felt it more than she would ever have suspected. More than she was prepared to. Because she felt its strange alarming similarity to her own past, to her own night of sheriffs and spinning cherry red police lights.

Frozen in the bed.

Immobilized.

Amid the choking heat, the pooling sweat, frozen. Immobilized.

Daddy, could I have saved you, if I weren't frozen in the bed?

The guilt. The self-blame. The self-doubt.

All of it the same.

My God.

It was a story Alyshia had clearly been waiting to tell. Waiting to tell a long time.

At its end, she looked at Julian, in disarray, in disbelief that these words, this tale, had come out of her.

And then the moment of consequence. Everything before it, rhythm, preamble, dance. The moment of consequence, as Alyshia's own father had himself discovered.

"So . . . you . . . you killed him?"

Alyshia screamed aloud at the idea, the sound piercing in the little room.

She wailed at the very thought.

And nodded her head yes.

"Rick's gun?"

Another nod.

She looked at Julian imploringly, as if asking her to somehow change it, alter it, erase it. Make it bearable.

But of course, Julian could not. She could only witness it. But witness it significantly, and rectifyingly. She could not release Alyshia from it. But she could right it somewhat.

Alyshia Ryan leaned forward, put her forehead to the metal desk ungently, and stayed there very still. Somehow telegraphed her wish to remain there, in the temporary, ineffectual safety of the dark of her own shut eyes, at least for a little while. Numbly, uselessly, Julian placed a hand on Alyshia's shoulder.

The posture, Julian noticed. The posture of Alyshia's father. Collapsed at his desk.

———

While Alyshia Ryan slumped head down on the storeroom's metal desk, Julian and Edwards looked at her through the door's small panel of glass. Julian knew what she had to do. And where she had to begin.

"Now to tell the widow," she said, a dead feeling in her stomach, a deadness in her face and eyes.

"Now *you* tell the widow," said Edwards. Ever himself.

38

Once again, Julian stood on the porch of the Ryans' house.

She sensed this would be the last time.

She'd been here so often the house had become familiar. For its aura of disaster. Of calamity.

Julian was beginning to feel right at home.

She rang the doorbell.

Nell Ryan opened it, gestured her in.

Julian shook off the invitation, indicating she would stand here. She would not be welcome with this news.

But then she thought that Nell Ryan had better be seated for this, and followed her into the living room.

"I could tell it's important by your tone," said Nell as they both sat down. "I realized you wanted to keep Alyshia at the station so she doesn't have to hear any of this. And her sister's out at a sleep-over, so we're alone." Mrs. Ryan looked hopefully at her. "Is this it? Is it solved?" It was as if the question, the need to know, jumped out of the woman unbidden, on its own.

Julian nodded a heavy yes, then looked up at the woman from beneath heavy eyes.

Mrs. Ryan picked it up. "But what?"

Julian breathed. "We think it's solved," she said carefully. "But Nell, it's solved itself in the worst way possible."

Nell Ryan waited, preparing herself, Julian could see.

Julian looked around at the chintz chairs, the pretty carpeting, the perfect room, for some way not to continue. Some way not to say it. But there was none.

"Mrs. Ryan, it appears that your husband was killed by your daughter. . . ." Without pausing, without seeing, purposefully blinding herself to any reaction, Julian pushed on. She could not let that sentence, that thought, hang in the air alone even for a moment. Attach it to anything, anything at all, to take away its rawness. Of course its attachments were hardly softening or assuaging. But what should she do? Wait till the force of the punch had been absorbed and then punch as hard a second time? Better it should be a single punch. "She killed him because he was having sexual relations with her." *Go—fast—don't stop—hope she hears.* "In the state of New York, case law weighs in heavily with mitigating circumstance, extenuating factors. There'd be a hearing . . . her age . . . there'd be no record, she'd be remanded and released to you . . . so you could begin to rebuild your lives."

Julian looked at Nell. *Did you hear it? Did you hear it all? Any of it?* That was the question, what Julian had to gauge. Had she gotten it all, or had her mind shut down earlier on?

Nell Ryan stared. Stunned. Jolted. Fighting for consciousness. But something else, too. Something Julian had not expected, though she had expected anything. Furious. A rage, immeasurable, unfathomable, barely contained behind her eyes.

"But he did not do that," she said, formally, austerely, no emotion and all emotion packed into that sentence.

"Mrs. Ryan—"

"You don't understand. He did not do that," she said again. "I know that's what you'd expect me to say, and I'm saying it, but you need to listen to me." She was so strangely cool, clearheaded—as if in a last moment of normalcy, before collapse, before ruination. "I'm here. This is my family. I don't understand this. I don't know what Alyshia is doing. But Frank did not do that. You need to hear me. He did not."

"Nell, she's pregnant," Julian said.

"He did not," she responded. As if not hearing. Perhaps unable now to hear.

"Mrs. Ryan." Julian sat up, took a breath, held her back straight against the resistance of this terrified battered woman, and as resolve against her own terror, ramrod straight against the ugliness she was about to perpetrate. "Mrs. Ryan, we need to examine her bedsheets, her clothing. . . ."

Press on, don't stop, say it all. "Have any sheets or clothing been disposed of in the past several months, to your knowledge?" Julian was a machine, an automaton now, outside herself. Could not hear herself, could not believe herself.

"He did not do it," Nell Ryan repeated. Then screamed it at her, furious, enraged, neck and eyes bulging, veins popping, words burning, *"HE DID NOT!"* And she collapsed in the chair, then slumped toward the hardwood floor of her living room, her arms knocking a couple of the objects off the sofa table next to her as she slid.

Just like Frank, Julian thought vaguely, jumping up from the chair to help her.

The EMTs tended to Nell Ryan in her own bedroom, getting her comfortable in her own bed, monitoring the effect of the sedative.

Julian had already stepped out onto the porch, and signaled to Ng, Mendoza, and the others, waiting in their cars in the driveway. They had trudged up the porch steps wordlessly, and were already at work inside the house, their kits open beside them.

She had stood on the porch after them for a moment, looking out at the surrounding thick, shadowy woods that had at first seemed to hold some connection to the murder. But of course, it had come from within.

"Carpet around the study," she reminded them, moving briskly through the downstairs of the house. "Floor around the chair." They'd only run tests on the bloodstains before. *What's that? A coffee stain? Then I'm looking at a coffee stain,* Edwards had said. Now they were running a different test on it. It might be only coffee. It might be blood. Or it might be another substance, another human substance, entirely.

"Upstairs linen closet. Her sheets. All the bed linens," she told them.

Now. Before an attempt to hide something. To alter, burn, or destroy crucial evidence. Before anyone—a loyal sister, a quick-thinking relative—was tempted.

She went over in her mind a checklist of fiber samples she wanted to have, went over the individual processing times, the various New York labs that processed the various tests. "Get fiber samples from the desk chair. Take an REA from the floor."

She was another person. Would be unrecognizable to Mrs. Ryan, or either of the Ryan daughters. Was unrecognizable to herself. Not imperious or domineering or officious, but efficient, machinelike, an investigative juggernaut not to be derailed—a locomotive, and don't place any obstruction on the tracks.

"Laundry room. Dirty laundry. Especially underwear."

And with each reminder, the ugly picture soared, vivid in the minds of each of them, made more so by the formal, matter-of-fact verbalizations to one another, their own sordid imaginations animating each phrase, assuring that Julian would have to mention each only once.

"Bathroom hamper."

It was the demeanor she adopted, the demeanor she took on, in the search for truth. The search for truth was primary.

She wore her efficiency like clothing, to keep her own feelings at bay.

She would vindicate Alyshia, she thought coldly and ruthlessly. She would vindicate her, she thought with cold irony, even if it destroyed the girl.

As Nell lay in bed, and Ng, Mendoza, and the technicians moved through the house, Julian entered Alyshia's room.

The stuffed animals. The teen-star posters. The pink and lavender little-girl hues.

Julian double-checked through the linen closet and then opened Alyshia's chest of drawers herself. Wordlessly, she took each pair of panties. Bears. Hearts. Giraffes. Leopardskin. Placed each in its own plastic bag, sealed it, labeled it "Alyshia Ryan." Alyshia was still at the station house. They had to work quickly, couldn't unduly detain a minor. A judge could ask about timing. It could potentially be held against them if there ever were a case.

Once everything was bagged she stepped back. She took a breath. In her heart, she knew they wouldn't find evidence on the garments or the sheets. In Nell Ryan's physically orderly household, they were all washed regularly, no doubt.

She looked around Alyshia's little room. *But you do have something here*, Edwards had said. *Something you're goddamn lucky to have.*

Her connection to Alyshia. Her identification with her. Older daughters, both of them. Older daughters of disaster.

Think. Feel. Be twelve again. Julian tried to somehow inhabit, melt into, her connection with Alyshia. *If I were twelve. If I had this secret to hide . . .*

Without thinking, Julian went back to the chest of drawers. Bent down, opened the lower drawers, felt around and beneath the folded sweaters and the pairs of jeans.

In the bottom drawer, buried beneath the pants and jeans, she found a bedsheet. Poorly folded. A lone bedsheet, separate from any other linens in the Ryan household.

She stared at it a moment, before removing it carefully, to bag it. She winced at the possibility—the possibility that she knew was more than that. That on those horrible nights—before he would appear at the door, or maybe it was his idea—Alyshia would put this sheet on the bed. And then, after, tuck it back into the drawer, and remake the bed with the sheets that had been on it. So her mother would not see the stains. So her mother would not know.

She entered Nell's bedroom. Where Nell lay on the bed with her eyes closed.

Julian opened up the top bureau drawer. Looked at Nell's undergarments, went to a second drawer and found Frank Ryan's underwear. Opened the first plastic bag, lifted the first pair, deposited it into the bag. Nell Ryan opened her eyes.

Nell looked at her. Saw the plastic bag. Saw Julian holding Frank's underwear.

Julian stood frozen. Wanted to walk away. To walk out of the Ryan home, and out of her cramped sixth-floor office, and out of the crummy sadly furnished apartment, walk down the cracked sidewalk and keep walking and never look back, never think back. See what looking back and thinking back had brought her, and cost her. She'd found a young friend with whom to somehow salve and heal the past, and look what had happened. Walk out. Walk out finally. Walk out at long last.

Sedated, Nell moaned quietly with pain. Closed her eyes. Turned away.

Julian reached back into the drawer and took out another pair.

She held the front door open for Ng and Mendoza, carrying out armfuls of linens familiarly like hotel staffers.

When they were gone, Julian showed herself out. Carefully shutting the door.

The light was beginning to die. She had to get back. They couldn't detain a minor.

A minor. A murderer. A victim.

He did not. Nell Ryan's desperate insistence echoing, as Julian drove back alone. *Frank did not do that.* But people were blinded to their own families. She'd seen it a thousand times.

At the station house, nobody asked Julian how the widow took it. Nobody needed to. They could imagine well enough. They didn't dare incur Julian's wrath, or invade her gloom.

Julian, for her part, was lost for the moment in the dark bedrooms and corridors, the dark shadowy psychologies of the Ryan home. How could a marriage sustain that? Ignore that? And yet it happened all the time. It went, not surprisingly, underreported and unreported, yet the police knew it happened more than anyone would be comfortable thinking about. Now, of course, they had to think about it. Now they were forced to.

———

In the office where Alyshia waited, a video played, unwatched. There was a Coke, undrunk. A hamburger, uneaten. Alyshia looked at her and through her, little girl and event-swept ancient all at once, a dead-eyed vacancy that disconcerted Julian more than the dizzy fall in the bowling alley. Their relationship, whatever it would now become, Julian knew, would bear only a contorted resemblance to what it had been. Would be only an echo, a distorted version, despite any struggling to preserve it.

Julian sat silently with Alyshia for another moment, seeking to keep some piece of that budding friendship, before delivering a simple message that would, she knew, be fraught with emotion and peril and reckoning for a twelve-year-old girl.

"Alyshia, we're going to release you to your mother."

"No!" screamed the girl, with more power than Julian had expected of a twelve-year-old body and will. *"Please . . . no!"* Terrified to see her mother again, the secret now revealed.

It proved her fear of her mother, and left little doubt about her father's actions, or maybe it was a fear independent of and beyond those.

"She'll be here soon," said Julian. *As soon as she's stabilized. As soon as she can walk again, move again, function even marginally.*

Nell Ryan stepped into the station house in sunglasses and an overcoat, grim and businesslike and uncommunicative. Julian met her at the door, escorted her upstairs, where her presence seemed to garner little interest, Julian having extracted promises from Ng, Mendoza, and several of the staff to pretend to pay no attention, not to even look up if they could help it.

Alyshia Ryan was released into her mother's recognizance outside Julian's office. Only Julian watched, only Julian was witness, in the moment when mother and daughter exchanged looks, exchanged unspoken understandings and unspoken bafflements, unspoken loves and wearinesses and hopes and hatreds.

And just as she had on seeing the strange flower on the coffin lid, Julian suddenly experienced a premonition, a sense of something not fitting, something not right. It was as if neither mother nor daughter actually believed it had happened. It felt like a meaningless, victimless bust. A disturbing the peace. Mom coming to collect her mildly errant daughter. Maybe a laugh about the whole thing later.

Or was it, for the moment, simply a mutual denial? Which in the initial contact between mother and daughter, made perfect sense.

She'd been wrong, completely wrong, about the flower. The flower had led nowhere, meant nothing.

Her instincts seemed useless. She was in uncharted waters.

She walked Alyshia and Nell Ryan down the corridor toward the parking lot. She could see, with an annoyance spiraling quickly up into rage, that every eye in the station house had given in, had disobeyed her edict, and was watching the tragic, funereal stroll. She wanted to strike out at any and all of them, and realized it was because of her own past, how she had been thrown into an equal, awful glare, the same harshly aimed spotlight.

At the glass exit doors, nothing was said. No looks were exchanged among the three of them. Only a standing there, three women, cast together more by circumstance than three such different women could ever imagine. And each made more alone by circumstance than they could imagine, as well.

There were no good-byes. Not even a mild nod from Nell. Though Julian was ready to give one. Julian wanted the contact. Wanted to help.

She watched Nell and Alyshia walk to the car. Silent, never looking at each other.

Love her, she wanted to call out to them. *Love your daughter, Nell. Love your mother, Alyshia.* But she did not.

Julian let the door close, turned back in toward her office.

Push it away. Push it away for now.

What a night. What a world.

A general sense hung over Ng, Mendoza, Julian and the rest of the stationhouse, that the case was ending, coming to conclusion. Revulsion and relief blended and spun in the stale, hot, near-visible station-house air. A mixture of emotions that life doesn't generally serve up to civilians, and does to police officers often.

There was a sense the case was drawing to a close.

They could not have been more wrong.

It was only beginning.

And only Edwards, wizardly outcast—lying on the single bed in the dingy motel, beefy, white-haired ancient, mottled arms crossed behind his head—only Edwards sensed it.

39

Lawrence Cooperman, Esquire—dapper, wealthy, cuff-linked and collar-pinned, regal and infamous—pondered a life of retirement while he sorted through the mail in his rococo, velvet-upholstered office.

He was going to play a lot of golf.

He was going to get back in shape.

He was going to play the market and the ponies.

Oh, and he was going to let his wife and two daughters know that he was gay.

It was time to be straight with the world. Ha-ha. Time to make amends. Time, ha-ha, to come clean.

He neatened his desk. He went brusquely through the pile of accumulated envelopes.

The double life was over. Or ending.

He performed the morning rituals of his legal life as he always had. This morning, with tears wistfully in his eyes. Good thing Mildred wasn't in yet.

He read his e-mail and played his voice mail simultaneously.

"Hey, thought you'd get a kick out of this," said a voice message from a crony at the end of a quick briefing on a legal matter. "Heard through the grapevine that this Winston Edwards—guy you represented on that closed-door settle a few years ago?—he's actually working for his former accuser, that weird dishy young cop, what was her name? Julian Palmer . . . Don't that beat all. . . ."

The attorney's traditionally frozen heart clenched for a moment.

That stupid cunt, he thought. How stupid could a cunt be?

He was putting his life in order. He was making amends. He was retiring, so his practice could no longer be jeopardized.

He was going to let her know.

He'd save the stupid cunt. If there was still time, that is.

Jesus, how stupid could you be?

Edwards happened to be sitting opposite Julian in her office, shuffling once more through the pictures, when Julian answered the phone.

The voice was at once disconcerting and familiar. A rifle-crack of memory, a new wave of sickness. "Julian. It's Lawrence Cooperman. Don't say anything. Don't hang up," the voice said, with an urgency and force she recognized from its closing argument and summation five years before. The voice pressed on with importance. "Is he there in your office? Edwards? If so, don't look up."

"Yes," she said guardedly.

"If you send him out, he'll only be suspicious, and if we can avoid his suspicion, you'll be ahead of the game. Pretend I'm an old friend," he said. "Smile. Lean back. I'm calling from a phone that'll work for that. He'll check phone logs, you know, if he's suspicious at all."

"Sure! Hi!" said Julian expansively, "Well, well, well . . . a blast from the past!" she exclaimed. And in a way, of course, it was.

She held up a finger for Edwards's benefit, indicating give me a minute, this shouldn't be long.

Edwards gestured questioningly with his hands over the chair arms: should he leave?

Julian offered a shrug. Doesn't matter, either way, indicating its unimportance, and hoping of course that Edwards would go.

He didn't.

"I'm calling," said the attorney, "because I have heard, as one does, about your idiotic hiring practices, and to tell you why I do not approve," he said nastily and testily. "Ask me if I have kids."

Julian asked him aloud, with a smile, even added a surprised "Three!" for Edwards's benefit.

"Two actually," said Cooperman. "Not bad, considering I'm gay."

"Really!?" said Julian, managing to make it cheerful and bright. "How 'bout that!"

"Touché," Cooperman complimented. "And I will be announcing that, as well as my retirement. Now, despite the animosity that you know I feel for females in general and a certain kind of female in particular, I would find it unseemly to bear the responsibility for the death of even one of them."

She smiled, froze her smile, and listened.

"It is time to make amends, and knowing that you had taken Edwards on I felt compelled to convey certain facts which I may have chosen not to convey at the hearings but which become extremely relevant. He still there?"

"Uh-huh," she said brightly.

"Tell me a little about yourself," he commanded.

"Well, you know, same old same old. Police work. I'm a lieutenant, now."

"Congratulations," said Cooperman, mockingly.

"It's been challenging, interesting. For better or worse my work is my life. For right now, anyway."

"That should be enough," he said, cutting her off.

Edwards was again studying the photos.

"I have proof of what happened in the snow. Something that takes it beyond he-said-she-said."

"You don't say!" she said brightly. "Sounds neat!"

"Nice and neat," he said coolly. "The thing is, I will not put anything in writing, I will not risk being involved in any way, which is why I'm calling, which is why I will arrange a drop, and this proof will not have my name attached to it in any way. But it's powerful enough that you won't need it. It's incontrovertible."

"Oh, come on, tell me," she said with a plastic smile.

"I'll send it to you. Judge for yourself," said Cooperman. Given the situation, of course, she couldn't ask him more. He probably preferred it that way. "It got to us quite late in the process, I assure you. I'll arrange for you to receive it in a way that puts both of us at least risk." He asked suddenly, brightly, "So when are we going to get together for our reunion?"

"Let's do it . . . I don't know . . ." She looked at her calendar for Edwards' benefit. "First week in January? That's when you're north?" She wrote the name of an old classmate in her calendar, in case Edwards checked.

"Watch yourself, for God's sake," said Cooperman.

Incontrovertible. Not a term that golden-tongued counselors like Cooperman used lightly, when to them, almost everything was mutable, arguable, changeable.

Incontrovertible. There was one thing that would be incontrovertible.

Her heart started to pound.

"Yeah," she said brightly, cheerfully. "Really great talking to you. You take care."

40

Ng brought in the envelope as he had carried the laundry out of the Ryan's house, with a seriousness and sense of high purpose that his huge size did not offset or lampoon, as at other times it did.

The grim set of his face, the unblinking, untwinkling, affectless stare of his normally blinking eyes telegraphed the import of what he had to say.

"Well?" she asked, her insouciance masking nothing.

"Semen stains on the desk chair," he said.

Christ.

"Semen stains on the sheet found in the chest of drawers in Alyshia's bedroom," he said.

"Where on the sheet?"

"Right where you'd think," said Ng. "And semen stains on a pair of her underwear."

It was exactly as bad as they had imagined. It made it easier, but made it harder too.

"Go on?" Ng asked, begging not to have to.

Julian nodded, gestured silently. Go on.

"Pattern of stains indicating," he paused "copius amounts, according to the lab."

"Meaning he came outside her," said Edwards bluntly.

"To not get her pregnant," said Mendoza, up to Edwards's bluntness.

"Knowledge aforethought. Premeditation of abuse," said Ng, who'd clearly been thinking about it.

"Guess he missed once, didn't he?" Mendoza observed grimly.

"Thanks to the semen, the lab report indicates retrieving a number of very clean DNA samples," said Ng, leafing through the report. "Once we have samples from Alyshia and the fetus, it'll give us a fifty percent match to Alyshia Ryan's own markers, and a seventy-five percent match to the baby's." Ng looked up. "You don't often get it that easy. A match like that. Something like a one in twenty trillion possibility," he said, unable to hide his fascination and satisfaction with the mathematics. "In the age of DNA, you make cops' work a lot easier when you knock up your own daughter."

"The DNA profiles would lay over each other perfectly. A jury would see pretty graphically how Frank Ryan's the father," Mendoza observed, unable to hide his fascination either.

"That's the beauty of it," said Ng. He shook his head. "The only beauty of it. We don't need the deceased. We only need linens."

Mendoza watched a paper clip spin around on his thumb and forefinger. "So she'd put out that sheet, then fold it up."

"It was her fear of her mom knowing that let the DNA markers set," said Ng.

He gently closed the thick folder of lab reports. "Pretty strong circumstantially. Add the baby's DNA, and it's a lock."

"The hardiness of come stains," said Mendoza. "They muss your sheets. But they sure do make for a strong case." He leaned back. Stretched his arms above his head, breathed in and out deeply. "Case closed," he said, uncomfortably close to exuberance. "That's it, right, Lieutenant?"

Julian, on the other hand, felt tense. Guarded. "Yes . . . it seems to be closed. . . . That seems to be it."

So she could reasonably dismiss Edwards. Edwards, whose only use had been his instincts in the harshly lit diner. Whose only service had been his very presence, his dark view, which had led her to understand who was the father. But a use, a service, nevertheless.

She could dismiss him, having so far miraculously avoided their past's coming out, having so far avoided embarrassment to her reputation. She could get him out of here, begin perhaps to concentrate again on another case. A case that with a mysterious phone call had rematerialized.

Or, concerning that same case, she could keep him here.

Keep him close. Have what might turn out to be the added advantage of his close proximity. Of his presence again.

Flying in the face of what Richie had warned on his deathbed. Of what Cooperman had warned on the phone.

She managed not to look at him while she instructed Ng and Mendoza. "Yeah . . . case closed, I guess."

"You talked to Nell Ryan yet about that baby?" Edwards asked suddenly, brutely.

Now, given a reason to, Julian regarded him. She sighed. "Christ, Winston. It hasn't been the time to yet," she said. "I know I have to. And I will." She'd figured that in a few days, she'd help the Ryans with abortion options, and arrange both a placental and fetal DNA sample at that time.

The Ryans were churchgoing Catholics, it was true. But she knew that Nell Ryan—prim, proper, devastated by humiliation already—was not going to subject her family and herself to further humiliation by having or raising such a child. It was, furthermore, what statistically would be an extremely high-risk birth. Although amniocentesis and other prenatal testing could nowadays screen for many conditions and determine probable outcomes more accurately, the odds of serious mental and physical handicaps and outright deformities in a father-daughter pregnancy were significant. Even the fairly strict local Catholicism must allow the termination of such high-risk pregnancies, and this was legally one, to say nothing of ethically.

"Talk to her about that baby," said Edwards, pressing her on it with a focus that indicated he would think or say nothing else until she did.

Julian managed to smile. "You seem very concerned with the baby, Dr. Spock. Perhaps a new career in pediatrics . . ."

"Talk to her about that baby," said Edwards, glumly, without humor, annoyed at the lightness of her reply. "Just talk to her. That's all."

41

In certain neighborhoods in her jurisdiction, incest barely raised an eyebrow. In those cramped and chaotic and desperate blocks, it recurred in its multiple but finite forms: father-daughter, mother-son, brother-sister; grandfather-granddaughter, uncle-niece, aunt-nephew. In such neighborhoods it was sternly and roundly frowned upon but grudgingly acknowledged. Wrong but inevitable. And in the rare instances when it was commented upon aloud, railed against by a minister from a pulpit or duly noted by the few remaining churchgoing elders, it was only to furnish proof of the neighborhood's general condition.

But incest in a pretty stone house, incest connected to patricide—the newspapers weren't long in their ecstatic, gleeful discovery of the case.

She'd asked those in the station house not to talk to reporters, not to discuss anything, knowing that it was akin to asking them not to look up when Mrs. Ryan walked by.

Julian stood in a conference room, in front of a roomful of reporters.

She talked about semen, and millileters.

She talked about stains and underwear, bedsheets and DNA.

It was not her finest hour.

Her crisp three-minute report would send them swarming over the Ryans, vultures over carrion, screeching and cawing above the tragedy, lifting it into the air to carry it digitally across the sky.

There was nothing she could do. If she set up a police barricade, got an injunction, the local media's legal staffs were all very adept now at reversing the orders in court in the course of an afternoon.

There was nothing she could do. Except imagine life in the Ryan household.

She left several messages on the Ryan answering machine, taking her place, she knew, among the dozens of reporters and inquiries and promises, hoping against hope that one of these times Mrs. Ryan would relent and pick up. She spoke loudly and clearly at the start of each message, hoping that Mrs. Ryan would dignify her call, place her in a different, higher category, and reach for the phone. Typical of answering-machine frustration, each message she left was slightly more explicit.

"It's Lieutenant Palmer again. Please, Mrs. Ryan, let the state give you a hand with this. We can, you know . . . help as far as the pregnancy . . ." There were several excellent clinics. Professional, aboveboard, certified staff, with counseling services.

Suddenly, there was a rattling on the other end of the phone. It confused Julian momentarily, it was so unexpected.

"We'll take care of the baby," said the voice of Nell Ryan, briskly, confidently.

"Oh. Mrs. Ryan." Recovering from her surprise. "Oh. You will. Okay . . ." Julian paused, frowned. "I'm sorry. When you say take care of—"

"I mean take care of," said Nell Ryan. "Meaning, she's having it."

Julian felt herself suddenly sitting at her desk, when she'd been standing a moment before. "But, Mrs. Ryan, the risks—"

"We're Catholics. Devout Catholics, as you know." Her voice was clipped, formal, officious. "She's having it."

Twelve years old. Julian knew. Alyshia would disappear into a convent, into an order, not be seen again. It was none of her business. But her young friend, her young troubled friend, now to be locked away . . .

Having your own father's baby: it was tangling with life's natural order. Challenging it, daring it, as recklessly as Frank Ryan had.

Julian tried to recover. Stumbled around, trying to salvage the contact. "It's of course your decision. But at least let the state set you up with amniocente—"

"We don't believe in any of that," Nell Ryan cut her off.

At the Convent of the Frozen Heart, the Convent of the Broken Spirit, Sister-to-be Alyshia would see her own deformed child for a moment, before it was taken away.

There was pure challenge in Nell Ryan. Something far apart from and beyond religious belief or moral conviction or the welfare of a child. It seemed for Mrs. Ryan a way of wresting control, or getting even, in a mathematics that Julian could understand. Nell Ryan was a woman who valued appearances. And it was Julian, after all, Julian and her department, who were the instruments of Nell Ryan's ridicule and downfall. Nell Ryan was impatient and angry when they hadn't solved it. Now she was furious that they had. So there was challenge, antagonism from her, and Julian felt it, resented it, and heard herself say,

"Mrs. Ryan, I have to warn you. The state can exercise its authority. They almost certainly would in a situation like this. They can press for termination of the pregnancy on medical grounds. Even a second-trimester abortion is allowed, even encouraged by the state in a case like this."

"Not in a case like this, I'm afraid. My lawyer and I have examined it carefully." There was resolve in her. A way to control the situation, and enormous satisfaction in that control. To even things out with the authorities a little.

"I don't understand. Mrs. Ryan, I know the law fairly well on this—"

"My children were adopted," said Mrs. Ryan. "I'm surprised you never looked into it. But then, why would you?"

Julian listened silently, felt a pressure in her temples, a dull pain in her stomach, as Nell Ryan continued. "There is no blood relationship. The baby would be completely normal. Completely healthy. As normal and as healthy as it can be, in this insane world." And then she revealed herself in a rush—offering justification? asking understanding?—"We never had our own children, Lieutenant, but it didn't matter to me because Frank was here. Now Frank is gone. But he'll be here again, don't you see, with this child."

Was she crazy? Or was it, on the contrary, the only thing she could do to keep her own sanity? If sanity was what you called it.

Crazy, thought Julian. But crazy and fierce and self-righteous. A tough combination.

It was clear in the records. Alyshia and Anabelle Ryan.

Catholic orphanage in Upstate New York. A Canadian adoption. Adoption records in Ontario, Canada. Which is why it never flagged automatically in U.S. records.

But the girls looked alike. Well, of course. Because they were sisters. And they looked very much like Nell Ryan. Because they happened to. Because beautiful women and beautiful girls sometimes do. Because you wouldn't think about it. You'd never question it. And so Julian never had.

Having the baby. Nell Ryan delivering the shock for once, instead of receiving it. Maybe she would come to her senses. Maybe she had lined up the abortion already. But as a public Catholic, a media Catholic, she would never say that.

And what *about* the media? If she had the baby, the story would never end. The child would be in the news forever. How could Nell be entertaining the idea of a normal life for it?

The DNA test of the fetus would still be meaningful. It would still reveal Frank Ryan's fatherhood, thanks to the semen samples.

But adoption . . . motives . . . She felt a new complexity, an unfinishedness, creeping in.

42

She sat with Edwards in the diner. She was reluctant to tell him. She sensed it as a victory for him. *Talk to her about that baby.* He had predicted more to happen with the baby, and more had come to pass. Although he had never specified what with the baby exactly. Maybe that was his technique—one of his little tricks.

"Alyshia Ryan and her sister were adopted." Julian told Edwards gloomily. "Nell wants Alyshia to have the baby. Who knows what Alyshia wants."

It seemed to hold no surprise for Edwards. He sipped his coffee, dimly satisfied. "Having the baby. Good," he said with a surprising vague approval.

"And what's that supposed to mean?"

"Means if that baby ever becomes evidence, you want the evidence around." He looked at her, a sardonic glint in his eye. *You want the evidence around.* Referring to the evidence against *him*, the telltale serrated knife, that had disappeared years ago? Is that what he meant?

"Why would the baby become evidence?" she asked.

"I don't know." He shrugged. "But I do know this: Nell Ryan talked to a lawyer, she said? Well, if you want a DNA sample of that fetus during pregnancy, they'll never let you near it, amnio or any other way. With the baby alive in the world, at least you'll have a shot. Although I get the feeling they'll still try to keep you away."

To avoid the proof—to the world, to themselves—that it was Frank Ryan's.

And without that proof, Julian Palmer and the State of New York would have a more difficult time making the case. The baby's paternity being, after all, technically unproven, though circumstantially over-whelming.

"Thinking awfully far ahead, aren't you?" she said.

"Accent on the awfully," he replied.

With a sinking feeling, Julian realized Edwards might be exactly right.

He was frustrating. Continually frustrating. Unforthcoming, blunt, closed in. He had operated by hunch and instinct all his life, instinct largely unexpressed and unshared, and it had always worked for him, and she was not going to change that now.

And yet for reasons like this, she still sought him out. Still found value, eventually, in their rendezvous. Meetings somewhere between seminars and trysts, brusque, tense, dimly lit no matter what the lighting actually happened to be.

It was the second time she had met him alone in the diner, she realized. She looked at him as he sipped his coffee. He had grown old. Infirm. It was clear to her by now he carried no weapon. But her gradually increased comfort with him, her receding worry, went beyond those. Was apart from those.

Why was she growing slowly comfortable with him again? It was her *own* instinct. Ironically, the instinct that he had been teaching her to recognize in herself, to nurture and respect in herself, when she'd spent that remarkable internship with him five years ago. The instinct that had been borne out, when she had seen Alyshia on the floor of the bowling alley, when they had decided to bring Alyshia into the interrogation storeroom, the instinct that told her that in his own difficult way, he would help. It was her own instinct, more developed and more seasoned now, which told her—more with every day, more with every exchange—that he had no intention of harming her. That his attachment, his intention, recognized by him or not, was instead connection, regret—something, in his odd, gruff, emotionally inexpressive and mute way, approaching at least respect. It had both times, after all, been her suggestion to meet here at the diner. Not his. Never his.

He is evil, Julian. Evil incarnate. You know that, don't you? Chief

Richards lying on his deathbed, looking at her, waiting for a confirmation that she understood.

And why had she allowed him back in? Why, really? Maybe because he was her messenger to the underside. Vizier of the dark. Because it was *his* dark instinct—more masterly, more seasoned than hers—that knew who the real father was. Simply intuiting it that night from these diner chairs.

Maybe it was because he took the work as seriously as she. Was imprisoned, preoccupied by it to the exclusion of all else. Maybe that bond overrode all their conflict, all their confrontation, all their barriers of gender and age and education and outlook.

Or maybe there were no barriers of outlook. After all, they saw many things the same.

Ng had finally asked her gently, carefully, one evening as they left, "What exactly was it between you two?"

"Good question," she said. Deflecting it politely. The answer beyond her.

"But something," Ng ventured. "You can still see it, you know."

Yeah. Something. Despite everything, something.

Julian pushed into the dingy, ill-lit diner restroom.

Her first thought was that it was not to code.

That's how her mind worked now, she noticed briefly, gloomily. Not what the restroom looked like, no reaction to it emotionally or aesthetically, but legally. *Not to code.*

As she bent down to wash her hands, she was aware of the door opening behind her. She dimly pictured the few female patrons in the coffee shop.

And suddenly felt the object held hard to her sternum, and the heavy male breath beating on her neck from behind her.

This is it.

A single thought, instant, primitive. A single pulse of fear. As clear as the knife's edge so hard against her, she needn't look down to know it was there.

In the following milliseconds, she processed more. He had followed her in. Cooperman had been right. Richards had been right. *Don't ever forget. Don't drop your guard. He is evil.*

To any diner patrons, it would look as if Edwards went to the men's room when she went to the ladies'. He would come back out, pay the check, leave. Her body might not be discovered for hours.

The heavy breathing behind her neck paused, became only smell. "Don't move," she heard, heavy, but whispery. And not Winston Edwards's voice. "Don't turn around."

She felt the object—it had to be a knife—pressed even more firmly against her sternum.

"How does it feel?"

"How do you think?" she said.

"Good," the whispery voice said. "Don't forget the feeling."

Suddenly the knife was resting on the sink in front of her. Entirely sheathed in plastic, she saw. Blade and handle protected. "That's what Mr. Cooperman wanted to convey." The whisper harsh. "He said it was important. That you don't forget the feeling."

In the tiny, poorly-lit restroom, the mirror was on the wall to the right side of the sink. She tried now to angle herself to get a glimpse of whoever was behind her. But whoever it was had thought that through, was smarter, quicker than that. Just to be sure, the hulking figure was gripping her neck hard from behind, to keep her from turning. Julian now realized that the whispery voice was only to keep her from ever identifying him.

"You're assaulting a police officer," she hissed furiously. "You are using physical force against a police officer."

"I'm providing a police officer evidence she'd do anything to have. So I'm sure this police officer is going to disregard the manhandling."

The back of her neck still in his grip, he was shifting the two of them closer to the rest room door.

"Don't forget," he said, and quickly turned away, hunched over in a long black coat, out the door, slipping out the back undoubtedly, before she could see his face or any other defining feature.

Her first impulse was to go after him.

Her second impulse was not to know. To let him go. Instead, to look again at the weapon now in her hands.

"So where is the knife?" the judge had asked, annoyed.

"It seems to be misplaced within the system, Your Honor." The bailiff's assertion, loud, proud of an important role in the proceedings, rather than what Julian thought should be the appropriate embarrassment and humility . . .

He took it! He had it taken! He is the system, don't you understand? She'd wanted to scream it, and screamed it with her eyes at Edwards across the courtroom, but Edwards had kept his gaze studiously even, studiously away. . . .

The eight-inch serrated knife. The weapon that would tie Edwards to the waitress's murder. Here in her hands. Prints intact, if Cooperman's assertions were to be believed. And why shouldn't they be? Incontrovertible.

The knife that would prove his complicity. The knife that had been in evidence, and disappeared. One more moment of upcounty lassitude, of backwoods incompetence, of functioning outside observation or judgment, as Edwards had for years, as Edwards had forever. One more moment of operating in the margins, close to the border geographically, well over it morally. One more moment, unremarkable, except for its particular importance to Julian.

The years had begun to soften the facts in Julian's mind. Or at least, soften her feelings about the facts, lend a cooler distance to them. Cooperman's dramatic courtroom arguments had so successfully limned another side, so brought alive another point of view, that she had begun at last to see it. And even knowing it was a concoction, an aromatic brew by the defense, its scent had been long enough in the kitchen for her to whiff its possibilities. Saying something doesn't make it so; but the problem is, it does. Saying it long enough, saying it a certain way, makes it begin to be so, or at least, makes the hearer entertain the picture so frequently that it begins to be. Maybe Edwards hadn't done it there in the snow, there in the confusing wind and snow.

The knife changed all that.

Incontrovertible.

Here now. Hers.

Whatever shape its blade was in, it certainly sharpened perceptions.

She glanced over, and saw herself in the bathroom mirror suddenly, abstractly.

Not as Lieutenant Palmer offering evidence. But a girl named Julian, brown haired, olive skinned, a darkly pretty Southern girl miles and years from home, older now but still young looking, almost strangely so, holding a strange plastic-sheathed object.

Had the crafty Cooperman thought of that too? Told his mysterious hulking deliveryman to wait until she was in front of a mirror, wait until she had to confront herself?

Her. The knife. The mirror.

A reduction of elements.

Like the letter opener. The photograph of the daughters. The CD player. Greatest Hits.

After the first shot . . .

Before the second . . .

The violence of her past . . .

The warnings about her future . . .

But Winston Edwards hadn't tried anything. Or was he waiting only for the right moment? A moment like this? An even better one?

She stood between the shots, between past and future. Who was this in the mirror? Who was this truly?

She felt suddenly, eerily, an unnerving connection with Frank Ryan, a parallel moment, but could not sort it exactly, could not work it through.

She returned to her seat in the coffee shop. Sat opposite Edwards. The knife shoved quickly into her purse in the restroom, and transferred beneath the table—amid diversionary female fussing with purse and contents—into the purse's deepest pocket.

The knife with which Edwards had killed a waitress more than five years ago. The knife, that would simply, finally, irrefutably prove it.

What to do, exactly.

She wasn't sure.

But she couldn't manage a second cup of coffee when Edwards suggested it.

43

Amid the newspaper articles, the local swarm and frenzy, the Ryans kept to themselves. They closed in, cut off communications. When the local frenzy wore off, when the reporters moved on, and the free security of press attention died down—the natural protection of reporters at the end of the Ryans' driveway, angling for film snippets outside the girls' school—Julian assigned a plainclothes watch outside their home and a plainclothes watch of the girls during school. They weren't a big enough police force to use manpower that way, but she felt she had no choice, and it was at least something she could do. She'd seen newspaper coverage capture local imaginations in unpredictable ways, and it only took one simmering unstable imagination to boil over. The plainclothesmen she had assigned were new to the Ryan case, the girls might not even realize they were there. Nell Ryan hadn't asked for the protection, but it didn't matter, Julian could have it assigned anyway, regardless of what Nell Ryan might want.

Julian expected not to see or hear from them until the court dates. She had advised Mrs. Ryan by note to keep Alyshia in school. To try to keep her grades up. To ban visits from Rick. To look as good as possible for the preliminary hearings and court appearance.

She had Ng contacting the juvenile courthouse assiduously, to track judge selection, and breathed a sigh of relief when Alyshia drew Caramore, a woman.

Julian didn't know whether a judge could force a test of the baby's DNA to prove Frank's fatherhood. Bu a juvenile judge like Caramore might find the circumstantial evidence enough, and not put the family through any more pain.

She carefully explained by letter what the Ryans could expect in the courtroom procedure. How it would look. How it would feel. How to behave. How to prepare.

She felt the passion of wanting to bend the rules a little at least, tailor the proceedings, as if for the benefit of her own daughter. Filial passion and loyalty—she recognized it. As she equally felt the irony of trying to arrange for a twelve-year-old to get away with murder. Justifiable homicide, to be sure. But homicide nonetheless. A first. A career first. A career last, God willing.

Of course, Julian wondered at what point—whether after or even before the hearings—Alyshia would be taken out of school, transferred by Mrs. Ryan to some facility, to become a mother by the age of thirteen. She felt sure Nell Ryan was working on it now. Julian had just been feeling the first pull, the first impulses of her own temporary, safe, proxy motherhood, and in the next instant, in a bowling lane, her proxy daughter was suddenly a mother-to-be.

44

Julian stood in the Captain's office. The Captain, dapper as always, examined his cuff links closely, minutely trying to adjust them to face the right way, to appear correct, then looked up and examined her as if she were a difficult pair of cuff links herself.

"The murder is solved," the Captain said. "So why is he still here?"

Because having him here, I may be able to get a conviction in another murder. The one he committed.

But Julian was silent. Because on a practical level, the Captain had asked a good question.

Ng and Mendoza had gathered it was Edwards's insight that had led to breaking the case. It was Edwards who suddenly knew Frank Ryan's role. Probably word of Edwards's contribution and ability had spread across the sixth floor, whispered and muttered its way up the ranks, to where the Captain now had a sense of it too.

Unfortunately for the Captain's original plan, Edwards seemed to have proved useful.

The Captain looked somewhat distraught, more than mildly annoyed. "It's time to cut him loose, Julian."

Because the longer he's around, Julian thought, *the less excuse there is for a police captain to pretend to not know who he is or what he's doing here.*

"This story has the press here, and as soon as the press is on it, there's a logarithmically increased chance that someone's going to find your old connection, someone's going to figure out who he is, and how's that going to make you look?"

Meaning, how's that going to make me, your Captain, look.

Repeating his words, the Captain went one degree harsher in tone.

"Cut him loose, Julian." From collegial discussion to firm command, in a single, smooth, practiced moment.

"I will," said Julian. Just shy of Yes, sir.

Very soon now, thought Julian—obedient, disobedient, both impulses alive and strong—a theme of her police tenure, of her life. *I promise. Very soon.*

45

Given the angry silence, the brusque isolated inward turn while waiting for the court appearance, Julian was understandably surprised when within the week, there was a call for her from Mrs. Ryan.

Ng, who picked up Julian's line in the outer office, covered the receiver, leaned into her doorway, and mouthed "Nell Ryan," holding the receiver aloft.

Julian picked up her own phone, listened silently a moment before saying, "Lieutenant Palmer."

"Lieutenant. Nell Ryan," the voice said crisply.

"Well . . . hello . . . I'm glad you—"

"I have some news for you," said Nell, abruptly, officiously.

What now? What possibly? Julian, for weeks, always bringing the news. Nell's satisfaction in now reversing that.

But Nell's tone softened suddenly. She said it quietly, flatly, somehow intimately yet distantly. "She lost the baby."

Julian felt the relief flood instantly through her. *Thank God.* She felt Alyshia's life—*her* life—simplifying. "I'm . . . I'm so sorry . . ."

"Of course you're not," snapped Nell Ryan. "You were horrified at the thought of a thirteen-year-old mother." Indicating to Julian, at least, that the darkness of the thought had crossed Nell Ryan's mind, as well.

Julian was studiously quiet a moment. Then: "How . . . how did it happen?" To be polite, to be concerned, to rebuild a bridge to Nell, to Alyshia.

"It just . . . happened," said Nell Ryan, frustrated, annoyed, it seemed, at having lost a trump card, a weapon. A burdensome way for a baby to begin life, thought Julian. "The way it just happens with these things. The way God tests us," said Nell.

"Well, I mean—"

"She came downstairs in tears yesterday morning," said Nell suddenly, and it seemed that she did want to tell it, longed to, in fact. "Happened in the middle of the night. But she wouldn't wake me. Said she knew I'd be angry." It took Julian a moment to understand that the sound she heard next was weeping. Nell Ryan weeping. "Can you imagine? Didn't want to wake me because she thought I'd be angry."

Julian realized that Nell had no one to talk to. Suddenly realized how alone Nell Ryan was. When you turn to your enemy, to the technicians of your downfall, simply because that is who knows you best, because that is who you're closest to, it's proof of how alone you really are.

"Nell—"

Nell cut her off. "I'm calling to invite you to the funeral."

Wait. "Funeral?" Julian was confused.

"That child deserves its place with God," said Nell Ryan. "Saturday morning, ten A.M." A pause. "You know which cemetery."

Julian cradled the receiver. Stared at the phone, the objects on the desk, uncomprehending. They looked strange, out of place.

Do you have a funeral for a fetus? But really, it was a funeral for an unborn child. Hardly customary. But hardly illegal. And she could see it from Nell's point of view: trying to legitimize the child in every way possible. It was consistent, made immediate emotional sense: it was the one thing Nell could do for it, now that she couldn't raise it. Julian was surprised that Nell's church, Nell's faith, was going to condone it. But who was going to deny a grieving widow? A widow who had suffered the double indignity of an illegitimate pregnancy of her own daughter, and by her own husband. Let her grief play out, sayeth the Church. Some psychologist priest, perhaps. And it was probably the right thing. Maybe Nell needed it to serve as public proof of God's hand, and not public medicine's latexed fingers, and not the state's unfeeling paws. And if Nell's heart was set on it, maybe it would release her somehow.

Nothing could be more brutal than the funeral of a murder victim.

Except, perhaps, the funeral of an unborn child.

The Ryans were two for two.

———

"Baby aborted," she mentioned to Edwards.

His eyebrows went up. "Know the doctor?"

She looked at him. "No, no. Spontaneously."

"Says who?"

"Says Mrs. Ryan."

"Twelve-year-old girls are young and healthy," pronounced Edwards. "Forty-year-olds, that's who miscarries."

"Now, wait a second. Twelve-year-olds miscarry too . . . thank God."

"Don't thank God," instructed Edwards briskly. "And don't think God's will. There is no God."

"Jesus Christ, Winston. You're ridiculous! Twelve years old, for chrissake! If there's no God, then we should be thanking our lucky stars."

Edwards took a beat. "Actually, we should be investigating," he muttered.

Julian ignored the comment. "Nell's going to have a funeral for it."

"You're kidding," said Edwards.

"I'm not kidding."

"I'm going."

"You're not going."

"I'll be good," Edwards promised suddenly, a ridiculous schoolboy assurance and plea. "I never saw the first funeral, don't forget. Don't make me miss all the fun."

46

Lying on the narrow bed in the little rented room, thinking about Philip Smithers's life, Edwards couldn't help but think about his own.

In the twenty years since Vernon Blood's murder, Smithers had apparently never uttered a word about it. Carefully—or carefully enough, anyway—he'd constructed an alternate past for his own daughter. Smithers, it appeared, was quite competent at keeping a secret. Seemed to have no problem living with a secret for a lifetime. So while Edwards didn't know him, despised him without knowing him, he sensed that they had a lot in common.

And though he'd never met him, he felt he knew him well.

Knew the discipline. Knew the sense of mission and purpose. Knew the stealth of conversation. Knew the pained, silent bouts of drunkenness. Knew the rigid silent world, the human fortress, more locked up and locked away than any physical prison. Knew the impulse to paranoia, and the recurrent need to check it. Knew the alternate universe, the lively world that one had to create inside one's mind instead, a world that was cheerful, perfect, bearable.

Why did he know it all so well?

Julian Palmer, Chief Richards, and other steady-eyed, restless antagonists would answer that one way. Edwards himself would answer it another.

They would say it was a matter of Edwards's experience. Of the raw facts of his existence. Of acts committed.

Edwards would say it was a mind-set, a natural ability. Not an intellectual ability but something deeper. Something instinctive. And nothing more sinister than that. He took a slug of whiskey neat from the bedside glass, to set aside the thought, to refocus on the matter at hand. Acts, if there were any, were beside the point.

How would Edwards ever get Philip Smithers? Get him so it could be a conviction? So it was not only solved, but solved in the eyes of the law?

For that, he realized, there was probably only one narrow possibility.

There were, after all, two figures in Vernon Blood's living room that night. Two assailants. Smithers and someone else.

And the other assailant, whoever it was, was the only one who could implicate Smithers.

Smithers had had help.

Edwards sagged. It meant, in a sense, starting over. Hunching over the computer again. Finding a way down South again. Digging in again. Looking all over, for whoever would have had a reason, an impulse, to help Smithers, to assist, to risk murder.

One of the good old boys who was sleeping with her? But if you trusted Arteris's instincts, and Arteris's research, they stayed away. Weren't involved. But maybe Arteris's abilities went only so far. Not even one? One renegade?

He put aside the whiskey, dialed the phone.

"Arteris?"

"Hello, old friend," came the singsong reply.

"Anything at any point, anything at all, on who was the second assailant? Who helped Smithers that night?"

"Sylvia Blood only saw them fleeing," Arteris replied gloomily, apologetically, knowing how useless the information was. "Barely discernible figures in the night. One of them slighter, thinner than the other, 'cording to Mrs. Blood," and then morosely adding, "as would almost have to be the case, any two people together." There was a silence. "Sorry," offered Arteris.

Edwards was running out of time. Julian had taken him on to help solve Frank Ryan's murder, and although he still felt other possibilities there, could still sense it in his bones and being as unsolved, could see it and feel it going another way—based on evidence, on means and motive and opportunity, it was solved. So she wouldn't be keeping him on payroll for long, that he could see.

But imagine simply telling her that he had solved her father's murder.

Handing her the name of the murderer. The name and address.

Here he is, here's where he works, here's where he lives, he's got an average life.

Then what was the point?

He recognized that it was as it always was for him. "Solved" was too abstract, merely intellectual, a game board victory. "Solved," by itself, had no passion, no primal completion.

Merely solved? No. He needed it—*all* of it—completely taken care of.

And it was clear, he would simply have to take care of it all himself.

Like he always had. Like it always was for him. After five years in prison, and more years as an outcast, he was no different.

I'll show her.

And why had he done it? they would all ask. And would find every reason in the world. Closure. Proof. To even the cosmic balance. No one would ascertain it in finer terms than that. Why had he done it? To continue down the only path he knew? To prove by his actions that he had not killed that waitress? To prove by his actions that he had? Those would be the speculations, he knew, the hushed discussions.

He was old. His body was failing him. His mind, his memory—he could feel them pulling away from him like vessels set adrift. His infirmities were closing in on him like a police tail, threatening him from behind. His wife was gone, swept up in years of hardship and ill feeling. His money was gone, swept up in his defense. His reputation was taken from him. Everything of value, done and gone.

It was time for a last act. He qualified perfectly for a last act. And last acts, well, they had to be considered, they had to be weighed, for their symbolic content. Because the last act was your legacy. It could contain everything. It could contain nothing. You had to take care with it.

Twenty years after the fact, he probably couldn't pull together a valid, legal conviction. It wasn't going to happen.

So he'd have to improvise. Another way would have to reveal itself. And in the bare, tiny, grim motel room, another plan unfurled. As always with Winston Edwards.

And Julian Palmer? She would be part of that last act, of course. Audience. Actor. Star. It wouldn't be that hard to get her there, he thought. And it wouldn't be a last act without her.

He leaned back in the little room. He closed his eyes. He watched the events play out as he knew they would. As he would make them. Last act. He smiled.

I'll show her.

47

Another funeral. Another rainy day. They stood together in the drizzle once again.

This time, the casket was minuscule. Like a jewelry case on a bureau top, gleaming, buffed with tragedy.

A few photographers and reporters stood together outside the iron gates. They weren't allowed into the cemetery. At a funeral ceremony, the wishes of the family for privacy overrode any news value. It was an argument the reporters knew the police lieutenant would win, so they stayed at the entrance, a photographer occasionally raising his camera lens for a moment with nervous energy, then dropping it back to his chest, like the eye of a creature intermittenly aroused to interest, and then discouraged, subdued.

"But there's nobody in there, right?" whispered Ng, gesturing to the tiny polished black box.

" 'Course not," muttered Mendoza sidelong, brusquely annoyed. "What would be in there, anyway? Think about it," he said. Adding, "But not too hard."

Julian overheard Mendoza.

She stood in the drizzle.

She *did* think about it. Hard.

The baby gone now. The baby suddenly gone.

Alyshia and Annabelle Ryan in their long blue coats again.

There was no contact now between Julian and the Ryans. Nell Ryan sent the signal strongly, *Don't talk to us,* and Julian respected it.

So Julian only looked. She looked at the Ryans, in those long blue coats, that she'd known were new at the funeral of their father, that were now amortizing their cost over more than one tragedy.

Alyshia looked the same, she noticed. Exactly the same.

Not that she'd expect her to look different, really, so soon after losing the baby. Not that she'd expect her to have already lost some of the weight.

But Julian's thoughts began to run like the rain itself—wet, dense, fragrant, pervasive. And just as the strange crisp neon flower had appeared suddenly atop Frank Ryan's casket, a strange, crisp, neon idea seemed to perch atop this one.

She came downstairs in tears yesterday morning, Nell had said, telling how Alyshia lost the baby. *Happened in the middle of the night. Didn't want to wake me.* Only words over the phone, after all. The details sketchy, because Nell hadn't been there herself. Which was a perfect way to stay sketchy on details.

No, no, spontaneously aborted. No doctor involved, ever. No doctor at all.

Forty-year-olds miscarry. Not twelve-year-olds.

Was Alyshia Ryan still pregnant? And keeping it a secret from her mother?

Or was Alyshia Ryan still pregnant, and was Nell Ryan creating and managing the secret herself?

A way, after all, to avoid the DNA paternity test. To avoid such insult, such proof.

Julian instantly felt she knew. Knew thanks to all the time spent with her twelve-year-old friend. Alyshia, in her symptoms, in her confession, had seemed to understand little about her own pregnancy. She was unlikely—as prim Nell Ryan's daughter, in that incommunicative household—to understand much about miscarriage, either. So it was highly unlikely, in her fragile state, that she had the capacity to make one up. Whereas Julian had observed Nell's own steadily growing capacity for the challenge of convention, for insolent silences, and for the fierce defense of her daughter.

Was Nell's phone call about losing the baby merely the first volley in pushing off the critical world before sending Alyshia away to have it? The first volley in reshaping the world, reforming it for the entrance of the baby of a thirteen-year-old girl?

A funeral to throw everyone off?

Did Nell Ryan have the capacity to pull off a lie like that?

If so, it would explain something else that had been tapping at Julian incessantly since the gruesome fact of Alyshia and Frank Ryan had emerged. Namely, how could Nell not know? Not know what was going on down the hall? Was it really possible to have no idea, in the neat stone house, in her own home?

Or *did* she know? Did she know at some level about her husband and her adoptive daughter . . . know it, even condone it at some level, consciously or unconsciously, for providing some connection or satisfaction that her husband had craved and she had failed to deliver. In a house like that, wasn't it possible that Nell had her own sick complicity as well? Unthinkable . . . except in the realm of Frank Ryan's actions.

Ask them about that baby. Just ask them, that's all. Edwards's instincts. Unsorted, harsh and pure, still echoing in her mind.

A funeral, staged to keep them all away from the baby.

Pretty brazen. Bold.

Lying on behalf of her daughter?

Or lying as a pattern, on behalf of herself?

"What would be in there, anyway?" muttered Mendoza. "Think about it. But not too hard."

Winston Edwards overheard Mendoza.

He stood in the drizzle, a step behind the others.

He watched Julian watching the funeral.

What's in there? Nothing. An empty box.

Like a grave I know in North Carolina.

Edwards, listening, standing in the drizzle, began to entertain a further thought about that missing baby.

About that empty box.

He watched Julian standing watching the small box with sorrow, with sympathy.

The box empty. But full of power. Full of imagery. Full of deception. A vessel for the imagination.

He thought about that empty box.

She came downstairs in tears. She wouldn't wake me, Julian had reported Nell saying.

The empty box. The empty grave . . .

He was a seer of emptiness.

And the more he thought about it, and watched Nell Ryan, and watched Alyshia, and watched Rick, the more sure he was. The clearer it got.

By distant uncles and hired attendants, the little coffin was lowered by hand into the ground.

The mourners stood silent, numb.

Julian looked at Alyshia Ryan. Alyshia Ryan, unchanged.

Julian suspected it was a funeral for a baby they were still having.

Edwards could see how it was a funeral for a baby that never was.

48

"I think they're going to have that baby," Julian said aloud on the way back from the funeral, the rain beating down on the old Skylark, Edwards in the passenger seat, Ng and Mendoza watchful in the back.

"What?" said Mendoza. "What are you—"

"I think she's still pregnant," said Julian.

She could feel the stunned silence from her two colleagues behind her, as she knew she would. Their reaction was predictable. She glanced at Edwards beside her. No indication. No response. Which was the response she'd expected as well. *Ask her about that baby,* he'd said. Showing that he half expected it. Had had similar thoughts himself. He couldn't be surprised. But he wasn't saying anything this time, she noticed. She could feel Edwards's doubt.

Ng looked confused. "But what makes you—"

"She looked the same," said Julian defensively.

"But you wouldn't see any physical change in her yet," Ng said, somewhat amused, when he'd thought for a moment. "The baby just aborted—"

"I'm telling you. I just feel it. . . ." Instinct.

They rode silently.

"It is their right to have it," Mendoza pointed out, gloomily. "After all, it is their right."

"I want to call the Ryans in. I want to do a pregnancy test," said Julian.

"They can have the baby if they want to," said Ng. "Legally. She told you—"

"But it's not in the interest of the child."

"Twelve-year-old kid. The mother decides what's in the interest of the child," said Ng after a moment, shifting uncomfortably, hunching another way, simply too big for the backseat.

"A mother whose husband was just murdered by her kid? Her kid who's going to have her husband's baby? Nell Ryan's not equipped right now to decide the interest of her child," Julian complained, assertively bitter.

"Motherhood's a powerful right," said Mendoza.

"I'm terrified it's going to screw up Alyshia's hearing," said Julian. "A funeral? And still pregnant? What if that comes out? What's a judge going to think?"

Ng smiled slightly. "I think it'd help her, actually. Judge will see why Alyshia couldn't go to her mother. A religious fanatic. Throwing funerals like parties. I think it'll help her."

"Then can't the state at least insist it be healthy? Can't the state insist on an amnio? An exam?"

"The state probably can't force an amnio. No legal reason. No sound medical reason. She's way under thirty-five. Not a high-risk pregnancy," Ng, their scientist and six-time father pointed out. "The father is a healthy male, genetically unrelated. Amnio's an unnecessary danger."

Edwards, staring out the window at the rain, finally spoke. "Look, we know how you feel about Alyshia, we know what this little girl's welfare means to you." Although he was turned away—or maybe because he was—it was one of those rare, brief moments of connection with Edwards, moments that were growing more frequent, she'd noticed. Moments that confused her, making her wonder whether some part of the evil she'd seen had existed only in her imagination. "At the funeral, she was wearing that blue coat. It was all heavy coats. You'll see her better at the hearing," Edwards said, simply, authoritatively, not dismissing her notion at all but suggesting a reasonable next step. "At the hearing, you'll get a better look."

49

We know what this little girl's welfare means to you.

Her heart froze.

Replaying the words that night alone in her apartment, terror sliced into her.

Had he slipped? Was this his purpose? His plan inadvertently revealed at last, in a brief aside out the passenger window?

Was this why he had made no threat, no attempt on Julian?

Because killing Julian outright meant no suffering, no pain?

Instead, hang around long enough to see what she cares about most, and take that, destroy that.

A way to create far more suffering.

A far more effective way to get even. For five years of prison. For the collapse of his life.

We know how you feel about Alyshia, he'd said, faced away, looking out the passenger window.

Julian was stabbed by terror.

Remember, he is evil. Evil incarnate.

What could she do? Only watch. Watch fiercely like a mother hawk.

50

All rise.

Juvenile court judge Judith Caramore entered, a huge stout woman, her black robe trailing, a mother figure, a projection of stern compassion.

Julian orchestrated the hearing, as much as within her power, to reflect the State's position that this was a tragedy, pure and simple, of the sort we are bound to see periodically in the atomized and alienated society we have constructed for ourselves, and let's not compound one tragedy with another. Let's not compound the loss of a life, the life of a father—with the loss of another, the daughter who still stands a chance.

Even though she had fully expected it, she was still relieved to learn, weeks earlier, that the State, through the assistant district attorney assigned to the case, would take a stance of extreme leniency. It was their custom in cases like this, but nevertheless, there was always judgment on a case-by-case basis. The State, however, could change tactics at any moment. If there'd been a school shooting the week before, or a gang incident, and the political temperature changed, the DA's office might not proceed as it had promised—and the case could be prosecuted suddenly aggressively. You never knew for sure, until you were there, until the DA's office aimed their questions and made their recommendations.

In helping the young DA arrange an expedient presentation of state's evidence, and in her own brief testimony, Julian did everything she could to project, to convey to the bench, the State's posture of not wanting to inflict any more harm.

A juvenile court judge holds broad powers, and Judge Caramore exercised those powers to keep the doors closed, keep reporters and all additional parties out, given the sensitivity of the issues and in the interest of the child. Her own closed hearing, Julian felt, might have been a mistake, a tactical error that her inexperienced lawyer had too quickly agreed to. But here, the closed door, the smaller chamber, only lent an air of common interest, the welfare of a child, an air of wise counsel and consideration, and Julian felt reassured by the very tone of things.

It was the State functioning as it too rarely did, justly, sagely, mercifully.

Flanked by two youth counselors, the assistant DA proceeded as dispassionately and as technically as possible. "Semen stains positively matched to the decedent were found on a bedsheet in Alyshia Ryan's bedroom in the Ryan home. Testimony established this was Alyshia Ryan's bedsheet." But the young assistant DA—scrubbed looking, sober suited—remembered his forum, and soon dropped his habits of evidentary presentation. "Judge, the State is satisfied with the police version of events in this case. There is a full confession on record, in folder C there. Fetus spontaneously aborted"—he checked his notes—"on eleven twenty-eight in the Ryan home." Julian could practically feel the man's sigh of relief. One less heartbeat, so one less problem, in the juvenile system. "In light of the circumstances, the State is satisfied that it is not served by a further prosecution in this matter. We officially recommend for leniency under the juvenile code of the State of New York, and gladly defer to Your Honor at this point in Juvenile Matter ten nine oh one, State of New York versus Alyshia Ryan." He looked at the judge as if to say all yours.

The judge nodded.

"Disposition of the murder weapon?" Judge Caramore asked suddenly.

"Murder weapon cleaned of identifying marks, Your Honor."

Her Honor raised an eyebrow and smirked. "What, are we dealing with a professional here?"

"Twenty-five-caliber weapon was purchased by a male friend of Alyshia Ryan's, one Ricky Boyko, thirteen, purchase effected with contacts Ricky Boyko had through Mr. Boyko's father, Richard Boyko, Sr., a gun enthusiast. It has been established to the satisfaction of the State that Boyko, Sr., had no prior knowledge of his son's activities in this regard. Ricky Boyko, Your Honor, had acquired the necessary weapons knowledge in his father's home as well as having purchase contacts through his father's associations. State has established that gun was wiped and cleaned because that was the procedure Ricky Boyko learned from his father, a self-styled paramilitarist. Firing tests established this was the weapon." Here the assistant DA allowed himself a small smile as he continued. "Richard Boyko, Sr., initially reluctant to cooperate with authorities, did so readily when a state probe discovered several weapons violations. Mr. Boyko, Sr., was thereupon instrumental in helping locate the seller and the gun itself."

Gladly gave up his son, whatever the boy's involvement might or might not be, Julian had noticed grimly, in favor of his cherished arsenal. Just as quickly and gladly had given up a gun-dealer friend as well. When she'd first interviewed Boyko, she'd thought he might be trying to protect his son. But that, it turned out, was too high a motive to grant him. He'd only been protecting his weaponry.

The elderly judge stared over her bifocals, remained silent. Something seemed to be vaguely bothering her, but if it was, she kept it to herself for the moment.

"I'm inclined, in cases like this, to be lenient. As I'm sure you are all well aware . . ." Caramore paused, and Julian felt a sinking in her stomach. *Inclined, in cases like this* . . . Did that mean that in this case it would be different? Caramore seemed to have a slight annoyance at her reputation for compassion preceding her.

Caramore looked over her bifocals at Alyshia, then at Nell, finally at Julian. The hearing room remained silent. Her pause continued, clearly purposeful, clearly intended to stop them all in some way, to make them all uncomfortable and alert enough to take notice. Julian was suddenly aware of the stuffiness in the hearing room. Suddenly aware of the perspiration at her temples.

"I'm inclined to be lenient in this case as well," said Caramore, and she paused again.

Julian felt the tension in her shoulders, down her back.

"I'm inclined to be," Caramore repeated, pausing once more, tantalizingly, excrutiatingly, "and I will be lenient in this case. In light of the considerable weight of extenuating circumstance, I herely suspend any requirement for detention . . . and I hereby recommend the minor Alyshia Ryan to community service of two hundred hours to be mutually agreed upon by counselors assigned to her case, and two hundred hours of psy-chotherapy to be scheduled by counselors assigned to her case." She unceremoniously shut the case document in front of her. "Juvenile matter ten two nine hundred and one is closed."

Julian felt as much relief as if she had been sitting at the hearing table herself. She felt the tension drain away, evaporate into the thick court-room air and disappear, felt her shoulders sag in relief. Such relief that she could not for the moment stand up.

She looked to Alyshia. Alyshia looked at the judge, smiled. A small smile, but a warm smile. A smile of relief. Of thanks. Of escape. What any prisoner would smile, would feel, on finding themselves suddenly, finally, outside the fence.

"Lieutenant?"

Julian turned to the pleasant voice, after standing with counselors in the hall outside the hearing room finishing her coffee with them, and was surprised and delighted to discover it was Caramore's. Less commanding, a friendlier presence without her robes, even her voice different, lighter, more conversational.

"Judge Caramore."

"How are you?" She smiled at Julian cursorily, in a way that told Julian she had something to say beyond pleasantry.

"You care about young Miss Ryan, yes? Hence your presence here."

Julian nodded.

"You noticed my pauses."

"Of course."

"And?"

Julian didn't know what to say exactly. "They were dramatic."

Caramore frowned. "They weren't for drama," she said.

Julian looked at her.

"I've seen a number of these cases, you know," she said.

"I'm sure."

"My pauses," continued Caramore, quietly, "were because something, well . . . gives me pause." She looked up over her bifocals at Julian, sternly, assertively and yet inquiringly at the same time. "Something isn't right, Lieutenant. I don't know what, and if I don't know, I really can't act on it." She shrugged. "But something."

And then looked at Julian, with a challenging, you-figure-it-out look, before turning to head down the ancient marble corridor. "Nice seeing you, Lieutenant."

And finally, Alyshia and Nell Ryan emerged from the hearing room into the corridor. It would be Julian's first physical encounter with them in weeks. Julian didn't know what to expect from it, but she expected, given the outcome, that there'd be some thaw, some concession to the moment, to the accomplishment of their shared goal for Alyshia. She found that she could not keep herself from smiling, and she expected that mother and daughter would find the same. In fact, she had seen them smile in the hearing room, Nell in broad relief, Alyshia something less bold and apparent. The question was, would they smile in front of Julian?

The answer was no. Nell Ryan was making sure to wear her coldness toward the police officer who had escalated her troubles, to model it for all and anyone to see.

"Nell," said Julian in greeting.

"Lieutenant," said Mrs. Ryan in distant return. Julian got the message.

Julian looked at Alyshia. Did her best to look without studying. Looked again to see if there was any change physically, but also in behavior, in outlook, in bearing. But Alyshia looked the same. Was that true, or was Julian just trying to confirm her own theory?

And Alyshia's expression. A begging. An imprisonment. A smile that was stopped within itself.

Julian simply knew. Alyshia was having this baby. And no one was going to believe it except Julian.

51

Holding her morning coffee, Julian opened the door to her office, and bobbled and nearly dropped the steaming Styrofoam cup, on seeing who was perched on the chair in front of her desk.

Alyshia.

Julian was reminded immediately of the surprise of Edwards suddenly being there, but mostly by the contrast of feelings. Because now she experienced a sudden and distinctive flood of protective, maternal instinct. She felt a lightness, a release. It seemed that Nell's hostile silence toward Julian had not poisoned Alyshia, after all.

"I had a taxicab bring me," Alyshia explained. "I took the school bus for two stops, to where there's a pay phone, and I called the cab from there, and I made sure I sounded older," she said, with a quick smile.

"Very resourceful," said Julian, pleased by this expanding confirmation of her opinion about Alyshia's intelligence. "It's so great to see you. I've been wondering about you." An understatement. "But I'm . . . I'm really glad you came," Julian gushed. It was all she could think to say, and all she wanted to say. She closed the door behind her. Let the room bathe the two of them privately in light.

"I have to get back to school. But I really felt like I had to come here and tell you," said Alyshia.

Julian raised her eyebrows. Had an inkling, a satisfied sense, of what she was about to hear. *I knew it,* thought Julian. *I was right.* She wished Edwards were here. But she was glad he wasn't. She was glad it was her alone.

"It's about the pregnancy. And it's between you and me," said Alyshia.

I knew it.

"I feel a little more comfortable telling you this now that the hearing's over with," Alyshia confessed, curling up at a slightly different angle, knees drawn up to her chin in the chair.

There was a silent pause between them.

"You're still pregnant, aren't you?" said Julian, gently, motherly.

"I look it, don't I?" said Alyshia shyly.

Julian shrugged to avoid saying it.

"I look as heavy as I ever did, don't I?" As if insisting on an answer.

Julian deflected it by pressing on. "The funeral was your mom's idea, wasn't it?"

Alyshia nodded. "Of course. What do you think?" The twelve-year-old inflection of parent predictability, yet over such an unpredictable event.

"You're having that baby."

She put her hands to her stomach, almost reluctantly, and looked away. "Sure looks that way, doesn't it?" Depressed, resigned, seeing, it seemed, the life ahead of her.

"You never told your mother you lost the baby, did you?" Julian said gently. "It was her idea, wasn't it? That's why she was so sketchy about how it happened. Not because you didn't want to tell her the details. But because there were no details. Because she was making it up."

"I told her I lost the baby," Alyshia explained. "But my mother . . . you don't know . . . she just wouldn't accept it."

"Wait. I . . ." A blurriness seemed to gather around Julian. "What do you—" She blinked, confused. "You *did* lose the baby? I don't—"

"My mother won't accept it." Alyshia looked at Julian. "She wants that baby, Miss Palmer. Wants it more than anything."

We're having it, Lieutenant. With this baby, Frank will be here again, don't you see. We're having it.

Tucked, curled into the chair, Alyshia fiddled nervously with the top button of her cheerful blue flower-print dress. Amid her confusion, Julian noticed the bright, surreal colors of the flowers. They reminded her . . . *Lilius macrophylla lupidus.*

The cramped office was hot, stifling as always. Alyshia unbuttoned the top button.

Then looked up at Julian, and unbuttoned the second button of the dress. "You've been good to me, Lieutenant Palmer, so I want you to know . . ."

Julian felt off-balance, unhinged.

Alyshia unceremonially unbuttoned the third button, and the fourth.

Julian's confusion and panic rose like flood waters. "Alyshia, wait." She got up, went to open the door as a way to stop her.

"No. Please. Look."

At what? Your skin? Your growing belly?

"My mother doesn't know anything about pregnancy. She was never pregnant," said Alyshia.

I know, Julian thought, but didn't say it.

"Twelve-year-old Catholic girls have a lot of personal privacy. My mother, my sister, never see me naked, that's just the way our house is."

What?

"And I don't think you really know anything about pregnancy either, Lieutenant."

All the buttons of Alyshia's blue dress were now undone.

Allowing Alyshia Ryan to pull rags—carefully wadded, Julian saw, and folded into a thin, smooth, visible layer that had been carefully, adeptly taped in place, it appeared—out from around her belly.

My God.

"You thought I was still pregnant," said Alyshia. "So you can understand that's what my mother thinks." She held the rags carefully in both hands. Weighed them. Regarded them with as much care and affection as if they were a child themselves. It looked like old pajamas, strips of old sheeting. Maybe sheeting her father had attacked her on, Julian thought. Semen samples they had missed.

"It's what my mother thinks, and what she'll keep thinking," Alyshia said resolutely. After a moment, she began to place the rags carefully back inside her dress, settling them, taping them skillfully. "After I told her I lost the baby . . . a while after . . . I told her it was just blood that I'd seen. That I thought the baby might still be in me. My mother was so happy. . . ."

Alyshia's face and weight, Julian realized vaguely. Just continuing to overeat. To help the deception along.

"Look what was done to her, Lieutenant Palmer," Alyshia said, the dress now rebuttoned. Her eyes were studiously down at the seat of the chair, trying perhaps to look up at Julian, but clearly unable to. "Look what my father and I did." She paused, shook her head heavily, as if it contained pure burden, pure weight. "This is the least I can do."

Keeping the baby alive for her mother. Guilt. My God.

"I'll figure something out for later," Alyshia said gloomily, quietly, "for when I should be having the baby. But I wanted you to know. You've been good to me. You've cared about me." She looked apologetic, shifted uncomfortably. "I had to wait till after the hearing to tell you. I didn't want this to change the good things you'd tell a judge. I know you think good of me."

Julian was still trying to process it. There was a throbbing at her temples. But at the same time a sense of sorrow washed over her. Overwhelmed her.

It's not your fault, Alyshia. You're only twelve. Twelve . . .

"I'm trusting you with this," said Alyshia. "You won't tell her? It's between you and me. You'll keep it a secret, right?" An edge of desperation in her voice.

Julian would never have to say anything to Nell Ryan, because Nell Ryan would soon enough, of course, discover her daughter's deception.

If Nell was even deceived at all.

"Yes," promised Julian, "I will keep it a secret, but Alyshia, honey . . ."

Yet before Julian could form the thought, Alyshia Ryan began to cry. To cry again as she had in the old storeroom.

Julian came around from the other side of the desk, put her arm around Alyshia's shoulder, was surprised and overcome by the sense of its smallness.

Pretending to be pregnant to satisfy a mother's wish for a baby. Julian tried to see into the psychology of a household where an adopted daughter would do this. Was this the degree of Alyshia's desperateness for acceptance? Maybe her unconscious motivation for becoming pregnant in the first place—offer Nell the baby Alyshia sensed her adoptive mother always wanted. Julian knew that the strange pathologies of the Ryan house were in full play here. The strange pathologies whose result was incest by one parent and denial of it in the other. And when she had lost the baby, a desperate twelve-year-old had concocted this.

In which case, Nell had thought Alyshia *was* still pregnant, and proceeded with the funeral as a way to deceive everyone else, to let her daughter have the baby in privacy—unseen, unhumiliated—just as Julian had theorized, standing there in the drizzle, watching the baby's funeral.

Most young girls would try to hide their pregnancy. This one was trying to show it. To re-create it. The lengths Alyshia had gone to offered some clue, Julian sensed, into how and why Alyshia—adopted, after all—would tolerate the incest. Was she that desperate for her adoptive parents' approval? Was she that insecure in a world without her real ones?

Questions that went beyond this investigation, and into the subtler reaches of psychology. Adoptive mothers, adopted daughters. Desperation. Insecurity. The sense of belonging. The sense of isolation. Julian was out of her depth. This was terrain beyond her.

Eventually, Alyshia got up. She carefully checked the padding once more, as she must every morning, secretly throughout the day.

Blaming herself.

Once you knew, it was absurd of course. An absurd, heartbreaking charade. A twelve-year-old's plan, to make it right.

Could Nell Ryan actually believe there was still a baby, after her daughter had told her she'd lost it? Why not? A tale of spotting. A twelve-year-old's confusion. A frantic reaction on seeing some blood.

Or was it Nell simply accepting her daughter's charade? The mother seeing it as the daughter's need. Just as the daughter saw the pregnancy, the baby, as the mother's need. Each trying in their mute, uncommunicative way, to help the other.

The lack of communication, the distance, the indirection, that helped create the disasters of that house to begin with.

She stepped with Alyshia to the door, opened it, said good-bye.

Closed the door again. Sat down heavily into her fraying, worn-out desk chair, stunned. Amazed. Lost in meditation on the power and the paradoxes, the cramped, twisted, locking power, of mother-daughter connection.

Push it away. Push it away for now.

It was absurd, really. Low comedy, farce, on the heels of tragedy. Tragically absurd. And of course, she thought, shaking her head, she had fallen for it.

So why couldn't the prudish, standoffish, unbalanced Mrs. Ryan? She might very well be falling for it too.

Edwards wandered into the station house an hour later.

Just between us. You'll keep it a secret, right? She weighed her promise to Alyshia. But a promise to say nothing to her mother, really. Edwards seemed outside the promise, outside ordinary human interaction.

Telling him, of course, would only bring his superior smile. His unspoken smug I-told-you-so. She didn't need to tell him, really. It would only make her look a fool. But it was the fact, after all. The startling truth. And even in her own embarrassment, probably deserved to be shared.

She could keep it to herself. Respect Alyshia's wishes, and make herself look good. But something told her not to. To take the path of most resistance. As usual.

"You won't believe it," she said to Edwards. "But then again, you will."

He sat in the chair Alyshia had occupied. Menacing, huge, an absurdly, comically contrasting presence in it.

She told him. The wadded rags. Alyshia's explanation. Her confessing. Her crying.

Desperate for her adoptive mother's acceptance, Julian speculated. The power of filial connection. The astonishing power of guilt.

"So I was wrong, I guess," Julian admitted. "She's not pregnant. She did lose the baby. How about that?" she said, conclusively.

Edwards wore a strange expression. Gave no response.

"So . . . what do you think of that?" she asked again, this time looking for some observation, some confirmation, anything from him.

Edwards remained silent. Was very still, Julian noticed, almost poetically, religiously still, in a kind of trance. Julian felt unnerved. Then he smiled. "What do I think?" His smile deepened. A look of transformation. Of strange bliss. "I think Alyshia Ryan just made her first mistake."

"What?" said Julian.

"She just revealed how smart she is. And more than that, what she's capable of."

And in a moment he began to lay out the astonishing possibility.

Means, motive, opportunity.

Converging. Three wind-tossed crafts from separate seas, pulling to shore together, snugly and safely in harbor. Their long-planned rendezvous.

Singing their three-part harmony at last.

52

He shut the door.

"Julian." He looked at her.

It was a look she'd seen before. A look, an expression, that the oblique, difficult, irascible Winston Edwards exhibited only rarely. An expression that said he needed to be listened to.

"Let's say . . . let's suppose for a moment, that Frank Ryan's in a bad marriage." He said it slowly, deliberately, gauging her. "I mean, you've met, you've dealt with Mrs. Ryan. She can be very . . . I don't know . . . rigid. Stiff."

"She is nothing but loving toward those children," Julian jumped in, defensively, reflexively.

"I don't dispute that," said Edwards. "My question is how loving she was toward her husband."

Julian shrugged. Frank Ryan had been handsome, upbeat, hardworking, gentle. Why *wouldn't* she be loving? But something had happened, clearly, with Frank Ryan and Nell. Something had gone awry, so Julian, reluctantly, was listening.

"A young, good-looking, healthy guy. Two young daughters. Both adopted. Why? Why is a young Catholic couple adopting two girls at once? Less than a year after marriage? Check the dates. That's not much trying on your own," Edwards pointed out.

Julian shrugged. "I'm sure they couldn't have children. I'm sure that's why—"

"Maybe you're sure. But Nell Ryan's OB-GYN wasn't so sure. Nell Ryan's OB-GYN was sure they could—and was pretty mystified by the adoption."

Julian felt the fury surge in her instantly. "*When* . . . when did you find this out?" She paused, realized. "A doctor would never tell you that. That's privileged, confidential, he could lose his license."

"Good for you, Lieutenant," said Edwards, "absolutely correct. But the doctor's oldest nurse was not so cautious. And the doctor had mentioned it to her. Meaning it was odd enough to mention."

Julian was still incensed. "Why—why were you doing this without me?!"

"Because a sharp young police lieutenant coming into a medical practice all official, her big scary-looking detectives in tow, versus an old broken-down investigator sidling up informally to the nursing staff . . . I thought I might have a better shot at actually learning something." He looked at her. "Plus I knew you'd never sit still for where I was going with it. Never in a million years."

They stared at one another.

"The lab," said Edwards, continuing suddenly. "The lab said copious amounts of semen, right?" He shook his head, clearly angry with himself. "Ng and Mendoza just jumped in. Reasonably assumed that Frank Ryan was pulling out and missed once. But those copious amounts . . . maybe he wasn't ever inside Alyshia Ryan. Maybe he wasn't ever sexually near her at all."

"What are you *talking* about?" said Julian. "The semen—"

"Young handsome guy, and his beautiful young wife won't have sex with him," said Edwards. "Maybe only a prim little bit, maybe none at all, but not enough to even give them the chance to have children. Or maybe she won't because she's afraid of pregnancy—of becoming a mother—good Catholic, can't use contraceptives . . . whatever the reason, sex terrifies her."

Julian began to shake her head, annoyed. Edwards held up a hand, to please let him finish.

"Two stationery businesses, starting a third. I don't know if you have to be up at four in the morning every morning to stay on top of them. In fact, if you're a smart young guy, I don't think you do. I think he's up at four in the morning working just because he can't sleep." Edwards looked at Julian now, a deeper power emanating from him, the passion of an idea. "Four in the morning, young, alone, frustrated, pent up," said Edwards.

Julian watched him.

"Let's say Frank Ryan masturbates."

Julian looked at him—didn't flinch, didn't move; listened.

"Maybe only once in a while. Maybe a pattern. Maybe masturbates in that little bathroom off the office, and comes into the toilet, which he doesn't flush, doesn't want the noisy plumbing of the old house to wake his sleeping family at four in the morning. Maybe just masturbates into a tissue at his desk, and wads it into the trash, who knows?"

The tiny bathroom off the office . . .

The blue box of tissues on the desk . . . semen stains on the desk chair. . . .

Something isn't right, Lieutenant. Judge Caramore's shaking head. *Something isn't right. . . .*

"Why am I even listening to this?" Julian said.

He did not do it! Nell Ryan screaming. *I'm telling you! HE DID NOT!*

"Point is, Alyshia Ryan stumbles onto what her dad's up to," says Edwards. "Sneaks down quietly at four in the morning, discovers the pattern. Is shocked and disgusted, or giggles and tells her friend Rick, who knows? But whatever she first feels about it—seeing that semen, that little milky wad, floating in the bathroom lavatory or wadded and buried in the trash, she hatches a plan. Scoop it up, scoop it out, spread it on a sheet set aside for just that purpose, on her underwear, do it often enough for it to really take, to work itself in . . ."

Julian can't breathe. She feels a tightness in her chest, in her throat.

"To implicate the sexually frustrated, weakling father she hates," Edwards says, "the father who's not really her father. To destroy the prim dysfunctional mother she despises, the mother who's not really her mother. To escape the childhood and the life she can't stand."

He did not do it! I'm telling you. He did not!

Julian, stunned, confused, can only partly absorb the images, only partly absorb the meaning. "Wait a second—what are you saying?" And she realizes. "There was *never* a baby?" Julian regarded him incredulously. "Come on."

Edwards looked at her. "No one of any medical authority ever told us there was. Nobody but the Ryans ever told us there was."

"She was dizzy, growing huge, fainted in the bowling alley, for chrissake!"

"All planned."

Smart. She was smart.

Noticing, admiring, how smart she was . . .

"You're out of your mind! She's twelve!"

"A twelve-year-old has seen plenty of TV, movies, and parents' pregnant friends. A twelve-year-old knows how to act pregnant. Particularly a twelve-year-old who coolly collected and redistributed her father's semen. Onto a sheet she hid where the police could find it."

"But this is a twelve-year-old who . . . who didn't even *know* she was pregnant!"

"Who pretended not to know. Pretended very well."

"A twelve-year-old can't act like that."

"I think this one can. Because I think this one has for years. Because I'd say for years there have been two Alyshia Ryans. The Alyshia Ryan who is Nell's daughter. Who pretends to be Nell Ryan's dutiful daughter. And the Alyshia Ryan who is someone else entirely."

Edwards leaned forward. Looked at Julian, studying her.

"That visit to you here this morning. You really think she was coming here after the ruling just to tell you she's faking it for her mother's sake? Come on. That's what she's saying. But she's coming here to show you that she never *was* pregnant. How she pulled it off.

"That's what she wanted you to know—that she never *was* pregnant. Wanted to rub your face in it. Laugh at your gullibility. Revel in the victory. A typical twelve-year-old would have bragged about it. But she's not a typical twelve-year-old. She's smarter. Much smarter. So she finds her own clever way to brag. To prove how well she pulled it off."

Smart. She was smart.

Julian felt herself suddenly back in the storeroom, listening to Alyshia's confession; to the story of the rape.

Clearly a story she had been waiting to tell, Julian had thought.

Because she'd been rehearsing it?

The story pouring out of her. Disorganized. Jumping in time.

Because it hadn't really happened?

A startling, sudden similarity to Julian's own story.

Because Alyshia had stolen elements from the story Julian had just told her?

Julian felt a pulsing, a shuddering inside her.

Edwards leaned in even closer. "That school assignment of hers. Her so-called report. That was just a way to get in to see you. Get to know you.

Get a good report from *you*. Keeping her enemies closer, as they say. Just something she told her mother, so her mother's asking you the favor would legitimize it. Call the school. See if there was any such assignment."

"Meaning . . . meaning you already have?"

"Go ahead," he said. "Call," said Edwards. "Her teacher's name is Mrs. Harkavy."

Julian picked up the phone.

Stared at the numbers, not dialing.

She didn't want to know just yet that there was no school assignment.

She couldn't handle that just yet.

She put the phone receiver down.

She felt slightly sick, she noticed. Sick from the whole notion of the scenario. Sick from Edwards's ability to imagine it.

But sick especially from its possibility.

53

She leaned back, gripping the beaten-looking arms of the desk chair. Steadying herself.

In trying to completely dismiss the idea, the idea played completely in her mind.

"You're nuts," she said finally, conclusively, angry and insulted by such a wild-eyed interpretation of events. "This is insane."

"I thought it was insane, too," he admitted. "I was sure it was insane," he said. "Until you told me about the wadded rags."

She shook her head. "It's nuts."

"But not so nuts that you've tossed me out of your office. I see that I'm still sitting here. The chair is still under me," he said with a wry, dark edge.

"It's . . . preposterous." *An idea out of your hatred of women. Your imagination coupled to your rage. Or some hidden agenda I'm missing completely.* "There's not an ounce of proof," she said, annoyed.

Though she noticed she was searching her own mind, hoping for some quick way to prove or disprove it.

It was true. No doctor had checked to see if there was a baby, as far as they knew. It might have simply been Alyshia convincing her mother there was, adding the credibility of her mother's beliefs to her own ruthless plan.

There had been no official reason to investigate the existence or nonexistence of the fetus. For the incest case, there had been, it seemed, sufficient DNA evidence without it. Particularly for a juvenile judge.

Until now. Until semen stains were insufficient.

It showed how easily they could all be fooled by a twelve-year-old.

A different appearance. A change of behavior. Wadded rags and ice cream.

She was unable to dismiss Edwards's scenario out of hand. But she wanted to. Indeed, was about to. "All that hatred of her adoptive parents? It could explain wanting to humiliate them. Wanting to escape them. But wanting to *kill* one of them? Something more would have to . . ." *Something more.* And she looked at him, her eyes opening, slowly realizing. . . .

Edwards seemed to see it at the same moment. His eyes went wide. He looked awed. Absorbed. "What if you were right about Rick? Right from the start, right all along, and I was wrong."

He shook his head numbly. "What if she *is* still carrying a baby? The rags are just to make *you* think she's not."

My God . . .

"Rick's baby. Her thirteen-year-old boyfriend, who gave her a baby when she needed it."

Needed it? What are you . . .

"Like you said. There had to be something more. If the hatred has simmered for so long, there's got to be some precipitating event." He looked at her hard. "Like pregnancy. Look. How does a twelve-year-old girl like Alyshia Ryan get hold of a gun? Only by convincing someone to give her one. Maybe Rick's the boyfriend only because of his dad's hobby. Maybe she asks Rick, and terrified Ricky says no way, or maybe she just senses he won't get it for her without a damn good reason."

"So how does she change his mind? Make him a proud father. And then tell him his fatherhood's being threatened by her own father, who's going to take away their baby, going to tell Boyko, Sr., about his son's activities, going to tell the police that Ricky raped his daughter, who knows? Whatever she says, it's enough to get that gun from him." He pauses. "Maybe even enough to get Ricky to pull the trigger."

She thought for a moment. "It would help explain why she could do such a good job of acting pregnant," said Julian. "Because she *was* pregnant."

"Pregnant not *just* because she needed a gun," he added, "but would need a way to get the police—her new best pals, the police—to make their logical way to those semen stains of her father's, should an investigation ever get that far, should that ever be required."

And Julian, despite herself, despite her skepticism, her procedural stubbornness and care, felt a tinge of excitement.

They're having that baby, she'd told them in the car. *I just know they are.*
Trust your instincts, he'd always said. Maybe her instincts had been right.

And now there was a way to prove or disprove his theory.

A way to see whether Edwards was a crazy old cop, or an intuitive genius.

Get the DNA of Rick's baby.

If there was a baby.

If it was Rick's.

54

Getting DNA evidence of an unborn child was in most cases fairly simple, but in this case impossible on several levels.

If it was six months or so later, if the baby was born, it was easy. You didn't even need permission. Just a cell of skin, a strand of downy hair, anything, though a cotton swab of saliva was best.

But getting the DNA of the fetus now was considerably more complex. It meant amniocentesis. Which required the approval of the guardian. Who, even if only learning of the baby's existence from the police, could be expected to do her utmost to defend it, and its young mother.

Even if Nell could be convinced that the baby was an underage boyfriend's, and not her husband's, she'd realize that granting permission for amnio would risk abandoning Alyshia's role as victim, and begin to pave the way for her daughter to go to jail, or at best do tough juvenile time. A mother like Nell would do whatever she could to keep her daughter out of either. Faced with swapping one sordidness for another, Nell might stay with the one she'd dealt with so far, and not invite a new one. Not open up a new field day to opinion and the local newspapers.

And if you could even get them to admit there *was* a baby, the Ryans could argue that amniocentesis is not recommended for mothers under thirty-five, exposes mother and fetus to unnecessary risk. Modest risk, but extra risk nonetheless.

The whole matter could wait six or so months. But the state would hardly allow a twelve-year-old and her fate to wait that long. Particularly a twelve-year-old with existing DNA evidence—gobs of it, as it were—on behalf of her version of events. A completely credible version. Not some harebrained theory.

And what judge was going to let them get it from the unborn child anyway? What, on a hunch? The contrary existing DNA evidence of Frank Ryan's semen was already so compelling.

If Edwards was right, little Alyshia had pulled off a good one.

If she had cold-bloodedly killed her father, without the fetal test it came down to we-said-she-said.

Just like *State of New York* v. *Winston Edwards,* Julian mused. A tough one to win. Particularly if the weight of DNA evidence is against you.

"The State won't wait six months. And Nell's not going to send her daughter to jail," said Julian. "And competing DNA evidence alone doesn't make a case in the State of New York, so we couldn't obtain it without something convincing to show cause." Still skeptical, still doubtful, wondering aloud, "So what do I do? Get Alyshia in here? Try to break her?"

"Wouldn't work on two counts," Edwards said gruffly. "One, she probably wouldn't break. If she's been lying, as I think she has, then she handled your little storeroom just fine the first time, thank you, and on her second visit she'll be even more at ease. Second of all, let's say we did break her. Breaking a twelve-year-old? Pressing a twelve-year-old to change her story? A judge would disallow it. It'd never hold up in court, in a juvenile hearing, anywhere."

If Edwards's version of events was true to any degree at all, then Alyshia had acted so well, played them all for such fools, she would never break. If his version of events was true, it proved Alyshia was too confident. Too amoral. Because she'd know that if she didn't crack, there was no way they could get her.

Smart. Real smart.

Alyshia.

And Edwards.

Julian had to be smarter.

55

"Elinor Banning?"

"Yes?" Cautiously.

As soon as Edwards had stepped out of the office, she had Ng get her the name of Nell Ryan's OB-GYN, and the name of the senior nurse in the practice.

"This is Lieutenant Palmer. I need to speak to you about a patient, Nell Ryan, in connection with her husband's murder."

"You know I can't do that. We currently see her in this practice."

But Julian pressed her, gently, insistently, behind her the vague threat of authority, of action.

Elinor Banning felt cornered, trapped. "Look, I told that big guy too much already. And he said no one else would call. Don't you people talk to each other? I'm sorry."

She hung up.

Edwards had indeed been there.

But what, Elinor? What exactly did you tell him?

"Mrs. Harkavy? Alyshia Ryan's teacher?"

"Yes."

"Mrs. Harkavy, this is Lieutenant Palmer."

"Oh, Alyshia's report on you! Did you see it? It was wonderful!"

Julian felt a flood of relief. So it really *was* a report for school. Alyshia had never talked further about it. Julian hadn't thought much more about it. Now she was curious to see it.

Mrs. Harvaky lowered her voice. "You know, Lieutenant, she turned it in, and that was her last work before, you know, the thing about her father came out."

"Yes, I see," said Julian, and after a polite beat of understanding, "So it was a specific assignment, then."

She could feel Mrs. Harkavy's puzzlement. "No, no it wasn't. It was her own idea. I was very impressed. That's what was so wonderful about it. And so unusual for Alyshia. So uncharacteristic, given, you know, what she'd been going through."

Her own idea.

"Mrs. Harvaky, were you ever contacted by our office before?"

"No."

Go ahead. Call her school. Daring her? A bluff? Or simple knowing, sure, that Alyshia had made it up.

"You're sure?"

"Lieutenant," slightly offended, "you know I'd remember."

She finally reached a Dr. Caliban, in the Binghamton labs.

"Dr. Caliban, Lieutenant Julian Palmer. I understand you did the DNA workup on a matter we submitted, uh, samples, uh"—checking her paperwork—"forty-seven oh one oh through forty-seven oh one nine."

"If you say so."

"Can you pull the records?"

"Sure. One sec." Brightly, cooperatively. A pause. "There it is." Another pause. "Oh, yeah, I remember this. That was a hell of a lot of sample."

Her antennae went up. "Meaning what?"

"Meaning stain patterns indicated large amounts of semen, which we duly noted. I'd make the leap and say there was a lot of fun being had on those sheets, but given that we're running these tests for your department, something tells me in the end it wasn't much fun at all."

" 'Copious' is the word in your report."

"Then copious it was," he said genially.

She paused. "Would it be consistent with someone ejaculating onto the sheets?"

"Consistent?" Mild puzzlement. "What else would it be?"

She paused. "Would it be consistent with the ejaculate retrieved from elsewhere, and rubbed into the sheets?"

"Now, there's an idea," he said. After a moment, Caliban said, "In fact, I like that idea."

"You do?"

"Makes me feel a little more manly," he joked. "A little more secure."

"Because?"

"Judging by the stains, see, those are awfully copious amounts for coitus interruptus."

"But you can't say conclusively it was one or the other."

"Afraid not. But I like the idea that the semen was imported to look good. Have fun with that," Caliban said cheerfully.

She was no longer a naive recruit. No longer a blind worshiper of talent and reputation. She didn't know what might be in Edwards's dark heart. Was beginning to accept that she might never know. But she suspected there was something. Some agenda there.

But this was all the checking she could do. And it was inconclusive.

As Edwards knew it would be? That was the question.

He wandered into her office again a few minutes later. Sat mutely, as if by his mere presence to push his point of view on her. She didn't know what to say. How to deal with him at the moment.

To avoid it, she turned to the pile of mail.

Opened the envelope on top.

56

Edwards saw the envelope as she did so.

Saw and read the return address as Julian, brow furrowed, tore it open.

St. Mary Southwest Virginia Rehabilitative Center.

Deep in his ursine chest, his tired heart punched him hard enough to make him flinch.

She'd of course been informed of her mother's death. Presumably by phone. But still she had said nothing about it to him. She had kept the news to herself, driven up to see Richards with no mention of it, hadn't shared it with him or anyone in the station house that he could see. It seemed equally clear to Edwards that, for whatever reason, details of the death, so far at least, had not included him. Not on the phone, anyway.

The relationship had been distant, strained, because of her mother's mental illness, he now knew. But he had expected a reaction of some sort. Maybe there had been, and he was simply excluded from it. Why would she share it with him? Why would she trust him?

But now, was there something written from the St. Mary staff, something sent, that they had chosen not to speak?

As she read, he saw her eyes well up.

She looked up at Edwards.

Her jaw set.

She shook her head.

He felt his heart punch him again. He was intensely aware of her service revolver holstered in the gun belt, suspended as always from the coat tree a few feet behind her.

He thought of the first day, when she had pressed him with its muzzle, held him splayed to the floor. He had prepared for this. Expected it for days now. He'd thought it would be in a phone call, a phone call that unleashed her rage. Now, maybe, it was in written form.

He looked obliquely at Julian's gun again. It wasn't such a terrible end, he thought. There was some justice to it. Justice in a police station. Imagine that.

"My mother died," she said, jaw still set. She put her fingers to her eyes. "Killed herself," she told him. She held her fingers to her eyes, seemed to consider gouging them out, as if to gouge away the information, the knowledge.

Edwards waited. Nothing. Nothing more.

"She was in a sanitarium in the South," Julian explained. She shook her head mildly, unthinking, side to side. "I rarely spoke to her."

He tried to remain calm, unstartled. Something wasn't right. Why wasn't she saying anything more?

"Never got to see her down there."

"No?" he volunteered, weak, dumb.

"Nobody did. She wouldn't allow visitors. That's how she wanted it."

Wouldn't allow visitors. That's how she wanted it. He realized that the hospital had screwed up. She wasn't supposed to have visitors. So they would never admit in writing to the next of kin that she had had a visitor coming, and that the disregard of her wishes had indirectly resulted in her death. He couldn't believe it. Was that possible? Was this luck even possible?

Edwards looked at the correspondence still in Julian's hand.

It was two sheets of paper.

She hadn't yet read the second.

She read it now.

And looked up at him, directly, pointedly shook her head, seemed to fill slowly with rage. "Goddamn, goddamn," she said, looking at him, shaking her head.

He bowed his head, exposing his neck to the pistol shot . . .

She tossed the two sheets of paper on the desk in disgust. "It's the final bill," she said.

Okay for now. Saved for now.

He'd stayed silent, unable to say a word, in some basic instinct of self-preservation.

The sanitarium, embarrassed by their failure of procedure, had not revealed his involvement. Or else he was simply lost or forgotten within the event. He had escaped implication. He could not tell what the Fates meant by this intervention. His famous instincts gave him no direction, revealed no clue. But he knew—never doubted—that something more was in store.

He was definitely running out of time.

He had to get this thing taken care of.

57

"Let's look at the pictures again," Edwards said. "It's true, it's all just possibility at this point. Speculation. But sometimes a new emotional investment, a different energy . . ." The thought, the words, surprised her, as he must have known they would. Was it a glancing, inadvertent insight into how he worked? "Maybe we'll see more. Maybe something new."

She looked at him.

He had fooled her before. His versions, his interpretations.

Why should she trust him? Why should she give him the chance?

What was the point? Why make the leap of faith?

"Have Ng bring in the pictures," she said.

The sixteen-by-twenties and eight-by-tens were splayed across Julian's desk again. They examined the pictures once more.

The gold letter opener on the floor; the Lucite-framed photographs of the daughters knocked out of place. The desktop CD player. The pencil holder.

They looked silently, mutely, uselessly.

Julian felt like sweeping the pictures off her desk in exasperation. Maybe that's what had happened with Frank Ryan, she thought wildly, maybe that's what those objects were doing on the floor. Knocked over, swept off, in exasperation, in frustration, with a bad marriage, with his hateful daughters, with his imprisoning life. Maybe knocked out of place, swept to the floor well before any murderer appeared.

And if she swept the photographs to the floor of her office? She could imagine herself looking at them. Searching for a clue in how they landed.

Looking for them to reveal something in their accidental new configuration, like an oversized, black-and-white set of tarot cards. Because you never stopped looking. Absurdly, you never gave up. Maybe the very action of the sweep of her arm would reveal something. Would replay the moment as Frank Ryan had experienced it, and show them something they missed.

"My God," said Edwards, barely audibly, a whisper, "I'm an idiot."

Ng, Mendoza, Julian looked at him.

"Idiot!" he exploded suddenly in self-accusation.

He swept up the photographs like a deck of cards in his bear-paw hand, clenched the pile and shook it in punctuation. "These police photographs were taken in the day, and the murder was at four in the morning, right?"

"But you thought about that already," reminded Julian. "You even simulated his office at four in the morning." Closing the shades. Stuffing the trench coat in the octagonal window. Putting on the CD player.

"But I couldn't simulate what it was like *outside* at four in the morning." He looked into the confused expressions of his audience, and confused, half-amazed himself, said, "Maybe he really did know what he was doing, reaching for the letter opener or the picture frame." Julian knew instantly that Edwards had never really believed it before. "It's possible Frank Ryan knew who his assailant was *before* the first shot was fired." Edwards's look was climbing irrepressibly into a kind of satisfaction. "That he knew without even turning to see who it was."

Ng and Mendoza and Julian stared at him, uncomprehending.

"Because at four in the morning, pitch-black outside, Frank Ryan's office window was a big, clear mirror."

A mirror.

Julian sat silently a moment.

The murder scene—immutable and unalterable for so long—suddenly opened up before her, took on a new appearance in her and all their minds.

"But he wouldn't necessarily have looked up," Julian said. "Remember the CD player playing? He might not have heard."

"But the CD player shuts itself off, right? Well, look here, in this photograph . . . you can see how low the volume is. And remember how low and tinny it was when I played it in his office. No one's ever touched the volume. Point being, at four A.M., with his family sleeping, he played it *quietly*. Look!"

She looked closely at the photograph. It was true.

"That old wooden floor outside his office . . . it squeaks loudly when you walk on it, you can hear it over the CD player. Like *we* did, Julian. Like Frank Ryan would have."

She remembered Edwards standing there, rocking mysteriously on the floor outside Frank Ryan's office when she had first brought him there. Only now was she aware of the squeaking.

"These aren't necessarily the same objects anymore," said Edwards, guardedly, holding up a photograph of the letter opener, another of the picture of the daughters. "These could be entirely different objects now." He looked at them. "Because these could be objects arranged in a mirror. . . ."

He continued, not processing the thoughts, unable to stop. "First shot, second shot, sentient, not sentient. Maybe doesn't matter anymore. The message to us, if there is one, may have been left *before* the first shot.

"If he happened to be looking out that window, into that black mirror, then he knew how smart his killer was. Because he saw it was his own daughter. And he knew he had to be smarter. And could only hope that the police would be smarter too."

And thanks to this strange, broken-down old cop, she thought, maybe the police would be at last.

。•.

Looking out the darkened window six floors above Police Plaza . . .

Staring out the window of her tiny apartment to the street below . . .

How many times had she looked out both those windows into the waning light, into the windows' black, in moments of intense concentration, trying to see into the event, trying to figure out Frank Ryan's murder.

Both those windows, at those times, big clear mirrors, too.

If only she had looked out . . . differently. If only she had looked . . . at herself.

Staring into the bathroom mirror, holding the knife, thinking about, feeling, eerie connection to Frank Ryan . . .

Yet missing it completely.

Edwards was up, moving around the tiny office like an uncontainable force. "Think. Go back. If he *is* looking at that window, at that black reflection, what does he see? Some combination of three elements, let's assume: his daughter. Ricky. A gun.

"Now, let's say for a moment he *does* see the gun," proposed Edwards. "Then why doesn't he turn?"

"Because she never lets him? She fires too quickly?" said Mendoza.

"Or he simply can't understand what he's seeing," said Ng. "I mean, it's his daughter. Maybe . . . I don't know . . . he can't comprehend it. Can't believe it."

"Or maybe the first shot is fired, and *that's* what prompts him to look up," said Mendoza. "What you said the first day, Winston. It's still possible."

Edwards enthusiastically fanned the pictures out again on her desk. "Once we knew it was Alyshia," Edwards said, "once she'd confessed, we should have checked these photos again immediately. Looked again at the gold letter-opener photo. The framed photograph. But see, just when we learned it was her, we also thought we learned that Frank Ryan had raped her, and, figuring we had the whole story, we never went back to the photos."

Yet for all his fresh insight and enthusiasm, the pictures were revealing nothing more. "Think," said Edwards, "think." Amid his pains, despite his bodily miseries, he continued to shift and move restlessly around the little office, never taking his eyes from the spread of crime photos.

And then, he suddenly stopped moving. Stood perfectly still. Smiled wanly. Shook his head with self-rebuke. "We're doing it again." He cocked his head slightly, regarded the pictures as if for the first time. His eyes glimmered. "For chrissake." He shook his head again, more forceful, more angrily now. "Look at Frank Ryan's office window in this photograph. The photograph's taken in daylight, so obviously it doesn't show the mirroring effect, right?"

They nodded.

Edwards's thick forefinger tapped the photograph insistently. "That window is a lesson. A lesson that apparently we haven't learned yet." He shuffled through the stack of pictures until he came to the photo of the framed picture of the daughters. He began to tap it even more insistently. "We're sitting here, looking at these photographs day after day. Looking at what's in front of us. That's why we never thought about the window.

"But it's *also* why we never thought about the picture of his daughters. The *double-sided* picture frame. We've been to the house, we've seen this picture of his daughters, which just confirms for us that what we're seeing in these photographs is correct. That we're looking at the same double-sided frame. But we're looking at one side of it! We keep looking at one side! Sitting here with all these photographs, we've never looked at the other side."

His eyes narrowed. Then closed for a moment. And though it was only brief—mere seconds before they opened again—he seemed for those seconds to inhabit a strange, suspended, trancelike state. As if recognizing something. Connecting to the crime in some new and fundamental way.

"What we've been seeing," he said on opening his eyes, "it's the same view the killer would have seen. But Frank Ryan, between shots or before the first shot, could have turned the frame around."

"A picture the killer *wouldn't* see," Ng noted, intrigued.

"Maybe *that's* what he'd been doing holding the frame. He'd just *turned* it," said Mendoza.

"So the killer wouldn't see it. And we wouldn't see it in the crime photos," Edwards said.

"But the other side of that frame," Julian protested. "We know what it is. It's . . . just . . . another picture of his daughters." ·

Edwards shrugged.

"And that mirrored window," said Julian soberly, finally. "We don't really know if it means anything at all."

He looked at her imploringly. The taut animated enthusiasm of his face seemed to suddenly loosen and drop, as if with the full and sudden knowledge of his crumbled, vanished world, his diminished existence beyond the walls of Julian's office.

His huge shoulders, his whole frame, sagged. He seemed to deflate visibly before her eyes. "It's obviously all just . . . speculation."

He looked now at Julian. Only at Julian. As if there were no one else in the room. As if there were no room. As if there were no one else in the

world. Held his bear paw hands out as if in supplication, as if in surren-
der. "You know me, Julian. You know how I work." *A dinosaur. Another
era.* "I go"—he shrugged—"by this . . . instinct. It's all I know how to do."

Julian had thought long and hard, repulsed and fascinated, literally for
years, about Edwards's famous instincts. Instincts that, it had sometimes
seemed, came close to actual perception. Instincts that had caused whis-
pers of wonder and resentful muttering and brought convictions for thirty
years. Instincts that were, she'd eventually realized, just another term, just
a more acceptable-seeming interpretation, for his strange complicity with
the criminal.

Then was it a strength or a weakness? To be desired or feared? Had it
made him or ruined him? And after thinking about it for so long, had she
now perhaps observed it literally, seen his instinct literally at work, in that
strange closed-eye interlude a few moments before?

Or was he just using it, capitalizing on what he knew was her fascination? Playing on it again?

"I'm not saying there is a clue," he said, the note of defeat unmistakable, "I'm just saying *if* there is, if Frank Ryan had the chance to think that
way, he might have left it in the mirror for us, turned away from his
assailant," and for the flicker of a moment Edwards's eyes closed once
more, and he was once again suspended, trancelike, too quick for Ng or
Mendoza to see, but not too quick for Julian, before opening them again.
"I'm just saying if there *is* a clue, seems like that's where it would be."

And he seemed to Julian, strangely, eerily—to be actually seeing it.

The other side of the double frame.
    Another side of Edwards.
    Unexpected. Revelatory. As always.

58

Once more, they entered the Ryan home.

They headed en masse—Ng, Mendoza, Edwards and Julian, like a lumbering trench-coated beast—directly for Frank Ryan's office.

They stood in the office doorway, on the squeaking wooden floor, before the desk of Frank Ryan. Accountant, stationery-store owner. Husband, father. Victim, mystery.

All of them were looking at the double-sided Lucite picture frame, neatly placed back where it had always been on Frank Ryan's desk, where they had memorized it from some of the crime-scene pictures, as well as seeing it knocked over in others.

Ng and Mendoza stayed in the doorway, as if conscious of the hierarchy of the moment. Julian and Edwards went together around to the far side of the desk.

Edwards bent down laboriously.

Squinted at the back of the frame.

Stood up, wordless. Frowning.

"What?" asked Ng, the syllable bursting from him.

"There are marks. Red marks," Edwards announced. Then shook his head. "But they're random. Incomprehensible." He closed his eyes, snorted. "Must be one of the daughters with a red marker when she was younger." He looked up with a rueful smile. "I guess that's why this side of the frame was turned toward the window."

He looked out the office window, Frank Ryan's much-discussed office window, and shook his head again. "I could see those marks," he said in a whisper of deep confusion and disappointment, a whisper so hoarse and low that only Julian was close enough to hear it, and his partial, sidelong look at her revealed that he wanted her, needed her to. "I could *see* them."

He smiled grimly. "So I was right," he said—pridelessly, a statement of fact—staring off now, "and I was wrong."

Julian had been standing silently next to him, looking at the red marks too. One red mark horizontal across the heart of the younger daughter. The other vertical across the heart of the older one.

Her knees were wobbly. Her breath was short. Frank Ryan's office seemed to be closing in on her.

"Those are ledger marks," she said, remembering what she learned, what she'd been taught, going over Frank Ryan's books with the forensic accountants. "Accountant's marks." Now she picked up the framed photograph, pointed to each mark. "A credit mark on Annabelle. A debit mark across Alyshia." She looked up. "All he had time for. A quick accounting of the moment. A quick accounting of the truth."

59

"You said . . . said with such conviction . . . that Frank Ryan was the father."

"I know," Edwards said, shrugging. "So I was wrong."

The diner was empty. As if its familiar low yet glary, flat, and unflattering light had driven everyone else away. Better for them. A mood of privacy. In a place remarkable for having no mood at all.

Originally only a convenient location, a place to meet outside the office, to minimize Edwards's office presence and her superiors' awareness of him, she had grown to at least respect the diner, to value what it afforded her, if not exactly to like it. It seemed to foster a directness difficult to achieve with Winston Edwards otherwise.

"That whole second-shot thing," said Julian. "In the end, it meant nothing. You were wrong about that too. Totally wrong."

Edwards shrugged again.

"What bothers me," she said slowly, realizing at last, "is you *knew* you were wrong."

Edwards said nothing.

"You said it just to make things confusing, to throw us off. To take a stalled investigation, and make it go backward, for chrissake." Her anger was rising.

Edwards looked at her. Didn't dispute it.

"You even had me hire an expert, to add legitimacy to your point of view, to make it look good," she realized. "When you *knew* there was nothing to it," she said. "Ida Cornell—"

"Ida Cornell. Good prison reading," said Edwards.

Why? Why? To be with me? But she had invited *him*, after all. Whatever it was that held them together, it involved both of them in some bond that maybe neither could understand. She wasn't clear about it. Why should she expect that he would be?

The friendship with Alyshia she'd begun to imagine—showing her new places, new things, laughing together, helping her—like a cruel lesson, like swift and brutal biblical justice, the wishful images were severed and sharply clipped. Had Alyshia played her from the beginning, played her for all she was worth? Or had Alyshia's feelings been at some point authentic, sincere, and discovered too late, in an intenable situation? It still seemed possible that her affections were genuine, that Julian was a remedy, simply arrived at too late to save her from fate. On the other hand, if you had the confidence to con a police lieutenant, you were also probably capable of shooting your own father and coolly watching the funeral and investigation proceed.

Alyshia . . . now held close in the encompassing, smothering arms of the State of New York. The tenuous, promising connection was gone, the mute loneliness had returned, and it had left Julian in this diner with Winston Edwards again.

"You want to be the hero, so you throw everyone else off," she accused.

He smiled. "Maybe you learned too much interning with me five years ago," he said. "You see the madness to my method." Genially, playfully, letting her feel that she was right, so making her freshly doubt that she really was. "Look, I'd read about the Cornell research," he offered, more seriously now. "Sounded intriguing. And it was, wasn't it?"

True. It was.

He took another sip of coffee, put the cup down, looked at her suddenly seriously. "Lieutenant Palmer," he said, "you called it two shots, pure and simple. But I saw it differently. Saw it with all the possibility of a second shot." He looked at her. "I think a second shot has to be looked at. Has to be weighed. Has to be considered and reconsidered in light of the first shot."

Julian slowly understood. Slowly realized—a dawning, an unfolding. "You mean, *your* second shot, don't you? This was *your* second shot."

"Everyone deserves a second shot. Every case. Every person," Edwards said, archly, meaningfully. "A chance to correct. To rectify. To realign things, somehow."

It would make historic sense, of course, if his offhand speculations, proposals, suggestions, had all been merely his hostility toward women— a female police lieutenant, even a twelve-year-old girl-woman at that. It would make sense that these speculations, these challenges of his, had been nothing more than a way to stay on the case. But to Julian, it always felt like more. Or was it just Edwards's expertise at making it feel like more? Was it just her experience of him as, well, experienced? Knowledgeable. Insightful. Had he used that experience of him against her?

"Then, don't you see, it *was* just to be a hero," she said again, with fresh understanding. "To set the investigation back so you could leap ahead. Contact the nurse. Work on your own. Using my department and my resources and my faith in you." She felt the annoyance, the anger, rise— controlled, contained but strong, surging. "To exert influence and control, just for their own sake. You're the same power monger. As egotistical, as selfish, as ever."

"Egotistical. But not as ever," he responded. "Not as ever." He spun the coffee cup in the saucer. "I make mistakes," he said, obliquely. "I make mistakes," he looked up, "but I correct them."

Not "*try to* correct them," she noticed. Just "correct them." Said not with arrogance but as a statement of fact.

And as she sat staring at him, she saw a different look come over him, an entirely different expression for a moment, than she had ever seen, that she would realize later was the expression of the truth from him, unaccustomed, unadorned, brief. "I brought all that up about the letter opener, the picture, the neurology expert, to join you. To have . . . a place." But he suddenly pulled back, colored it and shaded it, as if he couldn't mete out even a little truth, as if it wasn't in his nature. "And to jump-start the investigation, don't you see? To light a fire under all of you."

And then he became intense. Leaned forward with two hundred eighty pounds of meaning. "But don't you see? Don't you see the amazing thing?" he asked. "That when I finally realized about the window, it turned out so much of it—about the letter opener, the two-sided picture frame, the clues—it turned out so much of it was right."

Egotistical, haughty, intuitive to the end.

Preserving his own myth. If only for himself.

But she was finally understanding him, she thought. His ego. His desperation. The small man behind the large exterior. The frightened man behind the myth. Frightened into ingenuity. Frightened into wild scenarios, and salesman enough, desperate enough, persuasive enough, for those around him to follow him anywhere.

Understanding him, of course, had been part of her purpose in taking him on. So he had served it. In that sense, then, the investigation had been a partial success. But of course, it hardly felt successful. Alyshia Ryan had coldbloodedly killed her father, and was now in the machinery of the state.

There might never be any full understanding of Winston Edwards.

And that was his own loss. His own prison.

With his own ego, his own hubris, his own layers of secrets and opaquenesses and black walls, he had confined himself to aloneness.

And no one could reach in there. Much as he might want them to. Much as he might yearn for, even arrange for, people to try.

And a shiver went through her. Because that, right there, might be the reason for a man like Winston Edwards to kill a woman he wanted to love.

For her failure to reach in. Her failure to soothe his soul. Her failure to save him. In desperation, disappointment, freshly imprisoned, he would destroy the one he'd hoped to love.

Was the investigation a "success" for him too? Had he accomplished what he wanted? To prove useful again? Valuable? Alive?

Or was there something more he wanted?

She thought of the knife, the knife still in her purse, wrapped in plastic. A quick shudder went through her. But it wasn't that, couldn't be that. There had been opportunities, hadn't there? It wasn't as simple as that. And she should have realized—with Edwards, it was never that simple.

The knife, still in her purse.

An ordinary kitchen knife.

An extraordinary kitchen knife. In its appearances, disappearances, reappearances. A dark, variable history of its own. Not unlike that of its original possessor. Its original wielder. Which, Cooperman had assured, would be proved when it was run through fingerprinting.

So what was stopping her? Why hadn't she done it already?

Was it the feeling of controlling his fate? Holding the control of his fate literally in her hands? In that sense, wielding the knife, wielding power and control.

Yet she hadn't felt an enormous sense of control.

The murder weapon that Cooperman had assured would be proof. Incontrovertible.

What was stopping her? Why hadn't she done it already?

The same thing stopping him? The same reason he hadn't done it already?

She looked past Edwards to the black sheet of diner window behind him. A mocking reminder of the reflective window in Ryan's office, that she'd failed to see or consider. This time, she looked into the mirror created by the blackened window to see her shape, her presence, but not her face or expressions, the angle of the diner lights not allowing it. She could see her soft outline, but no detail, no features within it. See that she was there, but not to see who she was. See that it was someone, but not exactly who.

"So much of it was lies, wasn't it? Misdirection." She looked at him. "The lies . . . generate an energy of their own, don't they? Like a power source. Self-propelling. Perpetual." A gathering, accumulating, unstoppable force. "They create their own energy, their own heat." The thought condensed, coalesced, in her mind, in her mouth. "The heat of lies."

The lies to others. But the lies he told himself, too. And out of those lies, he'd stumbled onto the truth. But that was the mystery of Winston Edwards. Certainly the luck of Winston Edwards, certainly the intuition, but the perpetual mystery of him too.

Maybe there was no understanding him. But she felt sure, at least, that no one had come closer.

———

He sat looking at her. Looking at her smug, snide expression of understanding. Of trying to reduce him. Feeling she'd succeeded. He could
see it.

Wishing that he could say more. Wishing that he could explain more.
But he could not. Not now. Not ever. He wondered if she had heard him
at all. He felt inarticulate. Inadequate.

He looked at her. Looked in the flat, hard light of the diner. Looked at
Julian Palmer—her pain, her triumph, her still astonishing beauty—for
what he knew was the last time.

60

She'd heard other cops—older cops—refer to "death season," like a climatological condition. She'd figured they meant a certain time of year, until she realized they meant a time of one's life. Everyone had one, they implied. And this—this was clearly hers.

Since as far as they could tell, it was principally the two of them—Julian and her sister, Stephanie—and since they had no family burial plot, they had made arrangements to cremate the body, and Stephanie had acquiesced to her sister's wish to put off the memorial service till Julian felt out from under her current case.

It was Julian, Stephanie, Stephanie's opaque, cipherous husband, a local clergyman, and that would be it. It wasn't appropriate for Stephanie's kids, who'd hardly known their grandmother anyway, who'd met her only a couple of times before her craziness, and never since. Julian had thought briefly about inviting Mendoza, or Ng, just to have someone there, but then thought why? If the service was small, if it was just them, so be it.

After the press at the Ryans with cameras whirring, mourners and onlookers crowding into the tragedy as into a circus tent or a hot new restaurant, she saw—dare she even think it in this context?—the pleasure in a small event. When it was her own family, she wanted it small. Small was personal. Small was meaningful.

As kids, they'd vacationed at the Virginia beaches. She and Stephanie had been very happy there, and though they could not remember or be at all sure, they theorized that their mother and father had both been happy there too. Away from the constant pressures of the newspaper. Away from any enemies.

Stephanie still vacationed there. She knew a pretty curve of shoreline that framed the blue gray sea, looked out uninterrupted on its vastness. She'd checked with the owner of the land, who'd been immediately accommodating and understanding. There was a knoll of high grass at the edge of the rocks that was truly spectacular. A geography, a last place, of inarguable physical beauty—fitting for the woman they were memorializing.

The Virginia beach was situated fairly and conveniently between the two of them geographically as well.

And something—anything—that was far away from that little North Carolina house and town.

Julian was surprised to see two women there in nuns' habits who she had never seen before.

"They're her nurses from the hospital. They called me," Stephanie said. "They really wanted to be here." She shook her head amazed. "I told them we probably weren't going to say a word, just stand here with the ashes, and then scatter them. They didn't care. They drove up two hundred miles anyway." Stephanie couldn't suppress a small, warm smile. "See? She did have friends."

Julian looked at the two women. They smiled and nodded. Julian smiled back, appreciatively.

"They knew that Mom never wanted us to visit. While we were waiting for you, Jules, they told me a little about her life there. It's true, she was out of touch. But you know, she did have her routines, and her contacts. Interestingly, they said the day she . . . you know . . . the day she did it, someone was actually coming to see her."

Julian looked up at her sister.

"A gentleman caller." Stephanie smiled, summoning up with the phrase a regal Southern past. "Who knows who from her past found her there?" Stephanie shrugged and smiled.

But Julian looked dagger eyed at the two women again. Who had it been? Was it their father's killer, after all these years? Had she met him? Spoken to him? What had he said?

The trim, attractive, but hard-eyed police-officer daughter was standing next to the two nurses in a moment. Something in her focus, in her urgent, hard expression, told the nurses to set aside their condolences and sympathies, and answer this daughter's questions immediately. Their mother wasn't supposed to have visitors. This daughter obviously knew that. They'd better answer directly, accurately, satisfactorily.

"I don't remember his name," said the younger nurse, upset, unnerved, by the look in the daughter's eye. "I know I told her, we'd always announce a visitor, but I don't remember the name. . . ."

"Showed up eventually, then left," said the older nurse nervously, trying to clarify. "Huge guy. White hair."

Huge guy. White hair.

Retiring to Florida, are we? Going back to see the missus?

Julian's mother must have known. Must have remembered, through her self-protective cloak of craziness, through her numbness and haze, the name from the trial, from the years of hearings her daughter was involved with, that it was the man who had tried to kill her daughter. The man who tried to kill your daughter: even crazy, a name you don't forget.

Had she died frightened, terrified once again? One last time?

Huge guy. White hair.

Stephanie watched Julian turn silently, begin to walk purposefully, wordlessly, to her rented car.

Stephanie, confused, frightened, held the urn of ashes.

Held them for another time. To put their mother to rest, she somehow sensed, when she finally could be.

Stephanie hoped.

61

Edwards stood at dusk across from the Smithers's farmhouse.

He'd been dropped off by a taxi driver, a different one this time. They had made a quick stop at the same little pharmacy, where Edwards made a phone call. The driver had been a little nervous, Edwards saw, at being this far out into countryside, but like the first taxi driver, to his credit, he had nevertheless offered to wait.

"No need," said Edwards.

"What 'bout your ride back into town?"

"Don't worry about it," he'd told him.

When the taxi driver had opened his glove compartment, searching for something on the trip over, Edwards had seen the gun. He considered it for a moment, but felt more confident about what he'd seen in the Smithers' barn garage last time.

In a moment, he slipped carefully into the same garage's side door. The same side door where he'd found the shovel and hammer and post to check the grave. The empty grave.

There they were. Right where they'd been before.

Along with everything else he'd seen. Peat. Commercial fertilizer. A couple of good-sized containers of gasoline for the tractors.

Perfect.

He'd grown up on farms. Always lived near them, had done his summer jobs on them, best friendships were formed on them, knew them well. It's how he knew exactly what to do with the fertilizer. Knew from law enforcement, but knew also from being a farm-town teenager. Farms were his past. His beginning.

So it was fitting.

Full circle.

With a fatalistic feeling, a soaring feeling of finality, a feeling of relief, a feeling of freedom and escape and flight and victory that he recognized from brief occasions before—occasions as brief as the pull of a trigger, as the twist of a knife—Winston Edwards went quietly to work.

62

Julian raced the rental car north toward the airport, cell phone glued to one ear, dialing madly, screaming frantically.

Rage and fear, evenly mixing, frothing, overflowing.

We know how you feel about Alyshia, he'd said. *We know what this little girl's welfare means to you.*

So she'd been right. Her fears seemed confirmed.

And the plan now seemed deadly clear.

To kill Julian's mother, when Julian was with Alyshia.

To kill Alyshia, when Julian was with her dead mother.

Killing Julian outright—too easy, too painless. No wonder he had made no attempt.

But hanging around long enough to see what was most meaningful to her, and destroying that. Her mother; her young friend.

That would inflict the maximum pain.

His whole theory about Alyshia spreading the semen. A mockery, she realized. An outrageous, mocking version of events. When she'd first been sent to interview with Edwards years before, he'd opened the interview with a lewd aside about her having masturbated that morning. It had been calculated to shock her, she knew, to test her in some way, and she had met the challenge. But how could she not have thought of that, not remembered it, in the context of his version? She could have seen—*should* have seen—that he was mocking her again. And buying himself time.

Dialing madly. Screaming frantically into the cell phone.

But Ng and Mendoza assured her. Triple-checked with the authorities. Alyshia was safe. Closely watched. Deep in the guardianship of New York State.

"Then where the hell is he?" she raged.

Ng and Mendoza swiftly proved their excellence and worth once again.

Within fifteen minutes, they established that he'd been ticketed on an afternoon flight to Charlotte, North Carolina.

In five more minutes, they confirmed he'd been on the flight.

Less than a minute later, they'd patched her through to the Charlotte police, who accepted immediately and at face value that this was a police emergency. All the good ol' boys needed to hear was the term "manhunt."

Charlotte, North Carolina. Close to where Julian had grown up.

Charlotte, North Carolina . . . right after trying to see Sylvia Blood . . .

It took Julian only a moment to realize: he might not have gone to kill her mother. He might have gone to *talk to* her mother.

She realized: it might not be about retribution at all. It might be about solving. It might not be about hatred. Maybe she hadn't understood his motives, or where he was, or who he was. It might not be about hate.

Rage versus love, he'd said that first day, looking at the photographs of the letter opener and the Lucite frame. *The aggressive versus the protective,* he'd said. *What's their relationship? What's their interplay? What are they trying to tell us?*

Rage versus love.

Before she'd even hung up the cell phone, she had turned the rental car around in the highway median, and was heading south.

Had her inability to understand made her too late?

The local police proved excellent too. Picked up his trail from the Charlotte airport, kept in constant touch with her via her cell phone or dialed back immediately, as they located each of various witnesses who recalled seeing the big, white-haired man some time back. They carved a clean, clear, crisp path of remembrance, from a curbside airport worker to a pharmacy checkout girl, to someone who saw a shiny red pickup, leading them to local motor vehicle registration. But that's where it stopped, because Motor Vehicle Department computers were temporarily down. Happened occasionally. Back in a jiff, then we'll run it and call you.

When the computers come back up, when you have the red pickup's registration, you may surround the residence, Julian told them, you may observe, but you may not go in.

She held the cell phone as she drove. Dialed the number she knew so well by now.

Please. Please, no answering machine, she prayed: *Please, please pick up.*

"Hello?"

"Nell!"

"Yes? . . ."

"It's Lieutenant Palmer."

"I don't want to speak—"

"PLEASE . . . I'm begging you—don't hang up—it's an emergency—"

"What?" suspicious, puzzled, but willing, tolerant.

"Please. The big, white-haired detective. Did he—did he ever come out to the house without me?"

"Once, yes."

Heart pounding. "What did he ask you?"

Nell, confused. "He . . . he didn't ask me anything. He just went into Frank's office, to have another look, he said."

"Alone? He went alone?"

"Well, yes. You said he's an expert."

Oh, he's an expert all right.

The marks. The accountant's marks.

Goddamn him. Goddamn.

"Thank you, Nell. That's all I needed. Thank you."

His own trial, five years ago. Forensic accountants on both sides, tracing what happened to the money. *Red marks on the photograph. Incomprehensible.* He knew very well what they were, she realized now.

She slammed the cell phone down onto the seat.

Rage versus love. What exactly was he going to do?

Her cell phone rang once more.

"Yes?"

The momentary silence at the other end told her immediately.

"It's solved," the gruff voice said.

"Where are you?!" she fumed. She could barely speak. She felt like ramming the cars in front of her, running herself off the road. *"Where are you?! Tell me!!"*

"I want you to know it's solved," he said calmly.

"She's dead! *Dead!*" she screamed into the phone. To make him feel again, whatever guilt, whatever pain about it she could. To release it, send the rage into the world finally, let it land anywhere, everywhere.

He was silent.

Then, still calmly, and somberly now as well, "I'll take care of everything," he said. "Everything."

Winston Edwards's two obsessions—Julian Palmer and police work. Their intersection.

She should have known.

And now he had solved it, he said.

The man who'd tried to kill her. . . .

Who had caused her mother's death. . . .

Had solved her father's murder.

Ambassador of mortality. Vizier of evil. Meddling in her private life. Fiddling with her soul.

At last she understood the degree of his obsession with her. That he would try to solve a decades-old crime, to right wrongs with her, in some ineffable balance.

And then her mother had died. And the wrongs could never be righted, and the balance could never be restored. Unless he employed extremes.

And when obsession itself resorts to extremes, then all bets are off.

63

He finished spreading the fertilizer and gasoline, looked up at the house, breathed deeply. He was sweating profusely, breathing hard. The physical pain was consuming, yet he was hardly aware of it at all.

His body couldn't handle this kind of effort anymore. Of course, it wouldn't have to.

He figured the whole thing should go up in seconds.

Conflagration. From the Latin, no doubt. Important sounding. The word large enough, high-toned enough, to accommodate symbolism. The word *murder,* on the other hand—Anglo-Saxon, tree-swinging, spear-chucking Anglo-Saxon in tone—no such symbolism, no such weight in it, no such stature. Nor the word *kill.* But conflagration. Menace and hell and the devil, evil and fire and explosion—conflagration had it all.

He had watched the lights come on within. Had seen Tammy Smithers and her father moving through the rooms inside.

He was going to have to get her outside, he knew, somehow, at the last moment. He hadn't quite worked out how to do it, and he was counting on brute force, which he'd relied on unthinkingly and countlessly in the past, and knew it was a mistake to rely on now. He found a rag in the garage and a length of rope, stuffed them into his pocket in the garage, vaguely figuring to gag her and drag her out bodily if necessary, tie her to a tree or post while telling her in a blunt sentence or two what her father did, before heading back in for Philip, back to stay, the two of them going up together. *Conflagration.*

It was a poor plan. Ill conceived, thought up on the fly, complicated by too many steps and variables. A poor plan. But it didn't have to work very well.

And now, it was all set.

He looked up at the windows, searched the windows, to see where she was now.

Something cracked huge and bluntly against his head.

He saw nothing after that.

64

"I'll take care of everything. Everything."

The words, the tone, the layers of meaning, echoed in her.

Was he going to kill himself? First kill her father's killer, and then himself?

His last act.

Hence the call. Hence the lies. To stay a step ahead. To give him the time, the resources he needed.

As well as she now understood that he had solved the crime, she was also sure he couldn't make the case. It would no longer stand up in court, and then her father's killer, apart from being discovered, would be free. Free and known.

And Winston Edwards would never subject her to that.

Winston Edwards would never accept it himself.

And given what had happened to her mother, he would never face her with the matter half-resolved.

Solved was not enough. The case had to be . . . what would he say? . . . taken care of.

She still didn't know him. Not fully. Not really. Not at all. And yet she knew him enough to know that he might kill himself. Had nothing left to do. No greater opportunity.

He had been around death for thirty-five years. Death had become a familiar.

And as opposed to the deep cowardice and frightened self-protectiveness of most killers at heart, he would have no remorse about killing—and killing himself—in the bargain.

His was a chivalrous evil. Evil with a code.

She simply sensed it. That he was arranging his own justice. His own redemption.

And damned if he was going to let the laws of the land interfere with that.

She realized, if she was right, that it was her duty to save him.

To stop him from murdering her father's killer.

Her sworn duty. Her ironic duty.

To save him, and as soon as possible after saving him, to destroy him, by presenting the State with the evidence of the knife.

She realized that she was driving hell-bent south, heart pounding, the clock ticking, to try to save the life of her father's killer. And to save the life of the man who in some way had precipitated the death of her mother—and who, incidentally, had once attempted to kill her too.

The badge on her chest was asking a hell of a lot.

Would she feel bound to duty in the moment?

With any luck, the moment wouldn't come.

65

Winston Edwards awoke duct-taped to a chair, standing by itself in the middle of the Smithers living room, nailed to the middle of the living room floor.

Tammy Smithers stood several feet away, sneering at him.

Edwards looked at her, and it did not take him long.

A *slighter build,* Arteris Shore had said, with a shrug. *That's all they knew. One smaller than the other. Like any two people would be.*

"You're the second figure. The accomplice," he said.

Proof that he could never have gotten the second witness. Tammy Smithers wouldn't have testified against her father.

All her questions about being a detective. She must have guessed, or at least been on guard, against what Edwards was after. Must have put it together once he was already at the Smithers house, when it was already too late for her to wrangle out of his staying, to avoid him.

Julian's half-sister. Killer of Julian's father.

"How old were you? Fifteen?" he guessed.

"Old enough."

"And did you know what you were doing? Who you were killing?"

"The man who had killed my mother."

"That's what you think?"

"That's what I know."

The story must be elaborate, deep in her, part of her being.

To tell her she was wrong would get him nowhere. He would try, of course, he would try everything, but not just yet—save it for when he needed it. Give it its best shot—when her father was there, and she could see his expression.

Tell her there's no one in the grave. To check it herself. No one in it and there never was. But save it, save it for when you need it. Save it for when Daddy is here.

Tammy Smithers looked at him in disgust. "You're a fool. I just saw you out there, you know. I looked out the window, and I saw you, and I knew who you were, of course. And I went outside and followed you around and watched what you were doing. You don't see or hear too good, you know. You're an old man. Which you don't seem to understand."

"Where is he?"

"He's out now. Gettin' a few things we need." She smiled obliquely, meanly. "Says you didn't have what you needed to do the job right. He's gonna sweeten' the deal." She checked the tape on his wrists and ankles. "Neither of us loves this place. It can go up, maybe we'll get insurance, maybe not. Good time to move on."

"And what are you running from?"

"We did kill a man, case you forgot. You came tryin' to get us for it. And there might be others." She looked at him. "It was justified. But the law don't see it that way, and never will."

He heard footsteps coming up the porch steps. A jostling at the front door. "And why," said Edwards, more urgently, "why didn't you tell him about me? Why'd you whisper into the phone to me so he wouldn't hear?" he whispered to her now. Establish a rapport. A secrecy. A connection.

She looked to the front door nervously, and looked back at him with pity, as if he were a sorry specimen of reasoning and logic. "I didn't want you to die. I don't want anyone to die. 'Less it's necessary. Like you made it." He watched her momentary remorse harden and vanish. "I was warnin' you. And you didn't listen."

She looked toward the front door again. As it opened, she drew a piece of duct tape forcefully off the roll she'd been holding, set it carefully, firmly, over Edwards's mouth, pressing it hard against his cheeks and into the creases of his sagging jowls.

He'd been fooled. Fooled by Tammy Smithers, just as Julian had been fooled by Alyshia. He'd been able to clearly see the blindness in Julian. But not to see it in himself.

His fabled instinct, his mythic intuitions. Clouded when there was feeling. When it was personal. A lesson he'd taught Julian. A lesson he'd forgotten himself.

He'd been a fool. A fool for Tammy's resemblance in looks, for her reverberating beauty. A fool for feeling and memory. And now it was going to cost him.

It would have taken Julian to tell him, to warn him. It always took someone else to warn you. That was the risk, working alone. That was the risk, being alone.

He didn't make many mistakes. Given how he worked—by instinct, intuition—he didn't make many at all.

But he'd made a mistake now, and it was going to cost him everything.

Some mistakes he hadn't paid for.

For this one, clearly, he would pay full price.

Which, after all, he'd been planning to anyway.

It's just that it looked like Philip Smithers wasn't going to pay at all.

And he hadn't been planning on that.

Julian had been driving for hours now. The motor vehicle computers were still down. The local police were trying to be optimistic. She could hear the embarrassment in their voices. They called her cell phone every ten minutes and updated her. They'd traced Edwards's call to her cell phone. It had come from the pharmacy where the shiny red pickup had been seen. The pickup they needed the registration on.

By her map, she figured she was now about ten miles from the pharmacy.

She was back in the South. The South she had tried to escape. Dirty trucks, ribbons of dusty road, the heat hovering above the macadam outside, surrounding the air-conditioned rental car like a lurking predator, like a disease, silently awaiting its opportunity to invade. For her, there was a poverty of heart and of soul, though others, she knew, found a richness, a charm, a sense of home here. Here she was, back. Back just long enough to save a life? Or two? And then to escape it once again.

It occurred to her that she didn't have her service revolver. It would have been inappropriate—unthinkable—to bring to her mother's funeral.

She hoped not to spend any time here. Much less an eternity. She swallowed.

Night was falling, flat and featureless. She had no sense of where the sun was setting. There were only a few vehicles on the road, roaring by occasionally from the opposite direction.

She was getting desperate. The motor vehicle computers seemed down for the count. She was feeling choked, cramped, tight, anxious. Running out of time.

A shiny red pickup came roaring past the other way. Gleaming in the gathering dark.

Shiny red pickup . . .

Her heart jumped.

She jerked her head violently left to see. Spun back, riveted her eyes in the rearview mirror.

Something in the back, she could just see. Barrels.

Ten miles from the pharmacy.

She wanted to turn, felt the impulse to, the instinct to.

But how many pickups were there? It was a county of them. Every other vehicle. It was ridiculous.

Shiny red pickup.

She realized it with a jolt: all the other pickups she'd been passing were dusty, dirty, from the country roads.

A shiny red pickup had to be some nut who constantly cleaned his. How many of those were there likely to be?

Trust your instincts, he'd taught her. *When instinct intersects with evidence, trust it.*

She hit the brakes, threw the wheel. A violent mechanical screech and shudder. She crossed the double-yellow median as she had when she'd turned the rental car south.

It was a gamble.

She headed up the road.

In a few minutes, the red pickup was in view.

It was a huge chance.

She figured it was her only chance.

She realized vaguely she'd be alone.

Thought again about the fact that she had no gun.

She'd be alone.

But then, that's how she always was.

Philip Smithers appeared at the wide entrance to the living room. Lean and alive, clearly energized by recent events.

"Well, well, nice to put a face to the voice," he said, leaning forward to check the tape across Edwards's mouth, not coming too close. "Nice to make sure that voice stays stopped." The furniture had been moved away from Edwards. All objects. Smithers's life of criminal caution was clear in his careful movements now.

Edwards would have only his wits.

None of his strength. None of his physical power.

And no words. No power of lies. No power of truth. None of it.

He tried to stay calm. Focused.

He had just his eyes.

Might be enough.

Not likely.

But might be.

The highway turned to a dirt road. Then another.

She followed the best she could. She needed to stay farther behind now that her car was kicking up dust, and her presence on untraveled dirt roads might seem more suspicious to the red pickup.

They began to head through a swampy wooded area. The dirt road turned muddy. The pickup wasn't kicking up its own dust anymore, so it was harder to see.

She came around a turn, to discover she'd lost it.

She'd lost the pickup.

Shit. Shit.

She looked frantically through the windows. Searched the tree line in front, behind, to both sides.

Pulled the rental car to the side, leaped out, jumped up onto a rock to look for even the tiniest plume of dirt or dust in any direction.

It was gone.

Shit. Shit.

Or had she at some level, meant to lose it?

Meant not to know what Edwards had discovered.

Meant to let him mete out his unjust justice. The brutal brand of it she knew he delivered. As if his call was to say only that: *The crime is solved. I'll handle it. I'll take care of everything.*

To know that he had solved it. Never having to know more.

She stepped back to the rental car slowly, deliberately, watched each footstep she took in the mud.

She sat back down heavily in the driver's seat.

What would she accomplish anyway?

She thought of the barrels she'd seen in back of the red pickup.

What could they be?

Think Edwards. Think Winston Edwards. He'd solved the crime. But probably, after twenty-five years, could not bring justice legitimately. So what would he do? How would he cover up what he was about to commit? Some way to not leave a trace. Some way for no one ever to know.

Explosion. The thought itself exploded inside her.

When she'd interned with him, she and Edwards had hired a psychic once. It had led them, naturally, to discuss the whole idea of psychic ability. Edwards had categorized it as only intuition, a highly developed sense of it. And he'd demonstrated a number of times in his career that startling level of intuition, in instances that had become legendary, that had melted and evolved into anecdote, in police instructor's colorful asides ("There was a Chief Edwards up in Canaanville, New York, working a double homicide about fifteen years ago, and he realized . . ."), in police academy dormitories. He'd maintained that like anything, intuition got better with practice, the more you trusted it, the more you tried it.

It's what she was feeling now—some high degree of intuition, it seemed. Because for no reason she could explain, she was picturing a woman about her own age, standing near, too near, when this explosion occurred.

The woman was a stranger, but somehow familiar. Julian couldn't see her face. Could only feel the familiarity.

Julian found herself shaking in the rental car at the side of the road. It was an unsettling, upsetting feeling. Like awakening in the middle of the night knowing a relative has died.

She pushed the image away.

Because the familiar woman, after all, could only be her.

Philip Smithers was as focused as Edwards. Had no desire to talk to Edwards, seemed to have no desire to gloat. Seemed only eager to move on, to silently attend to the situation, turn it to his advantage, and flee.

He pulled off extra strips of the duct tape, pressed them over Edwards's mouth. Was he so afraid of what Edwards might say?

"You did a pretty good job with the fertilizer. But I sweetened it up a bit. Just to make sure it all goes up."

Smithers moved around behind him. Edwards heard the hollow pull and rip of two more strips of duct tape.

"We figure you wouldn't be here tryin' this if you had a legal way to get us. So we're pretty damn sure you're here alone, on your own, and nobody else knows it."

He felt the extra strips being wrapped much more tightly around his wrists—calculated, he guessed, to cut off circulation to his hands.

"You got no legal way to get us. But we still ain't gonna take our chances with the law. Guess you weren't gonna take no chances either—the law wasn't good enough for you. Guess we understand each other on that."

Tammy, there's no one in that grave.

He had only his eyes. His eyes behind his wrinkles, searching hers, searching the face that was so like the one he had dreamed of.

Tammy, I nearly met your mother two weeks ago.

But his eyes wouldn't do it.

Tammy Smithers came over to him. Fingered the duct tape teasingly. "So much you want to say to me, so much you want to convince me of, so many words," she said. Her features narrowed into focused fury. "You were going to kill me, burn me and my father alive."

I was going to kill him. And save you.

"You're no cop. You're some kind of rogue, figuring you can just burn us out. That's why we figure we can do it to you. You seem outside the law. So we figure we're safe, doin' anything to you."

Some kind of rogue.

What kind exactly?

"So many words to say, huh? So many deceptions."

She was smart, Tammy. Smart enough to know that that's what a man about to die would be doing, trying to concoct anything.

Smart like her half-sister. Streetwise like her father, Philip, seemed to have been.

Smarter than she knew. Because it was words that Edwards had been living by. Words that had landed him here.

His plans, his deceptions, coming back to haunt him.

He was old. He wasn't so strong. He'd miscalculated.

You know I'm right, Tammy. Let my eyes tell you. Let my eyes speak it if it's the last thing they speak.

"You ready?" her daddy asked her, not looking.

"Am I ready?" she asked.

She looked at Edwards waveringly. Weighing, surveying . . .

Then leaned over him.

A stance, an expression, exactly like Julian's that first day in her office, with Edwards on the floor.

"Yeah, I'm ready," she said, and picked up the carton that was hers to carry, and headed for the door.

Mouth taped, limbs taped, mere seconds from the incineration that he had planned, Edwards helplessly watched Philip Smithers and his daughter Tammy grab their bags and boxes, as if off on a vacation or jaunty adventure, and head for the front door.

He knew all the steps, because he knew that Smithers was careful.

First he'd hear the truck start. They'd drive it up to the front porch, light the fuse on the porch (placed there to be destroyed in the explosion and not left as evidence), and drive off, reasonably, carefully. They'd have about a minute, maybe more.

He was taped to the chair. The chair was nailed to the floor. There'd be no way to get to the fuse in that minute.

Even his old self, strength superhuman sometimes, probably couldn't lift the chair from the floorboards.

Not that he had the will, either. He had expected to die. Been prepared to.

It's just that he'd been planning to take Philip Smithers with him.

Philip Smithers and his daughter, Tammy, hefted their bags and boxes, and headed for the front door and a new life.

They never glanced back at Edwards. Maybe their refusal to look was some final remorse, maybe some final insult, he'd never know exactly.

Edwards watched the last two people he would ever see head for the farmhouse door.

Maybe it was justice that these were the final specimens of humanity he'd see.

Clever, manipulative evil in one representation of it.

Devoted victim, in the other.

In the final accounting, hadn't he been both?

66

As Edwards watched Philip and Tammy Smithers step toward the door, it flew open before Smithers touched its handle.

Lieutenant Palmer burst in.

The Smitherses, laden with bags and boxes, had no instant access to a weapon.

Julian, Edwards saw, had no weapon either.

Edwards could only watch and admire Julian's quick thinking as, seeing Edwards tied and taped, she leaped at Tammy, grabbed her from behind and with one arm around Tammy's neck and throat held her as a shield against Smithers before Tammy had even dropped her boxes. A position from which to at least assess what she'd found.

Smithers, at the same time, had dropped his bags, and retreated to behind Edwards. Edwards suddenly felt steel at the side of his head, the barrel of a revolver Smithers had grabbed from inside his coat jacket.

Maybe Smithers thought it raised the stakes. But Lieutenant Palmer was up to keeping them even.

Because suddenly there was a knife at the throat of Tammy Smithers.

A knife, oddly, wrapped in plastic.

It was all she had. Still in her purse. Undecided what to do with it, or when. But it was at least something. A weapon of proven value. A weapon of proven lethalness.

If the evidence was destroyed defending herself, maybe that was the best use of it.

Maybe it could defend her, and still be evidence.

The man holding the gun must have found the plastic-sheathed knife odd.

The man with the duct tape across his mouth, unable to utter a reaction, no doubt found it particularly fascinating.

In fact, the duct-taped man figured the odds for Lieutenant Palmer were now better than even.

Because the duct-taped man figured Smithers was holding a gun to the head of someone Lieutenant Palmer wanted dead anyway.

Julian's knife at Tammy's throat. Smithers's barrel at Edwards's head.

Smithers looked at Julian. Julian looked at Smithers. Each with their shield, their victim, their bargaining chip. Each trying to sort out where to begin. . . .

For Edwards, it was a richer scenario, a deeper mathematics. He moaned, powerless against the duct tape, exploding with frustration. Neither sister could see the face of the other. Julian gripping Tammy tight from behind, her face in Tammy's hair. Tammy facing out, unable to see Julian behind her.

If they could see one another, would they recognize anything? Would they recognize the resemblance that had bowled him over, that had been his break in the twenty-year-old case? Or was it too strange, too odd and too far from the everyday, for either of them to even imagine?

Were they only—would they only seem—attractive strangers to each other?

And then his eyes, his searching desperate eyes, saw it.

My God . . . maybe . . .

On the wall opposite Tammy and Julian. Wood framed, askew. There, of course, near the front door.

A mirror.

Don't you see? At four in the morning, Frank Ryan's office window was a huge clear mirror.

If they would just look in the mirror, each could see the other.

Next to each other. Face to face. Maybe, looking like that . . . a chance . . . a chance they'd see the resemblance . . .

My God. A sudden portrait. Sisters, faces framed next to one another.

The photograph on Frank Ryan's desk.

He had only his eyes. Eyes seeing, knowing everything. Accomplishing nothing.

Julian was looking hard-eyed at Smithers behind him. Tammy was too. Waiting for Smithers to make the first move.

Edwards opened his eyes wide suddenly, in abject alarm, in terror, in desperation, trying to pour all his emotion, all his abilities, all his brutal experience, all of his soul into them.

At the risk of having it blown off, he jerked his huge ursine head to the left, shooting an alarmed, terrified, loaded look toward the mirror on the wall.

Julian and and Tammy both looked over to it in reaction.

Edwards saw the knife Julian was holding begin to tremble at Tammy's throat.

He saw Tammy's eyes go as wide as his own.

Just like Julian's were.

Naturally.

Sisters.

If they didn't know, couldn't process exactly what they were seeing, they knew they were seeing something. Something powerful. Strange.

They continued looking.

They knew something.

Now it would get interesting, thought Edwards, with a fatalistic calm. Even more interesting. If that was possible.

Of course, it wasn't only Edwards who knew.

The man behind him knew too. The man holding the barrel to Edwards's temple. The barrel now warm from its contact, its growing familiarity, with the folds of Edwards's skin around his tired forehead.

Barrel against skin. The way it had begun for Edwards in Julian's office. And given a rational assessment of the chances, the way it would end.

"Daddy?" The two Southern syllables rising questioning, frightened, from the woman Julian was holding. A little girl's voice, so sudden, so odd from an adult figure and from amid the tensions.

"It's nothing. Forget it," her father said, but Edwards sensed from the cool and collected and controlled Smithers he had observed minutes before, that Smithers was now rattled, open to error, and indeed, in the brusque, dismissive response to his daughter, he might have made one already.

"It's not nothing." The words clear. The voice Edwards had always loved. The directness he'd always yearned for. The voice a version of Tammy's; even in those syllables, even over lifetimes, the voices versions of each other. Could they hear it?

Julian looking in the mirror, at Tammy, at herself: "It's not nothing."

"Daddy?" the word rising again, the same, but more forceful. Meaning, *Tell me, please tell me.* . . . Fearful, questioning, tenuously keeping the panic at bay.

"When he says forget it, you know it's not nothing," said Julian, logical, reasonable, inarguable, adding to the weight of her questioning. The detective in her, everything in her, needing to know.

Quietly, carefully, "Ask your daddy to take the tape off his mouth."

Tammy looking at her father now. Saying nothing.

"I'm pulling this trigger," said Smithers.

What someone says when they don't want to, Julian instantly thought—trained, mechanically.

"Take the tape off his mouth." Julian said it this time to Smithers directly. Not a demand. But more than a request. Poised perfectly some-where between them, as if merely a suggestion, almost friendly, but not.

Smithers did not respond.

"Take the tape off his mouth," said Tammy Smithers. The sentence sounding identical.

Edwards heard Philip Smithers breathe deep behind him. He felt the pis-tol barrel shift its angle against his temple.

With the fatalistic calm of the already dead, Edwards processed it: Smithers wouldn't want to lose a daughter. The living, devoted embodi-ment of the woman he had once loved so much. Smithers's carefully laid deceits had worked until now. How would he handle this one? What was he going to say?

But Smithers surprised Edwards once again. By saying nothing to Tammy. By speaking instead to Julian.

"The man Tammy and I killed was not your father," said Philip Smithers to Julian gravely.

Admission . . . but negation . . . A single charged moment both confirming and denying a lifetime of Julian's belief. *The man Tammy and I killed. Not your father.* Her mind went numb. It was too much to understand.

"He was the man who raised you, yes," Philip Smithers's words swiftly gathering force, energy, validity, "but he was not your father," he said, pausing to make room for the significance, the inevitability, of the next thought. "I am."

He raised you, yes. But I am your father. The lie delivered along with the truth. To glide in its wake into the ocean of belief. Edwards's ancient eyes bulged. The skin around them stretched. He moaned his disbelief loudly. But it wouldn't matter. The possibility that Smithers was dangling was much louder than Edwards's moaning protest. He felt the gun barrel pressed closer into his temple.

"What you see in that mirror is no lie. Mirrors don't lie. You're sisters," said Smithers.

The power of blood. The shock of sisterhood.

A gamble Smithers was making to convince both women at once.

Julian stood silently. Stunned.

Holding a knife to the throat of her sister.

One of her father's killers . . .

Except that it wasn't her father . . .

Her real father . . . across this room? . . .

Somewhere beneath her sense of reeling, somewhere safely below her dizziness, someplace in which she was always a cop, she understood instantly, at last, why Vernon Blood had been killed.

Jealous rage. Humiliation. The loss of Southern honor. The loss of the life envisioned, and the beauty briefly known by the man now holding the gun.

Means, motive, opportunity.

Singing their three-part harmony once more.

Trust your instincts. Go with your instincts, he'd always said.

She felt the knife push almost reflexively against the throat of Tammy Smithers, the throat of a killer, felt Tammy's sharp intake of breath, sudden, terrified, defenseless.

Trust your instincts. Go with your instincts.

Julian eased the knife off Tammy's neck.

Still holding her tight, she felt Tammy exhale in relief.

Julian looked hard at Edwards, who could only look fixed, unblinking, back at her. In that brief moment, in that exchanged look, so much judgment, so much conclusion, to distill, to condense.

Winston Edwards. Prince of deceit. Master manipulator.

Yet solving a twenty-year-old murder case.

Her first. His last.

Solving it for her. For himself. For both.

Prince of deceit. And knight-errant of truth.

And the man holding the gun to his head behind him . . . her father? Or was it a lie that only had to stand up long enough to save his daughter Tammy? To gain the upper hand. To get him through the front door. To finish Julian off. Could anyone lie that agilely? That boldly?

She looked hard at Edwards. Yes. Someone could.

Prince of deceit. And knight-errant of truth. But which one now?

Trust your instincts. Go with your instincts.

She didn't know Winston Edwards. She would never know Winston Edwards. But looking for that brief moment into the dark brown eyes behind the folds of ancient skin, she knew him well enough to know: he had one last tale to tell.

All of it in an intuitive instant. "Take off the tape," said Julian, in reality only a moment later.

Smithers looked at Tammy.

"Take off the tape," Tammy said to her father again, evenly, unchanging, insistent. Whether from a long mistrust or a new inkling, or from only an instinctive, ironic trust of the woman holding the knife to her neck, Tammy Smithers was apparently as ready as Julian in this accidental, hastily assembled forum to hear the other side.

Philip Smithers answered with swift, blunt, wordless admission.

He fired once, behind the Bear's huge back, and stepped forward briskly, gun held out. Toward his daughter, toward the door.

Edwards's head pitched forward.

Smithers advanced toward Tammy and Julian.

My God . . .

"Let her go," Smithers shouted.

In response, Julian visibly tightened her grip on Tammy.

"It's your sister," said Smithers fiercely, then dismissive, snide, superior, "you're not going to hurt her," holding the gun up higher and clearer, for physical and psychological advantage, as he stepped toward them.

"You're not going to hurt her either," said Julian evenly, pulling Tammy violently closer, stretching her white neck near to choking, staying behind her.

"Oh, no?" Smithers said.

She watched him set his feet. A gesture of experience, a gesture of intent.

"Daddy, put that thing down," said Tammy, frantically, the fear rising in her. Until now, Julian had felt little struggle in her. And it occurred to Julian now, suddenly, that Tammy might have been standing here for Julian's benefit.

But now she feels Tammy's struggling. Now she feels the nervousness. Tammy seems to fear, with what she has always known or with what she has just learned, that her father will do it.

He levels the gun at them.

"Daddy . . . *Daddy, PLEASE!*"

In an instinct of self-preservation, Tammy curls downward. Struggling to hold her up will mean gashing her with the knife, so Julian lets her go, Tammy curling toward the floor.

There's an instant of shared shock at the new dynamic: Julian and Smithers facing each other with nothing between them.

Unobstructed, Smithers smiles, and confidently, almost lazily, levels the gun at her.

While Julian crouches and lunges with the plastic-sheathed knife . . . the knife arriving well ahead of her, her messenger . . . plunging into his ribs, her other arm knocking the gun from his hand—trained, unthinking, automatic . . .

The plastic sheathing of the knife breaking . . .

All fast, slow. An instant, a lifetime. Filled with judgment and chance. And to some yet indeterminate degree, with family.

Tammy screams, curled on the floor in shock. . . .

Julian looks over to Edwards. The slumped head. The corpse, of Winston Edwards.

Who lifts his head up, and looks clear-eyed, blankly, back at her.

Alive, as always.

And the evidence against him gone forever. Buried in her father's killer.

Or buried in her father.

Tammy keeps screaming.

In tense, pulsing minutes, has gained a sister. Lost a father.

Julian drops to her knees, puts her fingers to Smithers's neck, feels quickly and ably for his carotid vein. Feels Smithers's pulse pound twice. And stop.

Feels him die.

Justice. Swift. Unjust.

The first person she has killed in the line of duty.

A jagged, twisted line of duty.

She feels nothing but remorse.

In the weeks that followed, the flash of events—all in seconds, in moments—would replay in a thousand questions.

Her frantic search of the dirt roads. Her lucky sighting. Or unlucky, if that's how you saw it.

Seeing the barrels of fertilizer, the fuse on the porch, ready but unlit. Bursting in, thinking there might be only seconds . . .

Would Smithers really have fired at his own daughter? she would wonder. The daughter he loved? The daughter he lived for?

Would he really have fired at his daughter's half-sister? Or was he only leveling the gun in warning? In threat? To carve out a path of escape.

She lunged at him to save herself, of course. But what part of it was to not let him get away? Not to let him out that door? Not to let her father's killer get away with it again?

The questions, the second-guessing, the doubts, would never have arisen—any of them—if not for the preceding question. The larger question.

Why had he not shot Edwards?

Because it had been only a warning shot. Into the floor behind him. It was Edwards who turned it into more. Edwards who had slumped forward, upping the ante, spiraling the tension. Making the armed police officer feel she'd witnessed a murder. Edwards, with mouth and body taped, with only neck and head and eyes, had managed to tell one more useful lie.

Why had he not shot Edwards?

Did he want Edwards alive to witness the Smithers's escape? Had he imagined Edwards, envisioned Edwards in the explosion, and could not imagine another fate for him?

Why had he not shot Edwards?

Maybe because there was no need. Taped up, old, immobile, silent. No threat. The only nonthreat in the room.

And yet the greatest threat of all.

Why had he not shot Edwards?

Maybe he somehow knew, she would speculate weeks, months later. Somehow sensed that Edwards was dead already.

Or that Edwards could not be killed.

67

In a single motion, she ripped the tape from his mouth. The sound echoed through the front hallway in hollow punctuation. Edwards winced. The skin across his jaw was seared instantly red. Clownlike. Painful.

She had already brought Tammy over to the ripped brown living room couch, laid her down; Tammy stared up at the ceiling now, silent, immobile.

Julian stood over Edwards, looked at him, bound tightly, thoroughly, to the chair. "Say it, damn it!" in a violent hiss, leaning forward toward him, so Tammy wouldn't hear. "What he said . . . being my father . . ." She swallowed. "I need it to be a lie."

"It was a lie," he told her, flat, immediate, expressionless. In a way for her to know that was the truth.

Thank God. Thank God.

Julian stood over him. Didn't move yet to cut the other bands of tape.

"You slumped forward," she said.

Edwards didn't look up at her.

"To make me think you'd been killed," she said. Anyone else would have jerked reflexively at the sound of the gunshot. Edwards must have been ready—ready to do it, thinking to do it. Only someone fully prepared to die could do that. Only someone who didn't care. Only someone ready to slump forward anyway.

"You slumped forward. So that I'd stop him. Swift, brutal justice. Winston Edwards style."

He didn't answer.

"You knew I wanted you dead."

He looked steadfastly away.

"And so you managed to be," she said, the whimsy despite her exhaustion. "And by being dead for a moment, you probably got me to save your life."

She'd got to see him dead for a moment, she thought. And in that chaotic instant at least, she had felt nothing about it, nothing beyond a rudimentary wrongness.

Edwards stared at the bands of tape around his wrists. "Sylvia had started over," he said with a sudden mildness. "Met your father, had two daughters with him, a nice new life." He seemed to study the floor. "Tammy's father couldn't stand it."

The police sirens had begun to wail outside, the squad cars to pull squealing in. The Motor Vehicle Department computers had obviously—finally—come back up.

Julian looked at him. "I know you didn't hurt my mother."

"I know you know," he said.

She looked at him. Looked a moment longer at the tired, broken Winston Edwards.

"You saw it," she said to him. "Exhibit A. It was found."

"You buried it in your father's killer." He looked up at her finally. "It's useless against me now."

"It's still the murder weapon," she said.

"It won't prove anything now. You'll only look foolish."

She looked at him. She knew he was right.

He gestured with the huge ursine head. "Go to your half-sister," he said. "She needs you."

She looked at Tammy, lying on the couch.

"Lieutenant Palmer?" a young cop called out nervously from the porch. "You okay?"

"Come on in," she called back. "And real slow, for chrissake. You see what's rigged out there."

"Yes, ma'am." Obedient. Dutiful.

They entered carefully. Two of them. Both young enough to make her feel far from it.

She stood looking at Edwards. Looking at him in such a questioning and unclear way that the young cop who had called out to her, not knowing the disposition of events, who was who or what was what, felt compelled to ask. "Should we cut him loose?"

Cut him loose?

Should we cut him loose?

Good question.

It was true. The knife would no longer serve as evidence.

There was no choice. He'd done it again.

By solving, ruining. By ruining, solving.

"Yeah," she said with some indefinable, inseparable mix of authority and resignation, "go ahead. Cut him loose."

The two young officers still wore questioning looks. This old man, infirm, immense, his chafe-red, near-bloody mouth.

"Go ahead," she reassured them, nodding slightly. "He's a cop."

She sat in the back of a squad car with Tammy Smithers—Tammy still heaving, whimpering, stunned and shell-shocked.

It was a crime scene, and a still dangerous one. The fuse was still armed. They'd had to decide whether to remove Philip Smithers's body, or leave it and vacate the crime scene until a bomb squad arrived. In any case, it was too dangerous to stay inside. Julian had taken Tammy by the shoulders, guided her out of the farmhouse, out to the squad cars, leaving those decisions to the local police. It was their jurisdiction.

Exiting with Tammy out the front door, supporting her bodily, she had seen Edwards, finally loose, standing with one of the young cops.

Now she watched the cops milling in the front yard.

For no reason, simply by instinct, she began to count them.

The explosion rocked the squad car they were sitting in. Its concussion pressed hard against their ears and heads and chests.

Through the car window, she saw two of the young cops thrown to the ground.

The farmhouse was instantly a magnificent wall of flame.

"*Omigod! Omigod!*" one of the other young cops screamed, the one who'd called out from the porch in to her. "Omigod! He said! . . . He said he knew what he was doing! . . ." Frantic, stunned, near tears.

Edwards. Tired. Dispossessed. Nowhere to live. Nowhere to go. Righting what he could right. Accepting what he couldn't. Final chores done.

Was he in there?

A curtain of smoke rose now from the magnificent wall of flame. Rose perfectly, a final scrim, a flawless effect at the end of a magic show.

The heat of lies.

Or was he at that very moment retreating through the woods, to Florida at last?

Body at the epicenter of an explosion of that magnitude. Nothing left. Investigation would be inconclusive.

The heat of lies.

So she wouldn't know.

Would never know.

Which, she sensed, would be just how he wanted it.

"Omigod!" the young cop wailed. "He told me! He told me to wait outside by the cars! He told me he knew what he was doing!" Frantic, pacing, inconsolable. The flames simmering and popping, licking, hissing mockingly.

She waited a long, careful moment for any further explosion. Got out of the squad car in a cautious crouch. She felt the heat of the wall of flame against her arms and neck and face, heard the strange hollow roar and hiss of the immense burning. She made her way crouching over to the frantic young cop, who was still shaking, rocking in place, overwhelmed, powerless. A country kid, she could see, a smooth-skinned, baby-faced kid in a spiffy cop's uniform. She grabbed him by the shoulders, and made him look at her.

"He did," Julian told him, calming him, assuring him, the fresh-faced young cop clearly confused by such calm amid the heat and chaos, amid the crackles and bursts of mountainous flame. "I promise you," she told him. "He did know what he was doing."

68

The letter came with her morning office mail. No return address.

She sat up smartly in the new leather-and-chrome desk chair. The new chair's springs, its action and response, were mechanically crisp and prompt and professional—and annoying. Its chrome twinkled in the morning light. Its leather scent was sumptuous. A chair like the Captain's. She missed the old one. But it was gone. Tossed into a Dumpster at the back of Police Plaza. Landfill by now.

A surprisingly mature hand-writing, she noticed. The note didn't say much. Light news, some pleasantries. And only in closing, making its request—asking that she please come pay a visit. That it was important.

"I'm gonna be upstate Thursday morning," she called out to Ng. "Back around lunchtime, probably."

Ng grunted acknowledgment. Her dutiful, amiable keeper. She smiled.

Julian and Alyshia sat on the bed together in Alyshia's tiny, bright bedroom in the halfway house, regarding with quiet and equal wonder the huge belly between them. It looked about to burst. Alyshia smiled. She glowed. Seemed to glow all over.

"How long?" Julian asked.

"Two weeks," she said, still smiling. "They'll take me to this nice facility about ten miles down the road. I got a tour a couple of weeks ago." Now adding a hint of wryness to her smile, which nevertheless did not diminish it.

"How is it here?"

Alyshia shrugged. "Fine. Not bad. Grades are back up," she said brightly. She smiled a little. "There's time to think."

Julian nodded.

Alyshia looked at her belly again, then up at Julian. "So listen."

Julian was listening.

"I've been doing well here. So I'll be out of here in a little while. As I'm sure you know."

The reports that Julian had read had been excellent.

Alyshia took a breath. "So I'll have my life ahead of me," she said.

Julian nodded agreement.

"I'm not dumb."

"You were never dumb," assured Julian.

The startling image returned to Julian suddenly. The wadded rags over a pregnant belly. The fake pregnancy, to hide a real one.

Alyshia smiled. "Maybe I was always smart in a certain way. But I feel a lot smarter now." She looked down. "This baby. I'll still be thirteen. Then fourteen . . . fifteen . . ." She shook her head. "I couldn't. I couldn't raise it. It . . . wouldn't be right . . . for the baby or me."

Incest. A young girl's retaliation. A gun supplied by a thirteen-year-old friend. *What seems complex . . . turns out to be simple.* But the simple can also be made complex. The extent of Edwards's manipulation was at first hard to absorb—his tale of Frank Ryan's lonely self-relief and Alyshia's strategic placement of the semen; the red accountant's marks he had drawn on the girls' photograph. But once Edwards's deception was fully understood, Alyshia's official fate had been retrieved from the machinery of adult prosecution and returned to Judge Caramore's chambers.

Alyshia looked up at Julian now. "How old are you, Lieutenant Palmer?"

"Midthirties."

"You're not seeing anyone right now, are you?"

Julian shook her head, smiled.

"And there's no one really on the horizon, is there?"

Smart. Really smart.

"You've had . . . an unusual life. It says so in the report I did." Alyshia smiled impishly. Then turned suddenly serious. "So you're not afraid of the unusual. . . ."

She dropped her head, looked away. And then, eyes filled with weight and meaning, looked straight at Julian, straight and direct and proud. "I want you to take the baby. I want it to be yours. You'd be a great mother to it. You know you would."

The voice of a twelve-year-old. The words of an adult.

Very calmly and evenly, gently and respectfully, Julian asked her, "What would your mother say about something like this?" Calmly, respectfully. "She's still your guardian, you know."

"My mother," said Alyshia, "she wants the baby with her. But"—she looked darkly—"I don't want my baby raised in that house."

Nell had denied knowing Alyshia was still pregnant when she'd held the funeral for the miscarried child. But the prospect of that "staged" funeral—and obvious questions about the stability of the Ryan household—had led Judge Caramore to add a stipulation to Alyshia's juvenile sentencing: residence in a halfway house for the duration of the pregnancy, with Alyshia's own option to continue it for a period afterward. To Alyshia's immense relief, at not having to return home.

Alyshia's visit to Julian's office with the padding that day seemed to confirm Nell's denial about knowing. The stunt had been Alyshia's idea. She wanted to fool Julian. Convince her there was no baby. Because, well—Alyshia looking down, hands folded, body curled in embarrassment—she'd just wanted their friendship to somehow go back to how it had been. Before Julian—or Alyshia—had been aware of any baby.

Julian sensed, too, the deeper psychological element of Alyshia's office charade. Trying to pretend the pregnancy simply hadn't happened. That it was all a mistake. A twelve-year-old's wish . . . a twelve-year-old's solution.

And Julian—already suspecting Alyshia was still pregnant—had fallen for it.

The North Carolina events had soon made their way to the Captain, of course. Julian was sure she'd lose her job. But her hot-headed actions and questionable judgments got dissolved in the compelling story of solving a twenty-year-old crime. The story of her brave behavior at the scene. The glowing report of her quick responses and selfless actions from the impressed and appreciative officers of the North Carolina police.

The brutal murder of a police lieutenant's father, solved after twenty years. A felonious former cop, presumed killed in the blast. And the discovery of the lieutenant's half sister, amid it all. A vast blue tide of fascination, satisfaction, and sympathy washed over the events. The dapper Captain had no choice but to let his private resentment simmer.

The discovery of that half sister, Julian had found, seemed to temper her sadness over losing her mother. And Tammy—suddenly alone now—seemed to need Julian and Stephanie. Tammy lived nearer to Stephanie, so Stephanie saw more of her, but Julian and Tammy would always share the moment of their mutual discovery. It would always be something miraculous between them.

All preamble, in a way, to the absurd request before Julian now.

"What happens to this baby, it's my decision," Alyshia said, in the little bedroom. "My mother accepts that. And the idea of your taking it . . . well, I don't know if you can tell this, Lieutenant, but I can, 'cause I know her. She really admires you."

"My God . . . you've discussed this with her that thoroughly?"

Alyshia nodded, and rushed on. "Don't say anything yet. Just think about it, okay? Just promise me you'll think about it."

Julian happened to look up then, and noticed it with a shock on Alyshia's bedside table. *Lilius macrophylla lupidus.* In full bloom. Its black piping. Its startling scarlet. Its neon green. But what? . . .

But of course. It was from Nell. For whom the flower meant the color of memory. The South American florist had said *another death.* Julian saw now that was wrong, but not entirely off track. It stood for another *life.* She reached out, lifted the flower from the vase, held it, looked at it.

Julian looked back at Alyshia. "The truth is, I have thought about it," she said. "I thought about it all the way up here."

Alyshia looked puzzled.

"Don't forget, I'm smart, too," Julian said. "A sudden letter to me, a few weeks before you're due. After months and months alone to think. A letter that says a visit is important. I thought about it all the way up here."

Looking out the window at the trees. Imagining if the responsibility was even possible. If such a life was possible. A life outside normal boundaries, to be by this act and this commitment forever outside those boundaries. And yet, a life at the same time pulled into normal boundaries, by the needs, the wishes, the world of a child.

Childhood robbed from two little girls a generation apart . . .

To be generously resurrected, for this new child.

Yes, she'd thought about it.

"And?" asked Alyshia. The twelve-year-old again. Direct. Curious. Forthright.

Julian sighed deeply. Listened to, felt, her own breath go in and out of her.

"I think it's a plan," she said.

Smiling, they both started to cry. Sat together silently, Alyshia's belly between them, for a while longer, the morning sun pouring through the dirty windows of the small bright bedroom, warming it, bathing it in angled light.